S0-AWC-934

"Trailing you about town today, and missing you at every opportunity, seems to have addled my wits.

"No matter. Let me see if I can do this properly." He swept up her hand and dropped to one knee. "My dear, my respect and admiration have grown and deepened. Would you do me the honor of becoming my wife?"

Sarah stared at him. Like nonsense syllables babbled by a babe, his words didn't make sense. She must be hallucinating—lack of sleep and endless worry had affected her brain. That had to be the reason she thought she heard the Marquess of Englemere proposing to her.

"No, 'tis ridiculous. You can't be asking *me* to marry you."

"Nonetheless, I believe I just have. Twice, in fact. Though I admit, I made a botch of the first attempt."

"But why?"

"Why not? You need to marry, do you not? As do I…"

Dear Reader,

Heroes come in many forms, as this month's books prove—from the roguish knight and the wealthy marquess to the potent gunslinger and the handsome cowboy.

The widowed Marquess of Englemere, Nicholas Stanhope, will steal your hearts in *The Wedding Gamble* by Julia Justiss. This book won the prestigious Golden Heart Award in the Regency category, and we think that Julia is one of the best new writers in the field. Be prepared to laugh and cry in this anything-but-typical "marriage of convenience" tale of duty, desire—and danger—when two friends so perfectly suited must deny their love....

You *must* meet Sheriff Delaney, the smooth, mysterious ex-gunslinger who inherits a house—and a young widow—in *The Marriage Knot* by the talented Mary McBride. And in *A Cowboy's Heart,* an adorable Western by Liz Ireland, the magnetically charming wrangler Will Brockett uncharacteristically finds his soul mate in tomboy Paulie Johnson.

Fans of roguish knights be prepared for Ross Lion Sutherland and the lovely female clan leader he sets his sights on in *Taming the Lion,* the riveting new SUTHERLAND SERIES medieval novel by award-winning author Suzanne Barclay.

Whatever your tastes in reading, you'll be sure to find a romantic journey back to the past between the covers of a Harlequin Historicals® novel.

Sincerely,

Tracy Farrell
Senior Editor

Please address questions and book requests to:
Harlequin Reader Service
U.S.: 3010 Walden Ave., P.O. Box 1325, Buffalo, NY 14269
Canadian: P.O. Box 609, Fort Erie, Ont. L2A 5X3

JULIA JUSTISS

THE WEDDING GAMBLE

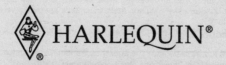

HARLEQUIN®

TORONTO • NEW YORK • LONDON
AMSTERDAM • PARIS • SYDNEY • HAMBURG
STOCKHOLM • ATHENS • TOKYO • MILAN • MADRID
PRAGUE • WARSAW • BUDAPEST • AUCKLAND

ISBN 0-373-29064-0

THE WEDDING GAMBLE

Copyright © 1999 by Janet Justiss

Look us up on-line at: http://www.romance.net

Printed in U.S.A.

JULIA JUSTISS

wrote her first plot ideas for twenty-seven Nancy Drew stories in the back of her third-grade spiral, and has been writing ever since. After publishing poetry in college, she served stints as a business journalist for an insurance company and editor of the American Embassy newsletter in Tunis, Tunisia. She followed her naval-officer husband through seven moves in twelve years, finally settling in the Piney Woods of east Texas, where she teaches high school French. The 1997 winner of the Romance Writers of America's Golden Heart for Regency, she lives in a Georgian manor with her husband, three children and two dogs, and welcomes mail from readers. Reach her at Rt. 2, Box 14BB, Daingerfield, TX 75638.

In Memory of
Marsha Ballard
Critique partner and friend.
We shared the dream.

Prologue

"Just because that opera dancer got her clutches into you your first year on the town—" Edmund Stanhope paused to shoulder his creel "—doesn't mean all women are mercenary."

"You're dumber than a trout." Nicholas Stanhope, Marquess of Englemere, picked up his fishing rod and gave Edmund a mock-pitying look. "Take care, baby brother. A wench can bleed you dry faster than a Captain Sharp."

"Cynic." Shaking his head, Edmund kicked the hall door closed and set off across the rain-drenched lawn.

"Perhaps," Nicholas muttered as he followed in his brother's matted footprints. "Though I have excuse enough."

Rising sun gilded the grass and set off diamond sparkles among the dripping trees. They reached the lawn's edge, and leaving behind the stately bulk of Englemere Hall, turned onto a narrow wooded path.

Nicholas picked his way around the boughs strewing the trail, mute testaments to the violence of the previous night's storm. "About the wench," he continued, keeping his tone light. "Do try to remember, once she lands you, not to pay the trollop more than she's worth."

"She's not a trollop, and I won't have you speak of her so!"

Astonished at Edmund's vehemence, Nicholas nearly tripped over a fallen branch. Alarm coursing through him, he fixed his gaze on his brother. "'Tis a lady, then, who's caught your eye?"

"A lovely one, Nicky. Fair, blue-eyed and innocent as an angel." His earnest look faded to a frown. "Her father is the dupe of the Captain Sharps. Forever gaming, and never winning. I fear the debt-ridden bastard means to auction Angela off. I might have to bolt with her."

"You mean marriage?" Nicholas whistled. "All the more reason for caution, then."

Edmund opened his mouth as if to retort, then closed it. After a moment he said, "She's nothing like Lydia."

"Lydia was nothing like Lydia when first I knew her," Nicholas replied grimly. "I promise you, Edmund, no matter how enchanting her face, you'll never know what's really going on inside that lovely head. How can you be certain about her? Forgive me, brother, but you're rather young, and have hardly seen anything of the world yet."

"I've seen enough to know what I want," Edmund said quietly. "Besides, if I marry and set up my nursery, 'twould take the pressure off you."

"Don't be immolating yourself on the altar of matrimony to save my hide." Nicholas forced a smile. "I admit, since Lydia's death I've more or less handed over the duty of the succession to you. I'd not have you rush into it, though."

"I'm not rushing—I've thought carefully about this. Besides," he added, flashing Nicholas a grin, "surely you can't rest easy with only my poor mortal self standing between your title and Cousin Archibald."

"The Odious Archibald?" Nicholas shuddered. "Last time I saw him, he was swathed in lavender from head to toe. Tried to borrow some blunt from me too, the quiz. Indeed, if they distanced Archibald from Papa's honors, I might grow rather fond of a passel of grubby nephews leaving handprints on my Hessians."

They heard the roar of the river even before they reached the path's end. The Wey, flowing fast and full of floating debris, foamed high against its banks.

"Better not fish the point." Nicholas raised his voice above the din. "The stream's been undercutting that old stump."

"Growing cautious as well as ancient, my lord Englemere?" Edmund called back. "I always fish the point."

"Well, don't blame me if you sink up to your elegant thighs in muck."

Chuckling, Nicholas watched his brother straighten the creel on his back and slowly approach a jagged stump that jutted out over the stream. Reaching the edge, he sent Nicholas a triumphant smile.

A portion of the bank beneath the stump crumbled. Before Nicholas could even shout a warning, the old trunk shifted downward.

Clawing at the downed tree's weather-worn smoothness, Edmund scrabbled for balance. He twisted off his creel, teetered on one foot—and tumbled sideways into the water.

In the flash of an instant, Nicholas saw his brother's head strike the sharp stub of a projecting root. Saw blood against the dark hair before Edmund went under.

His heart stopped, then hammered in his chest. He threw down his fishing gear and raced toward the river.

Shedding his jacket as he ran, Nicholas slid and stumbled up the potholed bank beside the stump. More earth dissolved under him as he tugged frantically at his boots and watched for his brother to surface. When Edmund bobbed up, he jerked the second boot off and dived after him.

He came up sputtering, grit in his mouth and his eyesight blurred by muddy water. The current swept him blindly onward, scraping him against a hidden boulder as he dug at his eyes with his knuckles. Then his vision cleared and he spotted Edmund.

A whirlpool of swirling debris caught him. He fought free, battled downstream, grabbed Edmund and jerked the supine head out of the water. Clutching his brother's body, Nicholas let the torrent carry them over the rocks to the pool below, then struggled ashore.

Exhausted, he dragged Edmund onto the slimy bank, the wet-dog stench of soggy vegetation filling his gasping lungs. With shaking fingers, Nicholas turned the head to the side and pushed with all his remaining strength against his brother's chest. A trickle of muddy water drooled from the slack lips.

"Come on, bantling, help me!" Over and over he slammed his linked hands against his brother's chest, blew air into the unresponsive mouth. Long after any rational hope died he continued, his tired muscles burning and tears blurring his brother's face into a grotesque kaleidoscope of white skin, blue lips and river muck.

Sometime, moments or hours later, he pulled himself to his feet. As golden sun peeped over the treetops, he hefted Edmund's body onto his shoulders and stumbled toward the distant towers of Englemere Hall.

Chill wind whipped the scarf at Nicholas's neck and threatened to dislodge his curly-brimmed beaver. Pulling his greatcoat closer, he watched the slight, black-robed figure of his mother, the Dowager Marchioness of Englemere, as she arranged the bouquet of sweetbrier roses on the simple marble gravestone.

"Please, Mama, come along now. You'll catch a chill. Edmund wouldn't want that."

"In a moment, Nicky. Just one last prayer." The dowager dabbed at her eyes with a lace handkerchief. "By now—" she made a gesture toward the three graves flanking the dank raw earth before her "—one would have thought I'd be prepared for the uncertainties of life. Still, it is so hard to accept."

"If I'd reached him sooner," Nicholas replied, his throat tight, "maybe I could have—"

"Nicky dearest, you mustn't torture yourself!" She reached over to grasp his arm. "You did everything you could. I know that."

His jaw set, Nicholas helped her rise. "Come back to the Hall now, Mama. Your fingers are frozen. Martha will have a hot brick waiting."

"Oh, Nicky, don't fuss. I must go back, I know. I just wish that wretched Amelia would leave." She gave him a slight, sad smile that caught at his heart. "It's been ten days since the funeral, and still she lingers. With my Edmund barely cold in his grave, she has the effrontery to refer to that foppish son of hers as 'the heir.' It's almost more than I can bear, her snooping about, mentally rearranging furniture and redecorating rooms. Can you imagine, she told me the library would be much handsomer done up in puce. Puce! I cannot credit what possessed your uncle to marry that vulgar, jumped-up cit's daughter."

Nicholas smiled grimly. "The Odious Archibald already touched me for a loan. Wouldn't look right for the Stanhope heir to fall into the clutches of the cent-percenters, he said."

His mother's eyes widened, and he patted her cheek. "Don't fret, Mama, I have no intention of pensioning my cousin. Nor do I plan for him to remain much longer my heir." With a sigh, he turned his face away. "I may have been avoiding my duty these past four years, but only Aunt Amelia could be cloth-headed enough to think I'd eschew it."

The mittened hand on his arm tightened. He heard a rustle of silk, and knew his mother looked up at him. He couldn't bring himself to meet her concerned gaze.

"There's been so much pain in those years, for all of us. Give yourself time, Nicky. There's no need to rush."

He winced at the unconscious echo of his words to Edmund. Taking a ragged breath, he squeezed her fingers.

"What good would waiting do, Mama? No, 'tis time to go forward."

Gently disengaging his hand, Nicholas placed it on top of the hastily carved headstone. "I swear to you, by next Season's end, I shall bring home a bride."

Chapter One

Sarah heard the angry voices as soon as she entered the library hall. Or voice, she amended, frowning. Though she could not make out the words, the high pitch of the feminine tones warned The Beauty was in a rare temper. How could Clarissa be tiresome enough to quarrel with her fiancé on the very morning of their betrothal ball?

Coming around the corner, she nearly collided with a footman, his ear to the door and a grin wreathing his freckled face. Seeing her, he sprang back.

She raised a quelling eyebrow. "I believe Timms sent you to polish the silver, James. If that is complete, Cook needs you to help Simmons bring up the wine."

His face reddening, the young man bowed himself off. Sarah watched him retreat, thinking ruefully that the delicious details of Clarissa's latest outburst would be all over the servants' hall by luncheon.

Sighing, she grasped the handle in front of her. A smile pinned to her lips, she knocked lightly and entered.

In that first instant, she saw Clarissa's flushed face, Lord Englemere's back and a missile flying toward her. Instinctively she ducked. The object whizzed past to strike and shatter the vase behind her. As Sarah straightened, Clarissa stormed toward the door, thrusting aside her fiancé's outstretched hand.

"Beast! How could I have agreed to marry you? You're a detestable tyr-rant!" Bursting into tears, The Beauty brushed past Sarah and fled sobbing down the hall.

Sarah stole a cautious look at the man who had just been subjected—if the small sample she'd witnessed were any indication—to one of The Beauty's famous tantrums. Similar disagreements with Clarissa's mother normally left that unfortunate lady collapsed upon her couch. And afterward gained Clarissa whatever she wanted.

Her fiancé appeared made of sterner stuff. Evidently Clarissa had neither cowed him nor reduced him to red-faced embarrassment or white-eyed fury. He stood motionless, and Sarah could not glean from the sober face he'd turned to the window any hint of his thoughts.

Grudging respect stirred, followed by the reflection that if his lordship were as shrewd as he appeared, Clarissa was a looby to be flaunting her temper before the wedding ring was yet on her finger.

Uncertain how best to break the silence, Sarah knelt to tend the broken vase. She saw in the shards a glint of gold, and her fingers froze. *She couldn't have.* The large ruby winking up at her informed her Clarissa could indeed.

Fury displaced shock. Did that wretched girl expect her to smooth *this* over? When Sarah caught up with her—!

The polished boots beyond her shifted, jolting her back to the present. Swallowing her anger, she raked the rubble under the hall table and slipped the ornate ring beneath her cuff. Rising, she searched for the proper phrase. How does one tactfully return to a gentleman the betrothal ring his intended has just pitched at his head?

He turned and studied her, as if trying to assess her place. Even while anxiously weighing apologies, she had to appreciate what a work of perfection he was.

The coat of dark green superfine fit without a wrinkle over his broad shoulders, with nary a crease to show impatient hands had pulled at his immaculate sleeve. Nor had impetuous skirts dragged across the spotless Hessians disturbed their shine, or left a speck of lint on the tan inexpressibles molded over those muscled thighs.

The only sign of disorder was a lock of dark hair hanging upon his brow. She felt a ridiculous desire to brush it back, and almost laughed. The richest prize currently gracing the Marriage Mart, the widowed Marquess of Englemere had no need of *her* help.

When he smiled, as he did now, she had also to acknowledge him the handsomest man of her acquaintance. As she'd thought upon first seeing him years ago... She pulled her thoughts together and smiled cautiously back.

"Lord Englemere, I must apologize! With the ball, I'm afraid the whole household is rather...upset, and—"

"Miss Wellingford, is it not? I met you at Lady Rutherford's ball. Wearing something, ah, white." His smile deepening with a hint of humor, he bowed.

His unruffled composure, after what must have been an unpleasant scene with Clarissa, surprised her. She dipped a curtsy, her respect deepening as well. Perhaps more lay behind his typically bored aristocratic facade than she'd credited. Though if so, why had he offered for Clarissa?

Dismissing that disloyal and irrelevant thought, she nodded. "Yes, I remember. Lady Beaumont escorted us."

"Clarissa wore her usual flame red. 'Fire and Ice,' the *ton* calls the two of you. Having just been burnt, I could use some cooling. Is that what you were sent to do?"

Taken aback, she evaded his too perceptive gaze. She could hardly admit that Clarissa's abigail, lingering outside the door, had heard the quarrel and come flying to find Miss Sarah before her mistress did "something awful."

"Some 'cooling' refreshment, then, my lord?" she evaded. "Sherry? Or would you prefer brandy?"

"Brandy."

She poured a glass. "I was coming to fetch Clarissa, merely." She settled for a half truth as she handed the glass to him. "Lady Beaumont is a stickler for the proprieties. Until you wed, she must limit your time alone together.''

''You and I are alone. Will that cause gossip?''

She looked up quickly, but his face told her nothing. Surely he wasn't flirting—not with her. He wanted reassurance, she decided. ''Of course not. I am an old friend of your betrothed and a guest in her house. I—''

''There ye be, miss!'' A maid rushed into the room. '''Tis an uproar below stairs, and that's a fact. Wine in the cellar's two cases short, and Timms be shouting at James over it, and then the lobster for them patties were bad when Cook opened the crates, and she went into a swoon. Oh, and Ruddle says as Lady Beaumont's laid down on her bed with the headache and needs you to fix one o' them p-powders.'' Out of breath as she finished, the maid bobbed a belated curtsy.

''Oh, dear,'' Sarah murmured, embarrassed to have the household's problems blurted out in front of the marquess. ''You'll pardon me a moment, my lord?'' At his nod, she ushered the girl into the hallway.

Sarah kept her voice low. ''Lilly, tell Timms he must return to cleaning the ballroom, and I will handle James. Send Willy to Gunter's—inform them Lady Beaumont simply must have lobster, and counts on them to procure it. I shall return in a moment to make up Lady Beaumont's powder.''

She hesitated, fighting a craven desire to call farewell to the marquess from the hallway and retreat below stairs. The ring pressed her wrist with the heavy weight of Duty.

''Go along, Lilly. I shall be down directly.'' The maid eyed her uncertainly, then bobbed a curtsy. As the girl departed, Sarah forced herself to reenter the library.

''You said you are a *guest* in this house?''

''Why, yes. Oh, you mean—'' At his raised eyebrow, embarrassment flushed through her again. Evidently her voice hadn't been lowered enough. ''I'm very grateful for Lady Beaumont's sponsorship, and I do like to be useful.

Domestic details are fatiguing to one of her delicate constitution, she says, and I'm happy to spare her. I'm quite accustomed to managing a household."

"You're Wellingford's eldest, aren't you?"

"Yes. With a houseful of servants and siblings, I have vast experience." She took a deep breath, her fingers clutching his ring. "But with the ball tonight, you must forgive me for leaving you, after I—"

"Give back something that belongs to me?"

Again he surprised her. She'd sworn he'd not noticed her retrieving the ring. Feeling somehow guilty, she opened her hand, holding it out on her palm.

"I should return it. But I beg you, let me return it to Clarissa instead." She paused, seeking the most persuasive words. "She is...high-spirited, I grant. Having lost her father when so young, she's been given her head much more than is good for her. When her temper cools, she will wish to beg your forgiveness. Will you allow her to?"

He looked at her steadily. "Does she often fall into such, ah, 'high-spirited' freaks?"

Sarah stared at the ring in her hand, seeking some response short of blatant falsehood. "Clarissa has the disposition often reputed to go with her coloring," she replied carefully. "But she is also generous, courageous and loyal. Granted, her—exuberance—needs curbing. She should have learned that years ago, but no one ever troubled to teach her. The small effort of guiding so beautiful and accomplished a lady would be well worth the prize. Do you not agree, my lord?"

She dared not even contemplate Lady Beaumont's reaction should her appeal not convince him. Swallowing hard, she offered the ring again, praying he would not take it.

She didn't realize she'd closed her eyes until she felt his hand on hers. For a horrified moment, she thought he meant to gather up the ring.

"You may open those solemn silver eyes, Miss Wellingford." He curled her fingers back around the ruby. "I will spare you the task of informing Lady Beaumont her daughter just jilted her fiancé, mere hours before the ball that was to present them to the cream of the ton."

A vision of the piteous shrieks and burnt feathers that must have followed such a revelation shook her. "Thank you, my lord," she said faintly. She looked up to see him smiling at the relief she hadn't managed to conceal.

Feeling better, she smiled back. "I'm sure Clarissa will write you, wishing to meet before the ball to apologize. I must go, but please stay and finish your brandy." She held out her hand. "Good day, sir, and again, my sincerest thanks for your understanding."

He shook her hand, but to her surprise, retained it. "Bear me company a moment longer, if you will." As she looked toward the open door, a protest on her lips, he continued, "Your domestic crises will wait, and I dislike drinking alone." He turned on her his very charming smile.

When she nodded reluctantly, he brought her fingers to his lips for a brief salute. "Thank you, my very cool and calm Miss Wellingford."

His breath seemed to have ruffled the tiny hairs below her knuckles. She took the hand back, feeling less than cool and calm. Not at all certain it was the thing for her to entertain him alone, even with the door open, she seated herself at the edge of a wing chair.

He settled on the small sofa and grinned at her. "I shan't ravish you, you know, and I'll send you off before there's any irreparable damage to your reputation."

"Don't be nonsensical," she replied, nettled that he had perceived her unease. "I'm hardly a green girl in need of a chaperon, and your passions are elsewhere engaged."

His grin widened. "All right, I'll behave. But after observing you fling yourself—quite decorously, of course— into the breach of a distressing scene and handle it so neatly, I admit a juvenile desire to see what might ruffle that calm veneer. Are you truly 'Ice,' Miss Wellingford?''

"Certainly not. I have a full share of all the warmer emotions. Wexley cursed us with that silly sobriquet before you came to London, and I hoped, since you've replaced him in Clarissa's regard, we might escape it.''

"Not if you continue to wear white gowns and Clarissa her red. With your fair coloring, and her fiery hair, the ton is constantly reminded.''

Sarah couldn't admit that new gowns were, for her, an impossibility, but with a trousseau to plan perhaps Clarissa could be persuaded. "You might suggest you should like to see Clarissa in emerald, to match her eyes. She refuses to wear the so-called 'insipid pastels' generally required of girls in their first Season, but she's fond of bright hues.''

"Would she change from her favorite russet for me, do you think? I wonder.''

Before Sarah could frame an unexceptional answer to that leading remark, the marquess laughed. "I'll ask no more questions that force you to choose between truth and loyalty. Clarissa has a good friend in you, indeed. But since you are, as you put it, not a green girl in her first Season, how did two such opposites as you become friends?''

"Do not men ever befriend their opposite? And we met as you probably met your closest companions, at school.''

"True, but my friends from Eton were of an age. You must be—four years older than Clarissa?''

"I'm three-and-twenty, my lord,'' she admitted. "We were schoolmates at Mrs. Giddings's Academy for Gentlewomen.''

"And?''

Sarah looked up with a tiny frown. Surely he wasn't interested in schoolgirl reminiscences.

"I'm eager to learn everything about my betrothed,'' he said blandly.

"Of course,'' she replied, still puzzled.

"You were telling me how you came to be friends."

Wary, she took up the tale. "We met, as I said, at school. As you might expect with one of her commanding personality, Clarissa was her form's acknowledged leader. After several—incidents, we came to admire each other's strengths, and grew to be friends."

"'Incidents,' Miss Wellingford? You alarm me. What sort of mischief did my future wife brew?"

"Nothing significant." Sarah was sure Clarissa would not thank her for revealing details of her hoydenish youth. Even if he did wish—belatedly—to learn "everything" about Clarissa, she hardly felt it her task to enlighten him.

His lordship, however, continued to stare at her with a wide-eyed expectancy that positively begged her to impart all manner of ill-advised confidences. Well, she would not.

"We had a few, ah, disagreements over strategy, but resolved them. And later indulged in the normal sorts of high jinks schoolchildren enjoy."

"She was volatile, and you were the cautious one?"

"Something like that. I always favored the prudent approach, while Clarissa tended to be more adventuresome."

"Passion and Prudence, eh?" His shoulders shook. "What a pair you must have been."

"Oh, we did not long collaborate. The next year, things, ah, grew difficult at home, and I had to withdraw. We lost contact until we met by chance this spring at Lady Moresby's rout. Clarissa invited me to call, and I assisted Lady Beaumont with several trifling matters. Then—"

"Wexley made his infamous remark?"

"Yes," she said shortly, not wishing to pursue the point. The very day after Wexley's comment, Lady Beaumont invited her to reside with them in Grosvenor Square. Revealing that detail, however, might insinuate Clarissa resumed their friendship because their continued appearance together would give The Beauty a unique cachet to set her apart from the other Diamonds of the Season. Though Sarah privately suspected as much.

"As I was saying, learning I was staying with an elderly aunt, for Mama was too ill to sponsor me, Lady Beaumont graciously asked me to spend the remainder of the Season."

"Where you would be closer at hand to 'assist with trifling matters'?" Englemere asked dryly.

Sarah drew herself up. The fact that he echoed her own opinion merely made her more uncomfortable, for he must know she could never agree to so shockingly uncivil an assessment, regardless of its truth. "In this house," she replied stiffly, "I have been treated with every kindness, as a favored guest. If I have said anything to make you think otherwise, then I have expressed myself badly indeed." Rising, she nodded to him. "I must bid you goodday."

He rose too, rueful dismay on his face. "Now I have offended you. You *said* nothing, and I meant no disrespect, to you or your gracious hostess. I spoke out of turn, as I sometimes do among friends." One corner of his mouth turning up, he offered her an apologetic half smile. "Pray forgive me, Miss Wellingford."

A dimple creased the skin next to his mouth. She had the absurd desire to touch it, and gave herself a mental shake, annoyed both at his uncommon perspicuity and his effect on her. Of course he was charming, she told herself crossly. He probably practiced in front of his glass.

"Miss Wellingford?" he repeated, looking grave now.

She nodded shortly, but before she could reply, the maid reappeared at the doorway.

"I be so sorry to disturb you again, but, oh, please, miss!" Lilly gasped. Her expression as desperate as her voice, she stood on the threshold, breathing gustily and pleating the edge of her starched white apron.

"Yes, Lilly, I'm coming. My lord." Sarah curtsied.

As she rose, he once again caught her hand and brought it to his lips. "Thank you for the conversation, Miss Wellingford." Craning his head to ascertain the maid had already started down the hall, he added softly, "I must also apologize for being so—inquisitive. It was just borne upon me rather forcefully that the events of a Season don't allow one to gain a very clear insight into another's character. I was casting about, I suppose."

She drew back her hand, trying not to let the unexpected prickling sensation fluster her. "Indeed, my lord, I've sometimes thought all the busyness was expressly designed to *prevent* couples from getting to know each other." Belatedly realizing that was hardly a fortuitous remark, she looked up to catch him grinning at her.

Torn between exasperation and humor, she shook her head. "Now, before you trick any more impolitic comments from me, I must go."

"To make yourself useful?"

"I like to be useful," she said at her loftiest. His throaty chuckle followed her into the hall.

She'd brushed through that tolerably well, she decided as she hurried after the maid. Once she settled the household, she would search out Miss Clarissa. The peal she intended to ring over that damsel should echo in her flighty friend's ears for a week.

What a charming, intelligent woman, Nicholas thought as Miss Wellingford departed. Not that one could trust appearances, of course. He'd met her before, but she always seemed to withdraw into the background, and he'd not taken much notice of her.

Though she lacked the sort of vibrant loveliness that instantly captured masculine attention, her gray eyes and classic profile crowned with a coronet of white-gold braids were nonetheless attractive. And her womanly form merited much more than a second glance. Would that ice melt if one loosed those heavy plaits from their pins, fanned the silken strands free to play down—

In a wash of heat, he squelched his wayward thoughts. Best concentrate on the problem at hand.

The lady who'd just left him was about as different from his volatile betrothed as one could imagine. He'd chosen Clarissa Beaumont for her beauty, breeding and the fact that, of all the eager young misses crowding the Marriage Mart this Season, she alone didn't bore him.

He hadn't bargained on a chit of her tender years being already a hardened flirt. Or a shrew.

Nicholas swirled the brandy in his snifter and frowned. Should he have forbidden Miss Wellingford to give Clarissa back his ring? But how could he have resisted the appeal in those lovely silver eyes?

He recalled his fiancée's ugly tantrum, and shuddered. He'd better devise an effective plan, lest he spend a lifetime regretting that bit of gallantry.

Having sorted out the wine, smoothed feelings, succored Lady Beaumont and supervised the unloading of the new lobster, Sarah at last sought Clarissa. Her anger had cooled, but she still intended to give that rash young lady a thorough dressing-down. The task was, how should she deliver it so that the increasingly unmanageable Miss Beaumont paid her any heed?

Drawing, for the moment, a blank in that suit, her thoughts wandered to the marquess. She reviewed their conversation, wondering again why a man of his obvious wit would choose to wed a lady as self-absorbed as Clarissa.

Sarah shrugged. He'd not be the first gentleman whose powers of discernment diminished in direct proportion to the beauty of the lady. Besides, as a leader of London society, he would naturally prefer a bride who flourished there.

Her conscience smote her at that dismissive assessment. To be fair, she must admit she'd learned at first hand seven years ago that he was also a man of honor and compassion.

Remembering that incident inevitably recalled thoughts of Sinjin, and she flinched. With habit of long practice, she took a deep breath, waited for the ache to ease and forced her mind back to the marquess.

Were the widower not society's most famous gambler, as well as its most eligible bachelor, she might find him wholly admirable. But he did gamble. Indeed, Englemere's Luck was a byword throughout the ton.

Coming to London from Oxford with an exalted title and only a modest competence, in a few years at the tables he'd amassed a fortune reputed to be second only to Golden Ball's. It seemed, regardless of the wager or the game, the lord marquess could not lose.

Clarissa, along with the rest of the Upper Ten Thousand, considered his gaming prowess just another manly trait. Sarah could not.

She had seen her father when the gambling fever seized him, knew only too well the feckless optimism that, when Lady Luck frowned, convinced a man that surely the next hand, or the next throw of the dice, would find her smiling again. One reckless wager would follow the next until nothing was left, and heaven help any who depended on him.

Never would Sarah entrust her future to a gambler. Since Clarissa obviously didn't share her reservations, she could only hope, for her friend's sake, that Englemere's Luck would hold for a lifetime.

Which brought her back to Clarissa. As vexing as her friend sometimes was, Sarah truly wanted the best for her.

In addition to striking looks, Clarissa had a keen wit and a tempestuous spirit as often sunny as surly, as soon generous as toplofty. However, Sarah worried, having become the reigning belle, she seemed to forget that even for an incomparable there were limits. Limits, Sarah must make her recognize, that Clarissa could disregard only at her peril.

In offering their home and sponsorship, the Beaumonts had done Sarah a singular favor. Despite Englemere's insinuations, and her own reservations over Lady Beaumont's use of her, she owed them gratitude, loyalty—and an unbroken engagement.

Entering upon her knock, Sarah advanced into the chamber and stopped short. Standing next to the crocodile-legged Egyptian-style settee, Clarissa's abigail fluttered her hands and cast Sarah an apologetic look. Her charge reclined upon the settee, skirts drawn indecorously up above her ankles while she painted her toenails with silver gilt.

Despite her good intentions, Sarah's sorely tried temper snapped. "Heavens, Clare! Do you now plan to appear as an abandoned woman as well as a shrewish one?"

Harris gasped, but Clarissa laughed as she sat up, apparently in high good humor after her earlier pet. "I think it vastly becoming."

"Certainly, if you wish to look like a Haymarket whore. Not, I think, quite the thing for a marchioness."

"Oh, Sarah, you're so…fusty." Her temper miraculously unimpaired, Clarissa waved her hand at the abigail. "Bring us tea or something, Harris. Sarah's going to read me a scold, and I'd as lief not hear it with you gasping and moaning in the background."

By the time the chaperon exited, Sarah had her ire under control. "At least you've sense enough to expect a lecture. Thunder and turf, Clare, what possessed you to treat Englemere so? Are you all about in the head?"

Clarissa settled her skirts about her ankles and gave Sarah a suspiciously penitent look. "I shouldn't have lost my temper, I realize, so you may save yourself the scold. There, now you can't say I'm never reasonable."

"I'm glad to hear it. And I hope—" Sarah chose her words "—you'll take care to be sensible in future. Not just in your dealings with Englemere, but in general."

"Oh, I'm always sensible," Clarissa replied airily.

Sarah bit back a sharp retort. "I cannot call it 'sensible' to tool a curricle down Bond Street—"

"It was eight in the morning, with nobody about to see, and Montclair dared me!"

"Or to let Wexley take snuff from your wrist."

"Oh, that." Clarissa giggled. "He was saying the silliest things, and oh, his mustache tickled." Her grin faded, to be replaced by a frown. "I think it beastly of Englemere to take me to task for that, and for allowing Arthur both my waltzes at Almack's last Wednesday. 'Tis my first Season. Why shouldn't I kick up my heels?" Her tone turned petulant. "I've promised to become his dull marchioness at the end of it. Isn't that enough?"

"Don't you wish to marry Englemere?"

Clarissa studied her toes, moving them so they sparkled in the light. "I suppose so."

"He does gamble," Sarah allowed. "Dearest, if you harbor any doubts…"

"Oh, I don't! Not about his gambling—faith, all the world gambles, and besides, Englemere always wins." A small frown wrinkled the perfection of her profile. "It's rather that…well, he can be positively *gothic* sometimes, acting as though I should have eyes for no man but him. However, he *is* enormously wealthy, and the catch of the Season."

Clarissa picked up a hand mirror, a self-congratulatory smile on her face as she patted her glossy titian curls. "Did you know, in the four years since his wife died in that carriage accident, Englemere never once showed a hint of partiality for any woman—a respectable one, that is—until he met me? I can't wait until he makes the announcement tonight. The other girls will be positively green!"

"Will there be an announcement? I thought you just rather, ah, dramatically ended your understanding."

Clarissa looked startled, but then her face relaxed. "I expect I vexed him, but he'll come round. I'll send him a little note saying, oh, that I became distraught because he seemed disappointed with me, or some such rot." She smiled sunnily, oblivious to Sarah's gasp of outrage. "Gentlemen are so arrogant, he'll believe it. Even better, you write it. You're cleverer with words than I am."

"I most certainly will not!" Sarah retorted. "Englemere's no fool, Clare. You threw his ring back in his face! What makes you think you're still engaged?"

Clarissa eyed Sarah as if she were a perfect dunce. "A gentlemen never cries off."

"No? But you were the one, ah, crying off. What if Englemere doesn't take you back?"

Sarah watched intently, but the reaction she was seeking—horror, remorse, penitence—never came. Clarissa shrugged. "I'll marry someone else, I suppose. Wexley perhaps, or Montclair—he's so amusing."

"Wexley?" Sarah echoed faintly, shocked to realize Clarissa had not lost her heart to her betrothed.

"Or Montclair, but 'tis no matter. Englemere *shall* marry me," Clarissa announced before Sarah could recover. "And if he thinks to keep me under his thumb like some obedient schoolgirl, I'll soon set him to rights."

"You'll not convince him to allow you free rein by shouting at him or painting your toenails like a trollop," Sarah countered bluntly.

"Mrs. Ingram paints her toes."

Sarah's surprise must have shown, for Clarissa sniffed. "I know gossip says she's his mistress. Well, he'll not look at her again once he has me."

The slight change of tone, from confidence to bravado, revived Sarah's flagging sympathy. If Clarissa felt vulnerable, who could wonder? The woman identified by the ton as Englemere's current ladylove was no girl out of the schoolroom, but a mature, sophisticated beauty.

"Englemere may indeed admire spirit—even gilded toenails," Sarah said gently. "But you may be sure he never asked Mrs. Ingram to be his wife."

"Oh, stubble it, Sarah, you're getting to be a dead bore. Just be a dear, and write me that note."

"I will not," Sarah gritted out, once more holding on to her temper with an effort. "I warn you again, don't try to run a rig on Englemere. He'll not stand your nonsense."

Clarissa turned to face Sarah, ominous signs of impending explosion in her flashing eyes. "And how can you claim to know what Englemere will or will not 'stand'?" Clarissa's tone grew saccharine. "That must have been quite a little chat you had after I left. If it weren't beneath me to make such a comment, I might say you were jealous."

Sarah stilled, fixing Clarissa with a stony stare. After a silent moment, Clarissa's gaze wavered. She lowered her eyes, a faint blush staining her cheeks.

"It is indeed beneath you," Sarah replied in clipped tones. "You had better find other, equally vulgar things beneath you in future, if you don't wish to make yourself such a byword nobody will have you."

Clarissa dashed an angry tear. "That's unfair! I could never be! You're supposed to be my friend, and I think you're being horr-rid!" She turned away, her voice breaking on a gusty sob that promised more.

Sarah watched her, wondering a bit remorsefully if she'd overplayed her hand. After a moment, she pulled her weeping friend into her arms and patted her soothingly.

"Hush, now. Here comes Harris with your tea. Let her console you while your wasp-tongued friend goes to check on the household." Sarah pushed Clarissa to arm's length and studied her face. "We are still friends?"

Tears bejeweling her emerald eyes, Clarissa nodded a little doubtfully. The fit of weeping had turned neither eyes nor even the tip of her perfect nose red, Sarah noted with chagrin.

She turned to go, then halted. "I nearly forgot." Producing the ruby, she grinned. "You were right, he didn't cry off. You must write your own note, though. Mind you make it a good one."

Leaving her friend to the efforts of her abigail, Sarah walked out. At the end, she thought she'd reached Clarissa. With grave problems of her own to deal with, Sarah could only hope the impression would last.

Chapter Two

Sarah inspected the deserted supper room: platters, punch bowls, posies all in place. She nodded approvingly. The ball was a great success, Clarissa seemed on her best behavior, and Sarah had every reason to be pleased.

Glimpsing herself in the pier glass over the sideboard, she sighed. The stylish white dress fit well, but the color failed to show her to advantage. She looked, she thought as she inspected her mirrored image critically, like a ghost, or an ice maiden carved for a frost fair.

"So this is where you've hidden away." Englemere's voice interrupted her thoughts. "You should rejoin your guests." Smiling, he approached her. "The gentlemen will be missing you, for you look very lovely this evening."

She turned startled eyes toward him. His expression seemed sincere, and she frowned slightly. This must be gallantry, she concluded, since she'd just determined that she looked about as lively as a statue—

"You shouldn't wince at compliments."

You will not explain, the stern little voice in her head commanded. Sarah closed the mouth she had opened to do just that and pressed her lips together. Drat, what was there about the man that prompted her to almost unthinkingly respond to him? With—worse yet—honest thoughts, not the socially acceptable ones she believed she'd long ago learned to plaster over the genuine.

His lips curved in a smile. She realized she was staring—nearly as sorry a breach of decorum as candor. "Y-yes, my lord," she stammered, feeling like a perfect dolt.

"I wanted to thank you for a lovely party."

"Prettily said, but that compliment is due Lady Beaumont." She managed a reproving look. "As you know."

His smile widened to the twinkle-eyed grin of a small boy succeeding in mischief. "I have this lamentable urge to give credit where it's due. Reprehensible, I admit."

A gurgle of laughter escaped her. "If credit were always placed where it's due, society as we know it would crumble." Sobering, Sarah asked anxiously, "Everything is going well, is it not? Clarissa is—"

"—a paragon of decorum. This afternoon, I received an exemplary note of apology. Only four misspellings." He gave Sarah a penetrating look. "You must have delivered a thundering scold."

A little flustered, she replied, "I did speak with Clarissa, but she needed no prompting. She already regretted the, ah, incident. As her behavior demonstrates."

"You really must allow matters to run their course."

Though softly spoken, she recognized the reproof. He had every right to reject interference, but after all her efforts she couldn't help feeling resentful.

"I did not intend to meddle in a private matter," she said stiffly. "If you feel I have done so, I must apologize. Now, as you justly observed, I should return."

She started past. He caught her wrist. Once again, the touch of his gloved hand sent a tremor up her arm.

"I realize you intervene from a sincere desire to help." With one finger he caressed her wrist. "You aren't 'Ice' at all, are you, Miss Wellingford? 'Tis only right you detest the nickname."

Trembling, Sarah stepped back and withdrew her hand.

No wonder he'd won such a reputation with the ladies. His eyes held hers still; his compelling presence mesmerized.

Her mind skittered, locking on sensation: the throb of her pulse in rhythm with the distant orchestra…the mingled scents of beeswax, roses and shaving soap…the midnight of his eyes and broad, black-coated shoulders silhouetted against the dancing light of the sconces.

Coloring faintly, she turned to fiddle with the perfectly aligned flatware. "I should hope," she managed at last, "I am neither shallow nor easily shattered."

"Not at all." He replaced the fork she'd just moved a fraction of an inch. "If one must compare you to ice, I'd describe you as the solid kind on which one skates. Dependable, and a pleasure to be near. Now—" he took her hand from the table and placed it on his arm "—let me escort you back to the ballroom." In a lighter tone he added, "I expect several faithful swains await your return."

Gallantry again. More comfortable with that than his compliments, she replied, "I don't know about 'several,' but one or two might wish for a dance."

"Which one or two?" He wagged a finger at her. "You've solved my romantic difficulties—let us consider yours. You ventured to London to make a match?"

At her nod, he continued. "From what you've said, I gather you have no male relatives to screen your suitors. Perhaps I should take on the post."

She shot him a glance. Surely he wasn't serious. Nonetheless, she replied politely, "You're very kind, but I couldn't think of it."

He looked startled, as if he didn't understand her refusal. Not wishing to appear ungrateful, she added, "You are funning, I realize, but—"

"Not at all, Miss Wellingford. I'm quite in earnest. After all, who better to judge than an experienced older man acquainted with everyone in the ton?"

"I being so young and green," she countered dryly. "'Tis most generous, but I wouldn't dream of imposing."

"No imposition. I should look upon it almost as…a duty to my fiancée." He drew himself up into a parody of a *pater familias*. "Come, Miss Wellingford. No secrets."

The absurdity of it—having that incomparable Corinthian, the Marquess of Englemere, pass her suitors in review—wrestled with proper reserve, and won. "'Tis ridiculous," she protested, laughing.

"Child, you wound me. Now, tell Uncle Nicholas everything."

For whatever reason—perhaps the same one that had led her to speak frankly before—after a moment's hesitation, she fell in with his game. Leaning closer, she said in confidential tones, "The first is rather young—Marshall Beckman, from Yorkshire."

"The coal magnate's grandson?"

"Yes," she replied, hoping she didn't detect a sudden coolness in his tone. "'Tis true, his grandfather was in trade, but his mother's family is unexceptionable. He's a nice lad, if a trifle…shy." As well he might be, she added mentally, with half the ton ready to cut him for his grandfather, and the other half mocking his tall, gawky frame and spotted face.

"I know nothing to his discredit, though I'd not judge him up to your weight. Who else?"

She chuckled. "The next is surely that! Baron Broughton must outweigh me by several stone. And though I suspect he's much more interested in a new mother for his six daughters than a wife, he has been attentive."

The marquess frowned with mock severity. "Family's acceptable, but for all his wealth, the baron is too fond of the green baize for unqualified approval."

She thought she'd masked her reaction, but Englemere laughed. "The pot calling the kettle black, you think? My dear, don't you know? *I* never lose. As for the baron, rumor says he spends his winnings on—well, I should think you would want more than a nursemaid's position.''

She gazed up at him appraisingly. ''Do you think I look for love, or some grand passion? I assure you, at my advanced age I've long since abandoned romantic notions. Should he honor me with a proposal, I am certain the baron would treat me with kindness and respect.''

''Paltry.'' Englemere dismissed the baron—or her sentiments—with a wave of the hand. ''If not grand passion, then devotion is a minimum requirement. I insist on it.''

One marble-perfect face flashed into her mind. ''I would rather dispense with the devoted one,'' she muttered.

''*Devoted?* Excellent. Who is this perceptive man?''

Sarah looked away, her enjoyment of their banter dashed. She didn't wish to discuss Sir James. When possible, she avoided even thinking of him. Chastising herself for having begun this silly recital of suitors, she reluctantly replied, ''Sir James Findlay.''

Englemere's smile vanished. ''Entirely unsuitable,'' he said flatly. ''Findlay's already buried two wives. Suicides, rumor says. He's received—just barely—but no matron worth her salt would let an unmarried daughter near him. I'm astonished Lady Beaumont permitted it.''

''She's been busy, and he can be charming.''

''Perhaps, but I still think it a shocking lapse.'' He looked steadily at her. ''No more funning, Sarah—Miss Wellingford. The man's a villain, and I say that based on personal experience, not rumor. Dismiss him.''

Despite her reservations about Findlay, Sarah's independent nature bridled at the command. ''I've heard the rumors, and I think it reprehensible that a man be condemned on that basis. Sir James comes from an excellent family and is, as you admit, everywhere received. To me, he has been all that is correct.''

''Excuse me, Miss Wellingford. I didn't mean to dictate. Please understand I spoke from genuine concern.''

Her resentment extinguished by his swift apology, she

felt foolishly churlish. "I do understand. Excuse *me* for flying into the boughs. And I must confess, for all that Sir James is handsome, well-bred and amusing, I cannot like him. Unfortunately, of my several suitors, he's by far the most persistent." Sarah sighed. "And he's very rich."

"They are all of them rich, aren't they?" he mused, as if just realizing the fact. "Is wealth *that* important?"

She sensed, rather than heard, the change in his tone. What matter if he thought her a fortune hunter. Was that not the bare truth? His disapproval should not have hurt, but it did. "Some of us do not possess the privilege of free choice," she said defensively.

"Naturally, one must choose jewels, and modish gowns, and fancy carriages," he replied, his voice sardonic.

"Jewels and gowns and carriages?" she gasped, truly stung now. "Try food, and clothing, and a roof over one's head!" She regretted the outburst the moment the words left her lips. Her face heating, she turned away.

"I had heard Wellingford was all done up." His quiet voice came over her shoulder. "Are things that bad?"

She was suddenly, furiously angry—at herself, for once again blundering into confession, at him for his well-heeled disdain. Even more, at that moment she hated Englemere for unleashing the burden of worry she struggled so hard to contain. Was it not enough that it haunted her dreams?

She turned back to stare straight into his eyes. "Lord Englemere, do you think me stupid enough to have thrown myself—a plain, penniless ape-leader—to the Marriage Mart wolves, were the case not *absolutely* desperate?"

"Tête-à-tête with Englemere? That will never do."

The mocking voice wafted to her from the doorway, and Sarah winced. *Not yet.* She needed to be at her best to deal with Sir James, and now her composure was in shreds.

"I wondered where you'd gone." Sir James strolled toward them. "Lady Beaumont sent you on another little errand, did she? I must return you to the party."

He took Sarah's hand. "'Evening, Englemere." He bowed. "I'm to wish you happy, am I not? Mayhap you will soon be doing the same for me." Sir James gave Sarah a significant look. "Come along, my dear. The next dance is mine."

Ushered out by Sir James, Sarah could do no more than nod a brief parting to Englemere. As he bore her down the hall, she found her voice. "'Twas presumptuous of you to speak so to Lord Englemere." She tugged at her hand. "You know quite well you have not asked, nor have I answered."

Sir James obligingly loosened his grip. Sarah felt a strong urge to remove her hand—and her person—from his presence, though she had no reason beyond an instinctive dislike to justify such rudeness. After a moment's inner struggle, she left her hand on his arm.

Smiling, as if in thanks, he patted it. "We both know I shall ask very soon. How much time have you left before the note comes due—ten days? I shall ask, and when I do, we both know what your answer must be."

Sarah glanced sideways at him, wondering not for the first time why she could not bring herself even to tolerate the undeniably handsome, elegantly dressed Sir James. Perhaps it was the coldness of that chiseled profile, which might serve as a sculptor's model for a Greek hero, or the disturbing light she sometimes caught flashing in his clear blue eyes. Or his irritating arrogance.

"You are not my only suitor."

"Sarah, surely you don't mean to compare my faultless breeding with that spotty-faced youth's. He's unworthy of you, my dove. In any event, I understand he's gone out of town—to Scotland, I believe. Inspecting a stallion."

"Indeed? He mentioned no such trip yesterday."

"Did he not?" Sir James shook his head. "Perhaps I'm mistaken, but I doubt it. 'Tis my stallion, you see."

A chill rippled through her. Resolutely she stilled it. "My resources are not quite exhausted."

"You refer to the corpulent baron?" Sir James smiled. "A sadly unreliable champion, my dove. Not only is he enamored of quite a different ladybird, he has a most unfortunate fondness for gambling." Sir James sighed. "It seems in recent days his luck has changed for the worse. From what I hear, he'll soon be barely able to afford that mistress, much less a new wife."

"I suppose he told you that?"

Sir James chuckled and tapped her nose with one finger, like an indulgent parent. "We gentlemen hear such things, in the wicked fastness of our clubs. 'Tis true enough, I vow. You do much better to have me, my dear."

Sarah pulled away. "I am not 'your dear' and certainly not 'your dove.' You will refrain from addressing me so."

An odd flash in his pale blue eyes sent a frisson of alarm through her. Then he laughed, leaving her to wonder if she'd only imagined it.

"But you *are* a dove, my dear. A lovely, fluttering dove dragging her wing across the ground to lead predators away from her nestlings. I shall save the nest—that is the bargain, is it not? Save Wellingford Hall and your brother's patrimony, and ensure your nestling sisters' dowries."

Before she could guess his intent, he brought her hand to his lips and kissed it. She jerked away, but he held on, his grip like iron. "My wealth I'll gladly expend to lift those burdens from your shoulders."

She tugged again and he released her, giving her wrist a quick, apologetic rub as if realizing he'd grasped it too tightly. "We shall deal well together. You will see."

"Perhaps," Sarah retorted, "but as you kindly remind me, I have ten days left. Mr. Beckwith may return from viewing *your* horse, or the baron's luck improve."

Sir James halted abruptly on the ballroom's threshold and gave her a long, slow smile. "I don't think so."

Mercifully, the movements of the dance separated Sarah from Sir James, precluding the need for conversation. For weeks she had suspected Findlay of toying with her, advancing, then retreating as he studied her other suitors with an amused and calculating eye.

Unease formed a little knot in her stomach. Twelve hours ago Mr. Beckman told her he was looking forward to this ball. Had Sir James indeed sent him to Scotland? Could he be gambling against the baron as well? Her attentive suitor was well-known to be infallible with the bones and unbeatable at cards, so much so that knowledgeable gamblers avoided him.

The music ended. She sensed Findlay's eyes on her. A sudden revulsion seized her, so strong she could barely prevent herself from bolting as he picked up her dance card.

"Baron Broughton's tardy," he announced after perusing it. "I shall claim his waltz."

"Sorry, Sir James." Lord Englemere materialized behind her. "You promised me this waltz in the supper room, remember, Miss Wellingford? You'll not object, Findlay."

He swept her away before Sir James could protest. She clung to him through the steps of the dance, as if the ballroom were a stormy sea and he the buoy keeping her afloat. Gradually, the lilting rhythm began to relax her.

"Much better, Miss Wellingford. Though I could not blame one suffering Findlay's presence from stiffening up, it is rather difficult waltzing with a board."

She laughed, if a bit shakily. "Thank you for the rescue, my lord. I have had a surfeit of his attention."

"Ah, we are to have conversation, too. Excellent! Then I am well rewarded for my bravery."

"In cutting out Sir James?"

"Findlay?" He dismissed the baronet in a voice laced with contempt. "No, 'twas my lady fair I feared. You left me with a look that would have melted stone. Though I was shaking in my slippers, I felt I must face your displeasure, if only long enough to apologize."

"You said nothing for which you need apologize. I must marry for money." She offered a smile that almost succeeded. "A fact no less true for being unpalatable."

"Too often the innocent suffer for the sins of the guilty," he said with an intensity that surprised her. "And I do owe an apology, to think even for a moment that you might marry for shallow or selfish reasons."

"Don't make me out a martyr," she murmured, tears pricking her eyes. "My predicament is all too common."

"One does what one must. But Sarah—not Findlay."

"Let us abandon such a dismal subject. Come, this should be a joyful night! Thankful as I am for your intervention, should you not be waltzing with Clarissa?"

"I'm afraid I'm in her black books again. Wexley." The marquess rolled his eyes in exasperation. "I objected to her marked partiality for that fop. Of course, she had to go off immediately and waltz with him." At Sarah's look of alarm, his expression lightened to ruefulness. "You didn't expect her to behave for an entire evening?"

The music faded, and the marquess led her off the floor. "There now, remove that troubled look from your brow." Englemere brushed a fingertip across her forehead as if to do just that. "Lady Beaumont is waving—she must require your assistance. I can handle Clarissa."

"I have no doubt. Yes, madam," she called, and turned back to him. "Thank you again for *your* assistance."

He gave her fingers a lingering squeeze. "You're most welcome. Good evening, Miss Wellingford."

Sarah walked over to Lady Beaumont, her mind in tangles and her hand tingling.

Thoughtfully Englemere watched Sarah go. He must hunt up his betrothed and escort her in to supper. Things in that line were progressing nicely, and once he had his own affairs sorted out, perhaps he should devote some time to Miss Wellingford's.

The idle conclusion startled him. He'd thought himself

beyond becoming interested in a woman toward whom he harbored neither carnal nor marital intentions. But, he realized, Miss Wellingford intrigued him.

No, she wasn't "Ice." He noted her response to him in the supper room, the flare of mingled interest and confusion that revealed her innocence even as it hinted of a hidden passion. Not that he'd be the man to uncover it, of course.

He'd immediately regretted the casual offer to review her suitors, but before he could retract it, she'd piqued him by refusing. In his experience no woman, be she countess or courtesan, ever turned down a chance to further her own interests. Upon the spot he decided to pursue the game, fencing with her until she acquiesced.

He liked the way she spoke frankly to him, with a man's directness rather than a woman's wiles. Those changeable silver eyes that glowed when he amused her, that throaty little gurgle of a laugh, charmed him.

He remembered her frown at the fulsome compliment he'd paid her, and smiled. He'd give a monkey to know what she'd been thinking behind those expressive eyes, what she'd almost said before a lamentable caution stilled her tongue. Damn, but she'd be wasted on the provincial Beckman or the pompous Broughton.

Then he recalled her shudder at Findlay's approach, and his amusement faded. Perhaps more than anything else, he admired the courage and sense of duty that propelled her, for the sake of family, to even consider wedding such a one.

To allow her sweet loveliness into the keeping of that scoundrel would be a crime. But how to prevent it?

He must review the ranks of his friends, he decided as he set off to bring his recalcitrant fiancée to heel. Surely one of them was ripe for the parson's mousetrap, and would prove a more fitting match for the quiet elegance of Sarah Wellingford.

Chapter Three

The warm parlor fire lulling her, Sarah let Lady Beaumont's bright chatter and Englemere's occasional polite replies wash around her like the babble of a country brook. The chiming of the mantel clock brought her up with a start.

Lady Beaumont cast a worried glance at the timepiece. "Clarissa wished to wear the charming new gown you commissioned. Emerald shows to such advantage on her, and I know she wants to look her loveliest—"

"I'm sure our patience will be well rewarded." Draining the brandy from his glass, Englemere walked over to lean against the mantel. *He displays well in evening dress,* Sarah thought sleepily, taking in the elegant black coat and trousers, the pure white waistcoat and snowy cravat. Elegant and annoyed, with Clarissa forty minutes late.

She turned to find Lady Beaumont glaring at her. Her ladyship refashioned the glare into a smile and said pleasantly, "Sarah, dear, why don't you go assist Clarissa?"

"With Harris and her maid both attending her, I'm likely to be more a hindrance than a help," Sarah protested. For Clarissa to be this tardy must mean she'd find above stairs a minefield of frayed temper and wrought nerves that she would as lief not enter.

"I'm told Harris took to her bed with a nervous spasm."

Lady Beaumont's voice conveyed her irritation at this blatant dereliction of duty. "Doubtless Lizette is having difficulty managing alone."

"I'll go at once, then." Sarah suppressed a sigh.

Lady Beaumont patted Sarah's hand and turned to the marquess. "Allow me to refill your glass, Englemere."

Sarah plodded up the stairs, puzzled that Mrs. Harris would have allowed herself to succumb on such an important evening. Invitations to the Dowager Duchess of Avon's occasional entertainments were jealously sought, and tonight's ball would be one of the Season's most glittering.

She hoped her erstwhile suitors would be there. In the four days since Clarissa's ball, she had neither seen nor heard from Marshall Beckman. Worse, rumor whispered Baron Broughton was indeed gaming against Sir James— and losing.

The news worried her. She'd not survived a gamester father to pledge herself willingly to yet another. And should the baron propose, would he be able to provide the staggering sum she required to rescue Wellingford?

Her recent chat with the banker confirmed she'd not be able to beg additional time. While expressing sympathy for her unfortunate circumstances, he informed her the full sum due must be paid by the stated date, or the bank would be forced, regrettably but unavoidably, to foreclose.

Six days left. Three, really, for even with a special license—her cheeks reddened to think of conveying the news that there'd be no time for a proper calling of banns—her hapless bridegroom would probably require another two or three days to gather the necessary cash.

Sir James, however, knew exactly how much money she needed, and when. She'd detailed it early on, thinking to discourage him, but the knowledge had seemed rather to pique his interest. If only she'd not made that miscalculation.

The vision that greeted her when she entered Clarissa's

room drove all other thoughts from her brain. Draped in emerald satin, Clarissa regarded herself in the pier glass while her little French maid beamed up adoringly. "Ah, *mam'selle,* is she not *magnifique?*" Lizette breathed.

Magnificent wasn't the first word that occurred to Sarah. She understood now what had caused Harris's attack of the vapors and why Clarissa had so delayed what would undoubtedly be an unforgettable entrance.

The satin material reflected the glow of the candelabra and hugged every curve of Clarissa's voluptuous body, outlining in a sensuous ripple of light the movement of her thigh as she tapped her foot. The merest suggestion of a bodice confined her full breasts, and Sarah could swear she saw the dark shadow of nipples below the gown's edge.

Clarissa had seemed troubled, but at Sarah's gape-mouthed shock, her chin rose. "Englemere chose the modiste and material. Harris has already scolded, wept and been sent to bed for her pains, so don't start."

Sarah knew she ought to do something to dissuade Clarissa, but she was too tired to summon the effort. Instead, she was struck by the total incongruity of such a gown being worn by a supposedly innocent young lady of quality.

Her lips twitched as she thought of the look on the stone face of Mrs. Drummond Burrell should Clarissa trip over the threshold of Almack's wearing this. As for the reaction of Clarissa's slavishly admiring courtiers—Wexley would probably walk straight into a post. A suppressed giggle escaped, and then she burst out laughing.

"Heavens, Clare." She gasped. "Do you mean to make your rejected suitors expire of jealousy?"

After a surprised moment, Clarissa's defensive face relaxed. "They should. Is it not wondrous sophisticated? 'Tis not the gown of some First Season mouse, and Englemere will see he cannot prose and criticize as if I were."

Sarah thought the dress would incite the marquess to more violent reaction than speech, but refrained from saying so. "Clare, surely he didn't approve this, did he?"

Clarissa fingered the gold and emerald choker that provided the only coverage for the otherwise bare skin extending to her cleavage. "We looked at fashion plates. But he grew 'bored with feminine twaddle—'" her voice shaded with pique over this unchivalrous remark "—and left for his club before I found the design. Madame Thérèse argued 'twas not suitable for one of my 'tender years,' but I knew I must have it." She patted the matching earbobs. "The bodice is a trifle…briefer than I expected."

"Why not have Thérèse alter it for tomorrow night?"

"I ordered it expressly for the Duchess of Avon's ball," Clare objected, her tone turning petulant. "Besides, Englemere has been carping at me every evening. With me wearing this gown—" she stroked her hips with a satisfied smile "—he shall see that though *he* may only complain and chide, quite a number of other gentlemen find much to admire."

The two friends looked at each other. Sarah could tell from the mulish set of her chin and her sparkling eyes that Clarissa had set her iron will upon this.

Dispensing with the useless, she rummaged in Clarissa's drawer and pulled out a thin shawl of gossamer gold thread. "This would set off the gown nicely," she coaxed.

Clarissa considered the shawl and, apparently satisfied with winning the rubber, conceded the point. "Yes, it will be pretty, do you not think, Lizette?"

The maid murmured approval and draped the shawl loosely about her mistress's shoulders. Sarah motioned her aside, wrapped the gauzy gold twice around Clarissa and tucked the ends under her elbows. "Do you think you can dance in it?"

Clarissa twirled. "I like it. Quite understated."

Sarah smothered a choke. *Heaven help us if it falls off,* she thought as she propelled Clarissa from the chamber.

* * *

The two friends entered the salon to silence, the desultory conversation Lady Beaumont had been maintaining having evidently expired in their absence.

Clarissa swept a deep curtsy. Relief lighting her face, her mother turned to them. Englemere walked over with no sign of impatience, though Sarah noted by the mantel clock they were now a full hour late.

"Mama, Englemere, I'm so sorry to have kept you waiting! Truly we don't value Harris as we ought. I had no idea it would take so long to dress without her."

"You look charming, dearest. Does she not, my lord?" Lady Beaumont darted a nervous glance at Englemere.

The marquess brought Clarissa's hand to his lips. "Doubtless worth waiting for. Emerald and gold with your glorious hair are stunning. I'll be accounted the luckiest man at the ball tonight."

"Thank you, my lord." Clarissa preened at his obvious admiration. "Ring for our cloaks, won't you, Sarah?"

Sarah nodded and walked to the bellpull. Clarissa made to follow, but Englemere caught her shoulder.

"The gown is delectable, my sweet." Englemere toyed with the trailing ends of the gold wrap. "Let me feast my eyes before I must share you with all the world." His smile teasing, he began to unwind the diaphanous cloth.

"Englemere!" Clarissa squeaked, catching his hands.

"My dear?" He raised one eyebrow.

Clarissa must have realized she could summon no reasonable objection. To her credit, she made no attempt to wriggle away or explain, but released his fingers and stood proudly silent. Sarah's hand clenched on the bellpull.

"Beauty unveiled!" With a flourish, the marquess pulled the drape free. Slowly his smile faded. The shawl slipped from his fingers and drifted to the floor.

"Cla-ris-sa!" Lady Beaumont wailed. Clutching her bosom, she toppled back against the sofa.

Galvanized by Lady Beaumont's cry, Sarah let go the

bell cord. For the briefest moment, she saw on Englemere's face a look of profound weariness, succeeded by—
regret?

"Stunning indeed," he murmured.

Sarah fumbled through her reticule and pulled out smelling salts. While she patted Lady Beaumont's hand and
waved the vial under the moaning woman's nose, she
found her attention drawn irresistibly to the betrothed couple.

Clarissa, brave as Sarah had claimed, did not quail under
her fiancé's scrutiny. Drawing her breath in sharply, a
movement Sarah feared might drop the skimpy bodice to
a truly indecent level, she stared with haughty defiance
straight ahead.

"Any rumors you may have heard of my imminent financial collapse are grossly exaggerated, my dear," Englemere said at last. "I assure you there will be no need
for my wife to earn her bread on the stage—or the street."

Clarissa stiffened. "You are offensive, Englemere." In
one fluid motion, she scooped the shawl from the floor and
flung it about her shoulders. "Do get up, Mama. Timms
will be bringing our cloaks."

Englemere placed a hand on her collarbone. "No, 'tis
you who offend, my dear." He ran his fingers up the bare
skin to her chin and tilted her face toward him. "You've
had your little joke, shocked your poor mama and made
Miss Wellingford miss half the duchess's ball. 'Tis time
to behave. You have twenty minutes to change into something suitable and present yourself back downstairs."

Clarissa set her teeth and glared at him. "The gown was
commissioned for this ball and I mean to wear it. If you
dislike the style, 'tis your own fault. You should have
stayed at the modiste's until we made the final selection."

"You can't imagine I would have approved *this*." The
marquess met her glare. After a fraught moment, and despite her obvious anger, Clarissa dropped her eyes.

"Twenty minutes. Considering how little there is of it,

'twill be no great piece of work to remove. Lady Beaumont, if you please, send Miss Wellingford to assist."

Timms entered, the ladies' evening cloaks draped over his arm. The marquess turned to him. "Have the housekeeper summon Miss Clarissa's maid—Lizette, is it? She is to be discharged immediately."

Clarissa had been walking with sulky reluctance toward the door, but at this, she whirled around with a gasp. "How dare you presume to dismiss my servant?"

Ignoring her, the marquess continued, "Since 'tis already dark, the girl may stay the night, but I want her gone first thing in the morning. She may approach my housekeeper in Curzon Street for her wages."

Clarissa stormed up to him. Englemere silenced her with one contemptuous look.

After the butler withdrew, he drawled, "My dear, you can hardly expect me to nursemaid you through every social engagement. Since you've demonstrated so little sense of your own, you must have a proper dresser." He paused for a sip of wine. "I cannot permit my wife to employ a maid lack-witted enough to send her mistress out dressed like a Covent Garden drab."

Lady Beaumont moaned, and Sarah caught her breath in dismay. White-faced with fury, Clarissa stood stock-still, two bright spots of color burning in her cheeks. She made a movement with one hand. Englemere trapped her wrist.

"Don't even try," he breathed.

Clarissa jerked her hand free. Turning on her heel, she swept from the room and slammed the door.

In the hall Sarah heard the crash of splintering crockery. She wondered with numb detachment which of the Chinese vases had been sacrificed to Clarissa's wrath.

She started at a touch to her arm. "We leave in twenty minutes," the marquess said softly, and Sarah was struck again by his air of weariness. "If Clarissa chooses to stay home and pout, she may do so, but please do come down yourself." He gave her an apologetic flicker of a smile. "I shouldn't wish you to miss the ball entirely."

Quietly he moved to the sideboard. "Dear Lady Beaumont, you must need a restorative."

The door opened before she reached it, revealing a wooden-faced Timms and three footmen hovering in the hall. Jagged shards lay scattered about the marble floor.

Sighing, Sarah mounted the stairs once again. The state Clarissa would be in when she arrived didn't bear thinking of. Why could the marquess not have chosen to delay schooling his bride until *after* the wedding?

To Sarah's surprise, Clarissa completed her change with unusual speed, in even more unusual silence. However, anger radiated from her in palpable waves, and Sarah was unhappily certain that before the night ended, she would explode.

The marquess and Lady Beaumont awaited them in the entry, already garbed in their evening cloaks. As the two friends descended, Lord Englemere extracted a pocket watch from the folds of his cloak and made an elaborate show of consulting it. "So you can be punctual when you wish," he announced. "An encouraging sign."

Clarissa, engaged in adjusting the cape the footman had thrown over her shoulders, did not reply. Englemere strolled over to her. "Late as it is, shall we go?"

Clarissa looked through the marquess as if he weren't there. Ignoring his proffered arm, she walked past him to the door. Lady Beaumont and the footman both inhaled audibly, and even Timms's hands faltered on the door handle. Sarah thought she saw the flicker of a smile on Englemere's lips before he shrugged and gave his arm to Lady Beaumont.

The receiving line had long since disbanded when they finally arrived at the duchess's ball. Before they could attempt to find their hostess, a blond bear of a man accosted them.

"Thank God you're here, Englemere! Thought I'd mistaken the date."

"Sorry, Hal. Ladies, let me present my good friend Mr. Henry Mountbanke Waterman. Hal, Lady Beaumont, Miss Clarissa Beaumont and Miss Sarah Wellingford."

Clarissa turned on him a smile so radiant the young man's jaw dropped. "Charmed to meet you, Mr. Waterman. I'm in a positive *fury* to dance. Shall we?"

Before she could offer her hand, Englemere scooped it up. "Hal will be delighted to squire you later, my dear. First we must greet the duchess and settle your mama."

Clarissa tried, unsuccessfully, to pull her hand free. "Come along, my dear," the marquess said in the cajoling tone with which one humors a sulky child. He patted his friend's shoulder. "Hal, why don't you take Miss Wellingford for a turn? He looks ferocious," he said to Sarah with a smile, "but he's really quite tame."

Though Clarissa cast him a furious glance, the marquess bore her off. 'Twas one more match waved near a smoking fuse, Sarah thought as she smiled at the blond giant.

Mr. Waterman managed to cease gaping, but hadn't yet progressed to speech. With practiced ease, Sarah filled the gap. "I'm sure Clarissa will dance with you later."

Mr. Waterman shuddered. "No, thank you, ma'am! Don't like Beauties. Acid tongues, most of 'em. Like m'mother. Came to dance with you."

"Me?" Sarah echoed in astonishment.

"Nicky told us that bounder Findlay was making up to you. Said you needed some camfo—camfla—"

"Camouflage?"

"Yes, that's it. Nobody can see around me, you know. Avoid balls as a rule, but had to come. My best friend."

"Lord Englemere?"

"Why, yes. Did you think I meant Findlay? Bad man, that. Ought to avoid him."

With that sage advice, he led her onto the floor. "Big

lummox, but I dance well. No conversation, though. Nicky said you wouldn't mind.''

"There's no need to converse if you prefer not to.'' Sarah craned her neck up. Though his face and form were larger than an ordinary man's, her massive escort was quite handsome, once one adjusted to the sheer size of him.

If he were inarticulate, he also seemed kind. Curiosity got the better of her, and despite her assurance, she had to ask, "Why do you avoid balls, Mr. Waterman?''

"Women. Girls, actually. Terrified of 'em. So little and frail. Afraid I'm going to step on a foot, or hold an arm too tight.'' He peered down at her in sudden alarm. "You ain't fragile, are you? Nicky promised you wasn't.''

"I'm quite sturdy,'' Sarah assured him.

"Worse 'n that, they want to marry me. Oh, I know I'm not much to look at—or too much, rather.'' He smiled with self-deprecating humor. "Don't matter, though. Least not to the mamas. Rich, you see.''

Sarah felt a rush of sympathy. "Mr. Waterman, if you are pursued, I'm sure 'tis not for your wealth. I find you quite attractive, and I expect other ladies do as well.''

He missed a step and looked at her in amazement.

Sarah nudged him back in rhythm. "Your manner is, ah, comforting, and I find your size very—manly.''

The tips of his ears reddened, but he shook his head. "Nicky said you was a right'un, but that's doing it too brown, ma'am. Why, my valet's always complaining. Can't stuff me into any sort of fashionable rig. Sad disappointment to her, m'mother says,'' he added gruffly.

"How unfeeling,'' Sarah cried. Catching herself, she continued, "'Tis not my place to criticize, of course. I expect mothers always wish the best for their children. I'm sure I'm often a disappointment to mine.''

"Couldn't be,'' he returned firmly. "Not much in the bone-box—'' he gestured to his head "—but Nicky's a downy one. He likes you, and Nicky's never wrong.''

Suddenly Mr. Waterman stiffened. "Lord, m'mother! She'll try to push some little chit on me. Have to bolt."

He began to dance her rapidly to the opposite side of the room. "Promised Nicky I'd turn you over to Ned. Must go then. No offense taken?"

Sarah gave him her warmest smile. "Not at all, Mr. Waterman. Thank you for a lovely dance. And you're wrong, you know. You converse quite nicely."

"I do?" He looked startled, then a slow grin lit his face. "Tell m'mother, would you?"

"Why would Miss Wellingford wish to converse with your esteemed parent, Hal?" asked a quiet voice at her elbow. "Go on, introduce me," the man prompted.

Mr. Waterman grinned and bashed the newcomer on the shoulder. "Don't mind Ned. Always ragging me. Sir Edward Austin Greeves, Miss Wellingford. Guard her well, gallows-bait. Findlay's in the far corner." Nodding in that direction, he froze. "M'mother. Must dash. 'Servant, Miss Wellingford." With a speed unexpected in so large a man, he wheeled on one foot and fled.

Sarah froze too, and in spite of herself her glance went to the distant corner. As if waiting, Sir James caught her eye and made an elaborate bow.

Sir Edward grasped her trembling hand. "Shall we dance, Miss Wellingford?"

She stuttered something and followed him, taut as a bowstring at the knowledge of Findlay's scrutiny. The baronet simply stood, the mocking smile she hated fixed on his lips, watching them like a predator.

She forced herself to concentrate on Sir Edward. "Did Lord Englemere really send you? How singular of him."

"Nicky is a staunch friend, as I have good reason to know," he replied. "With his support, you need not fear—" his glance drifted briefly to Findlay "—unpleasantness."

In that instant she realized the full import of Mr. Waterman's terse words. Clarissa's quixotic betrothed had deliberately directed two eligible bachelors to attend, protect—and court her? A blaze of hope flared, as swiftly dying. Even had that been his intent, she had no time to ensnare a new suitor. Still, Englemere couldn't know that. Gratitude, regret and a simultaneous despair brought her close to tears.

"I don't recall seeing you before in London, Sir Edward," she said, forcing her mind to less dismal channels. "Do you, like Mr. Waterman, avoid balls?"

Sir Edward seemed to note her distress, and steered her so she could not see Findlay. "I don't trouble myself to attend often. At the risk of lowering what little credit I may have with you, I must admit I seldom spend the Season in London. I'm a simple countryman."

The last was said with the slightest touch of defensiveness, as if he expected her to take him to task for so unfashionable an admission. To Sarah, though, the country meant stability, security and peace. "How fortunate you are! I should thank heaven daily, could I but spend the rest of my life at Wellingford."

Her vehemence seemed to startle him, and she lightened her tone. "Where are your estates situated, Sir Edward?"

"In Kent. I breed horses and cultivate several thousand acres. But you can't be interested in that."

"But I am. Since our steward retired, I've managed Wellingford. Do you know anything of Mr. Coke's methods?"

"Why, I attended his fall session at Holkham just last year." His face lit with surprise and a dawning respect. "Shall I describe it?"

For the next few minutes Sarah drank in details of turnips and tares, barley and wheat, cattle-grazing and sheep. So absorbed was she that she forgot Findlay until she nearly collided with him at the edge of the ballroom.

"Miss Wellingford, good evening." Sir James bowed over her hand. "Our waltz awaits."

"The lady is thirsty, sir," Sir Edward interposed. "I am escorting her to the refreshment room."

"Then I shall take her, and claim my waltz after she is 'refreshed.'" The baronet extended his arm.

Sir Edward retained her hand. "Miss Wellingford and I are in the midst of a discussion. You may waltz later."

Instead of retiring, Findlay planted himself in their path and clapped a hand on Sarah's shoulder. "I, also, have much to discuss with Miss Wellingford. Our acquaintance being of longer standing, I insist on taking precedence."

Findlay's fingers bit into Sarah's shoulder until she winced. Sir Edward's gaze narrowed to Findlay's hand, and he took a menacing step toward the baronet. "If you choose to be impolite, sir, this is not the place to resolve the matter. I will be happy—"

"Please, gentlemen," Sarah broke in, indicating a gathering group of curious onlookers. "Let us not quarrel here. Sir Edward, I shall look forward to resuming our conversation soon. For now, I...I will go with Sir James."

"You need not," Sir Edward said quietly.

"At the moment, I think it—wiser." With reluctance, she withdrew her hand from Sir Edward's arm. Findlay's sardonic smile at her capitulation, though, provoked her to add, "I do thank you, Sir Edward, for the most interesting and enjoyable conversation I've had since coming to London."

He caught her hand and kissed it. "The gratitude is mine. When Nicky claimed he would present to me a lady I would find as intelligent as she was lovely, I bet him a monkey he couldn't. Never have I so thoroughly enjoyed losing a wager." He directed a hostile look at Findlay. "Your servant, Miss Wellingford, and do not hesitate to call upon me at *any time.*"

Findlay pulled Sarah from the room. In the relative solitude of the hallway, he extracted a lace-edged handkerchief and dabbed at his nostrils. "I never see that man without smelling the stables. I can't imagine what you could have found to converse with him about.''

''The stables.''

''How droll. No doubt you were secretly delighted by my rescue, then. 'Tis naughty of you to try to make me jealous,'' he said in a caressing tone that caused her teeth to clench. ''You nearly succeed, I vow. Though it is, you must grant, rather late for these last-minute champions.''

''''Tis all a game to you, is it not?''

''But of course.'' His smile became almost a smirk, and her fingers itched to slap it off his face. ''A game, my dove, I fully intend to win. Oh, yes, I remember,'' he said, raising a hand to forestall a protest. '' 'I have not asked, nor have you answered.' Yet.''

His face darkened with irritation. ''For some reason, Englemere intervenes. 'Tis no matter. You couldn't truly consider either of his friends, even had you sufficient time to enslave them. The first, in addition to his inelegant bumptious self, has a mother who makes the shrew you call friend appear an angel of amiability, and Greeves—! I'm astonished the man knows how to open a door that doesn't lead to a barn.''

''I happen,'' Sarah grated out, ''to be quite fond of the country, and find Sir Edward knowledgeable and amusing.''

''Indeed? Perhaps a very long, bucolic wedding trip is in order. I find myself envisioning it with anticipation.''

Findlay abruptly steered her into a small antechamber.

Alarmed, Sarah halted. ''Sir James! You must not—''

''Compromise you, my dove? You closeted yourself with Englemere willingly enough. 'Twould never answer, you know. He's too slippery a fish to be caught by such tricks.''

''Compromise Englemere? I should never!'' Sarah protested hotly as she retreated from him, stopping before a pair of French doors leading into the garden.

Findlay nodded his head in mock approval. ''Wise of

you. Should Silence Jersey herself discover Englemere's hand up your gown, he'd not be trapped into wedlock.''

''How *dare* you—!'' Sarah gasped, her cheeks flaming.

''Oh, I dare much for you, my dove. Have I not already sent two suitors packing?''

He pressed closer, until she felt the door handles against her back. Trapping her hands, he drew her to him. His glance traveled over her with insolent slowness, from her face down her bare throat to the modest décolletage of her gown. Deliberately he dropped his gaze lower, to rest on the breasts concealed under the thin veiling of muslin. ''You are mine, and no one else shall have you.''

Sarah held herself rigid, refusing to struggle. But when he raised a hand and traced her lips with a gloved finger, she had to fight the urge to flinch.

''No other man could appreciate you as I do. Your slender silver beauty. And that quick wit, my dove. One has only to suggest, and your nimble mind leaps to the accurate conclusion. I find the possibilities...arousing.''

He leaned closer still, his eyes glowing with unmistakable heat. She feared he meant to kiss her, and nausea coiled in her stomach. Though she knew she must not reject him, a desperate need to delay him seized her.

''Sir James,'' she choked out, ''I find it fantastical that you go to such extraordinary lengths to pursue me, when you must know I, ah, cannot return your regard.''

''Love? Hate?'' He shrugged one elegant shoulder. ''They are but two edges of the same slim blade. I could slice from one to the other in a heartbeat.'' He smiled at her, and the chill struck bone. ''I will teach you, little dove, and such pleasure it will bring us both.''

She pushed at him. ''You flatter yourself.''

He laughed softly. ''Of course I will please you. Without pleasure, there could be no shame.'' His breath quickening, he brushed his lips against her hair. ''And I will teach you to please me.'' He dragged her resisting hand up, peeled down her glove and forced her wrist to his mouth. The hot wetness of his tongue stroked her naked skin. Her resolve forgotten in a mindless panic, she tried to wrest her hand free.

With surprising strength, he held the hand motionless, as if to prove he could effortlessly control her. With a groan of distress, she went still.

He smiled again. "Good—you learn to submit. Now you will learn to kneel before me, to pleasure me, with your fingers—" he forced her hand down the length of the hard bulge in his breeches "—and with your sweet pink mouth."

Revolted, she somehow managed to rip her hand free. Beyond caution or rational thought, she slapped his face with all her might.

As the crack of the blow echoed, they both froze. His expression incredulous, Findlay slowly reached up to touch his reddened cheek.

Then his eyes blazed with heat of another sort, and before she could think or move, he seized her. Clapping a hand over her mouth, he dragged her to the side table and pinned her against the wall.

"That wasn't wise, my dear. Now I shall have to punish you." Prying loose the hand he had kissed, he forced it against the burning chamber candle. She screamed, the sound muffled by his palm.

His smile returned. "Pleasure and pain. So swiftly can one become the other. Remember that, little dove." He turned his body and rubbed his hardness against her as he held her wrist to the flame.

Tears dripped down her cheeks and she bit the inside of her mouth, but she refused to cry out again. The pain was itself a blinding flame, blotting out all else and sucking up every reserve of strength. When it abruptly lessened, her knees nearly buckled.

Findlay relaxed his grip. She sagged against the wall, and though he supported her, he made no move to bring her close.

"I came tonight to tell you I'd be leaving town for two days," he said in a conversational tone, as if nothing untoward had transpired. "I must make preparations to receive you. And transfer funds. How much will I require?"

He meant to complete her humiliation, for he knew to the last ha'penny what was owed. Instead, she felt a rage that stiffened her spine. "Nine thousand eight hundred and fifty-six pounds," she spat out. Deliberately, she straightened and stepped away from him.

Findlay laughed. "Courage, too. Damn, but you make me impatient for our union. Until Thursday, then—and try not to gather too many new suitors. 'Twould be wearying to kick their carcasses aside when I return to ask that question."

She accorded him a cold nod. He bowed, and with lightening speed plucked her burned wrist and brought it to his lips. Rather than kiss it, though, he ran the rasp of his tongue over the raw flesh. Pain exploded, and Sarah closed her eyes, once more biting her lip to keep silent.

"Remember," he whispered.

Chapter Four

The pain subsided to dizzying waves. When Sarah opened her eyes, Findlay had gone. She leaned against the side table, for a moment incapable of thought or movement, while nausea roiled in her stomach.

Staggering out the terrace door, she managed to reach the shrubbery before she was thoroughly, miserably sick. When the retching at last subsided, she pulled herself to her feet and fled down the dimmest pathway.

She burst into a deserted clearing and stumbled against a low iron railing. 'Twas the river landing, she realized. A thick fog caught and diffused light from a pair of torchères, as if inside the smoked glass of a lantern. Welcoming the privacy, she sank onto a nearby bench.

She couldn't marry Findlay. Frantically she searched her mind for an alternative.

Marshall Beckman was gone, and the baron probably lost. Mr. Waterman would take years to gather the courage to make an offer, even were he so inclined. She'd been immediately drawn to Sir Edward. Could she possibly approach him?

"Dear Sir Edward," she imagined herself saying, "you begged me to call upon you at any time. Might you do me the small favor of marrying me, to save me from Sir James? By the way, I shall need ten thousand pounds the day of the wedding, which must be tomorrow.'' No, 'twas impossible.

Must she marry anyone? She could hire herself out as a housekeeper and have Aunt Sophrina launch Lizbet. With her beauty and gentleness, though dowerless, surely Lizzie would make a decent match. Later she might assist her sisters.

Her aunt could shelter Elizabeth and one or two of the other girls, but where would the rest go? A potential employer would balk at housing his new employee's penniless siblings. The modest wages Sarah might earn would never suffice to maintain Colton at Eton, much less provide the wardrobe to launch Lizbet's Season. And Colton—stripped of his estate, what future could he hope for?

Whereas, if she steeled herself to marry Findlay, she could see her sisters well dowered and well presented, free to accept worthy men of their choice. Colton could complete his education at Oxford, buy that commission in the Hussars he was always talking about or assume management of his acres. She could replant and tend Wellingford's fields, refurbish or replace its worn or sold-off furnishings.

Wellingford. The image of it, achingly dear, rose before her: the Elizabethan great hall, its half-timbered walls adorned with climbing roses…the graceful stone wings with their Palladian windows…the glass galleries flanked with lilac and flooded with morning or afternoon sun. Unless she acted, Wellingford would be lost.

If she acted, it would be hers always. Perhaps, if she didn't please Findlay, he could be induced to banish her there. A vain hope, she thought sardonically. Did she not please him, he'd be far more likely, given the relish he'd just displayed, to punish rather than banish her.

No doubt he wanted an heir. Though once, in Sinjin's arms, Sarah discovered the joy of closeness with a man she loved, she'd long ago accepted this joy would never be hers. But Findlay? She thought of his cold, white hands pulling her close, touching her intimately. With chilling clarity, she remembered how he meant to have her "please" him.

Gagging, she leaned into the shrubbery. When her already-emptied stomach stopped heaving, she grasped the iron railing and handed herself along it to the river's edge.

Below her, the stream flowed peacefully. How wonderful to feel inside the tranquillity of the river, how soothing to sink beneath its welcoming surface and be no longer tormented by terrible choices and a bleak future.

"Miss Wellingford! Why are you out in this fog?"

She started and nearly lost her balance.

"Careful, my dear!" Lord Englemere jumped over to steady her. "You're much too close to the edge. Why, you might have—" His scolding voice died as he gazed at her.

Sarah knew she must look like the wild woman she felt: hair in disarray, eyes and nose red, bits of shrubbery caught in the lace of her gown. Turning her face away, she tried vainly to summon up some light remark.

"You look upset, Miss Wellingford. I hope my friends were not importunate."

Sarah blessed him for providing so simple a conversational opening. "Indeed not," she croaked. "I found them charming. So kind of you to send them to dance with me. Delightful dancers. But all that dancing—so fatiguing. I had to get away and find some, ah, cool air."

His raised eyebrow as he surveyed their chilly, damp surroundings helped her stop babbling. In a more normal tone, she continued, "What brings you out?"

He gave her a penetrating look before replying. "My lovely betrothed persists in treating me like a leper. After greeting the duchess, she ripped herself free and latched on to Wexley like a limpet. Having watched that charming display quite long enough, I came out to blow a cloud. Yes, I know, a disgusting habit."

"I'll leave you in peace, then. Enjoy your nasty little cigar." Managing a creditable smile, Sarah turned.

Englemere stopped her. "It was Findlay, wasn't it."

"I should get back."

Nicholas didn't release her. "Was your papa so desperately under the hatches that you must consider him?"

At the mention of her father, all her anguish focused, and the remaining restraint in her overwrought mind seemed to snap. "My esteemed father wasn't 'under the hatches,'" she spat out bitterly. "Oh, no, he *sold* the hatches. And everything else he considered even remotely of value. The silver. The furniture. All the estate's and my mother's jewelry. You may see the portraits of my ancestors gracing the drawing rooms of a score of different cits."

Once started, she couldn't seem to halt the angry words. "He sold all the land he could and sucked every possible groat from what he couldn't sell, never putting back a penny. So when he was finally merciful enough to break his neck in some ridiculous hunting wager, we had nothing left. Or nearly nothing." She gave a mirthless laugh. "Fortunately he never realized books were of any worth. I financed this Season by selling off our library."

"The Season's only half over. Dismiss Findlay! You can't *wish* to marry him."

"Wish to!" This time, her laugh bordered on the hysterical. "It makes my skin crawl when he touches me. But Season's end or no, I'm out of time."

He frowned, and suddenly it seemed important that he understand fully, that he not again suspect she was merely weary of poverty, impatient with making do.

"You see," she went on, "when there was nothing left to barter, he borrowed nearly ten thousand pounds, secured by a mortgage on Wellingford."

"How could he? 'Tis entailed, surely."

"But it isn't. Some long-ago ancestor, incensed that his son supported Cromwell against the king, petitioned to have the entail broken. It was never restored." She looked out over the river. "We knew nothing of the debt until six

months after his death, when the bank approached our solicitors. Out of compassion, they gave us three more
months to avoid foreclosure. The time expires Friday.''

"Good Lord."

"As gambling debts go, 'tis not so great a sum, but for
us, 'twas impossible. I hoped we could get by until my
sister Elizabeth came out. She's a true Diamond. But we
had so little time, it had to be me. Now there's no time,
so it has to be him.''

"Have you no other family to assist?"

Sarah shook her head. "Both my parents were sole sur-
viving children. We've only Great-aunt Sophrina—and if
we lose Wellingford, she couldn't take in all of us.''

She inhaled deeply and straightened her shoulders.
"While there's breath in my body, I can't stand by and
watch my family beggared, parceled out to distant relatives
like—outmoded furniture. See my sisters denied any hope
of marriage and my brother stripped of his birthright and
his future. I can't! Could you?''

Nicholas met her fierce, anguished gaze with a troubled
look. "No, I don't expect I could."

"Then you understand." She ought to be shamed, now
that he knew the full extent of her family's degradation,
but instead she felt...comforted. "I must go in. No, stay,"
she said when he moved to escort her. "You've not had
your cigar, and it wouldn't do for us to walk in together.''

Reluctantly he halted. "Go, then, but don't think I concede the point. There must be another way."

"I appreciate your kindness, Lord Englemere. But
there's nothing to be done."

"'Tis not yet Friday."

She smiled at that. He smiled back and took her hand.
As he lifted it, his fingers grazed the burn, and given no
time to steel herself, she cried out.

"Have you injured yourself? Let me see."

Grimacing, Sarah tried to wriggle free, but his fingers

were so close to the wound that the slightest twist fired the burn back to white heat.

"That's what you get, stumbling about in the fog," Nicholas chided as he held her arm up to the flickering light. He froze, expression draining from his face.

Sarah saw the wrist as he must—the blackened edges of the unbuttoned glove, the red, weeping wound. "I—I d-dripped some h-hot candle wax on it." Even in her own ears, the excuse sounded lame.

Nicholas's face hardened. Cursing softly under his breath, he eased his grip. "Where did you leave Findlay?"

She stared back at him. "L-leave?"

"I'll escort you to Lady Beaumont. 'Tis time the baronet had a swift but punishing lesson in manners."

His curt words finally registered. "Oh, no, you mustn't!" Sarah cried in alarm. She dared not imagine what retribution Findlay would wreak on her later if Englemere confronted him. "I…I'm fine. Besides, in no manner can this be considered your concern."

He raised her uninjured hand and kissed it. "But my dear, 'Uncle Nicholas' always protects his own."

"'Twas but a foolish game! Please, my lord, if my desires mean anything to you, do not pursue him."

He stood utterly still for a long moment. "Very well," he said at last. "It shall be as you wish—for now."

"Thank you, my lord. I—I should go in."

He retained her hand. "You must not marry Sir James."

"I must," she said softly. "Despite my momentary weakness, I won't go meekly as a lamb to the slaughter. Nor shall I 'submit'—" she spat out the word "—or remove myself, as those other poor creatures evidently did. Sir James will find I've a stronger will than ever he imagined. And I'm a crack shot with a pistol." She smiled without humor. "If neither of us survives the honeymoon, at least Wellingford will be saved."

"Sarah—"

"There's no more to say. Thank you, my lord."

This time, he let her go. When she glanced back from the turning of the path, he stood staring after her, a lit cheroot glowing in the darkness.

Her wrist bandaged by a sympathetic housekeeper whom she fobbed off with a glib story of an overturned candlestick, Sarah proceeded to repair her glove. She had just finished that task when Lady Beaumont burst in.

"Sarah, thank heavens I've found you! Wherever have you been this age, child? You must come this instant!"

"Calm yourself, Lady Beaumont." Sarah sprang up to assist her. "Let me find your vinaigrette."

"Never mind that, I shall bear up somehow. Oh, 'twas dreadful! You must seek Clarissa at once!"

So, the shot had exploded at last. Sarah braced herself. "What happened to overset you, ma'am?"

"That wretched girl! What must she do but snub, absolutely snub, the duchess, and go hang herself upon Wexley's arm. Three dances—three!—with him, at the center of the ballroom for all the world to see, Wexley clutching her against him in a positively indecent manner!"

"'Twas unwise, truly, but their friendship is—"

"Friendship!" her ladyship shrieked. "I should like to strangle the blackguard! Bad enough that he led her into such indiscretion, but after the second waltz—the two of them still at the center of the room—he pulled off her glove and kissed her bare wrist. *At length!*" Lady Beaumont shuddered. "Countess Lieven was standing not three feet away. Of all moments, Englemere chose then to appear."

"He wasn't amused."

"I should like to strangle him as well. What was he thinking, subjecting my poor darling to such Turkish treatment tonight?" Lady Beaumont demanded, abruptly changing tack. "Small wonder she arrived at the ball in such a pucker, after the horrid things he said to her!"

Sarah made a sympathetic murmur. Lady Beaumont rushed on. "I know not what he said—'twas done so softly none could hear, but it must have been something equally nasty, for—'' she faltered and began shredding her lawn handkerchief ''—for then my darling reacted rather rashly.''

With foreboding, Sarah held her breath and waited. After a silent moment staring unhappily at the far wall, Lady Beaumont said, ''She slapped him.''

''Right there in the ballroom?'' Sarah gasped.

''Full on the face,'' her ladyship confirmed with a little sigh. ''I daresay he will have a bruise.'' That thought seemed to cheer her, for she smiled briefly, but then recalling her mission, she sprang to her feet.

''Englemere didn't say a word, but dragged my poor child off the dance floor.'' Lady Beaumont in turn pulled Sarah toward the door of the withdrawing room. ''And such a look on his face, he's like to murder her! You must go at once!''

Sarah caught the door frame. ''Lady Beaumont, they cannot want someone intruding upon such a…private moment.''

''My darling's safety is in danger! And her future, of course. Have I not sheltered and succored you?''

Almost, Sarah would have preferred to meet Sir James than to interrupt the quarreling lovers. But as Lady Beaumont continued to gaze imploringly at her, she heard again the clarion call of Duty. Why, she wondered as she straightened her shoulders and braced herself for the inevitable, was Duty so often unpleasant?

''I'll do what I can.''

''My smelling salts,'' Lady Beaumont moaned as she released Sarah and tottered back to the sofa. ''No, I shall find them. Go save Clarissa!''

Could anyone perform that melodramatic feat? Sarah wondered as she descended the stairs.

A number of curious guests loitered in the hallway. Shooing them away, she proceeded to the anteroom door.

"...suffer the sight of my intended making a spectacle of herself with that overdressed, underwitted fop."

"'Fop!'" Clarissa's voice cried. "He dresses far more elegantly than you. As for wit, *he,* at least, knows how to treat a lady."

"Kissing another man's fiancée in the middle of the ballroom? Gentlemanly behavior indeed. And I do know how to treat a lady—when I encounter one."

Groaning at that, Sarah entered. "Please, I beg you, restrain yourselves! At least, lower your voices."

She might have been shouting into a gale, for all the attention the pair paid her.

"By God, I've borne enough carping and insult! 'Tis not a ring you gave, but a ball and chain. Saddle some other unfortunate female with it!" Clarissa jerked off his ruby.

"I'm perfectly ready to take it back, I assure you."

Horrified, Sarah leapt over and trapped the ring in her friend's fist. "No, you mustn't! You are overwrought!"

"Stubble it, Sarah." Clarissa brushed Sarah's hand aside and dropped the ring on Englemere's outstretched palm. "Dear Lord Englemere, *devastated* as I am to disappoint you, I've discovered we shall not suit. I'm not at all partial to tyrants." With a regal nod, she swept to the door.

"Shrew," Englemere murmured without heat.

Sarah lifted her skirts to run in pursuit. "No, Clarissa, you cannot—"

Nicholas grabbed her. "Sarah, *don't fix it.*"

"But she will be so sorry, once her temper cools! And you've been no help at all, pushing her so hard all evening! Why, 'tis no wonder—"

She read Nicholas's expression and stopped dead. A niggling suspicion crystallized into certainty. "You complete hand," she breathed. "You *wanted* her to cry off!"

Looking shamefaced, he dropped his eyes. "Well, yes.

But before you take me to task, remember 'twas my future at stake. Desperate measures were called for.''

"Indeed?" Sarah choked out, still astounded.

"Had the deuce of a time of it, too. I was beginning to fear her lust for a title would outweigh her vanity.''

"That's unfair, sir! Her character may need…polishing, but one cannot accuse Clarissa of coveting position. Why, the old Duke of Gresham has—''

"You're right, that *was* ungracious." Nicholas sighed and ran a hand through his hair. "Please believe, had I the smallest indication Clarissa truly cared for me, I should never have driven her to cry off. But 'twas obviously not my charming person she valued. So, seeing her reaction to that dress, I knew I had to end it.''

Sarah's jaw dropped. "Do you mean," she asked slowly, "you *arranged* the green dress?''

He had the grace to blush. "I hadn't meant to admit that," he mumbled. "You will think me beneath reproach.''

Sarah thought him rather ingenious, but wasn't about to let him off that easily. "You, sir, are a rogue. You conspired with Madame to fashion a totally unsuitable garment for your betrothed, just to judge her reaction.''

"I needed to know we had at least some chance for happiness. If not—marriage would surely bring misery to us both. The deception was meant for the good.''

"Equivocation, my lord. 'Twas a reprehensible act.''

"Would you have worn the dress?''

"'Tis not my behavior in question, and at any rate—''

"Would you have?''

"Well, I…that is—''

"No, you would not. Nor would any modest woman of sensibility." He gave her a coaxing smile. "So you *do* think me justified, 'reprehensible' as I was.''

She had to smile back. "All right, I feel some sympathy for your plight. Though that doesn't excuse you!''

His blinding, bone-melting smile seemed lit from within. "You forgive me, then. Thank you."

It seemed he valued her good opinion. That incredible realization robbed her of any further protest. "I must admit I never regarded you two as well suited. Though you must not think too harshly of Clarissa! She doesn't—"

"Spare me a recital of her virtues," Nicholas groaned. "She's a woman grown, and must answer for her own actions. Or her unlucky husband must, Lord help him."

Sarah sighed, knowing how truly he spoke. "Shall you take yourself off to savor your freedom?"

"I feel I've just wriggled out from under the Rock of Gibraltar." He laughed, the sound giddy. "I must remain in town, though. I shall have to begin all over again, you see."

"Surely you are not compelled to marry this Season."

He stared into the distance, rubbing her hand absently. "Mama took my brother's death very hard. It's time and past that I do my duty by the family." He looked back at her, his smile wry. "I can think of nothing that would cheer Mama more than dandling her first grandson on her knee."

"Shall I draw you up a list of eligibles? From *my* vast experience with the ladies of the ton," she teased.

"'Twould be very helpful, dear Aunt Sarah."

"Perhaps I shall. But not tonight. I expect you're anxious now to escape to your friends and your club."

"Excellent advice. Mayhap Clarissa has drawn the fire of the curious, and we can both slip by."

Sarah started. "Oh, dear! Lady Beaumont will be in a state. I must go to her."

"You'll not bear the blame for this fiasco?"

Sarah frowned as she pondered her sponsor's reaction. "Even Lady Beaumont must realize I can't work miracles."

"Are you sure?" He gave her another knee-weakening

smile and carefully clasped her injured hand. "Well, Miss List-Maker, is there nothing I can do for you?"

Her eyes followed his to her bandaged wrist. A wave of bleakness swamped her warm mood. Resolutely she slammed her mind shut against her worries and dredged up a light tone.

"If you *should* decide to gallop off on your white charger, you might ride up and fetch Mr. Beckman back."

He kissed her fingertips. "Perhaps I'll do just that."

With a curtsy and one last smile, Sarah left him. Euphoria swept through Nicholas as he collected his things and slipped out the entry. Free! Damn, he'd been terrified his beauty-blinded senses had lulled him into a blunder that would have blighted the rest of his life. This time, a merciful Providence had seen fit to spare him.

Perhaps he *would* take a trip to the country until the gossip died. He might even go in search of Mr. Beckman.

He recalled Sarah as she joked with him about Yorkshire, her worried face bravely light. His euphoria drained away, and he felt again the rush of fury that succeeded the shock of discovering her injury.

Had she not been so adamant he not intervene, he would have tracked down Findlay that very instant. *No, Sarah Wellingford,* he vowed silently, *you'll not wed Sir James, if I have to kill him to prevent it.*

Shooting Findlay wouldn't solve all Sarah's problems. She still needed to marry money, and she deserved better than the callow Beckman lad. Ned and Hal were both far preferable candidates—but how to get either to the sticking point before Friday?

He was halfway down the street when the answer came to him, so simple, so perfect and so blindingly obvious he wondered he hadn't tumbled to it immediately. No need to harry his friends: he would marry Sarah Wellingford himself.

Chapter Five

He stood stock-still, examining the decision from every angle. In one stroke, he could secure the wife he required and rescue a lady he admired from a difficult, possibly dangerous future.

A mature woman well beyond romantical illusions, Sarah Wellingford would be a skillful hostess, a capable manager, a congenial companion. Even better, they were friends. Their union could be grounded, not in some ephemeral notion of ''love,'' but in the solid base of mutual respect.

Best of all, Sarah totally lacked the flirtatiousness that demands a permanent coterie of admirers, nor was her beauty the breathtaking sort that might entice men to rash or adulterous action. No, it required a discriminating man of considerable refinement to appreciate her subtle quality.

Skillful, capable, congenial—and *safe*. Since he was forced to gamble once again on a woman's honor, he felt better gambling on Sarah's than on that of any other woman he could imagine. Yes, 'twas perfect.

He didn't think himself conceited to assume Sarah would prefer his suit to Findlay's. Indeed, he couldn't wait to see her relief when he offered such a simple, safe alternative. Small wonder she'd looked worried tonight, weighed down by the prospect of falling into Findlay's power. He should go back right now and end her anxiety.

He swerved around to do just that, and halted once more. At the moment, she was no doubt tending a swooning Lady Beaumont, awash in burnt feathers and vinaigrette. Any attempt to spirit her away for a private chat was about as likely to succeed as an attempt to reform her father's gambling habits. He'd have to wait until morning.

Nicholas peered at his curricle from beneath shuttered lids. He waited for the high step, dancing in the disturbingly brilliant sunlight, to steady before hoisting himself up. That movement intensified the pounding in his head to a clang that rivaled Magdalen's carillon, and he groaned. Perhaps the last bottle of brandy had been unwise.

He'd met Ned and Hal at White's, broken the news of his fortuitous liberation and toasted his deliverance well into the night. Despite a gag-inducing mug of his valet's infallible morning-after potion, his head still throbbed, his eyes felt as if someone had lit a candle behind them, and his mouth hadn't tasted so foul since his last bowl of the noxious pap served as breakfast gruel at Eton.

Yet here he was, properly rigged for a call—at least he trusted he was, Baines being an efficient valet—having nobly abandoned his deathbed to totter off at a positively indecent hour, all to relieve Miss Wellingford's anxiety. Nicholas hoped she would appreciate it.

After crashing through the third crater that saw his stomach rise in proportion to the distance the curricle fell, he pulled up the horses. Damn, he cursed silently, why were London roads in such bad repair?

He handed the reins over to his grinning tiger. Informing the lad he would walk, he lowered himself gingerly to the street. Six blocks later, feeling he'd hiked six miles, he at last mounted the steps of Beaumont House.

The brass knocker dropped with a bang that made him wince. As the last reverberations echoed through his skull,

Timms appeared. Nicholas donned his most charming smile.

"Good morning, Timms. If I might—"

"My lord." Timms bowed. "The ladies are not in."

Before he could utter another word, Timms started to shut the heavy mahogany door. Nicholas just managed to shove in a foot before the portal closed on his soft leather boot. Eyes watering from the pain, he gritted his teeth and smiled gamely. "A moment, please, Timms."

The butler looked down to Nicholas's intruding foot and back up, his expression wooden. "Forgive me, Lord Englemere, but I have express orders to deny you the house."

"I appreciate that, but my message is urgent, and—"

"Your boot, my lord." Hands on the door handle, Timms cast another pointed glance at Nicholas's foot.

With a sigh, Nicholas dug a gold coin out of his waistcoat. "Admit me for a moment only, if you please."

After a brief hesitation, Timms pocketed the coin. He stepped back, allowing Nicholas barely enough space to pass. Wondering if his boot were past repair and envisioning Baines's swoon when he saw it, Nicholas limped through.

"Would you summon Miss Wellingford? She'll be quite willing to see me, I promise you."

"Miss Wellingford is not in."

Nicholas's smile died. "Not 'in'! Why, you thieving old rogue, I'll—"

The butler fell back, his hands raised as if to ward off a blow. "Indeed, my lord, 'tis true, I swear it! Miss Wellingford has gone out. To walk, she said."

The butler's alarm was genuine, and Nicholas saw no reason to mistrust his word. Irritation pulsed in time with his throbbing head. "When do you expect her?"

"She didn't say, my lord. I'm sorry, my lord."

Nicholas tried to make his spongy brain function. "Where did she go?"

"Miss Wellingford did not vouchsafe her destination."

"Have you any idea? Where does she usually walk?"

Timms knit his brow. "The park, I believe, my lord."

"The park. Which park?"

Timms looked aggrieved. "I'm sure I don't know, my lord." A faint noise emanated from above stairs, and Timms hastily reopened the front door. "Good day, my lord."

"Tell Miss Wellingford I called and must see her at once on a matter of the highest urgency."

"I'm not sure I can do that, my lord. My, ah, instructions, you know." Timms looked carefully past him.

Stifling a curse, Nicholas fished in his pocket for another coin. When the butler extended gloved fingers, he pulled it back. "Make sure she gets the message."

"Of course, my lord." Bowing, Timms plucked the coin.

His temper as foul as his breath, Nicholas stalked out.

After jolting about in various hackneys, all piloted by ham-fisted drivers with ill-matched nags, to Hyde, Green, and Regent's Parks, Nicholas concluded either Miss Wellingford didn't walk in the park, or he had missed her.

With ill-managed impatience, he gave up and went home for some luncheon to pacify his churning stomach.

He presented himself back at Beaumont House in the early afternoon, to be met by the intelligence that Miss Wellingford had accompanied the Beaumont ladies on a shopping expedition, but was expected back for tea. Returning a third time, he learned the ladies had encountered friends and were taking tea with them.

Pressed about evening engagements, Timms was induced, with the aid of a few more coins, to reveal the ladies planned to attend a musicale at the home of Lady Standish. Seething with frustration, Nicholas returned home to partake of a Spartan dinner and a stiff drink, and await his chance to finally corner the elusive Miss Wellingford.

* * *

Having seen Lady Beaumont settled and Clarissa whisked off by her friends, Sarah stole away to a dimly lit anteroom. She'd slept badly last night, awakening time and again to a surge of panic, quickly squelched but unnerving.

It must be done, so just do it, she repeated to herself. Almost, she wished the waiting over, so she might deal with fact rather than her hazy, awful imaginings.

"So this is where you're hiding."

Distracted out of reverie, she turned to see Lord Englemere at the doorway.

"You realize I've slunk through every antechamber in the house looking for you? Interrupted two sets of clandestine lovers and one dozing housemaid."

She shook herself, trying to clear her groggy mind. "I—I beg your pardon?"

"Blast it, woman, I've spent the entire day trying to run you to ground. Will you marry me?"

A shock jolted through Sarah and she came fully alert. Involuntarily, she looked over her shoulder. No, the room was empty but for herself and Lord Englemere. Incredulous, she turned back to Nicholas. "Wh-what did you say?"

Lord Englemere groaned and ran a hand through his hair. "What a clutch. No—no, I meant myself!" He closed the door and crossed the room to her side. "Miss Wellingford, pray forgive me. Trailing you about town today, and missing you at every opportunity, seems to have addled my wits. I collect Timms did not give you my *urgent* message."

"I've not seen Timms since this morning. I left—"

"No matter. Let me see if I can do this properly." He swept up her hand and dropped to one knee. "My dear, as I have come to know you, my respect and admiration have grown and deepened. Would you do me the honor of becoming my wife?"

Sarah stared at him. Like nonsense syllables babbled by a babe, his words didn't make sense. She must be hallucinating—lack of sleep and endless worry had affected her brain. That had to be the reason she thought she heard the Marquess of Englemere proposing to her.

"No, 'tis ridiculous. You can't be asking *me* to marry you."

"Nonetheless, I believe I just have. Twice, in fact. Though I admit, I made a botch of the first attempt."

"But why?"

"Why not? You need to marry, do you not? As do I. You are lovely, witty, well-bred, capable, and it would delight and honor me to make you my marchioness. Whereas I am sufficiently wealthy, reasonably personable, and I hope less 'ridiculous' a choice than Findlay."

"'Tis no comparison." Sarah tore her hands free and took an agitated turn about the room. "But it makes no sense! You could marry anybody. I would wager my lost inheritance there's not an unmarried lady in London who wouldn't leap at the chance to become your bride."

"I can think of one," Nicholas said dryly.

"A sensible one, then. Wealth, charm, beauty—there are dozens who would bring you far more than I."

"Name one."

"Well—Miss Rollins, for instance. Impeccable breeding, beautiful, good dowry—"

"A lovely witch who manages, in a sweetly confiding voice, to never say a good word about anyone."

"Lady Elizabeth Barnwell. Pretty, wealthy, biddable—"

"And whose entire conversation consists of 'Yes, my lord' and 'No, my lord,' and 'Oh, la, my lord.'"

Sarah smothered a chuckle. "'Tis true, I suppose, but what about—"

"What about Sarah Wellingford? Fine family. A kind and compassionate nature. Also honest, loyal, as brave as any man I know, and possessing one characteristic no other woman in London can boast.''

She couldn't, wouldn't believe him serious, but amid the jumble of despair, shock and dawning hope, a strain of simple female curiosity won through. ''What that might be, I can't imagine.''

''I count her my friend.''

''Oh.'' Inane and superfluous, it was the only comment she could manage.

Nicholas grinned. ''Unusual in a marriage, I admit— friendship. Far as I know, though, there's no law *forbidding* it.''

''No, of course not! I am honored, but a true friend must wish the best for you, and I cannot believe that is I.'' She frowned, troubled by a new insight. ''You are concerned about my...situation, I know. Truly, you cannot consider it yours to rectify.'' She looked away, thinking of Clarissa and Chloe Ingram. ''Especially not, to be frank, when you might later regret such chivalry. I'm...I'm hardly the sort of spirited, passionate lady you seem to prefer.''

Nicholas shuddered. ''Lord save me from 'spirited, passionate' women! You, Sarah—your calm, dignified loveliness—are exactly what I want in a wife.''

Nicholas took her chin, lifting it so she met his eyes. ''This isn't a spur-of-the-moment whim. I've considered carefully, and think this would be a perfect solution for both of us. True, we can't claim to be top-over-tails 'in love.' But are not mutual respect, admiration and friendship equally good bases for a marriage—perhaps better ones?'' He gave her a deprecating smile. ''Besides, consider the crushing blow to my self-esteem were you to prefer Findlay's suit to mine. I should go into a decline.''

She smiled at his teasing. Despite her resolve not even to contemplate so unequal a match, a wild hope was licking through her veins. She tried hard to squelch it, to do the right thing.

"N-no, my lord. Your offer is amazingly kind, but I mustn't consider it."

"Sarah, do me the credit of believing I know my own mind. I want to marry you, and I will do all I can to make you happy. Will you not make *me* happy, and say 'yes'?"

"Oh, but you can't truly—"

"Sarah!" He put a finger to her lips. "Say 'yes.'"

He gave her a quick, encouraging nod and removed his hand. Could she seriously contemplate marrying Nicholas Stanhope—this surprising man who had somehow fashioned himself her champion? 'Twas unsuitable, impossible—and yet…to be forever free of worry, beyond Findlay's reach.

A euphoria of deliverance and relief swamped the last noble vestiges of self-sacrifice. "Yes," she whispered.

"Thank you." Nicholas grinned and led her back to the sofa. "I'll arrange for the special license and inform my mother. We can be married at her house, if you like. Shall I bring you by there tomorrow afternoon?"

Alarmed, Sarah swallowed hard. The dowager marchioness couldn't help but be stunned by her son's announcement. Yet if they were truly going to marry—fantastical as that seemed—she must certainly be presented to that lady.

She summoned up a brave smile. "Tomorrow would be fine." Memory stirred, and she gasped. "Oh, dear! Sir James is calling tomorrow! To make his proposal."

Nicholas smiled grimly. "Much as it saddens me, you will have to disappoint him." He lifted her injured hand, discreetly bandaged under its glove, and kissed the wrist. "Sweet Sarah, he shall never hurt you again."

A lump filled her throat and she blinked rapidly. Unable to trust her voice, she nodded.

"I must also send my secretary to settle the mortgage on Wellingford. What was the amount?"

The simple question hit Sarah like a rifle fusillade. She'd tossed the total off to Findlay with bitter bravado, but now, all the humiliation the baronet had meant her to feel rose up to choke her.

Though she knew the pride that shackled her tongue was false, and futile, still it took her two attempts to get it out. "N-nine thousand eight hundred fifty-six pounds."

"A paltry sum," Nicholas drawled.

"Paltry?" She gasped. "'Tis a fortune!"

"Hardly a fortune. Well, perhaps a smallish fortune. Certainly not a large one. Whereas *my* fortune is generally accounted to be somewhere between 'enormous' and 'obscene.'"

He grinned, and her discomfort slowly dissolved in a gurgle of laughter. "You are absurd."

He gave her a theatrically exaggerated look of reproach. "Absurd, me? Never. Arrogant, autocratic, spoiled, perhaps. You must work upon my failings."

"As if I should! You have been, as you well know, all that is noble. I can only promise to interfere in your life as little as possible, and to do my utmost—"

"If you thank me, sweet Sarah—" Nicholas once again stilled her lips with his finger "—I shall strangle you."

"I shan't tease you with gratitude, then," she replied when he removed his hand. "Still, I want you to know if…if you should come to your senses in the night, and wish to withdraw your offer, I shall perfectly understand."

"Sarah, Sarah," he admonished. "I promise you I shall not suffer second thoughts, cold feet, bridegroom's jitters or any other premarital malady you can conjure up. I shall come for you at Lady Beaumont's at noon tomorrow."

Her heart and mind churning with a riot of conflicting emotions, Sarah nodded. "Until tomorrow, then."

She started to rise, but Nicholas stayed her.

"Is it not customary to seal a betrothal with a kiss?"

While Sarah stared at him, mesmerized, Nicholas pulled her close. At first his lips gently brushed hers, tentative, questing. Then he deepened the kiss, and Sarah's stupor dissolved in a wave of remembered pleasure.

His touch ignited long-dormant desire to a flame that sputtered, caught and then blazed through her. Sighing, she opened her mouth and wrapped her arms around his neck.

He responded instantly, pulling her closer still until she felt the strong hard warmth of him down the length of her, felt the rapid beat of his heart against her own. His fingers caressed her back, curved toward her breasts.

He stopped abruptly, pulling away and leaving her bereft, every nerve afire with wanting. A little mewing sound of protest escaped her lips.

"Sweet Sarah," he whispered unsteadily, his eyes glowing with a heat she'd never seen in them before. "I'm beginning to believe short engagements have much to recommend them."

Nicholas tried not to grin as he awaited the return of his hat, cane and coat from Lady Standish's butler. After beginning a fiasco, this day had ended a complete success.

He relived the kiss that sealed their bargain, well pleased with her response. No reluctance or skittishness there. Marriage to Sarah was going to be a delight.

As he placed the beaver on his head and strolled out, the various sensory impressions suddenly coalesced into one startling realization. Someone had taught his spinsterish, on-the-shelf Sarah to kiss, and taught her very well indeed.

Chapter Six

For the fourth time, Sarah walked from her chair to gaze out the window at the deserted square. She glanced again at the mantel clock: five minutes to noon.

One daisy in the flower arrangement on the side table perched awry, and absently she plucked it out. 'Twas not until she returned from the musicale to the haven of her bedchamber that the shock, euphoria and confusion had diminished enough for her to realize the incredible truth. She, Sarah Ann Wellingford, had pledged her hand to the most notorious gambler in London.

Consternation seized her, and her first impulse was to dash back out to find Englemere and retract her acceptance. A moment's reflection squelched that notion. What could she say to Englemere, even should she run him to ground?

By society's standards, his was a brilliant offer. Despite his protests of their equality, Englemere surely recognized the disparity of the match. Her deeply rooted fear of gambling might be a valid concern, but 'twas also one she could hardly expect him to understand. As he had joked, to reject him would be to tender a humiliating insult. After his many kindnesses, such an action would be unconscionable.

But…marriage? Could she ever rest easy, knowing her

fate—and that of her eventual children—rested in the unreliable hands of a gambler?

There was Englemere's Luck, of course. But what would happen should it fail? Would he be able to toss down his cards and go home? What if he could not?

Even should that theoretical event transpire, the consequences couldn't compare to the immediate physical threat Findlay posed. Was she truly prepared to spurn Englemere's rescue and deliver herself back to the baronet?

For an instant, she felt herself again trapped against the wall while he forced her wrist into the candle's flame. No, she concluded, swallowing a wave of nausea, bankruptcy held no terrors worse than that.

Except for Englemere's gambling, she saw much to admire in him. Generous, intelligent, perceptive, he had been a kind and supportive friend. She enjoyed his company—and his kiss awoke her to desires she'd forgotten she possessed.

As for his late wife, she couldn't recall his ever so much as mentioning Lydia's name. If he still mourned, he kept his grief close. She could respect that.

He would remove the burden of debt from Wellingford and secure her family's future. With careful management, in time Wellingford could be restored to its former wealth and productivity. Having been willed to her brother, it would be there always—a safe haven beyond any gambler's reach.

So, she had concluded, she would marry Englemere. She might never be able to trust him enough to commit her whole heart—but he didn't want it anyway. She could offer what he did want: a well-bred, competent wife. And an heir.

Her mind skittered to the night of Clarissa's ball—the smell of his shaving soap, the warmth radiating from his tall body. And the betrothal kiss—her cheeks burned and a tremor spiraled down her spine as she remembered the hot velvet of his mouth, the liquid stroke of his tongue against hers. Marriage to Englemere might hold unexpected delights.

Assuming he still wanted her, of course. She looked down and realized she'd been methodically plucking petals from the daisy until only one silken bit remained. 'Twas nearly noon.

She'd advised Nicholas to think carefully, and think again. Sober reflection might well have convinced him the match was as unsuitable as she'd declared it. She thought of Chloe Ingram—violet-eyed, alabaster-skinned, voluptuous Mrs. Ingram. Why would a man sampling delicacies such as those want a tasteless pudding like Sarah Wellingford?

It appeared he wouldn't. The mantel clock began to chime the hour. As the last peal faded, Timms walked up. "Sir James for you, Miss Wellingford. Shall I show him in?"

Heart pounding, she nodded. She barely noted as the balled-up flower bits fell from her nerveless fingers, one lone white petal floating slowly to the floor.

Nicholas glanced at his pocket watch, cursing. Giving Jeb scarcely enough time to grab hold, he sprung the horses.

He'd had a devil of a time finding the bishop, and then the clerk who'd prepared the papers seemed to consider it a life's work. 'Twas already five minutes past noon, and he'd be willing to wager Findlay, that unspeakable cur, was probably never tardy. If the man so much as laid a finger on Sarah, Nicholas would beat him to a bloody pulp.

Narrowly avoiding two heavily laden carts and rounding corners with a recklessness that caused even his normally unflappable tiger to gasp, he arrived five minutes later at Beaumont House. He threw down the reins and took the steps two at a time, not slowing his pace until he reached the room to which an anxious Timms conducted him.

He entered and stopped short. Findlay had Sarah cornered on the sofa, his arms trapping her against its back, his head descending toward hers.

Stifling the urge to plant Sir James a facer, Nicholas said loudly, "Sorry I'm late, my dear."

Findlay halted and glanced at him. Surprise and irritation showed briefly before the faintly bored ton mask settled back on his face. "Englemere," he drawled. "Do you not realize you're decidedly *de trop?* Kindly pursue your red-haired vixen elsewhere."

While Findlay spoke, Sarah sat staring as if she'd seen a ghost. "N-Nicholas?" she whispered.

Englemere strode over and grasped one icy hand, pulling her up as he kissed it, and planted himself between her and Findlay. "I beg you'll not scold me for being delayed, darling. But I have the special license at last."

She nodded numbly. Nicholas turned to Findlay. "So, you are the first to offer us congratulations, Sir James."

Findlay looked from Sarah, who had retreated to the window, to Nicholas and back. "What farradiddle is this?"

Nicholas gave Sarah a mock-reproving look. "Did you not inform him, darling? How naughty of you! If you must dash a man's fondest hopes, you should do so quickly."

Sir James closed to a pace away. "I know not what your game is, Englemere, but enough joking. Miss Wellingford was about to accept my offer, so take yourself off."

"I'm afraid you're tardy, Findlay. Miss Wellingford has already accepted an offer—mine."

The two men locked glares. Sir James laughed harshly. "You? Marry the likes of Sarah Wellingford? I hardly think so." He cast her a dagger glance. "Your little jest does not amuse me, my dear. I fear you'll answer for it later. Englemere, if you'd be so—argh—"

Sir James gagged as Nicholas hoisted him off his feet by his neckcloth. "There'll be no 'answering,'" Nicholas hissed. He held the man suspended until Sir James's handsome face turned from white to blue, his arms windmilling as he tried to break free.

Nicholas dropped Findlay. "I fully understand your crushing disappointment. Naturally, you'll wish to take your leave. You'll excuse me a moment, my love?"

Nicholas clamped a hand on Findlay's elbow and propelled him toward the door. Coughing and clutching his throat, the baronet offered little resistance. In the hallway, the door closed, Nicholas released him.

Sir James fumbled with the limp folds of his ruined cravat. "Englemere," he croaked, "I'll—"

"You'll shut your vicious coward's mouth and listen."

Nicholas leaned toward Sir James until his nose nearly touched the shorter man's. "Neither you, nor any of your hirelings, will so much as approach my wife. Should you ever disregard those instructions, I'll do much more than wrinkle your pretty neckcloth."

Sir James did not retreat—Nicholas had to give him that much credit. "My, how bloodthirsty," he sneered. "Are you threatening to shoot me, Englemere?"

"I wouldn't waste a bullet on you. But rest assured, by the time I finished, you would wish I had shot you."

"So insulting. For that, and this atrocity to my person, I almost believe I should call you out."

"Name your seconds."

Anger blazed in the cold blue eyes, but Findlay was no match for Nicholas either with sword or pistols, and both men knew it. "I was speaking rhetorically, of course. So…violent you are, Englemere."

"You should know about violence."

Sir James brushed a spot of lint from his sleeve. "Indeed. You've crossed me before, Englemere. Remember the outcome of that little contretemps. I get what I want. Or no one does."

Nicholas held on to his temper, curbing the desire to finish strangling the baronet then and there. "Sarah's not a horse I've outbid you for at Tatt's. You found a way to have that colt garroted in his stall—''

"No evidence ever linked me to that unfortunate incident," Findlay protested, smiling. "Perhaps a careless groom left the check-rein too tight. When fire broke out, and the horse panicked..."

Nicholas gave him a withering glance. "You had best pray my bride enjoys robust good health and suffers not the most trifling accident. If anything at all untoward befalls her, you will pay for it. Remember that."

"Oh, I'll not forget. I'll not forget—*anything.*"

The mocking tone frayed the tattered edges of his control. As the man stepped past him, Nicholas whipped one limp end of the cravat around Findlay's neck and hauled him back. Finely woven linen, he discovered when Findlay gasped and clawed at his throat, made a rather crude but effective garrote. "See that you do not," he said in Findlay's ear.

"Y—your things, Sir James." Timms's high-pitched voice came over his shoulder. "If you please, Lord Englemere!"

Nicholas gave the cravat one last, savage twist, and had the satisfaction of seeing fear flash briefly in Findlay's eyes.

"It appears you win this round, Englemere." Settling his hat on his head, he managed a laugh. "You, and that ape-leader Sarah Wellingford. 'Tis almost amusing."

Before Nicholas could sidestep Timms to seize him again, Findlay slipped to the door. "Good day, my lord." With an insolent wave of his cane, he walked out.

Timms slammed the door shut, cutting off Nicholas's pursuit. "Miss Wellingford awaits," he urged, so distressed he abandoned decorum and actually tugged on Nicholas's arm.

Hands balled into fists, Nicholas took a deep breath and willed himself to calm. Satisfying as it would be to hunt down Findlay and horsewhip him like the scoundrel he

was, he had more urgent priorities. He'd savor that idea
for some later time—and keep careful guard over Sarah.

She still stood where he'd left her. "I'm so sorry you
had to deal with Findlay. The bishop was out, and his clerk
was slow, and—"

He stopped abruptly. Sarah was paler than her gown,
her silver eyes enormous, her face expressionless as she
stood clenching and unclenching her hands.

Fury roughened his voice. "Did Findlay hurt you?" he
demanded. She shook her head, displacing a tear that trick-
led down her cheek.

Her words from yesterday suddenly echoed through his
mind. *If you should come to your senses…I shall perfectly
understand.…*

"You didn't think I was coming, did you?" he asked
incredulously.

She opened her lips, but they were trembling so badly
she could not speak. She shook her head again.

He walked closer and saw she was trembling all over.
Any urge to chide her for lack of faith evaporated. "Poor
sweetheart, what a morning you must have had."

As he drew her into his arms, she threw herself against
his chest and clung to him. Her hands dug into his shoulders and her body quivered with stifled sobs.

"'Tis all right, sweeting," he said against her hair.
"He's gone, and he'll not trouble you again, I promise."

If he'd had any lingering doubts about the wisdom of
wedding Sarah Wellingford, they were swept away as a
wave of fierce protectiveness washed over him. Marrying
her was right; having her in his arms felt right. He would
guard her, and woe betide Findlay should he seek to do
her harm.

At last the tremors eased and her rigid fingers relaxed
on his shoulders. She drew herself back, though still within
the circle of his arms. "I'm s-sorry. I detest w-weeping
females." She swiped impatiently at a tear.

Nicholas stayed her hand and kissed away the droplet. "Let us get you ready to meet Mama." Seating her on the sofa, he produced a small box. "I wasn't sure of the size."

Looking bemused, Sarah watched him open it. The ring reposed upon a velvet bed, its large central pearl flanked by winking diamonds. Nicholas slipped it on her finger.

Sarah stared at it numbly. "'Tis not the ruby."

Nicholas laughed. "Did you think to have Clarissa's cast-off? No, I wanted something special for you—for my 'pearl of great price.'"

Sarah's eyes brightened, but she stemmed the tears. "'Tis beautiful, my lord. And how fitting. I only hope you didn't have to sell all your possessions to afford it."

"I've sufficient remaining. But when I arrived, you called me 'Nicholas.'" He pulled her back against him.

"Thank you…Nicholas."

As she whispered his name, he lowered his mouth. This time, she leaned up, parting her lips and winding her fingers into his hair. He deepened the kiss and she met him willingly in the sensuous dance of tongue with tongue, all the while caressing his neck with satin fingertips.

Completely absorbed in demonstrating his approval of her efforts, Nicholas was startled when she suddenly pulled away. Muttering a protest, he tried to draw her back and noticed her eyes were fixed on the doorway.

He turned to see Lady Beaumont standing stock-still on the threshold, jaw dropped, shock and horror on her face. "Sarah—Ann—Wellingford!" she gasped.

Nicholas looked back at Sarah. "You didn't tell her."

Sarah gave him a guilty smile. Moving apart from him, she reached up to smooth her tousled braids.

Sunlight flashed on the diamonds in her ring, and Lady Beaumont's gaze riveted on Sarah's hand. Her eyes widened farther, then rolled back in her head, and she fainted.

Clarissa helped Sarah revive and reconcile her prostrate mama. Though professing herself incredulous that Sarah actually *wished* to marry such a dull old stick as Englemere, she pledged eternal friendship and support.

After soothing Lady Beaumont, Sarah went to await Nicholas. To her mind, the worst was yet to come.

She recalled the unsmiling face of another highborn lady who had found Sarah Wellingford too poor and entirely unfit for the honor of wedding her son. Sarah struggled to banish Lady Sandiford's image and a sudden, searing longing for the tranquillity of her youth, her home—and Sinjin.

Nicholas's voice in her ear made her jump.

"I b-beg your pardon?"

"Calm yourself, sweetheart," he murmured. "Don't be imagining my mother an ogre. To be sure, she's quite astute." He chuckled reminiscently. "She'll see in a minute all your loveliness of character, and heartily approve my choice."

Sarah sighed. "And if she doesn't?"

"She will." He tipped her chin up so their eyes met. "But even should she not, *I* approve—and that's all that matters." Taking her arm, he led her into the hall.

Sarah rested her hand on his, marveling that it felt so natural to rely on one who a few short weeks ago had been a virtual stranger. Gradually in that time Nicholas had progressed in her regard from an amiable gentleman, to an admirable one, to the kindest of friends.

Yes, friends, she thought, the ache easing. Sinjin had grown up her dearest friend, the love she had always thought to marry. Then had come the debts of both their fathers, and the urgent duty to repair the respective family fortunes. Though she still wore on a chain around her neck the signet ring he'd pressed in her hand before leaving to join his regiment, she'd long known their union to be an impossible dream.

Reality was the enigmatic man beside her, whose thoughtful concern and careless kindness had saved her home, whose closeness even now soothed the ragged edge of worry.

She knew Nicholas didn't want words of gratitude, paltry payment in any event. In this moment she pledged instead to put away her doubts and give him unwavering loyalty, steadfast support—and the speedy birth of a son. *God keep you safe, Sinjin, love of my heart...goodbye.*

Waving aside the footman, Nicholas handed her into the carriage himself, a small courtesy that warmed her. *Careful, Sarah,* she cautioned herself. *Nicholas will never grow, as Sinjin did, from friend to lover. Accept his mistress, his preference for London life, and school yourself to be the "calm, dignified wife" he desires.*

Nicholas settled the carriage robe over her legs. "Now, when shall we tell Mama we wish to be wed?"

"Perhaps Friday evening would be convenient for her."

"'Tis not her convenience you need accommodate. Though I remain heartily in favor of the briefest of engagements—" he placed a lingering kiss on her palm "—there's no need to rush. 'Tis your day, sweeting. I know ladies put great store by weddings, and if you've always dreamed of a grand to-do at St. George's, with the usual crush of a reception after, I shall bow to your wishes."

"But—the mortgage!"

"Oh, that. I saw no reason to wait until after our vows to take care of it."

Nonchalantly he extracted a paper from his pocket and unfolded it: the mortgage on Wellingford, *paid in full* written in flourishing script across the top.

Sarah stared at that incredibly beautiful phrase, "paid in full," and then up at Nicholas. He gazed back, smiling faintly, tenderness in his eyes.

A swirl of strong emotion tightened her chest and forced her to blink rapidly. How compassionate he had been, teasing her out of her shame and pretending she was worth to him the considerable time, expense and trouble he'd gone to on her behalf. How compassionate now, to blithely hand back Wellingford and allow her to turn what she'd feared would be a hasty wedding into an event of taste and dignity.

"You could kiss me," he suggested, a glint coming into his eyes. "I know you wish to thank me, and I'm becoming quite fond of your kisses."

Carefully Sarah folded the precious paper and put it in her reticule. Placing her fingers on his cheeks, she caressed his face as she leaned up to him. She heard the hiss of his indrawn breath, then a muffled groan when she nibbled his lower lip and traced it with her tongue. He relaxed his jaw, inviting entry, and she slowly explored his mouth, until at last she claimed his tongue and stroked it.

With a deeper groan he bent her back against the cushioned seat. Once more the master, he devoured her lips and moved his hand lower, tracing her waist and the outline of her hip to her derriere. She pressed herself closer, letting desire flame beyond control.

As before, he pulled away first. For a moment, he simply held her, their hearts beating a staccato to the ragged whistle of their breath.

"Ah, sweet Sarah, that was the best yet. I've got the special license in my pocket. Do you think my coachman could marry us? No?" He sighed. "Call the banns, then, if you must, but I beg you, sweeting, let the wedding be soon."

Glendenning, a majestic silver-haired personage, announced them to the dowager marchioness and stood regally aside. Giving Sarah's hand a quick squeeze, Nicholas led her over to a slender brunette lady attired in black.

The dowager inclined her cheek for Nicholas's kiss, keeping her large green eyes, so like her son's, fixed on Sarah. She was much smaller than he, with a smooth skin and elegant bones that must have made her the reigning beauty of her day, and left her beautiful still. Her face showed no emotion beyond gracious courtesy. Sarah swallowed hard.

"Mama, may I present to you Miss Wellingford." He sent Sarah a warm glance. "My sweet Sarah."

"I'm honored to meet you, Lady Englemere."

"I'm quite anxious to meet you as well, Miss Well— Sarah," the dowager corrected at Nicholas's sharp look. "So, Nicky tells me you're to be married?"

"Yes, we thought to have the ceremony in a week, and the reception afterward at the home of her aunt, Lady Sophrina Harrington," Nicholas answered for them.

"I see," came the neutral reply.

With a quick glance at Nicholas, Sarah continued, "We envision a rather small gathering. Naturally, we should like to invite those of your friends or kinsmen whom you would wish to have present, if you would make me a list."

"Indeed."

A tense silence followed that monosyllabic utterance, deepening Sarah's unease. Then the dowager shivered.

"There's a chill in the air. Do you feel it, Nicky? Would you be a dear and fetch my shawl? I left it in the library, I believe."

She looked up at Nicholas with such bright entreaty he could hardly refuse, despite the blatant obviousness of her request. "Of course, Mama. I'll get it straightaway." Throwing Sarah an apologetic glance, he walked out.

"Now we can have a comfortable coze," the dowager said, with an edge to her voice that belied that warm prediction. "You've not known my son very long, have you?"

"Only a few weeks, ma'am."

"You've made quite a catch for yourself, young lady."

"Your son would be quite a catch for any girl."

The dowager inclined her head to that, and nerves already strained taut, Sarah lost patience with the subtle baiting. Better to just settle this for good and all.

"Your ladyship, let us speak plainly. 'Tis quite obvious your son could have done much better for himself than penniless Miss Sarah Wellingford."

The dowager showed no reaction. Taking a deep breath, Sarah continued. "I mean to make him the best possible wife. I don't wish to pull caps with you, but I can't change what I am. For your son's sake, I hope you will give us your blessing, regardless of any reservations you may have."

Head high, Sarah subsided into silence.

"Ah, there's Nicky," the countess murmured, after a long and rather uncomfortable pause. Indeed, Nicholas nearly flew into the room.

"Well, have you two finished shredding my character?" Though he smiled, his eyes looked anxious.

"Not quite yet," Sarah said dryly.

"Nicky, is Michael outside? Good." She turned to Sarah. "My dear, you must wish to freshen up before tea. Michael will show you to the blue bedchamber."

That stratagem was no more subtle than the shawl, but Sarah rose with graceful resignation. *Will she try to talk him out of it once I'm gone, or merely bewail his fate?* she wondered. As she started past Nicholas, he caught her hand.

"Though you look lovely to me, I suppose Mama must know best." Before the watching dowager, he gave her hand a lingering kiss. "Hurry back, sweeting."

A lump rose in her throat at his deliberate show of support. With a curtsy to the dowager, she left the room.

Nicholas's glance followed Sarah as she walked out. Though he could detect no distress in her composed face, he knew somehow the interview hadn't gone well.

"Are you sure you wish to be married so soon?"

He turned to his mama. "I should think after all the times you've urged me back to the altar, you'd be delighted at the prospect of seeing me riveted in a week."

"I don't think I ever precisely *urged* you," she replied. "When you broke the news last night, I was too shocked to respond, but it has since occurred to me there's no need for the unseemly haste of a special license. Why not have the banns read, and stage a proper wedding?"

"It will be a 'proper' wedding." Controlling his irritation, he tried for a lighter tone. "Given my broken engagement, any subsequent match is bound to set off the gossips. Neither of us wants the circus of a large ton wedding. Besides, I don't wish to wait." He gave her a wink. "Surely you can understand that."

She didn't smile, as he had hoped. Instead she continued in a thoughtful tone, "Miss Wellingford gains access to a great deal of wealth by this match."

Nicholas stiffened, as close to affronted as he'd ever been by his mother. "True, Sarah's family is in straitened circumstances, and I suppose mean-spirited folk might call her a fortune hunter. But having met her, surely you don't suspect her of that."

He was shocked to see cautious skepticism on her face. "For goodness' sake, Mama, she's not some social-climbing cit's daughter, like the insufferable Amelia!"

"I can't fault her breeding," the dowager admitted. "But you've always preferred the most dashing beauties, and she is rather plain." The dowager hesitated, as if sensing his growing anger. "Are you sure, once the pleasant glow of knight-errantry has faded, you won't regret this marriage?"

For a moment, he was too outraged to reply. "Sarah, *plain?*" he choked out. "I happen to think her lovely."

He looked at his beautiful mother in disbelief, feeling for the first time in his life that he didn't know her at all. "I'm astounded after what we've been through that you, of all people, would consider important the surface glitter of appearance. Or that having met Sarah, you could fail to discern the sterling character beneath her *plain* facade."

He broke off, fuming still, as Glendenning brought in a tea tray. When the butler departed, Nicholas strode to the fireplace, turning his back on his mother.

"I'll forgo tea. As soon as Sarah is ready, we'll proceed

to Lady Sophrina's.'' Over his shoulder he sent his mother a bitter glance. "I trust her aunt will accord me a warmer welcome than you have offered my chosen bride.''

In an instant the dowager flew to the mantel. "Oh, Nicky, do stay and let me apologize!''

He nearly shook off her hand before the words penetrated. "Apologize?'' he repeated stiffly.

"Yes, I've been a tartar, and though the ploy succeeded beyond my wildest hopes, you put me in an absolute quake!''

He stared at her in total incomprehension. "Ploy?''

The countess gave a musical laugh and tugged at his hand. "Come drink your tea, darling, and let me explain.''

Confused but still angry, he followed her to the sofa.

"First, I shall tell you straightaway your Sarah seems to be all you claim, and I couldn't be more pleased! But I needed to discover for myself whether you both were entering this engagement—so scandalously soon after the termination of the old—for the right reasons.''

At his incredulous glance, she added defensively, "Well, after Clarissa Beaumont, you must admit it was reasonable I entertain some doubts! Naturally, were I to just *ask* about your feelings for Sarah, you would give me the proper answers. I wished to see for myself.''

Relief coursed through him, and in spite of himself, his lips began to twitch. "I take it I passed your test?''

"Oh, famously,'' she affirmed with a reminiscent shudder. "I hope I shall never again see you direct me such a look.''

He laughed outright, and she frowned at him. "You may say I deserved it, but I had to be sure. When you told me you meant to wed a lady I knew to be in rather desperate financial straits, I did fear that, in your haste, you might have been taken in by a fortune hunter. It required but a moment to alleviate that concern.''

Nicholas grinned. "If you subjected my *plain* darling to

anything like the grilling you gave me, I expect you to offer her a most eloquent apology."

"I daresay you shall never forgive me that 'plain.'" The dowager sighed. "I *was* cool, but you would be proud of her response. She neither toadied nor explained. Nor, might I add, did she wilt under my supposed displeasure."

"I don't doubt it. I'd wager my stalwart Sarah calmly informed you that, though fully aware of the disparity of our union, she intended to make me a laudable wife."

"So she did." Hesitantly she took his hands. "From your spirited defense, I can dare hope she has truly engaged your interest. I'm so glad, Nicky! You're far too warmhearted to tolerate a mere marriage of convenience."

Nicholas stiffened. "Sarah is a dear and valued friend, 'tis all. We both need to marry. You may cease imagining some fairy-tale romance."

His mother remained silent a long moment. "Nicky dearest," she said at last, "don't let bitter memories poison your heart forever."

"Enough, Mama!" He pulled at his hand.

She caught his fingers and held on. "Call me foolish, with you a man grown, but to me you'll always be the darling son whose happiness I feel compelled to protect." The dowager smiled wistfully. "Perhaps now I can relinquish that role to your Sarah. She...she's nothing like Lydia."

"Thanks be to God," he said grimly. For an instant, the image of his late wife seized him—beautiful, vivacious, the undisputed center of attention as he looked on fondly.

Acid burning in his belly, he shook his thoughts free and kissed his mother's hand. "Thank you, Mama. I should marry her in spite of your disapproval, but I much prefer your blessing. You know, she reminds me of you."

"Rogue." The dowager made a face at him as she pulled back her hand. "What can I possibly do after such a tribute, than pronounce her perfect?"

* * *

When Sarah returned, Nicholas and his mother were tête-à-tête on the sofa. Suddenly she couldn't face any more sweetly barbed scrutiny.

She nodded to them and remained standing. "I don't wish to be discourteous, but I am rather tired, Nicholas. I should prefer to return to my aunt's now."

In a graceful swirl of black crepe, the dowager swept to her. "Sarah, you must not go until I apologize, as I already have to Nicky. I wished to discover for myself the true feelings each of you held about your union, and so I adopted that disapproving air. Do say you can find it in your heart to forgive a mother's concern."

Startled, Sarah looked at the dowager's hand clasping hers. As fatigued as she claimed, she found it difficult to grasp her words. "Of course," she murmured disjointedly.

"Thank you, my dear. Having raised only grubby boys—" she wrinkled her nose at her son "—I have always wished for a daughter to befriend. Now, thanks to my clever Nicholas, I have one." She caught Sarah in a scented embrace.

Over his mother's shoulder, Nicholas gave her a wink. Relaxing, she winked back. Perhaps becoming his marchioness wouldn't be so difficult after all.

Chapter Seven

Nicholas peered in the glass, straightened the white rose at his lapel and gave his cravat a quick tug.

"Nicky, if you fiddle with that cravat one more time, you'll ruin it." Ned's amused voice came over his shoulder.

Throwing his friend a black look, Nicholas turned from the mirror and moved to the small table before the mantel. Bowls of fragrant white roses flanked a gold cross, refashioning it into a makeshift altar. He repositioned the candles beside the cross and walked over to adjust a wing chair by the window, where bright afternoon sunlight filtered through sheer lace curtains.

"Leave it, Nicky, the room looks marvelous. Sarah's outdone herself." Ned indicated the neat line of chairs facing the altar, the white satin draping the mantel and doorway, the flowers on the mantel and side tables.

"Sit." Hal clamped one large hand on his shoulder and propelled him into the nearest chair. "Females'll be ready soon. You're wearing out the carpet."

Nicholas dropped into the chair but immediately sprang back up. Hal shook his head in disgust and Ned laughed.

Nicholas grimaced. Easy for them to mock. Bachelors both, they had no idea how quickly a wife could take a man's pleasant, well-ordered life and smash it. For one panicky moment, he considered calling the whole thing off.

Calm down, he ordered himself, taking a deep breath. His hands were sweating, and he wiped them on the chair's brocaded arm. He had chosen more wisely this time. And this time, he was on his guard.

He heard footsteps approaching. "That will be the priest. They must be ready at last, thank God."

Several moments later, they filed in formal procession back to the withdrawing room. Reaching his place by the mantel, he straightened his shoulders, and nearly tugged at his cravat again before he caught Ned's amused glance.

The opening chords of a Mozart piano piece startled him. The guests looked toward the doorway. His stomach doing a little flip, Nicholas's gaze followed theirs.

Sarah entered in a plain gown of gold satin. An airy breath of white net shot through with gold formed the tiny puffed sleeves, and a sash of the same glittering material tied at the high waist. Despite its simple cut, Nicholas detected the hand of a master, for the rich cloth clung to each curve of her body. The brief bodice, lower than any he'd seen her wear, offered a tantalizing glimpse of cleavage. Heat suffusing his face, he jerked his gaze up.

The glowing hue of the gown warmed her skin to cream and accentuated the delicate flush on her cheeks. Her coronet of braids was threaded through with wisps of gold net and circled by a ring of white rosebuds.

She raised her eyes, saw him waiting and smiled tremulously. By happy chance, at that moment a filtered beam of sunshine from the window touched her, gilding her fair hair and setting a thousand lights sparking on the sheen of her gown. She looked, he thought with a rippling shock, like a princess; she looked—beautiful.

Then she was beside him, a shimmer of gold in a scent of lavender, and the priest was intoning the ancient words of the marriage service. Sarah repeated her vows in a clear, firm voice, while, still shaken, he stumbled a little through his own.

Ned thrust the ring at him, he slipped it on her finger, and the priest proclaimed them man and wife. Sarah raised downcast eyes from their joined hands and gave him that shy half smile. He smiled back and leaned to kiss her.

Something twisted in his chest as he touched her soft lips with his own. Sweet Sarah, he thought, following the priest past the blur of guests. Sweet Sarah, *my wife*.

He had mastered himself by the time the other members of the wedding party signed the register, and penned his own name with a flourish. Sarah's fingers trembled on the quill. With a little frown, she steadied them.

"Gold becomes you," he murmured in her ear.

She glanced up, her solemnity softening into a mischievous look. "Well, 'tis certainly useful."

He chuckled and caught her chin. "When you joke like that, little flecks dance in those lovely silver eyes. You know what I meant. You look beautiful, sweet Sarah."

The pale apricot of her cheeks darkened. "More Spanish coin, my lord?"

"No, Miss Jokesmith. Except for one notable occasion—" he grinned, and knew she was also remembering Clarissa's ball "—I've always told you the truth—and I always will."

"Come along, lovebirds." Ned's voice interrupted. "Your well-wishers await."

Sarah gazed across the room to where Nicholas stood conversing with a cabinet minister, entirely at ease as he chatted with one of the foremost men in the realm. Several of Sarah's sisters hovered nearby, gazing up at him with incipient hero worship.

This handsome, charismatic man was her husband? So nonstop a blur of activity had this last week been, 'twas not until she'd begun to pen her name in the parish register, and realized after ''Sarah Ann'' she must now sign ''Stanhope,'' that the fact of her marriage struck home.

In an instant of blind panic, she'd nearly fled the room. Then Nicholas had murmured in her ear, his warm voice steadying her. Nicholas the gambler, but also Nicholas the friend who rescued her from Findlay, who saved her family from eviction and want. Hand wobbling only a little, she'd signed the page.

Married a whole hour now, she shook her head and stifled a giddy laugh. Despite any lingering doubts, she felt like the Cinderella of the French fairy tale, wearing the most beautiful gown she'd ever owned, awaited by a prince out of a dream. Perhaps this was all enchantment, and would dissolve when the clock chimed midnight.

She looked at her heavy gold ring. No, this prince had really taken Sarah Wellingford to wife—and by midnight, should have made her his wife in fact as well as name.

Heat warmed her cheeks and sent a rush of prickly anticipation through her veins. She recalled the kiss in the carriage when, overwhelmed by the gift of the Wellingford deed, she'd abandoned maidenly restraint. Drawing upon instinct, she'd tried to give Nicholas back some corresponding measure of delight.

Chloe Ingram's image intruded, and her warm glow dimmed. What had she been thinking, to kiss him like the veriest lightskirt? Had he not told her several times what he prized most was her calm, well-bred reserve? ''Lord save me from a spirited, passionate wife,'' he'd said.

She owed it to him to control herself and remember that preference. She also owed, and would bend every effort to give him, what Chloe Ingram could not: a son and heir. She sighed. Despite her best intentions, she suspected responding with well-bred reserve to Nicholas's touch was going to prove her hardest challenge yet.

Nicholas swung his mama through the last bars of the waltz. She fanned herself as he led her back to the table.

"No, Nicky, not another morsel! I declare, I've already stuffed myself outrageously."

"Sarah will be pleased you're enjoying it. She's been working like a Trojan."

"I daresay you don't know the half of it," his mother replied. "I talked with Lady Sophrina, and I'm amazed at what Sarah's accomplished. Do you realize none of these rooms have been opened for years, and just a week ago were shrouded in Holland covers? Half the furniture is hired—and the servants! She's been juggling three sets of them all week like a master acrobat at Astley's. My darling, you've not married a treasure, you've wed a miracle!"

"I'm beginning to believe that," he murmured.

Leaving her with a kiss, Nicholas strolled back to the dining room, where Ned and Hal awaited him.

Sarah appeared at the archway between the dining and dancing chambers, the gathering glow of the candles sparkling on the sheen of her gown. As the bride, she was the focus of all eyes, but she didn't demand that attention. Indeed, she seemed more the gracious hostess ensuring the comfort of her guests than the star of the festivities.

So modest and lovely, so serenely competent—everything he wanted in a wife. A mellow feeling of self-congratulation warmed him.

Ned looked in the direction of his gaze and smiled. "To think, someone once likened her to 'Ice.'"

"Not ice," Hal said. "Sunshine."

"She is indeed. Gentlemen, I'm a lucky man."

As Nicholas took another sip from his wineglass, he heard Hal's hiss of indrawn breath, and Ned's "Good God!"

Turning to see what had disturbed them, Nicholas choked on his wine. Before his astounded eyes, the midnight figure of Sir James Findlay led Sarah into a dance.

* * *

Nicholas leapt to his feet, upsetting his wineglass. "The bloody bastard! I'll rip his arms off!"

Ned trapped the spinning goblet while Hal grabbed Nicholas's shoulder. "Steady, Nicky! Can't mill the man down. Upset the ladies."

"Lord, yes," Ned seconded. "'Twas appalling ton for Findlay to appear uninvited, but you can't brawl over it. Not at your wedding dinner!"

His body taut with rage, Nicholas tried to brush off Hal's hand. "You don't know what he did to Sarah."

"Sit, then, and tell us." Ned pulled his sleeve. "Lady Jersey just noticed Findlay, and is looking straight at you. Don't offer her grist for the gossip mill."

Nicholas sat. Briefly he related the incident at the duchess's ball. As Ned muttered a curse and Hal turned a stony glare on Findlay, Nicholas ended with his warning to his wife's former suitor.

"He thinks himself clever, the miserable cowardly bastard, certain I won't cause a disturbance at my own wedding feast." Nicholas clenched his fists, the urge to pulverize Findlay making it nearly impossible for him to stay seated. "I must do something, surely you see that! 'Tis a clear challenge! I cannot let it go unanswered."

"You're right, something must be done," Ned agreed. The three men looked toward the waltzing couple. A strained smile on her face, Sarah appeared to be holding the baronet off while he leaned close to murmur in her ear.

Ned's jaw set in a grim line. "Something shall be done. But not by you." He rose and tapped Hal on the shoulder. "That's why a man has friends, eh, Waterman?"

Hal nodded and stood, his hard gaze on Findlay while with one large hand he held Nicholas pinned to his chair. Growling in frustration, Nicholas leaned back.

"'Tis bloody unfair for you two to have all the fun, but I suppose I must bow to discretion."

"That's the ticket," Ned said. "Play the happy bridegroom. Hal and I will handle Findlay."

Nicholas smiled grimly. "Don't kill him. I shouldn't wish my best friends to have to flee abroad. Short of that, you have my encouragement to deliver a memorable lesson."

"Bastard," Hal spoke up, startling them. His unblinking gaze never left the baronet. "You distract Sarah. I'll take Findlay."

Ned's lips curved in a slow smile. "Be gentle with him, Hal—for now. You sometimes forget your own strength."

"Time he tangled with someone *stronger*."

Despite his friends' wise counsel, Nicholas could not relax and mingle with the company. Wine, guests, music forgotten, he focused on the drama unfolding before him.

While Ned bowed and inclined his head to Sarah, Hal surreptitiously clamped a bearlike hand on Findlay's elbow and marched him toward the hall. Ned caught the sleeve of an Oxford friend, passed him Sarah's hand and motioned the couple to dance. Then he followed Hal.

Had Nicholas not been watching closely, he would never have noticed that while Hal bent down, seeming to offer a solicitous ear to some vehement comment Findlay was making, he delivered a vicious left hook to the baronet's stomach.

Behind the animated figure of Ned, who was playfully batting the shoulders of a friend he'd hailed, Nicholas saw Findlay crumple like a folded greatcoat over Hal's arm. Hal scooped the smaller man off his feet and bore him away.

Satisfaction warmed Nicholas, to cool at the memory of Sarah's distressed face. As soon as she finished this dance, he would escort Sarah off the floor, perhaps spirit her away to enfold her safely against his chest.

At last the music ended. As he walked to fetch his wife, a group of Wellingfords approached. Trying to recall last night's introductions, he decided the older girl must be Sarah's next eldest sister, Meredyth, and the younger two...? No, not the dazzling Elizabeth. Probably the six-teen- and fifteen-year-old lookalikes, Cecily and Emma.

"Lord Englemere, you must have some of this ice Timms just set out," one of the girls—Cecily?—cried.

Blue eyes starry, her twin—Emma?—made a sweeping gesture. "So much delicious food, the lovely music, and such elegant ladies and gentlemen. Surely not even Al-mack's or—or the prince's court could be any finer!"

The elder girl laughed and shook her head. "You must remember, Emma, Lord Englemere has doubtless tasted any number of ices from Gunter's, and probably visits of-ten at Carlton House. Our reception is not nearly so grand."

"Perhaps, but 'tis undeniably more elegant," Nicholas replied. Noting out of the corner of his eye that Sarah was being led into another dance, he accepted the bowl and waved them all to a seat. "'Lord Englemere' makes me sound old and cross. Why not—" the memory it brought back set him grinning "—call me 'Uncle Nicholas'?"

One sister gasped, and both turned round saucer eyes to Meredyth. "Might we dare?" Emma breathed.

"Are you sure, my lord?" Meredyth asked. "'Twould seem rather forward."

Nicholas shrugged. "I see no reason not."

"Capital!" Cecily clapped her hands. Emma giggled, blushing, and lowered her eyes.

"Here, Colton." Cecily waved to her brother. "Only listen, Lord Englemere has said we might call him 'Uncle Nicholas.' Is he not vastly condescending?" She turned sparkling eyes back to Nicholas. "I'm so glad Sarah mar-ried you instead of that nasty Sir James!"

Nicholas started as Meredyth murmured a reproof. How did the girls know of Findlay?

"Well, I am," the irrepressible Cecily was replying, "and you must be, too. He's just as rich, and surely nicer, and much handsomer, I dare swear."

"'Tis most unbecoming for you to discuss him so."

Meredyth gave Nicholas an apologetic look. "The girls need taking in hand, I fear. Sarah schooled them after we let—after our governess left, but I'm afraid in her absence their education has been rather neglected."

"That bang-up bay team is yours, is it not, Lord—Uncle Nicholas?" Colton asked as he joined them. "And the shiny black phaeton? Oh, to drive such a rig!"

"As if he'd let a cow-handed bantling like you handle them," Cecily muttered.

"Children!" Meredyth protested, her face flushing. "What must Lord Englemere think, to hear you brangle so?"

Nicholas smiled at Colton. "Perhaps we'll have a go at the ribbons sometime later." Suppressing a grin when Colton leaned behind Meredyth to stick out his tongue at Cecily, he continued casually, "I'm flattered you all prefer Sarah's final choice. Had she written you about Sir James?"

"Oh, no, Sarah never mentioned him in her letters," Cecily chimed in. "Lady Sandiford told us."

"Lady Sandiford is our neighbor," Meredyth explained. "Although she resides mostly in the country now—"

"No blunt," said Colton.

"—she has many good friends in town, who send her all the news," Meredyth concluded, frowning at Colton.

"Yes, and when her friends wrote her Sarah was about to make a match with a wealthy man, she came straightaway to tell us the good news," Emma expounded. Her brow crinkled thoughtfully. "Although she hardly called on us at all before, these three years since Sinjin left."

"That's her son—Viscount Sandiford, a captain in the Tenth Hussars," Colton inserted.

"And so handsome in his uniform," Emma murmured.

A handsome soldier. Nicholas's smile faltered.

"I don't think she was happy for us at all," Cecily objected. "Leastwise, not for Sarah. Why else would she tell us what a good match Sir James was for a plain, penniless girl, despite his *tarnished* reputation? And the things she hinted about his dead wives! Even if 'tis uncivil to say so—'' she glanced at Meredyth ''—she was always mean to Sarah, and that's the truth.''

''She likes Elizabeth,'' Emma put in. ''When we called on her together, Lady Sandiford was always quite gracious.''

Cecily snorted. ''Only if Sarah had just gotten a letter from Sinjin, and she wanted to pump you for news.''

''The grandest letters—calvary charges in the thick of the action.'' Colton sighed worshipfully.

''No, she truly likes Elizabeth.'' Emma returned to her point. ''Don't you remember she said how marvelous it would be if Elizabeth and Sinjin made a match of it?''

''Piffle,'' Cecily retorted. ''Just shows what a looby she is, when everyone knows Sinjin really loves—ouch!''

In the sudden silence, Cecily's small exclamation rang in his ears. His stomach lurched, and only with difficulty did Nicholas keep the polite smile plastered in place.

''Lord Englemere can't be interested in country gossip,'' Meredyth said quickly. ''Come along, children.'' She slanted him a glance. ''They are such chatterers. 'Tis quite…overwhelming, when one isn't accustomed.''

''I expect,'' he managed to choke out.

''Colton, you must fetch Faith, if she is to have some ice.'' Dipping a curtsy, she motioned her siblings away.

Nicholas leaned back against his chair, the celebrated ice melting to a sugary dribble in his bowl. Sarah's neighbor a handsome soldier—a handsome soldier who loved her, if the impetuous Cecily's unspoken assertion could be credited. God in heaven, this couldn't be happening.

Numbly he rose and stumbled past the chatting guests, down the stairs, into the garden. This time, he couldn't fend off the searing memories.

Lydia, the radiant bride reveling in the attention of the entire Upper Ten Thousand who gathered to celebrate their nuptials. Lydia, whose sweetness soured and whose pettishness grew week by week as she increasingly complained that he was neglecting her for his fusty papers, his friends, his library, his meetings with the solicitors.

Business compelled him to remain in town after the Season, and weary of the constant harangues, he rented her the town house in Bath for which she pleaded. And found when he joined her there, a week earlier than expected, not his beautiful, pouting wife, but a note she'd left with the butler a bare half hour before his premature arrival.

Recalling the words it contained still made his hands sweat and his stomach turn over.

> I never loved you.... I go to one who truly cherishes me, an officer of the king's Guards and a real gentleman.... Don't try to pursue us.

He had pursued her, of course. And perhaps sensing that pursuit, she must have driven recklessly along the twisting road that led from the city to the military encampment. He'd come upon her phaeton, one wheel off and its body smashed against the pale Bath stone of the sharp curve she'd not quite managed to negotiate. Arrived too late to arrest her flight, too late to beg another chance for their marriage. Like a fashion mannequin propped on a shelf, she sat among the ruins, her lovely neck lolling at an angle, her open eyes staring. *"I never loved you...."*

He realized he still gripped a glass of champagne and downed it in a gulp. *Be sensible,* he rebuked himself.

He should hardly find it surprising that Sarah once had a beau. She was too remarkable to have escaped the notice of some discerning gentleman, even buried as she'd been in the wilds of the country.

Had he not suspected some romance gone awry after she kissed him with such practiced skill? 'Twas an indigent viscount with a disapproving mother who'd schooled her responses, apparently. And then gone for a soldier.

But he'd loved Sarah, this dashing young hussar in his fur-trimmed blue coat. Had Sarah loved him as well?

Sapskull, he admonished. Why should Sarah have confessed a former love? After all, he'd not vouchsafed to her any details of his own disastrous entanglements.

She'd come to London to find a husband, was nearly pledged to another when he rescued her. Whatever her relationship with the soldier, 'twas clearly over now. To start suspecting deception behind her words, betrayal in her actions, would be unfair to Sarah and would sound a death knell to any chance of future happiness.

I will lock away the memories, he vowed, *and never compare Sarah's behavior to Lydia's.* 'Twas the only honorable course—not to mention the only path that would preserve his sanity. Nonetheless, he uttered a swift, fervent prayer that a certain hussar remain safely posted in the farthest reaches of the Peninsula.

Several hours later, Sarah stood in Aunt Sophrina's entryway in her smart new turquoise traveling dress to offer her family a final hug. In a shower of good wishes, she and Nicholas entered the carriage that would take them to the little cottage outside London Ned had lent them for their honeymoon.

Sitting beside Nicholas, his thigh warm and hard against hers as the rumbling carriage jostled them together, she thought with a shuddering thrill of the night ahead. This time, fear curdled the excitement. Her handsome husband was so powerfully male—and so very big.

Put Findlay's nasty words out of your head, she ordered herself. *He said them for naught but revenge, the wretch, knowing you couldn't pull away in the middle of a dance—*

She jumped when Nicholas patted her hand.

"Turquoise becomes you, too, my lovely wife. And as I know of no realm that employs currency of that hue, you can't possibly misconstrue this compliment."

She laughed nervously. "Th-thank you, my lord."

"My friends call me Nicky," he said softly, "and you may if you wish. But I rather prefer the way you say 'Nich-o-las.'" His fingers caressed her cheek as he tilted up her chin. "You make my name sound like music."

A deep peace settled over her. How could she fear this man, who had shown her naught but gentleness and affection? She might distrust his gambling, but she knew beyond question he would never harm her. Willingly she leaned up to meet his lips.

He didn't try to deepen or prolong the kiss. Ending it, he merely held her close. "You've had an exhausting week, sweeting. Rest now. I'll wake you when we arrive."

She ought to engage him in some pleasant conversation to while away the dull, dark minutes. But his arms about her were so comfortably warm, his shoulder so broad and inviting a pillow, that even as she murmured a protest, she felt her heavy eyelids descending. In an instant, she was asleep.

His hands cradling the brandy glass, Nicholas waited for his wife's maid to prepare Sarah for bed. His previous experience with initiating a gently bred virgin into the duties of matrimony had been distinctly unpleasant, and he frankly dreaded the task ahead.

Lydia had been all seductive enticement until the fatal moment. Apparently shocked by the pain, she pleaded with him to stop. Concerned and utterly frustrated, he had done so. Despite his efforts over the next few days to soothe and prepare her, she remained skittish and moody. After she finally permitted him to finish the deed, she wept. And kept her bedroom door locked for a week.

Well, this time he would go slowly from the very beginning. Fortunately, he'd noticed no signs of missishness in Sarah. Indeed, her kisses seemed to promise a rather receptive welcome. The thought cheered him, until he remembered her obvious nervousness during the drive.

'Twas only the natural trepidation of a virtuous maiden on her wedding night. Or was it? an insidious little voice asked. *"Everyone knows he really loves—"*

Uneasiness stirred. Might Sarah's distress have been, not bridal nerves, but the anxiety of a new wife who feared to be discovered less a maid than she should be?

Nonsense, he told himself, annoyed that he'd once again slipped into comparisons, and even more annoyed at the invidious suspicion. Sarah would never have offered herself on the Marriage Mart, were she less than a virgin. He was quite certain of it. With that reassuring conclusion, he downed the brandy and strode purposely from the room.

Sarah's nervousness returned later that evening as Becky, the sisters' former nursemaid, helped her into the shimmering gold nightrail and began unplaiting her hair.

A quick knock sounded. Clad in a satin-frogged dressing gown, Nicholas entered.

Becky curtsied. "My lord, let me but untangle—"

"Allow me." Nicholas reached for the brush.

Becky cast Sarah an inquiring look. Her stomach in knots, Sarah returned a short nod.

Becky handed him the brush and bowed herself out.

Acutely conscious of a partially clad Nicholas behind her, Sarah opened and closed her mouth, unable to dredge up a single conversational topic.

Meanwhile, Nicholas separated her thick braid into individual plaits. "Lord, Sarah, what glorious hair you have," he said, his voice a husky rumble. Slowly he combed his fingers through it to untangle the full length.

She shivered when he ran his thumb down the back of her head, parting the hair in two. Then he pulled the tresses forward over her shoulders and let them fall to her lap.

Stray strands brushed silken across her jaw, setting her nerves tingling. The tips of her breasts burned at the cascading caress of hair over satin.

Nicholas groaned deep in his throat. "Glorious," he breathed, and pressed his lips to the bare nape of her neck.

Sarah's heart leapt in her chest, and despite her best intentions, she stiffened.

Nicholas straightened. She gasped when he wrapped his arms around her, but he merely slid her over on the bench and seated himself beside her.

"What is it, Sarah?" He took her hand and looked closely at her. "You've been skittish as an unbroken colt all evening—and your fingers are like ice."

"'Tis n-nothing," she stuttered. Her obvious cowardice disgusted him, she thought miserably. She cast about for some calm, confident reply, but no words came.

The warmth seemed to leave him and his eyes narrowed. "Troubled thoughts, my dear?" he drawled, his tone slightly mocking. "Surely you don't fear what this evening will reveal? Or dare I hope 'tis delight makes you shiver— anticipation of the treats Findlay whispered about today?"

Sarah shuddered, closing her eyes as those far-from-delightful predictions once again assailed her. She felt a scarlet tide of shame and embarrassment mount her cheeks. Then Nicholas's hand under her chin lifted her face to his.

When she reluctantly opened her eyes, an arrested expression had replaced the coldness on his face.

"*Did* Findlay speak to you about tonight?" he demanded.

She stared at him, her high color making it pointless for her to deny it. With a sigh, she nodded.

"Bloody bastard!" His eyes blazed, but when he met her anxious gaze, the fierceness left him. He took her chilled hands and chafed them gently. "I hate that he upset you, sweet Sarah. What did he say to frighten you so?"

"I'm s-sorry, Nicholas!" she cried, still mortified by her cravenness. "I'm not frightened, truly!"

"Oh, no." He grinned at her, looking inexplicably relieved. "You always go round with frozen limbs and

cringe when I'm near, as if an ogre were about to attack.''
With a mock growl, he nibbled her fingers.

She had to chuckle. "He did say some…distressing
things," she admitted, "but I dismissed them."

"I can see you did." Wrapping his arms about her, he
drew her close. "What did he tell you, Sarah?"

"I'd as lief not discuss it."

He shook his head, adamant. "I think I need to know."

She exhaled in an unhappy little rush. "He said you
would not—" she flushed and turned away "—you would
not have a, a care for me, that you would…" Heavens,
she could hardly tell him Findlay had warned Nicholas
would be as quick as possible about the business, the faster
to return to his beautiful mistress. Nor could she bring
herself to utter the ugly, explicit words in which he described how Nicholas would go about it.

"That I would…?" he prompted.

She opened her lips, then firmly closed them. After a
moment, she said, "I'm sorry, Nicholas. I couldn't possibly repeat the rest." Straightening her shoulders, she
willed her body not to tremble. "He meant to spoil my
wedding night, but I shall not let him. I'm ready, truly."

"You're not afraid of me, are you?"

"Of course not."

He smiled at her unhesitating response. "Thank you for
that. Then believe me, sweet Sarah, I would never hurt
you. You do believe that?"

She nodded, unable to pull her gaze from his.

"You know what happens between a husband and a
wife?" When she nodded again, he continued. "'Tis unreasonable to expect to go from friendship to such intimacy
in an instant. We have Ned's little house all to ourselves,
for as long as we want. There's no need to rush."

"But I wish to be your wife now, tonight!" she cried.
Heavens, waiting wouldn't ease her anxiety, and besides,
perhaps this very night she might conceive a son. "Nicholas, please."

"Are you sure?"

"Oh, yes!"

A slow smile lit his face. "Far be it for me to refuse a lady."

Chapter Eight

Sarah smiled back tremulously, determined to yield to him with no more ridiculous missishness. But he didn't lead her to the bed. Instead he took up the hairbrush once more.

Her surprise must have shown, for he chuckled. Slowly he pulled the brush through her unbound tresses. "What happens between a man and a woman takes many forms, and is quite delightful, sweet wife. Being a greedy sort, I like to make it last."

She'd always loved having her long, thick hair brushed out. Sighing, she relaxed into the soothing strokes.

She was near to drowsing when Nicholas dropped the brush and began combing the heavy strands with his fingers instead. "I'd guessed your unbound hair would be like this," he whispered, "the sheen of satin with the feel of silk. I didn't dream it would be so beautifully thick and long, falling all the way—" his fingertips traced through the tresses from her collarbone down her chest, over her tautened nipples, her waist, her thighs "—to your knees."

He grasped a few strands and gently pulled her face to his. This time, it was she who made the first sound, a little shuddering moan as he kissed her forehead, the tips of her earlobes and finally her lips.

He made it last, just as he'd promised. At first his mouth

merely brushed hers. Then with his tongue he slowly outlined the slender, sensitive ridge where skin becomes lip. Deep within her, a hot, breathless tension coiled.

She was warm, so warm. Her nipples seemed to swell and ache, each gossamer touch sending a tingle of sensation to them, and lower.

She needed more of him, closer. Carried away by the liquid fire coursing to every vein, she opened her mouth.

His hands on her shoulders clenched and his tongue swept inside, probing deeply. Then his grip eased and he slowed to trace her tongue with light, quick touches.

The tension within her grew, her pulse throbbing to the teasing advance and retreat. The taste of him, wine-sweet, his scent of maleness and sandalwood, made her dizzy. She felt perspiration along her back, between her breasts.

She stretched toward him, craving the touch of his hands, the feel of his body against hers.

Kissing her more deeply, Nicholas carried her to the bed. He raised the hem of her nightrail, his hands tracing spiral circles of wonderment along her ankles, her shins, her knees. "Are you sure, sweeting?" he whispered hoarsely.

Her body burned, the very core of her molten with heat and pressure, like lava rising. "Y-yes, please!"

In one swift movement he pulled off her gown. Modesty abandoned, she parted her legs and urged him toward her.

He made a sound deep in his throat, half chuckle, half growl. "Not yet, sweeting." Capturing her hands, he drew them from around his neck, brought them to her sides and reclined his body beside her. Slowly he slid his fingers over her bare hip to cup her breast.

"Beautiful," he murmured, and bent his head.

His tongue circled her nipple, tasted it. She cried out, unprepared by anything she'd experienced for the surge of exquisite sensation that flooded her as he suckled.

His hand caressed the ridge of her hipbone, moved lazily

across the smooth curve of her belly, dipped to touch the warm, moist center of her parted thighs.

"When I come in you," he whispered against her breast, "I'll come here." He slid a finger into her intimate passage. "Are you ready, sweeting?"

She must truly be melting, for she felt herself wet against him. Beyond speech, she moved with him as he withdrew, pushed deeper. "R-ready," she answered unsteadily.

At some point he must have removed his own robe, for when he swung his body over her, his hard man's part probed where his fingers had been. He thrust down.

A clear flame of pain seared her, and she gasped.

He stilled, his rigid shaft a stretching, tearing pressure at her core. Murmuring soothingly, he braced himself on his arms and bent to lave one nipple.

Pleasurable sensation rippled through her faintly, then stronger. She sighed, her muscles softening.

His tongue laving first one breast, then the other, then drinking of her lips, he slowly eased himself deeper. The harsh burning within her subsided to a throbbing ache. As she relaxed, the coiling tension, momentarily suspended, started to build once more.

He began to move, and she learned his rhythm. The ache lessened, submerged under a simmering urgency.

His breath shortened, the muscles of his arms knotted. Then he cried out, his whole body tensing. After a breathless moment, he exhaled with a shudder. Holding her close, he rolled them over and settled her against him.

Sarah lay listening to the sound of their breathing as it steadied and slowed. She felt at once strangely dissatisfied, and elated. She was truly his wife now. And it had been nothing like Findlay predicted.

She thought of the gentleness Nicholas had shown, how he'd waited for her body to accommodate his. With a thrill that sparked her breasts and thighs to renewed throbbing, she remembered the incredible reactions he'd drawn from her with mouth and hands and tongue.

Nicholas pressed his lips to her shoulder. Propping himself on an elbow, he smiled down at her.

She smiled back. "Oh, Nicholas," she whispered, "that was wonderful!"

He chuckled and kissed her on the mouth. "Are you sure? I swore I'd not hurt you, but I know I must have."

"Only for a little. As for the rest—ah, 'twas as marvelous as you said."

He kissed her again, his tongue twining with hers as if to demonstrate gratification at her approval. That heated tension within her, which had subsided as she lay quiescent, began to build again.

"'Twill become more delightful still, sweet wife. For the lady, 'tis always better after the first."

His fingers played with the ends of her hair, feathering light touches across the insides of her thighs as he did so. The pressure grew more urgent.

"I can hardly c-credit it," she stuttered, the motion of his hands somehow hindering speech.

"Ah, I knew you were of scientific mind," he murmured. He moved his hand higher, dallying with the thicker, tighter curls nested there. "I think we should test the theory."

His fingers slid to her passage, now dewed with her essence and his. She moaned. Taking that for assent, he put his lips to her breast.

She shuddered and arched into him. This time, he traced with his tongue the pebbly edge of her nipples, holding her still when she would have moved. Against his exploring fingers she felt herself liquefy.

Instead of plunging deeper, he withdrew a finger and slid upward, painting her inner lips until he touched—there.

She jumped, even his slight pressure on that small, rigid

spot unbelievably acute. Murmuring, he suckled her harder and rubbed his slick fingers against it.

Over and over he stroked her, his fingers dipping to her throbbing wet passage and then back, the feel of it so piercingly exquisite she felt she must surely shatter. When the stroking suddenly ceased, she felt bereft.

He stifled her protest with a quick kiss, then moved his mouth to the place his finger had stroked.

If the sensation had been intense before, 'twas doubly so now—the soft pressure and liquid heat of his tongue sparking fire against her tender nub, and then lower as it slid into the passage his manhood had probed. Compelled to move, she broke free of his restraining hold and arched up at him, instinctively finding the rhythm.

She heard strange, feral sobs and realized they were her own. The deeply buried regret that it was not Sinjin who kissed her, Sinjin who loved her, flamed to cinder and disintegrated.

Nicholas entered her, his movement within this time all pleasurable friction and smooth, slippery delight. His body sheened, his breathing a harsh gasp, he filled her completely, advancing and retreating in urgent cadence.

In the next instant, he plunged deep and cried out. The world exploded around her into brilliant shards of sensation that shocked along her nerves for long, exquisite moments before dimming and slowly, slowly subsiding.

Sometime later, she opened her eyes to find Nicholas inclined above her. He held his weight on his hands, but his hips pressed hers intimately where their bodies still joined. She could feel the thunderous beat of his heart.

"Better?" he whispered hoarsely.

"Better," she breathed.

"Good." He bent and kissed her gently. "Sarah, my sweet wife," he murmured, the words a caress.

In the vicinity of her heart, her chest tightened.

Once again, he rolled to his side and pulled her against his chest. With a long, deep sigh, he nestled into the pillows. A few moments later she heard his slow, even breathing and knew he slept.

Awe and wonderment grew in her. He had taken her tenderly, given a pleasure as unexpected as it was profound. Even now, the miracle of that possession might be transforming itself into the miracle of new life.

'Twas no going back now. Though they had not exchanged words of love, the language spoken by their bodies had sealed a bond that for Sarah was permanent and irreversible.

A profound tranquillity settled within her. A scientific mind, Nicholas had said? She lifted a hand, tempted to trail it along the beauty of muscle and bone that lay beside her, see if she could uncover for him unexpected wonders such as those he had revealed for her.

Then her hand stilled. *Lord save me from spirited, passionate women.* No, he had married her to create a bond of flesh—the second miracle, not the first. She must remember that, and the fact that, as riveting as this experience had been for her, 'twas not the same for him.

He had known others before and might again. Though at this moment, suffused in the marvel of their joining, her mind refused to acknowledge that possibility in more concrete detail.

She moved her hand from the enticing curve of hip, instead brushing back the lock of hair that had drifted onto his brow. She must remember her place, and her duty.

This marriage, she thought sleepily as she snuggled her cheek against the fragrant velvet pillow of his shoulder, might be worth the gamble after all.

Smiling, Sarah seated herself at the desk in her sitting room, poured herself some tea and turned her face into the pale sunshine. Nicholas was in the library, but would be up shortly to escort her to yet another fitting. It seemed, at her husband's urging, she'd done nothing since returning to London but acquire the enormous wardrobe that he assured her was required for a lady of her position.

She sighed. She'd much enjoyed her more lowly position as temporary chatelaine of Ned's little cottage. Though Sarah had been the one to end the idyll of their honeymoon, reminding Nicholas of Lady Jersey's upcoming ball, she had been most reluctant to do so.

For idyllic it had been. They'd spent a profusion of lazy sunlit hours exploring the countryside, fishing poles and picnic basket stowed on their saddlebags. Rainy days they whiled away at billiards or chess. In the evenings they read aloud, or she entertained him with her repertoire of piano. They had even played cards.

Nicholas had at first suggested they wager chicken stakes. All her defenses springing to the alert, she sharply declined, replying if they played at all, she would prefer it to be merely a test of skill.

He countered by proposing they wager something more interesting than guineas. And proceeded to disarm all her apprehensions by suggesting, with a naughty-boy smile, that they play for kisses. By the time he demonstrated his expectations of what losing a point would entail, she could hardly recall which cards she held. She lost the first game with embarrassing swiftness, and he claimed his forfeit with such skill that cards were abandoned for the night.

Ah, yes, the nights… Her cheeks grew hot and a spiraling warmth uncurled in her belly at the memories.

She caught her wayward thoughts. However wrong he'd been about Nicholas's initial treatment of her, Findlay most likely spoke the truth when he predicted that, once she got with child, Nicholas would reduce his nocturnal visits.

Perhaps 'twas as well, for she found adhering to their bargain more difficult than ever she'd imagined. It had been all good and well to promise a calm, ladylike reserve in intimate matters while wholly ignorant of what that promise entailed. But now…

The powerful response he evoked made her burn to cry aloud at his touch, ache to follow his lead and to let her own lips and fingers explore his beautiful lean body.

Well, she would just have to manage it. She'd given her word, and she never went back on a promise.

Firmly redirecting her thoughts, she came across a note from the old steward's son she'd left in charge at Wellingford. Jenkins wrote of the repairs he'd effected over the winter and the preparations for spring planting. He'd do his best possible to stretch funds, he promised, but might she have available any additional monies?

A familiar mix of longing, frustration and shame filled her. Wellingford's land held such potential, could she but scrape together the funds to exploit it. She might apply to Nicholas—but no, she absolutely could not ask him for another groat. The quarterly allowance he allotted her was already more than generous.

With a tremor of excitement she straightened. A considerable sum still remained from that allowance, and her wardrobe was already stuffed to repletion. Why not send the rest to Wellingford?

Swiftly she estimated the amounts required for additional seed, roofing and tools. She set down the pen, her heartbeat quickening. She could do all, or much of it.

This very afternoon she would visit the bank. Taking up her pen, she mentally reviewed the instructions she must send Jenkins. But where did one obtain the rapeseed and the new curved plow Sir Edward had described?

Ned would know. Surely he would be willing to share his expertise. She'd write Ned first.

Her pen flew through the note, her mind whirling with images of Wellingford renascent. Not until she sealed it did a tremor of doubt trouble her.

The allowance was given her to fulfill her role as Marchioness of Englemere. But then, hadn't Nicholas several times assured her it was hers to spend as she liked? Besides—a gambler's passion had nearly lost her Wellingford. Wasn't it somehow fitting that a gambler's winnings rescued, and might now begin to restore it?

True, Nicholas might not appreciate her plowing yet more of his blunt into a farm—if he knew. Not that she'd dissemble, but she doubted he'd ask how she spent the funds, and couldn't imagine him troubling to inspect account ledgers. In a few short weeks, she'd have another shamefully extravagant sum to draw upon. Meanwhile, the sums she borrowed would buy a whole growing season's benefit for Wellingford.

Hours later, Sarah stood at the edge of Lady Jersey's ballroom as a teeming swirl of the haut ton passed by. She thought wistfully of Ned's cottage just an hour's drive away. Why ever had she urged Nicholas to return to London?

After one dance, she'd released him to make the rounds of his friends, while she sought out Clarissa. When Wexley claimed that lady, Sarah wandered back to the ballroom. Nicholas wasn't present, though, and Sarah wondered if she'd see him again tonight.

"The fair maiden doesn't dance? How can this be?"

She whirled to find Nicholas behind her. He caught her hand for a lingering kiss that sent a shiver of sensation from her fingertips to her toes.

She could feel her cheeks flush, and blessed the relative shadow of this alcove. "You found your friends well, I trust. And caught up on the latest *on-dits?*"

To her surprise, he threw back his head and laughed. "Indeed. Including this interesting tidbit. It seems a certain young lady, observing that her fiancé had fallen unaccountably but desperately in love with her companion, ended their engagement so those two persons might wed."

Sarah gasped. "She didn't! Oh, that wretched girl! Clarissa mentioned such a silly scenario, but I never—"

Nicholas put a finger to her lips. "Come, do you not find it amusing to figure in this affecting little tale?"

"But 'tis entirely untrue, and unfair to you, as well! As for your falling in love with me, 'tis a notion too preposterous for anyone to entertain."

"Ah, but entertain it they do. No less than three of my friends asked, in strictest confidence, if 'twere true."

Upset now, Sarah gave a helpless shrug. "What can I say, but assure you again how sorry I am."

"Don't let it trouble you, sweet Sarah. I did in fact abandon her—with no regrets. And I've been an object of gossip since the moment I inherited. Besides, I rather like the role of dashing knight discovering his one true love." His voice softened. "Do you not wish to be my lady fair?"

"I should be honored! But never would I wish to embarrass you."

"Then I must convince you this is ardor."

He peeled back her glove. With lips and tongue he slowly caressed each rounded pad of her exposed palm.

Sarah's heartbeat stampeded. "My lord," she said, gasping. "Have a care, else I shall start to believe it myself."

He nibbled the swell of her thumb before releasing it. "Would that be so bad a thing?"

"Shame on you, Englemere!" Lady Jersey tapped him with her fan. "'Tis bad ton to dance attendance on your wife—despite the interesting rumors I hear."

She cast them a shrewd glance. "Go along now, and let me chat with Sarah. Several ladies present tonight, I know, are dying for a dance with you." With a private little smile, Lady Jersey motioned him away.

Nicholas bowed and walked off, then turned to gaze back at his wife. The emerald of her gown accented the gold of her pale hair and seemed to set off jade echoes in her silver eyes. After a month, her subtle beauty still startled him, as it had dazzled him the unforgettable moment he'd first seen her in that gold wedding dress.

Their honeymoon had been emphatic proof of his brilliance in choosing her. Sarah never kept him waiting to fuss with her gown, or chattered at him over the breakfast table, or pouted if he left her alone to tend his accounts. Even better, with her ready wit and her many mannish accomplishments, she was…fun.

He'd expected her to be a bruising rider, but hadn't anticipated needing to use every trick to best her in their races. At their first billiards game, he deliberately missed a ball and found himself royally trounced before he could recapture his cue. And, he recalled with a grin, she was just as good with a pistol as she claimed.

She was also unexpectedly, delectably good at other things. The vein of sensuality he'd suspected beneath the calm exterior ran deep and pure. From their wedding night onward, Sarah entranced him with her delight in each touch, every sensation. 'Twas as if, he reflected in bemusement, her eager wonderment was scouring away his layers of jaded experience, making everything new for him—as if he, too, were exploring intimate pleasure for the very first time.

Equally amazing, she attempted none of the manipulation he'd come to believe inevitable in the sensual waltz of a man with a woman. Never did she entice and then refuse him; never did she hint that intimacy hinged on a gift or favor. She was just—Sarah, unaffectedly natural and willing.

Still, he sensed a banked passion smoldering behind a remnant of maidenly reserve. Though he was thoroughly pleased with the physical bond that already existed between them, it had become an intoxicating game to try to draw still more active a response from her. Faith, with a wife as arousing and arousable as Sarah, what need had he of a mistress?

The unexpected thought shocked him, his cautious head reining in his impulsive heart. 'Twas early yet, too soon for so far-reaching a decision. For now, he meant to just enjoy a marriage far more pleasant than he'd dared expect.

A wicked idea occurred, and he grinned. Damn, how long until they could leave this dull party?

"I should be delighted if I believed that—satisfied—smile sprang to your lips at the prospect of meeting me," a low voice murmured. In a swath of black silk cut low over her sumptuous breasts, Chloe Ingram glided to him.

"I'm certainly glad to see you, Nicholas, after all these weeks." She reached out a hand, then stopped. "That is, if you're still greeting your old…friends?"

It was a perfect opening, and for an instant he nearly seized it. But he and Chloe had been friends, as well as lovers. He owed her more than a cut direct in a ballroom.

"Of course I'm greeting old friends." Glancing past her as he brought one perfumed hand to his lips, he noted Sarah and Lady Jersey nowhere in sight. "Ladies dying to dance with him," indeed.

This explained Silence's cat-licking-the-cream-pot smile. He bet Sally Jersey would never send Chloe vouchers to Almack's, yet she'd included the lady in her ball tonight. A score he'd settle with the mischievous Sally later.

"You're looking exceedingly lovely." He dropped the compliment smoothly and looked back to Chloe.

"Flatterer." She made a moue at him and leaned closer. And thereby offered him, he realized critically, a better view down her brief bodice. He could easily make out the shadow of nipples barely covered by dusky silk.

She noted the direction of his eyes and drew a deep breath, swelling her ample bosom toward him. "London has been dreadfully dull. Indeed, I'm quite overwhelmed to see you again." She swept her glance down, like his, to her breasts, and her nipples under their silk veiling hardened.

In the past, he had found such innuendo about her passion—and its physical evidence—highly arousing. He thought now it was a cheap whore's trick. Surprised by that harsh judgment, he said brusquely, "Oh, I daresay you had much to amuse you."

He thought he saw a flash of pique in her eyes. Then, perhaps sensing his thoughts, she slipped out of the seductive pose. "I've been so lonely I fear I've been unwisely amused. Everly begged me most particularly to come to his party...." She sighed and cast him a look of appeal.

Lord Everly, the wild youngest son of an earl, hosted raffish affairs where, attracted by the possibility of casual liaisons and high-stakes gambling, one might find mingled both the haut ton and the demimonde. The beauteous Chloe had a weakness for gambling.

"Dipped again, Chloe?"

"I'm afraid so. Who could have believed that wretched ball would continue to favor the red?"

He shook his head at her. "Surely you know by now never to trust Lady Luck."

All wiles seemingly suspended, she showed him the repentant face of a schoolgirl. "I know, but I can't seem to help myself. I can still count on you—can't I, Nicky?"

The beautiful violet eyes looked at him guilelessly. She might only be asking about his readiness to stand her a loan—perhaps. Unwilling to be forced at this moment to decide Chloe's future, Nicholas chose his words with care.

"Send my secretary a note. But have some sense, Chloe. I may not always be able to rescue you. On the income Ingram left, you shouldn't game so freely."

She stiffened, and her eyes flashed. "'Tis easy for you to preach, circumstanced you are. Or has your little wife been preaching puritan restraint? Quite a prim and proper miss, I've heard."

Nicholas drew back. He supposed Chloe was angered by his marriage, but she should have been clever enough to realize he would never elevate a mistress to be his countess. Nor could he permit her to gossip about his wife.

Before he could deliver a set-down, Chloe put a hand

to one rouged cheek. "Oh, Nicky, forgive me! You are right, I am unwise, but it frightens me to consider the future...to think of being abandoned." Her voice wobbled on the word and her eyes looked suspiciously bright.

That concern at least was unfeigned, for Ingram had not left her well circumstanced. A fact that, Nicholas suspected, had weighed as much as his manly charms in deciding her to take him to her bed. Compassion stirred.

"Chloe, surely you know I never abandon my friends."

She swiped at the corner of her eye. "Of course. I'm just being foolish. You have ever been all that is kind."

She gave him a tremulous smile and put a gloved hand hesitantly on his arm. When he patted it, her smile warmed to brilliance and she squeezed his wrist.

Nicholas glanced up from that possessive little gesture to find Sarah's eyes resting on them, her face impassive. Swiftly he withdrew his arm, but at the moment he sensed her gaze, Sarah closed her eyes. As if blotting out some unpleasantness, she turned aside.

Nicholas simply stood as Sarah walked away. That she knew—or would be shortly informed—who Chloe Ingram was, he had no doubt. Cursing his luck, he wondered whether he should pursue her immediately, or let the matter rest. After all, a bit of jealousy never hurt.

At the far side of the room, Sarah stopped abruptly. Clapping a hand to her lips, she cried out and threw herself into the arms of a tall blond man in a hussar's blue coat.

A lightning bolt of shock immobilized Nicholas. As Nicholas watched in numb horror, the soldier hugged his wife tightly and rubbed his cheek against her hair.

Sensation returned in sharp tingling waves and nausea roiled in his gut. So much for the wilds of the Peninsula.

Chloe and the dancers forgotten, he strode across the ballroom. He was, he knew with a sour taste in his mouth, about to meet the man who had taught his wife to kiss.

Chapter Nine

Nicholas reached them in a moment. Apparently realizing what a spectacle she was presenting, Sarah stepped away from the soldier. "Sinjin, 'tis marvelous to see you! Why didn't you write you'd gotten leave?"

Then she saw Nicholas, and with a smile, led the officer over. "My lord, let me introduce my neighbor and dear friend, Captain St. John Stafford, Viscount Sandiford. Sinjin, this is Nicholas Stanhope, Lord Englemere, my husband."

The captain stopped short, friendliness draining from his face. "Husband?"

Her glow dimmed. "Yes, we've been wed this month and more. I wrote you, Sinjin. Did you not get the letter?"

In the ensuing silence, polite words of greeting stuck in Nicholas's throat. The best he could manage, his pulse still pounding and every nerve alert, was to twist his lips into what he hoped might be taken as a smile.

For a long, uneasy moment, the captain stared at him, his sunburnt face unreadable. Then he looked down at Sarah. "You know how uncertain the mails are. The last letter I had from you said you'd gone to London, for— urgent reasons. I demanded leave immediately, but we had some nasty set-tos with Soult before I could get away."

"Oh, Sinjin," Sarah murmured.

Finally managing to force the ritual of civility, Nicholas stuck out his hand. "Pleased to meet an old *friend* of Sarah's. I've heard of your gallantry, Captain."

"You have?" Sarah looked startled.

"Colton particularly lauded his abilities under fire."

Seeming to recover as well, the captain gripped Nicholas's hand. "Forgive my deplorable soldier's manners. Your servant, my lord. I'm sure whatever account you got from Colton was highly exaggerated." He tossed Sarah an amused glance. "The scamp's army-mad."

Nicholas found the captain's easy familiarity grating. And must the fellow be so tall, well-muscled and handsome? He looked across into blue eyes that, behind the smile, were as frosty as he suspected were his own.

"You're on leave from your regiment, then, Captain. Do you make a long stay in London?" He pushed the conventional pleasantry through tight lips. "You must call on us."

"Yes, do, Sinjin," Sarah echoed. "I should like you two to become acquainted, and we have—much to discuss."

For another long moment the hussar studied Sarah. A ripple of emotion crossed his face.

His tone, when he at last replied, was unexceptional. "So it seems. Yes, I shall certainly call upon you."

Lady Jersey descended on them in a flutter of pink satin. "Sarah, dear! Who is this dashing stranger you induced to visit my ball—and greeted with such warmth?"

"'Tis my wife's neighbor, Captain Lord Sandiford, just returned to London from the Peninsula," Nicholas answered.

The captain made her an elegant bow. "Forgive me, Your Ladyship! Even in the wilds of Portugal, my army mates traded tales of your beauty, wit and fascinating entertainments. How could I help but present myself? Raff Peterson assured me you'd greet an old soldier kindly."

Lady Jersey tinkled a laugh and preened herself. The

captain had taken her measure at a glance. Nicholas wasn't sure whether to be relieved or annoyed at his perspicacity.

"Marcus Rafferty Peterson, that devilish scapegrace? Well, if you are one of Raff's friends—as well as Lady Englemere's," she added with a penetrating look at Sarah, "then certainly I must bid you welcome."

Chloe Ingram stepped out of the crowd, startling Nicholas. Drat the woman, she must have trailed him.

She startled him even more by boldly inserting herself between her hostess and the newcomer. "You must present him to me, your ladyship," Chloe said. "I have a brother in the army, Captain. Mayhap you know him."

Someone gasped. The small circle about Nicholas seemed to hold its collective breath. Would the great queen of society punish or tolerate this intrusion?

Lady Jersey chose to be amused. After an ironic glance from Sarah to Nicholas to the hussar, she turned to Chloe. "Captain Lord Sandiford, may I present Mrs. Chloe Ingram. Certainly one of our, ah, loveliest London widows."

The captain bowed, and Chloe swept him a curtsy. "Chat with me, Captain. I believe we have much in common."

Lady Jersey trilled another laugh. "Oh, without doubt. Mrs. Ingram will lead you to...refreshment, Captain. Sarah, dear, let me steal your handsome husband. 'Tis my own ball, and I've not had a dance with him all evening."

The musicians were striking up a waltz. Avid curiosity lit her ladyship's face, and Nicholas knew he was about to be mercilessly quizzed. Bowing to his hostess and the inevitable, Nicholas offered an arm.

"I'd be honored, Sal. You must promise, though, if the gallant to whom you've bespoken this waltz calls me out, you'll leave flowers on my grave."

"Rogue," Lady Jersey reproved, and turned to Sarah. "I'll send him back intact, my dear. As for you," she said, placing her hand on Nicholas's sleeve, "should it come to grass for breakfast, I'd wager my blunt on you."

Nicholas cast a narrowed glance at a retreating blue-coated back. Fury sizzled through him. He felt a primitive urge to strike down the handsome captain here, now, in this very ballroom, to prevent with a preemptive blow even the possibility that the soldier might seek to wrest from Nicholas what was his.

The intensity of that battle instinct shocked and disturbed him. Like a blind man groping his way through unfamiliar landscape, he struggled to remember the place and time, to recover the normal pattern of behavior.

The matter of the dashing Captain Viscount Sandiford's untimely return couldn't be settled by fisticuffs in a ballroom. Though deal with it he must, and soon.

At a very late hour, Nicholas escorted Sarah back to Stanhope House, where a yawning footman admitted them.

The rest of the ball had passed uneventfully. The captain danced with Sarah only a proper two sets, after first honoring Chloe, his hostess and several other ladies. When Nicholas claimed Sarah's hand for the second waltz, she chatted amusingly and not once mentioned Sandiford.

He was thus unsure whether to be pleased or sorry when she asked if he would come speak with her before he retired. Though a discussion of the captain was undeniably necessary, once out of the man's troubling proximity Nicholas had half hoped to postpone it.

He smiled ruefully as he knocked at the dressing room door. He should know if difficulties loomed, in Sarah-fashion she would want to attack them head-on.

Sarah stood warming her hands at the hearth, her hair, in a loose braid down her back, gleaming in the firelight.

Nicholas tangled his fingers in the plait and leaned to kiss her. "Later," she murmured. A gleam of promise in her eyes, she urged him onto the settee behind them.

"What did the children tell you about Sinjin?"

His ardor vanished. "Does it matter?"

"I just wondered, that I might not bore you repeating

what you already know. After my rather—demonstrative greeting tonight, I thought you entitled to an explanation.''

''It did seem a trifle excessive,'' he said dryly.

To his surprise, she flared up. ''I'll not apologize for that! For forgetting myself in such a place, I do beg pardon—that was not well done. But Sinjin has been my dearest friend for as long as I can remember. His regiment is fighting in the Pyrenees, the journals say, and I knew he'd be in the thick of it. I was overjoyed to see him return uninjured. Just as you would be, should someone dear to you escape from that action.''

''Probably,'' he admitted. ''I wouldn't kiss him in a ballroom, though.''

She laughed, her heat dissipating. ''I didn't kiss him, merely gave him a hug. Let Sally Jersey make what she likes of it! The children told you, I expect, that his land marches with ours and the families have long been intimate.''

She looked up at him, waiting. With resignation, he prepared to offer up what else he'd learned.

''Yes, they said as much. After Cecily voiced her approval of your choice in husbands.'' He grinned.

''That child needs a curb bit,'' Sarah said, shaking her head. ''What other indiscretions did she let slip?''

''Apparently Lady Sandiford kept them informed of your, ah, progress in London. Cecily claimed the viscountess disliked you—'' Sarah groaned ''—but Emma insisted she had a fondness for you all.'' He paused, watching her. ''So much so that she favors a union between her son and your sister Elizabeth—now that she has a dowry, of course.''

If pain crossed her face, he didn't see it. '''Twould be a good match. He would make her a kind husband. And he could wish for no finer a wife.''

''Could he not?''

She studied her fingers. ''Not any longer.''

After a moment she continued. '''Tis true, we expected

to marry, though his mama never truly approved.'' A brief smile touched her lips. ''How could I blame her? She wished a beautiful heiress for her son, and I was hardly that.''

Nicholas instantly extended his dislike to encompass the captain's mother.

Sarah sighed, her gaze on the dancing firelight. ''In any event, our fathers were fellow gamesters. By the time I was old enough for a come-out, both estates were heavily in debt. We knew duty compelled us to marry elsewhere.''

''Did you? Sandiford seemed shocked to find you wed.''

''I had vowed never to marry. But one does what one must.'' She looked up at him, her eyes warming, then took his hand and kissed it. ''Never has a woman been so bountifully rewarded for doing what she must.''

A tightness gathered in his chest and he drew her into his arms. He'd been about to ask if she had loved her soldier friend. Why, he couldn't imagine. It didn't matter now, and quite frankly he would rather not know.

Despite these self-assurances, the tension in his gut continued to build. He discovered with dismay that it did matter, rather desperately, whether his wife had cherished a *tendre* for another man. Damn, he vowed, he'd bite off his tongue before he'd ask such a useless, green-sick question.

''I did love him,'' Sarah admitted. ''As the eldest of so many girls, Papa treated me almost like a son, and it was always Sinjin who challenged my skills at riding, shooting, hunting. The change from tomboy companions to youthful lovers came as natural as breathing, I suppose.''

I did love him. He barely prevented himself physically recoiling. Prickling shards of memory gouged at old wounds.

''I had hoped you were happy with me, Sarah.''

Her eyes widened. ''I have been happy! How could you think otherwise?''

The pressure in his chest eased a little. ''I'm glad for that. It has been a splendid month. But…now?''

"I'll not receive him, if you prefer."

The offer, freely given, loosed the tension still further, and he was vastly tempted to accept it. But he knew society too well.

"That wouldn't serve. Too many people observed us tonight. 'Twould be better for us all to be on cordial terms, as befits old friends." His smile twisted. "But only cordial. Though I would suffer much for your happiness, there are some things I simply could not allow."

She didn't pretend to misunderstand. "You must not worry the sudden reappearance of a former—friend—would make me forget my place, or my duty. Before ever I came to London, I set old loyalties aside. And now—you have treated both me and my family so generously, how could I think to look elsewhere?"

Her avowal helped, but couldn't completely reassure him. "Duty is a rather cold companion," he said gruffly.

Before he could look away, she reached up to cup his face in lavender-scented palms. "We may not be able to choose our fate, but we can make our own happiness. If I ever doubted that, this past month has convinced me."

Swiftly she encircled his neck, surprising him with a kiss. It was one of her best Sarah kisses, starting soft, then deepening as she parted his lips to tease his tongue and stir the smoldering embers of desire.

"You have brought me so many blessings," she murmured. "I only hope I may bring you half as much."

His turmoil flamed into another need. *Mine,* it said. *Now and always mine.*

"You will," he promised, and pulled her into his arms.

Sarah sat at the dressing table, inspecting herself in the glass. Her morning gown of deep blue, with its slashed rouleau puffs at the shoulder and gold military braid, was perhaps the most stylish of all her new gowns.

After their appearance last night, the news that Lord and Lady Englemere had returned from their honeymoon would by now have swept the ton. She expected a steady stream of the curious to come calling on his lordship's new bride.

When they breakfasted, Nicholas told her he must meet his solicitor over some matter that could not wait, and asked her to make his excuses to any callers. With his usual perception, Nicholas must have taken Sinjin's measure and known he would lose no time seeking her out for a full explanation. How thoughtful Nicholas was, to have arranged so unexceptional an excuse to allow them a private meeting.

How understanding as well. Until Sinjin's unexpected return shocked her into that emotional greeting, she'd not thought it necessary to inform Nicholas of her unhappy love affair. 'Twas past, and in no way affected him.

Last night she'd known she must acquaint Nicholas with the bare facts and reassure him of her commitment. After all, any husband must feel unsettled by such a public demonstration of his wife's feeling for another man. Even one, she thought with a sigh, whose heart was not engaged.

Some men might have berated their errant wives for such a lapse, but he barely reproved her. He even said, she recalled, that he wanted her to be happy. And demonstrated his trust by allowing her to meet her former love. Gambler though he were, she could not have asked for a more generous, considerate husband.

At the idea of meeting Sinjin her nervousness returned. Though the hour was too early for callers, she knew her childhood friend well enough to suspect he would call when he could anticipate finding her alone.

Almost upon the thought, a knock sounded. The footman announced a caller below.

Her stomach fluttered as she caught up a shawl. Downstairs she would see Sinjin alone for the first time in three years. 'Twas the moment she'd dreaded ever since steeling herself to the necessity of London, and marriage.

He said he'd gotten the letter detailing her plans, yet

he'd clearly been shocked to discover her wed. She feared he was not going to be as understanding as Nicholas.

Sinjin was gazing out the window, sunlight glinting on the gold of his epaulets, when Glendenning announced her.

"Some sherry for the captain," she instructed the butler. "And let Lord Englemere know we have a caller, that he might join us when he returns."

Betraying not a flicker of the curiosity he must be feeling at leaving his mistress alone with this stranger, Glendenning bowed. "As you wish, my lady."

Not until the butler departed did she turn, palms moist and heartbeat quickening, to greet her former love.

He had turned toward her as well. The bright light from the window illuminated every feature as the wavering candlelight last night could not. Her polite words of welcome dried on her lips.

He looked achingly familiar and yet changed. His tall frame was thinner than she remembered, his skin bronzed by a harsher sun than England's. A jagged scar running from temple to cheekbone showed whitely against the mahogany of his face. Tiny lines webbed the corners of his blue eyes and the edges of the firm, taut lips.

He'd left a boyish young man, but naught of youth remained. An aura of command surrounded him, the air of a man accustomed to giving difficult orders and being obeyed. His once-laughing eyes were hard, as if he'd met danger, privation and suffering, and conquered them all.

Then he smiled. Dimples creased the lean cheeks—the same dimples she traced with a finger before she kissed them, that happy summer she planned to be his bride.

"God, but you're beautiful, Sarah," he said huskily.

A bolt of pure joy shot through her, and she instinctively stepped toward him. At the last moment, some shred of sanity penetrated. She stopped just short of once again flinging herself into his arms.

Her heart pounding, she turned aside, aghast at the intensity of her emotions. After long bitter years, she thought she'd tamed the tumultuous love she once felt for him, toned it down to the limits permissible between friends. Yet it took every ounce of her control to keep her hands at her sides and her feet motionless. A great gash of pain tore through her heart.

Mercifully he made no move toward her. She thanked God for that and for Glendenning's swift return with the sherry. Uttering what she hoped were appropriate words, she went to pour, willing her hands not to rattle the glass.

By the time she dispensed his sherry she was calmer. Careful not to touch his hand, she gave it to him.

"You're looking well, too, Sinjin," she said, relieved her voice was steady. "Older, of course, but very handsome and commanding."

He raised his glass, took a sip and sat silent, twirling the fragile stem in his fingers. With a twisted smile, he looked over. "Obviously not handsome enough."

She winced as another shaft of pain lanced through her. "Surely you were expecting as much. I clearly remember writing you I could no longer honor my vow. That I must find a wealthy husband with all speed, lest we lose Wellingford—lose everything. You did get that letter."

"Yes, I got it. Indeed, I reread it so often I can still recite it, long after the paper fell to shreds. 'I have racked my brain, but can come up with no honorable way to meet our obligations save marriage to a wealthy man. Thus, I must break my vow and go to London. Repugnant as the idea is to me, the alternative is to lose Wellingford, and that I can never permit....'"

He turned to the window. "Was the idea truly repugnant? Or after three lonely years did you begin to yearn for marriage after all?"

She stared at him, not comprehending. "No, I had no wish to marry elsewhere! How can you think that?"

He turned back, his face impassioned. "If 'twas only to save Wellingford, why not launch Lizbet instead? She's old enough, and if she's grown as beautiful as she bade fair to do, should have met great success. Why seek a husband yourself—unless you truly wished one?''

"Oh, Sinjin, you have no idea how things stood, to accuse me of that!" Angered, she rose and paced the room. "Beautiful she may be, but you know the way of the world. With neither dowry nor important connections Lizbet could scarcely hope to attract the more desirable gentlemen. How could I bear to see that gentle loveliness bestowed on someone whose sole qualification was sufficient wealth? Sinjin, you know her. Of all my sisters, she would suffer most from a union in which affection played no part.

"No, if one of us had to endure a loveless marriage, I knew it must be me. I'm the eldest—'twas only my duty.'' She halted her restless pacing before the mantel and sighed. "Even had I determined to sacrifice Elizabeth, 'twould not have answered. You cannot image how little coin we had. I could not have come to chaperon her.''

She turned to face him, cutting him off before he could speak. "Surely you realize I couldn't let her go about London with only nearsighted Aunt Sophrina to guard her! Let us speak plainly. There are those who, seeing such a beautiful innocent unprotected, might seek to force her into something less than marriage.''

At length he slowly nodded. "I suppose you are right.''

"Then you understand why I came myself—regardless of my *inclination*,'' she concluded with caustic emphasis.

He stepped toward her, his hands outstretched. "I'm sorry, Sarah, I meant no insult. But the shock of finding you married! And to one I believe you might well choose.''

"I was lucky." She thought of Findlay and shuddered. "The man I was nearly forced to marry is an altogether different sort. During the course of the Season, Nicholas and I became friends. When the mortgage came due, and he learned I intended to marry Sir James in order to pay it off, he proposed a marriage of convenience.''

"Kind of him."

At Sinjin's mocking tone, Sarah fired up. "It was indeed kind! You cannot know society if you do not realize how far above my touch is the Marquess of Englemere! Not only did he condescend to the match, but he expended a great deal of blunt over it as well. He has been everything generous, even allowing me to see you privately that I might…explain the circumstances of my marriage."

"You mean that you would not have received me, had he not given permission?" He seemed to choke on the word.

"Certainly not. Not alone, at any rate. Despite our long friendship—mayhap because of it," she inserted with a tinge of sadness, "'twould have been most improper."

He stared at her. "You would be that obedient."

"Of course. He's my husband, Sinjin."

He looked dumbfounded, as if, despite the knowledge of her marriage, the reality of what it meant to her—and to him—only at this moment sank in. He sat down abruptly.

Sarah seated herself as well. Done, she thought with relief, her obstreperous emotions once more well in hand.

"Will you be remaining in England, or must you return to your regiment?" she asked, breaking the silence.

"I've a month's leave, though my business may take longer. I shall certainly rejoin my men after that. In good conscience, I can't sell out until Boney's routed."

"I see." Fear for him shook her, but she swallowed the words. "We must make your brief stay pleasant, then. A number of young ladies at the ball last night are both eligible and wealthy. I dare swear they would be only too eager to meet a dashing young captain." Though the words nearly choked her, she added, "And Elizabeth—"

"Don't, Sarah!" After a visible struggle, he seemed to master himself. "Having so successfully managed your own, do you think to play matchmaker for me? I've no interest whatsoever."

"Sinjin, what's done is done. We must go forward."

He walked to the window and stood, tilting his glass and watching the play of light on the amber liquid. "Yes," he said at last. "When one path closes, we find another."

"Yes," she echoed, relieved he seemed to understand. "Your mama would be pleased should you plan to wed. Have you seen her yet?"

"No." He tossed down the sherry. "I shall have to post down to Sandiford, I suppose, though I'd rather not. Seeing her brings it all back." He turned to Sarah, his face hardening. "Had she not been so opposed to our marriage, had she not harped so endlessly that I owed it to my family to marry an heiress with the means to restore our fortunes... Unable to marry you, unable to remain and resist you, the army seemed the only way out."

Sarah fought the memories his words recalled. "At least you got away! I used to pray I might find somewhere—anywhere—else to go. Anywhere but home where the walks, the glens, the very barns teemed with—"

His gaze shot back, and too late, she fell silent. She knew he was recalling, as she was, their last day before he went off to war.

They rode together as the sun was setting, and he walked her back to Wellingford's shabby parlor. They said their goodbyes under her mama's eye, exchanging proper expressions of mutual regard, and one chaste kiss.

But later that night, wild with grief and despair, Sarah stole out of the house and rode to Sandiford. She threw a pebble at his window, as she had in childhood when she'd bidden him to sneak out, and as in childhood, he came.

He met her in the stables, but unlike the many times before, she'd not had his horse saddled and ready. Instead, she threw herself in his arms, weeping, and covered his face with kisses. He laid her back against the sweet-smelling straw, and she molded herself to him, as if to burn into her skin forever the feel of his body against hers.

"I could have taken you that night, couldn't I?" Sinjin

said softly. "You wouldn't have resisted. I think perhaps you wanted me to. It would have changed everything, wouldn't it? And you knew it."

He laughed, the tone a travesty of humor. "But I was too noble—or stupid. I could envision no honorable choice but to leave, and how could I have ridden away, knowing you might carry my child?"

Sarah said nothing. She concentrated all her energy on drawing air in smooth, even drafts, lest dizziness overcome her or the agony in her chest rob her of breath.

Sinjin's expression harshened. "Damn, but I wish I'd not been so noble. Regardless of what happened after, I know one thing for sure. Had I taken you then, you would never have come to London—would you, Sarah?"

"Stop!" Sarah cried out, unable to stand it longer. "It makes no difference now! 'Tis long past and done."

Sinjin sighed heavily. "I thought to buy time when I rode away, time for—something—to happen. But in the end, love was not enough. You're lost to me—by your own choice."

Her torment exploded in fury. "*My* choice? How dare you talk to me of love, or choice? Yours was the first choice, Sinjin—and it wasn't me! I would have married you with us penniless both, worked happily my whole life to restore my home and yours. *You* chose to ride away."

He flung himself at her. "Sarah, how can you think—"

She held up a hand, halting him. "I'm sorry, Sinjin. That wasn't fair. Your choice *was* the honorable one, perhaps the only one. As was mine, when I had to make it three months ago. We can only live with both of them now."

"Then there's nothing left for us? I will not believe that! You still love me, Sarah—I know it. Surely we can work out something." His voice dropped to a hush. "I cannot live the rest of my life without you."

A lead weight seemed to bear down on her, hampering thought and making breathing difficult. "You must. Oh,

Sinjin, can you not understand? I'm Nicholas's wife now. He rescued my family and has treated me with such unfailing courtesy I would tear out my heart, if I must, before I would dishonor him.''

"And mine?''

"And y-yours,'' she whispered, her voice breaking.

His fierce face softened and he leapt to her side. "Ah, sweetheart, don't weep.''

His fingers barely grazed her shoulder, but she sprang back as if his gloved hand held burning coals.

"Don't touch me!'' she cried. "You must never touch me. How can I bear it, else?''

Sinjin froze, his hand still outstretched, his face bereft and pleading. Slowly his hand fell to his side.

Leaving him standing in the middle of the room, Sarah stumbled to the window seat. With an inarticulate growl that might have been anguish, or anger, or both, Sinjin walked over and dropped onto the sofa.

Sarah hugged herself, as if by holding on tightly she could contain the ravaging pain. She had thought in these three years she had learned every nuance of wretchedness heartbreak could offer, but she'd been wrong. Nothing compared to the soul-searing agony she felt now, her heart bleeding with love for him, half her instincts screaming for her to fly to him, and the other half telling her 'twas too late.

Desperately she listened to the faint voice of reason. Anything less meant scandal and dishonor. She would not—*she would not*—allow the love that had burned so purely in her for so many years to end like that.

"Glendenning said we had an early caller, my dear.''

Sinjin drew in his breath sharply, but Sarah could not even trust herself to glance up as her husband strolled in.

Chapter Ten

Taut with trepidation, Nicholas paused at the morning room door. He'd barely been able to mask his outrage when Glendenning informed him a Captain Viscount Sandiford had called on his wife.

He never dreamed the soldier would make a move so quickly. Telling the butler he'd announce himself, Nicholas dismissed him—and two loitering footmen.

What were they doing there, behind closed doors? Was Sarah merely filling in the captain on the circumstances of her hasty marriage? Or, if he were to walk in unannounced, would he discover his wife in another man's embrace? Sickness churned in his gut.

Hands sweating, he raised a fist to knock, paused, lowered it. If the worst were going to occur, better to find out straightaway. Taking a deep breath, he thrust open the door and strode in.

When he saw Sarah at the window, the captain seated on the sofa, he went almost dizzy with relief.

"Good day, Sarah," he called. "And—Captain." He couldn't bring himself to add "welcome."

The viscount rose lazily to his full height. "Lord Englemere." He sketched a bow. "Sarah's been telling me what a timely—*rescue* you made in marrying her."

The words, though polite, held an edge. Nicholas suppressed an urge to smack the slightly mocking smile off the captain's bronzed face.

"We rescued each other." He strove for a polite tone while he poured himself a badly needed sherry. "Despite the pleasure of greeting old friends, after your experiences London must seem rather tame. Do you make a long visit?"

That was direct probing after a bare minimum of greeting, but Nicholas couldn't help himself. The captain seemed aware of it, for the mocking smile deepened.

"I'm not sure as yet. My business here is—complex. It could take some time to resolve."

So the captain did not intend to fade away gracefully. What gall the man possessed! Nicholas's ire refueled.

And like a distraught parent whose anxiety over a missing child transforms, once the child is found unharmed, into anger, he fixed a furious gaze on Sarah.

Who had yet to glance up or utter a word. Whatever had possessed her to grant the bounder a private interview? Didn't she know the servants would be whispering? Just how warmly had she welcomed the brazen hussar?

Eyes narrowing, Nicholas crossed to the window. "I trust you've spent a pleasant morning, my dear?" he asked with barbed intent as he carried her hand to his lips.

As soon as he touched her, though, his anger lessened. Her fingers were chilled, her body rigid, and her eyes, when she finally looked up, spoke of an anguish too deep to hide. As she must have realized, for she quickly averted them.

"Oh, quite," she replied, her voice unsteady. "Sinjin and I caught up on old times. We mustn't keep him, though. Having just returned to England, I expect he has many friends to see and much pressing business."

Whatever was distressing her, she didn't want the captain to linger. Relief rippled through Nicholas.

"Yes, I mustn't outstay my welcome," said the captain, his lips twitching at the irony. He made them a bow.

"Sarah, Lord Englemere. It was truly good to see you, and I hope to enjoy your hospitality again."

Sarah remained at the window after the captain departed. She held herself stiffly, her eyes fixed straight ahead, as if she might shatter if she moved.

Nicholas stood hesitant. Distrust, fury and irritation at her indiscretion battled with compassion. His instinct to comfort, however, strengthened every moment he gazed at her obviously distraught figure. Finally, with a sigh, he drew her into his arms.

She shuddered, then clutched his shoulders and laid her head against his chest. His heart twisted. The remnants of his suspicious anger dissolving, he hugged her close.

After a moment she disengaged herself. With shaking hands, she smoothed her skirts.

Dimly he heard the clock strike. At any moment they might receive morning callers. Looking at her still-trembling figure, he knew she wasn't ready for that.

"Is a headache troubling you, sweet Sarah?"

"No, my lord." She managed a wan smile. "I'm quite well, thank you."

Her face was ashen and her lip bled where she must have bitten it. "Well" indeed. His smoldering anger toward the captain revived. Just how harshly had the man grilled her?

"I suspect the curious will be anxious to bedevil us this morning—especially after Clarissa's rumor. An appalling prospect," he said with an exaggerated shudder. "Shall we cry craven, and deny ourselves?"

"Would that not be dreadfully impolite?"

"You're looking pulled, sweeting. We've only just returned to town, and are unaccustomed to late hours. At least—" he winked "—late hours in a ballroom."

A genuine smile rewarded that quip. "I should like to rest," she admitted.

"I'll escort you up, then."

As they crossed the hallway, he told Glendenning to

deny them. Once inside the privacy of her chamber, he again embraced her.

"Rest well, sweeting. I'll look in on you later."

"Please, stay. I haven't yet properly thanked you."

"Thanked me?"

"For inventing that errand this morning. Somehow you guessed Sinjin would take the first opportunity to seek me out. We have been friends so long, I owed him at least a full explanation. You knew I could not have received him in private to give it, had you been at home."

He stared incredulously into her clear gray eyes, but he could find no guile there. Either she was the best actress he'd ever met, or she believed what she'd just said.

"You give me too much credit," he managed at last.

"You give yourself too little. Most gentlemen, I dare swear, upon anticipating a visit from a wife's former— friend, would forbid him the house."

Unable to invent a response, he simply stood silent. Should he confess that, had he in truth even suspected the captain might have the temerity to call, he would have locked her in her chamber and barred the front door?

"Thank you, Nicholas, for trusting me."

The simple words stabbed in his gut like a dagger. She seemed to believe him a better man than he was. The knowledge awed—and shamed him.

"You…you are welcome," he stumbled.

She studied him, and for an instant he feared she suspected the truth. Then she said softly, "What a puzzle you are." And kissed him.

Guilt, and a primitive urge to reestablish his claim on her, impelled him to respond. His original intent to leave her in solitude wavered, then evaporated altogether as with unprecedented boldness, she slid her hand under the linen of his shirt to stroke the bare skin beneath.

His last thought, before he abandoned all other efforts to free the excessive number of buttons on her bodice, was fierce and comforting. In her distress, she had returned not to her former lover's arms, but to his.

Several mornings later, as Nicholas worked at his desk over a dossier of papers, Glendenning interrupted him to announce a caller—Captain Lord Sandiford.

His first impulse was to deny himself. But for form's sake he really must attempt to be friendly to Sarah's dearest...neighbor. Even though he could barely stand the sight of the man.

"Show him in, Glendenning. And bring us some sherry."

He rose as the captain entered, looking splendid in his regimentals, drat him. "Sandiford, I trust you're enjoying your London sojourn. Can I do aught to assist?"

"To shorten it, you mean?" the captain suggested.

Nicholas pressed his lips together. He would not, he vowed, let this insufferable man annoy him. "You've missed Sarah, I'm afraid, but do stay if you like. Some sherry?"

The captain merely grinned. "You are too gracious, my lord. Yes, sherry would do nicely. And I waited until Sarah left. I wish to speak with you privately."

Nicholas tried not to let his surprise show. Uneasiness stirred as well. "Indeed? How may I serve you?"

The captain deposited his lanky frame in a leather wing chair opposite. After a sip, he looked up at Nicholas.

"First, it appears I owe you thanks. You've saved me the killing of this Sir James Findlay, who, by all accounts, is an out-and-out villain. I plan to return abroad in any event, but it will be more pleasant to leave England without a cloud over my head. Though I must admit the idea of Sarah being a widow has a certain appeal."

Nicholas choked on his sherry.

Seeming unaware, the captain continued briskly. "I must compliment you also. It seems your friend—a Mr. Waterman, is it?—did a highly satisfactory job of rearranging the bastard's face. Though he's left London, I understand, you might have a care. He's found himself another tool—a weasel-faced society fribble named Lord John Weston. Paid his gambling debts, which I hear were considerable, and now the man toddles back and forth from London to Findlay's country home. He'll bear watching.''

Nicholas shook his head, hostility battling with astonishment. ''You seem amazingly well informed, Captain.''

The hussar shrugged. ''One of the benefits of a military education. Gather intelligence poorly, and you die—or your men do. The skill has its uses.''

The frosty blue eyes met his. Nicholas had the feeling he was being sized up by one who'd learned, under fire, to judge men quickly and well.

Instinctively he straightened. ''Perhaps we should come to the point. I am not, you will find, a 'society fribble.' And I must ask—'' he kept his voice even but could not hide its animosity ''—what your intentions are regarding my wife.''

The captain smiled grimly. ''As well you might. Yes, let us dispense with further social niceties.'' He crossed one booted leg. ''I admit, my first thought after the horror of finding Sarah married was to carry her off to Spain.''

Before Nicholas could recover from that announcement, the captain had the incredible gall to laugh. ''What a splendid soldier's wife she'd make. I can see her now, babbling Portuguese as she ordered billets and saw to the wringing of chickens' necks.''

His fingers clenching at the thought of another neck he'd like to wring, Nicholas took a long sip of sherry. ''You have the audacity to think she would go?''

The captain grinned. ''I'd have to drug her, probably. Once I had her abroad, and she saw scandal would make it impossible for her to return, she'd come round. She loves me, you know—always has. I'd make her happy. To be sure,'' he admitted with an offhand gesture, ''she'd be upset for a while. She has such a powerful sense of *duty*.''

Nicholas winced. The captain saw it, and one eyelid flickered in triumph.

You conscienceless bastard, Nicholas thought, rage filling him. He envisioned swords, pistols—

"Like to spit me on your sword, would you?" the captain said with unimpaired good humor. "Can't say as I blame you. No doubt I'd feel the same, did I stand in your boots."

Nicholas took a deep calming breath. "Unlike you, Captain, I adhere to certain rules of morality. Which do not include, regrettably, murdering a guest in my library, no matter how much he might deserve it."

"Doubtless you are correct," the captain replied. "One of the drawbacks of war—it tends to blunt one's sensitivity to conventional moralities."

"Such as stealing another man's wife?"

"But for a mischance of the mail and a stubborn French general, Sarah would be my wife now, not yours."

Steering away from that shoal, Nicholas turned his attack. "Are you so certain you'd win her, despite your arrogant presumption? After all, you left her more than three years ago. And I can be rather charming."

The captain gave him another measuring look. "Would you choose to make yourself so? You prate of morality, but that seems shabby to me—to make Sarah love you, then slip away to Manton Street and the arms of Mrs. Ingram.

"I know," the captain said, waving a hand as Nicholas started to sputter, "you've not visited her since your marriage. Gallant of you to abstain for a whole month. However, the liaison is, I've discovered, of long standing. Judging by the ruby she sported when we talked and the fact that, just yesterday, you discharged a large gambling debt for the lady, I take it you've no intention of giving her congé?"

Nicholas found his voice at last. "Captain, you reach the limits of what I can tolerate, even of a guest in my home. That you investigated Sarah's activities is offensive enough, but to pry into my personal affairs—''

"Reprehensible, I agree. I've no real interest in your doxies, though I must say I've not seen such a coarse display of womanly charm since leaving Spain. 'Twould hardly tempt me—if I had Sarah.''

"Curious. It was my understanding you might have married Sarah. And declined the honor.''

The mockery left the captain's face and he flushed. Nicholas felt a savage surge of triumph.

"I cannot deny it," he said quietly. "'Twas the worst mistake of my life, though at the time I thought I was doing the right, nay, the only *honorable* thing.'' He punctuated the word with a savage look and flung himself to his feet.

He paced for a moment, then turned. "Yes, I spurned the fair lady and rode off to assuage my grief by dying gloriously in battle.'' His tone was self-mocking now, and his face bitter as he stared sightlessly at the bookshelves. "It took but one battle to discover there's naught of glory in dying, and naught to battle but dirt, anguish and fear.

"I must say this about it.'' He turned with a twisted smile. "There's something about standing surrounded by smoke, the roar of guns and the screams of the wounded and dying that clears the mind. Land, titles, wealth—none of that matters," the captain finished softly. "Only people do. And Sarah matters most of all.''

Did he speak of any woman but his wife, Nicholas might have sympathized. Before he could reply, Sandiford continued, "Had Sarah's letter reached me sooner—had Soult not caught us in the mountains, I should have reached England weeks ago, and we would not now be engaged in a conversation that cannot but be distasteful to us both.''

Nicholas raised an eyebrow. "You think so? Wellingford came at a rather high price.''

The captain shrugged. "I'd have sold off some land.''

"Land doesn't fetch much just now."

"Then I'd have touched up one of my wealthy army friends, or gone to the cent-percenters. Whatever it took to save Wellingford, and Sarah."

There could be no mistaking the sincerity of his words. Nicholas felt a reluctant tug of sympathy.

"But wishing cannot turn back the clock." The captain took another sip of sherry. "That is, I assume you wouldn't consider an annulment?"

Nicholas's infant empathy expired. "No."

"Divorce?"

"Absolutely not!"

"I feared as much. So, we come to the proposal that brought me here today."

Nicholas looked at him coldly. "The only proposal I expect to entertain is the one that tells me courtesy forbids my kicking your insolent ass down my front steps."

"Hear me out first," the captain persisted. "Yours was a marriage of convenience, not a love match. You take your pleasure elsewhere, and intend to continue doing so. I see no reason why we cannot both be accommodated. After Sarah does her duty by you, send her to me."

Through the sudden roaring in his ears, Nicholas stared at him. "You cannot have said what I think I just heard. You want me to keep Sarah as my wife until the succession is secured, and then—" he nearly choked "—let her go to you? By God, I should run you through where you stand!"

"Whatever for? Outraged vanity? True, she's your wife, and let no man poach on your preserves. But by God, she's more than that! Can you claim, as I can, to love her? Can you pledge yourself to making her happy?"

He gave Nicholas no time to reply. "Of course you cannot. You go your own way, as our society permits. As long as she satisfies convention, why not let her do so as well? For the sake of pride, would you deny her any happiness?"

Too incensed by now even to formulate words, Nicholas clenched his fists, restraining by force of will the impulse that shrieked at him to lay the captain out flat. Somehow he managed to hold himself motionless.

The captain ran a hand through his burnished hair. "Do you think I like the idea of taking to mistress the only woman I've ever wanted for a wife? But short of your demise, which I doubt you'd be willing to arrange despite my most fervent encouragement, that's all that's left to me. I'll take whatever I can get—another attitude war inspires."

He leaned his hands on the desk, fixing on Nicholas blue eyes burning with intensity. "Don't dismiss the idea out of hand. 'Tis no secret you're a creature of London. Sarah prefers the country. If you lived separately, 'twould cause little comment. And we would be discreet."

From the midst of Nicholas's fury an incredible, galling suspicion bubbled up. Sarah's distress on the morning of the captain's visit: had it been the anguish of tearing open old wounds—or unhappiness at the idea of waiting for her lover? Had she come to his arms for comfort, or out of guilt? Red spots danced before his eyes.

"And did Sarah agree to this charming little arrangement?" he asked through gritted teeth.

"Lord, no!" The intensity left the captain's gaze. "I wouldn't dare propose such a thing to her. She'd probably put a bullet through me for so maligning her honor." He laughed. "An impulsive lass she can be, as I suppose you've discovered. She'll take a deal of convincing. 'Twould be easier if I could tell her you approved."

"On a snowy day in hell," Nicholas retorted, though his anger cooled a fraction at discovering Sarah had no hand in this. "You must be a bedlamite to think I'd consider it."

"If you loved her as I do, you'd consider any alternative."

"You had your chance, Captain. I don't feel any obligation to provide you with another—certainly not the tawdry, illegitimate little arrangement you've proposed."

"You can't offer her love, or even fidelity. So give me no pious tripe about the sanctity of marriage."

Nicholas clenched his jaw to stifle a vicious retort and crossed to the bellpull. "I consider the subject closed. Thank you for your...*illuminating* visit, Lord Sandiford." He gave the embroidered cloth a ferocious tug. "I shall be cordial in public, but pray do not call again."

"My pleasure, though the matter isn't closed, merely pending. I've a score yet to settle with Boney, but when I return..." The captain smiled grimly. "You may hope some Frog marksman relieves you of my presence. The odds are with you."

"Never before have I favored the French."

The captain made an exaggerated bow. "Henceforth, I'll restrict my calls to Sarah. Quite conventional ones, I assure you. She thinks to make me a list of potential brides, and I'm willing to humor her." His voice softened. "I don't wish to hurt her more than I already have. Good day, my lord. Take care of her for me."

Nicholas gasped. "First you fit me for a pair of horns, then you instruct me to care for her until you choose to make me wear them! By God, Captain, you have gall!"

"A useful attribute in a cavalry officer, my superiors tell me. Your servant, sir."

As Nicholas escorted him to the door, an opening occurred, and he seized it. "A delightful business, this getting of sons. Chancy, though. One may end up with any number of daughters first. And as you so thoughtfully reminded, Sarah will do her *duty*." He let a lascivious smile play at his lips. "I promise you, Captain, I take great pains to ensure she enjoys it."

With an ignoble but satisfying rush of pleasure, he watched this shot strike target. The captain's mocking expression vanished, a muscle twitched in his cheek and the blue eyes blazed with rage.

But Sandiford hadn't been battle-tested for naught. Though his sword hand clutched at his side and his other hand balled into a fist, he made no move. Nicholas wasn't sure whether to be disappointed or relieved he'd failed to provoke a guest to brawl in his own library.

"Why not meet me at Jackson's?" The captain looked Nicholas up and down. "For a useless society fribble, you might strip well."

"Nothing would give me greater pleasure than beating your pretty face to a pulp. But then, I should hate to jeopardize Sarah's matchmaking plans."

Glendenning appeared at the door. "Show Lord Sandiford out," Nicholas snapped. With the barest of bows, he turned his back on the visitor and stalked to his chair.

Nicholas stared at his paper-strewn desk and counted to one hundred, then two. Fury, outrage and a brace of other strong emotions he'd not put a name to elbowed for room in his mind like noisy spectators at a cockfight.

Send him Sarah, indeed! he fumed. Rifle fire must have rattled the man's brain. How dare he suggest such a thing, or question Nicholas's fitness to be Sarah's husband. He really should meet the captain at Jackson's and pummel some of the effrontery out of him. The very idea of her in the arms of that hussar sent a shaft of torment through him.

He had never learned for sure if Lydia actually betrayed him. After the accident, her hysterical maid disclaimed all knowledge of the nameless soldier, and not wishing to arouse more speculation among the servants, he hadn't investigated further. Knowing that Lydia had always preferred wooing and gifts and pretty speeches to the physical act of love, he suspected she might have gone to her grave still technically faithful.

In truth, Lydia had always been somewhat chilly, especially before that ill-fated sojourn in Bath. Unlike his eager, sensual Sarah—Sarah, who even after an obviously wrenching scene with her former love, sought out rather than rebuffed his embrace.

He reviewed the encounter in fond detail, finding reassurance in each kiss, each sigh. If loving would keep her close and content, he was more than happy to provide it.

What else was it Sandiford said—that Sarah would shoot him for maligning her honor by suggesting an adulterous relationship? If Sandiford, who—God rot him—had known Sarah longer than he, discounted the possibility of her abandoning her marriage, why should he worry?

He wouldn't. He would forget the whole distasteful interview. Sarah would never consider such a sordid arrangement. In turn, he vowed, he would ensure she never regretted her loyalty. After all, contrary to the opinion of that fur-pelissed popinjay, Sarah's happiness *was* of great concern to him.

So why was he still troubled? The answer trembling at the edge of his mind unsettled him. Surely he wasn't such a coxcomb that he demanded both his wife's fidelity—and her love—without being willing to pledge his own.

Love. He'd thought he loved Lydia, that she loved him in return. But she claimed in her farewell note he couldn't have loved her and neglected her so—then abandoned him.

All he knew about for sure, he concluded bitterly, was the devastation of betrayal. And the simplicity of more businesslike arrangements.

From beyond the stack of musty ledgers where he'd relegated it, the cloying scent of a perfumed letter reached him. Twitching his nose in distaste, he picked it up.

Chloe's missive thanked him prettily for paying her gambling losses and hinted she lay ready at any time to offer thanks of a more intimate nature.

He stared at the letter, frowning. Despite Lydia's quixotic bedroom behavior, he'd never taken a mistress during their marriage. The captain's harangue on the subject pricked at him.

A ''coarse display of womanly charm,'' the captain had

uncharitably described Chloe. Truth be told, of late he was beginning to share the captain's opinion.

He could pen a cordial note assuring her of his regard, but terminating any future relationship. And yet…

He rolled the quill in his fingers. After Lydia, he had been relieved to settle on a straightforward exchange of cash for services rendered. Intimacy with Sarah was so sweetly different.

As friends, as lovers, they had grown close enough to make their marriage a comfortable and pleasant arrangement. Without Chloe, it would be all too easy to become— rather devoted.

The old, sick feeling stirred in his belly. Once he had thought Lydia devoted. Were he to be wrong again, he wasn't sure he could bear it.

His head was beginning to throb. With a growl he set the paper aside and stood up. Damn the hussar for reviving all his doubts.

No one would force him into a decision about this now, he vowed as he stalked from the room. Not Chloe, not Sarah and certainly not an obnoxious, adultery-minded captain.

Chapter Eleven

After a highly satisfactory visit to the factor, Sarah sat at her desk reviewing the agricultural supplies she'd ordered. There'd be a bountiful harvest at Wellingford this year—thanks to Nicholas. Perhaps she *should* tell him. 'Twas such a wonderful prospect, surely he would share her delight.

Her enthusiasm cooled. Perhaps she should tell him before someone else did.

After shopping for the usual fripperies with Clarissa, she'd intended to slip away to the agricultural factor. Scenting a secret, Clarissa had insisted Sarah reveal her mysterious destination. When she'd reluctantly confided her plans, her friend dissolved in laughter. Sobering, Clarissa swore not to divulge a word. Englemere would be a laughingstock, she declared, if the ton ever discovered his wife had spent her quarterly allowance on a farm.

Entering upon her knock, she found the library deserted. She paused, frowning. She could inform Glendenning she wished to see Nicholas when he came in. But no, she'd as lief not offer the servants any cause for speculation so soon after her meeting with Sinjin.

Write him a note, she decided. She walked to his desk, thinking to find paper and a pen.

The pale pink vellum scribed in a childish hand was

tucked in his blotter. A sheet of paper poised beside it, as if he were about to reply. Even at the distance of several feet, she could smell its cloying scent.

Something tightened in her chest. Even as instinct urged her forward, she retreated. No, she'd not stoop to reading letters from his mistress.

All thoughts of a note forgotten, she sped from the room. Not for anything would she want one of the servants—or worse yet, Nicholas himself—to discover her snooping.

When she got to her room, she found her fingers still trembling. Though she'd accepted Mrs. Ingram's position before she married Nicholas, lulled by the harmony of their honeymoon, she'd put the woman out of mind. She was, she discovered with mingled irritation and chagrin, woefully unarmed for the evidence of their continuing liaison that now sat conspicuously displayed on Nicholas's desk.

Don't be an idiot, she scolded herself, swiping at a tear that had the temerity to produce itself unbidden. *You neither asked for nor expected fidelity of him. How can you be foolish enough to hurt for it now?*

Her heart had an answer, and she didn't like it. Angrier still, she picked up a china shepherdess from the side table and hurled it toward the mantel.

The satisfying crash as it shattered brought her back to earth. Embarrassed, she hurried to gather up the pieces. *Let this be a warning,* she rebuked herself as she bundled the fragments.

True, her husband was kind and generous. Finding her closeted with Sinjin at that awful meeting a few days ago, he could have assumed the worst. Instead, he trusted her, comforted her, loved her so sweetly he brought more balm to her shattered heart than he would ever know.

But theirs was not a love match. In her need to distance herself from Sinjin, she must be wary of turning to Nicholas. She could never preserve the well-bred, unemotional facade Nicholas required of her if her affections became truly engaged.

Besides, she reminded herself, though he'd so far displayed only a milder form of the addiction, he was still a gambler and not to be trusted.

Could there be anything worse than losing her heart to one who not only didn't want it, but who with a toss of the dice could lose everything she possessed as well?

Lord above, help me to be wise. She sent the silent prayer heavenward. *Have I not known heartache enough?*

Nicholas sat in the parlor sipping sherry. Hal was joining them for dinner, after which they'd go on to the rout at the Sheffingdons'.

Restless, he glanced at the mantel clock, but instead of Roman numerals on a silver ground, he saw a gold-haired man in royal-blue regimentals.

No doubt they'd encounter the resplendent captain tonight. Since that first morning call Sandiford had been attentive but not overly familiar with Sarah, cordial and straightforward to Nicholas. Had the captain not paid him that incredible visit, Nicholas might have come to view his wife's neighbor as an admirable man, a valiant soldier who had rendered great service to his country.

But Sandiford had called, and Nicholas could never forget the look on his face when he said he would consider anything that would keep Sarah in his life.

'Twas better to be forewarned. Still, though Nicholas doubted the captain would attempt to fly with Sarah, and dismissed completely his absurd future plans, he could not shake a smoldering unease.

Damn, he didn't wish to think of the man. He'd go fetch Sarah. In the hall, he came upon Sarah's maid.

"Her ladyship'll be that happy to see this," Becky said as she took a letter from the butler. He got a glimpse of Sarah's name written in an unmistakably masculine scrawl.

The maid glanced up. Looking startled—and guilty, he wondered?—she hastily tucked the missive in her sleeve.

"Mistress will be down directly, my lord," Becky said, dipping a curtsy. "I had to match a thread on her shawl, but 'tis finished, and I'll take it right up to her."

Which, the shawl or the letter? Nicholas thought. A tremor of anger rippled through him. Was Sandiford sending Sarah letters, the blackguard? Did the note contain an avowal of undying love—or just the man's reactions to a list of the potential brides Sarah was supposedly compiling?

He turned on his heel and went back to the parlor, poured himself a brandy, and stared moodily at the clock.

"Sorry to have taken so long, Nicholas," Sarah said as she entered a few moments later. "I half expected to see Hal already arrived."

Did you linger to read his letter? he wanted to ask. "Collect any oddities on your shopping trip, my dear?"

For a moment she looked startled. "Only the ordinary," she replied at last. "Though it never ceases to amaze me the fripperies Clarissa finds she cannot live without."

"I hope you've avoided her example and retained some blunt," he said, forcing a smile. "Mama will be returning next week. You'll want to commission something suitable."

Sarah looked at him blankly. "Commission something?"

"Do you not recall?" He handed her a sherry. "Mama said since we'd had no engagement ball, and so small a reception, she must hostess a presentation ball—to properly introduce my wife to the ton."

Sarah choked on the sherry. "Good gracious! I'd forgotten all about it."

"Mama's so delighted with her new daughter she's happy to do this. You have only to select a gown splendid enough for a marchioness, and look lovely."

His words didn't seem to encourage her. "Nicholas, I,

ah, I've ever so many gowns. Surely I don't need another.''

"Nonsense, my dear. You're a marchioness now, and must dress the part, especially on such an important occasion.'' He patted her hand. "At the risk of putting you off completely, I must confess you should expect to greet most of England's nobility, from Prinny and his advisers on down. Something in gold and diamonds should do the trick.''

"Diamonds?'' she repeated, moistening her lips.

"Is something amiss? Not run off your legs already, I trust.'' Nicholas grinned at her.

"I'm afraid that's rather the case.'' She gave him a nervous smile. "I was going to inform you, but I'd not yet had the…opportunity.''

"Well, I daresay dressmakers' bills are more expensive than I remember,'' he allowed.

"I didn't spend the money on gowns, Nicholas. It was something quite different, something I doubt you'd guess.''

Whatever could she have purchased? Nicholas wondered. Articles so extravagant she suspected he'd disapprove them, if that troubled look was any indication.

A thought popped into his head, too outlandish to credit. Sandiford had as much as admitted he was short of funds. Had Sarah lent him money—Nicholas's money? Was the letter he'd seen Sandiford's note of thanks?

No, 'twas preposterous. Nonetheless, all his simmering anger reheated.

"Perhaps you'd better tell me the whole.''

"Hope I'm not late, Nicky.'' With a genial smile, Hal Waterman walked in. "Famished. Shall we dine?''

Nicholas grimaced. There'd be no answers now.

"Evening, Hal. Certainly we'll dine. Escort Sarah, won't you?'' He gave his wife a curt nod.

Nicholas watched Hal take Sarah's arm. With a light remark, she set him laughing. Moodily he followed.

Oh, she was good at nurturing, his lovely bride. He thought of the letter, and set his teeth. Just who else did she think to nurture?

Nicholas stared at the window and tossed the coin up again. He'd wandered into the Sheffingdons' gaming room to join in a hand of whist while awaiting his waltz with Sarah. But what tepid interest he'd managed to summon up for the game had already evaporated.

He simply hadn't been able to stomach any longer watching the country dance into which the captain had led his wife. Wasn't the man letting his hand linger on Sarah's? And Nicholas wasn't imagining the caressing look on the captain's face as he followed Sarah's movements, an expression far removed from brotherly regard. Had anyone else noted those all-too-fond glances?

Impelled by some sixth sense, he turned to see Sarah framed in the open doorway. The smile that automatically sprang to his lips died as he took in her appalled face. Before he could move or speak, she whirled around and fled.

Fear rocked him. Nearly running, he crossed the room, but by the time he reached the hallway she had disappeared.

He stood, perplexity and alarm coursing through him. If she were in trouble, why had she not waited for him?

Unless it were not he she'd been looking for. Unless she'd been rushing to rendezvous with another, and he was the last person she wanted to see.

Surely not. Had he not just left them in the ballroom?

He hesitated, then strode to the crowded dance floor. Neither the captain nor Sarah was among the revelers.

Acid burned in his belly. Pasting a society smile on his face, he set out to hunt for his wife.

Twenty minutes later Nicholas paused, trying to curb a rising outrage. He'd checked the refreshment room, the card room and several antechambers. That he was forced to progress slowly, speaking to the friends he encountered and maneuvering glibly to evade the invitations they pressed upon him to eat, chat or dance, only exacerbated his ire.

There was no sign of either his wife—or the captain. Wherever had they vanished? The only rooms he'd not checked were the ladies' withdrawing room—and the bedchambers.

Between the barely contained fury smoking in him and the sick churning in his gut, he had no taste for food or conversation. The waltz was long past, and by now he was too angry to face Sarah.

He'd go to his club, he decided. Perhaps after a bottle of brandy, he'd be calm enough to discuss this.

He went to the foyer and called for his greatcoat. He'd leave word for her to go home with a friend.

The image of Sandiford rose before him. Ah, yes, the captain would be only too willing to escort her home—and settle her in bed. A red mist of rage clouded his head.

Better make that two bottles of brandy, he told himself savagely as he awaited his coat.

Sarah sat in the ladies' withdrawing room, mopping her cheeks as she tried to make sense of what had just happened.

She'd gone to find Nicholas after the dance with Sinjin. He'd signed her card for the waltz, but she'd decided to ask him to slip away and talk with her instead.

She'd been berating herself for her stupidity in forgetting the presentation ball and her poor judgment in not consulting Nicholas about the Wellingford purchases.

Though well deserved, his coldness during dinner struck her like a chill wind, destroying her comfort. She suddenly realized how, in just a short time, she had come to rely on his kind and steadfast support.

She would make a full disclosure, endure his scold and pray all would be right between them again.

Pausing on the threshold to survey the occupants, she spied Nicholas across the gaming room and was about to approach him when a small movement caught her eye.

Nicholas was staring toward the darkened window, a troubled look on his face, while with one hand he tossed up a gold guinea, caught it, threw it up again.

The breath stopped in her throat. She stood riveted, unable to tear her gaze from the tumbling dance of the bright coin winking in and out of his fingers.

The image before her blurred, and she saw a slighter man, gray at the temples, standing before a darkened window at Wellingford, tossing and retossing a single coin. "I've lost it all, Sarah," her father said. "I've lost it all."

Beyond rational reaction, she fled blindly down the hall. Even now, recalling the scene made her stomach heave.

She mopped her brow again. *Calm down.* She was an idiot, letting a ghost of the painful past spook her. 'Twas not the disheveled wreck of her father who stood there, not the vacant stare of a man who'd gamed away everything.

But Nicholas gambles! her frantic heart replied. Maybe 'twas not him tonight, but it could be. Maybe tomorrow night. Maybe next year.

She dipped the cloth again in cool water. Yes, Nicholas gambles. Mostly, he wins. Should he lose, he's wealthy, much wealthier than Papa ever was. And even should he lose everything, there will be Wellingford.

Yes, Wellingford. A refuge for her—and her son. She put a protective hand over her stomach.

Should she tell him? No, right now she had a different confession to make. She'd best get hold of herself and find Nicholas.

She smoothed her braids and turned to leave.

Just then Clarissa tripped in. "Sarah darling, you simply must hear this! Oh, and could you help me with my lace? Wexley trod on it during our last waltz, the oaf!"

Resigning herself to the delay, Sarah pinned up the torn

bit, half listening to Clarissa's latest *on-dit* while in her mind reviewing her explanations to Nicholas.

Ten minutes later, arm linked with Clarissa's, Sarah at last strolled down the hall to the refreshment room. She would escort Clarissa back to her courtiers and then seek out Nicholas.

The first couple they encountered stopped chatting as they neared. Sarah thought the lady, one of the Season's Marriage Mart hopefuls, intended to speak, and smiled.

The girl turned aside and whispered to the young man. Both burst out laughing.

Sarah frowned and glanced at Clarissa. Her friend's chatter continued unabated.

When they reached the crowd outside the ballroom, a hush fell. Half the people in the milling throng looked toward Sarah and, avoiding her eyes, quickly turned away. Titters behind fans and ill-concealed chuckles followed.

This time Clarissa noticed, stopping her recitation in midsentence. A deep foreboding engulfed Sarah.

Clarissa bristled. "What the devil is going on?"

A slight, narrow-faced young man in a puce jacket and bright saffron waistcoat sauntered toward them. Sarah recognized the sharp-tongued Lord John Weston.

"Well, if it isn't the Farmer Bride. Did you leave the cows at home tonight, or do they await you in the street?"

Farmer. Cows. Alarm coursing through her, Sarah rapidly reviewed the passersby near the agricultural factor's shop. Surely this fribble hadn't seen her.

Lord John smiled, a thin curve of lip with no humor in it, and turned to several young fops by the wall. "We must watch our step after she passes, gentlemen. Something other than straw may still cling to her shoes."

She heard Clarissa's gasp, and several bystanders tittered. Sarah stiffened, anger replacing her chagrin.

"Lord John." Sarah nodded, head high and voice imperious. "And—gentlemen?" She invested the word with every bit of scorn she could muster.

Lord John swept her a bow. "How kind to acknowledge those of us so far beneath you." He gestured to the lounging men. "Alas, you think us a poor lot. All of London society, in fact. From the nouveau-riche hangers-on to the greatest hostesses, we are naught but a passel of idle gossips and mindless, pleasure-seeking dandies."

For a second, she was tempted to agree, adding sweetly he was the worst of the bunch. Good breeding prevailed. "Certainly not. I'm vastly grieved you could have invested me with so uncharitable a thought." Nodding her head once more, she gripped Clarissa's arm and swept past them.

More titters, though fewer this time. Then, in the silence that followed, she heard Lord John's voice. "Pawk, pawk, pawk, pawk."

Anger sizzled through her—not at his goading, for she cared naught for his opinion. But it rankled her that this worthless man should mock the humble farms whose revenues made his dissolute London life possible.

She turned her head back. "Chickens don't sound like that." She gave him a condescending smile. "But then, you wouldn't know. Being better acquainted with swine."

Squeezing Clarissa's arm, she resumed walking. By mutual, unspoken consent, they traversed the ballroom and proceeded out onto the terrace beyond.

Finding an unoccupied corner, Sarah let go Clarissa's arm and leaned wearily on the balustrade.

Clarissa slashed her fan again a pillar. "'The Farmer Bride' indeed! What a detestable worm! Oh, were I a man, I'd run him through for that."

Sarah laughed without humor. The Farmer Bride. Little as it meant to her, she knew Nicholas wouldn't be as sanguine. What the ton said of her would matter to him.

Then she remembered his angry face in the card room. Shock sizzled through her. He must have already heard it.

"Someone must have seen me at the farm goods emporium," she said with exasperation. "Damn and blast!"

"Perhaps, Sarah," Clarissa said, tears glittering at the tips of her long lashes. "But I-I'm afraid I mentioned something to Wexley."

"Oh, Clare."

"He complained his factor was taxing him over some matter about his estate, and how dare the man bother him while he was in agonies deciding whether to commission a waistcoat in daffodil or saffron? I scolded him, and told him some people not only listened to their agents, but sent them funds. When he swore it could not be so, I…" Tears slid down the porcelain cheeks.

Trying to stifle her annoyance, Sarah patted Clarissa's hand. Wexley was one of the worst rattles in the ton. Nicholas was going to be livid.

Clarissa straightened. "You trusted me, and I failed you. I shall make it right, Sarah, I swear it."

She took a few restless steps. "I shall cut Wexley completely. He swore he'd keep the news in strictest confidence, and surely realized what would happen if he whispered it." She gave her titian curls an angry shake. "He cannot hold me in much esteem, to injure my dearest friend. And I shall give the cut direct to anyone who dares call you that dreadful name, or so much as giggles in your direction. Let the despicable Lord John deal with that."

Sarah frowned. A public vendetta between Clarissa and Lord John would stir up just the sort of dust to fuel the gossips—and Nicholas's ire—for the longest possible time.

"Cut Wexley if you will, Clare, but leave the rest to me. The best way to deal with this is to ignore it. I am a marchioness, am I not?" She straightened and gave an imperious look. "What care I for the chatter of inferiors?"

Clarissa sighed. "Very well, I shall do nothing. Except—" her eyes glittered with anger "—deal with Wexley."

"What's done is done," Sarah said, trying to sound unconcerned. "We should get back."

"Yes." Clarissa unfurled her fan with a snap. "And if you'll excuse me, there's a gentleman I wish to see."

Silently they reentered the ballroom and scanned the dancers, Clarissa stiffening as she identified Wexley. Giving Sarah a militant nod, she set off.

Nicholas was nowhere in sight. Her chest tight with apprehension, Sarah left the ballroom.

As she crossed the landing above the entry, she saw a familiar figure collecting his greatcoat and hat.

"Nicholas," she called.

He looked up, his face hardening when he recognized her, and raised an eyebrow sardonically. "Madame." Making an elaborate bow, he settled his hat and stepped to the door.

His glacial tone shocked her nearly as much as the fact that he appeared to be quitting the rout without so much as a word. In a rustle of skirts, she flew down the stairs.

"You are leaving?" she asked, her cheeks pinking under the gaze of the butler and several hovering footmen.

"You have some objection, my *lady* wife?"

At his savage emphasis, her heart sank. Without doubt he had heard the story, and he was most definitely livid. So livid he intended to leave his disgraced wife to face a disdainful crowd alone. *Nicholas, how could you abandon me?*

"N-no, of course not. The evening is yours to command."

"At least something is," he muttered. "Don't let me keep you from your *admirers*." With another overcourtly bow, he turned his back on her and strode out the door.

Sarah swallowed the tears that clogged her throat. Damping down hurt and a burgeoning anger, she lifted her chin. If Nicholas did not wish to support her, so be it. Had she not always relied solely on herself? Perhaps 'twas only right. She'd gotten herself into this mess. She'd just have to get herself out of it.

Setting her head high, she made herself reenter the ball-room. And nearly bumped right into Sally Jersey.

Before Sarah could utter a word, Lady Jersey took her hand and tucked it under her arm. "Stroll with me a moment, Sarah darling. My, you do manage to get yourself talked about. Now, what's this I hear about a farm?"

Ignoring the queasiness in her stomach, Sarah raised an eyebrow. "Is something being said? If you'll tell me what you wish to know, your ladyship, I'll be happy to enlighten you. Though quite frankly," she added, trying to invest her voice with just the right note of boredom, "I can't credit you've any interest in a *farm*."

Lady Jersey eyed her sharply. Sarah held her gaze, maintaining a look of faint hauteur. After a moment, her ladyship's lips twitched.

"Very good, my dear." She patted Sarah's arm. "Despite your denial to Lord John, the ton does possess some dreadful gossips. Yes, Mrs. Drummond Burrell was standing by the hallway, and heard all. You're quite right. That Weston boy is a swine."

A vibrating hum in Sarah's ears muffled the rest of her ladyship's speech, and she felt faint.

Mrs. Drummond Burrell witnessed the encounter! Praise heaven she'd not succumbed to the temptation of seconding Lord John's assessment of the ton. Had that haughty woman—perhaps the greatest of London's great hostesses—overheard it, by night's end, her name would have been cut from the invitation list of every person of social standing in London. She dared not even contemplate Nicholas's reaction to such a catastrophe.

"...thought I saw Nicky sneaking away," Lady Jersey was saying. "How like a man to hie off to his club, just when one most has need of him. Well, never you mind." She gave Sarah a conspiratorial smile. "I shall support you."

And she did. Lady Jersey made a determined stroll through the entire ballroom, chatting as they went with various of the highest-ranking, most socially prominent people present. Any lurking sniggers vanished as Sarah approached on the arm of the queen of society.

At last they reached the ballroom doorway. "I expect you're ready for refreshment, Lady Englemere," Silence said as she released Sarah's arm.

"Since her husband has already gone—no doubt seeking refreshment of a more intimate nature," remarked a voice beyond the doorway.

A mocking smile on his face, Lord John stepped into the room. He stopped short, his expression changing to dismay, and bowed hastily. "Ladies."

Lady Jersey's eyes flickered over Lord John without acknowledgment. "I dare swear, my dear Sarah, one is continually astonished by the low sort of person one encounters at these parties. Whatever can the Sheffingdons be thinking of? Perhaps I must cut the connection.

"Christopher, darling." Lady Jersey plucked the Earl of March from the gaping onlookers, "you simply must accompany Lady Englemere." She wrinkled her nose in the direction of the frozen Lord John. "'Tis suddenly so *close* in here."

The captured peer dutifully escorted Sarah and remained with her, chatting pleasantly over a glass of champagne. By the time they returned to the ballroom, Sarah could sense the change in the atmosphere. Cordiality reigned now.

Though all she wished to do was return home to await Nicholas and the explanation she vowed she would not sleep until she had delivered, Sarah remained at the ball. 'Twas best to firmly face down the rumors.

Why Sally Jersey had chosen to help her, Sarah couldn't imagine, but she could only be grateful. Catching the lady's eye across the crowded ballroom, she sent her a nod of silent thanks.

At last, feeling she'd aged two years in as many hours, Sarah departed for the blessed solitude of Stanhope House.

* * *

Sighing, Sarah dismissed Becky, found a book and ensconced herself in a chair beside her bed. 'Twas no telling at what hour Nicholas would return.

Was he in fact at his club—or enjoying "more intimate refreshment"? A pain shot through her.

She seemed unable to summon up the explanations she'd used before to dismiss the matter of Nicholas's mistress. She was simply too weary, she told herself. Opening the book, she settled in to wait, and forced from her mind the searing image of Mrs. Ingram in Nicholas's arms.

Chapter Twelve

A banging in the hallway startled her. She must have dozed off, for her book had slipped to the floor and the candle at her elbow guttered. Unsteady footsteps clomped past to the adjoining bedchamber.

She crept to the door and put her ear to it, listening until Nicholas dismissed his valet. Then she knocked.

Eyes closed, Nicholas lay back against his pillows. He blinked them open as she approached the bed.

"I'm sorry to disturb you, Nicholas, but I should have spoken much sooner, and don't wish to wait any longer."

He put a hand to his temple and groaned. From the pungency of the alcoholic odor emanating from him, she could well believe his head hurt. "I'm in no state for confessions now. Leave me to my bed."

Resentment boiled through her apprehension. If he'd not abandoned her, she'd have finished this task much earlier. "'Tis but a moment I would have. As I've not seen my bed tonight either, surely you can spare me that."

He glanced up then, albeit slowly, a calculating look in his bloodshot eyes. "No bed at all, sweet Sarah?"

"No. I knew you were angry with me, so after Clarissa brought me home, I waited up for you."

"Clarissa brought you?" His eyes opened wider. "And you've been waiting for me since? Alone?"

She wrinkled her brow. Whomever would she have waited up with? "Y-yes, I sent Becky to bed."

"I suppose your maid or the butler can attest to that?"

She tilted her head, exasperated. He didn't seem to be making any sense. Perhaps he was more castaway than she'd thought. "You may have Glendenning inventory the tallows I expended whilst reading, but—"

"No, no." With another groan, he hauled himself up onto the pillows and folded his arms across his chest. "You've courage, to brave the lion in his den. Proceed."

She took the chair beside the bed. Now that the moment had arrived, her stomach was doing more leaps than an unbroken colt put under his first saddle. "I wanted to apologize. I'm fully aware I've been the most miserable sort of wife. First Clarissa's rumor, and then to have forgotten your mama's ball! Anyway, before spending what is, after all, your money, I should have consulted you."

"You wanted to apologize about *money?*" he asked, his tone sardonic. "'Tis of little moment. Your allowance is yours, to do with—" he grimaced "—what you wish."

She stared at him, trying to gauge the depth of his displeasure. If only she could bring him to appreciate her goals, she might make him sympathize. "Oh, Nicholas, the money will bring such benefit to Wellingford! Surely you cannot begrudge the poor tenants that."

"Tenants?" He opened his eyes wide again. "Wellingford? What have they to do with this?"

"Did whoever told you the—the rumor not tell you about the seeds?"

"Seeds? Rumor? What the devil—?" Hand to his head, he sat up straight. "Sarah, are you trying to tell me you spent that allowance money on seeds?"

"You did not know? When I saw you in the card room looking so displeased, I was sure someone had told you."

His intent gaze devoured her. "You ran away before I could speak with you—because you thought I was angry?"

"Y-yes. I wanted to explain, but after I'd composed

myself, I couldn't find you. And then you left, so I...I waited up for you," she finished in a small voice.

He flopped back against the pillows, looking dazed. "You thought I was angry. About seeds."

"Well, there were also plows, and roofing thatch—"

As she spoke, a smile lit his face, then his lips twitched. Finally he threw back his head laughing.

Her words trailed off. She gazed at him first in wonder, then with growing resentment.

He seemed to be deriving great amusement from her expenditures, she thought grumpily. She was just about to retreat with injured dignity when he seized her, and laughing still, dragged her onto the bed.

"S-seeds," he stuttered between gasps. "Oh, Sarah, if you only knew what I thought—! God's blood, what an idiot I am!" Fiercely he pulled her into an embrace so tight she could scarcely breathe.

All her disgruntlement dissolved as he clutched her to his warm chest. After the miserable evening she'd endured, the sound of his laughter and the feel of his strong arms were a precious gift.

Then a dismaying fact struck her. "But—if you didn't know how I spent the money, then you couldn't have heard—" She drew away, consternation flooding her.

"Heard what?" He kissed the tip of her nose.

"Oh, Nicholas," she whispered. She detested having to jeopardize the blessed sweetness of their reestablished rapport by telling him the rest, but he must know.

"You're going to be truly angry with me now. You see, Wexley found out I spent my allowance on estate needs, and thinking it vastly amusing, spread the story all over town. Some...wits have started calling me 'The Farmer Bride.'

"I've ignored them," she went on quickly, "and Lady Jersey was kind enough to stand by me, though I believe she more than half suspected 'twas true." She sighed. "Even so, I very much fear there will still be whispers."

Unable to bear his scrutiny, she covered her face with her hands. "I'm so sorry, Nicholas. Rumor upon rumor! What a sorry bargain I've been as a wife."

"Hush, sweeting." Gently he pried her hands away and kissed them. "What matter to us what the gossips say?"

"I care what they say about your wife," she said in a low voice. "For once, I should like to be a source of pride rather than an embarrassment."

"I am proud of you. Did you not use your pin money to better the lot of some distant tenants? No other lady I know would have done so." He chuckled. "My farmer bride."

She shuddered.

His face sobered. "'Tis almost nothing you could do that would truly anger me, Sarah. You can't imagine the start you gave me when I saw you in that doorway looking so distressed. I followed you, searched everywhere, and when I couldn't find you I was...beside myself."

How like a man, to translate upset into anger, she thought, touched by his concern. "Clarissa cornered me in the withdrawing room begging help in repairing her torn lace. I'm so sorry you worried."

He took her hand and kissed it earnestly. "Promise me, Sarah, you'll never run from me again."

The image of her papa with his coin recurred. Should she confess the whole? Perhaps he might understand.

"You were in the game room, if you'll recall, flipping a guinea?" When he nodded, she continued. "The night Papa lost the rest of our capital, our dowries, everything, I found him staring out the library window, tossing a single coin. Oh, 'twas foolish, I know, but seeing you do that brought it all back. Gaming—frightens me so, Nicholas."

He looked at her gravely. "I'm not your papa, Sarah. I've worked too hard for my fortune to throw it away."

"But you like to gamble! You cannot continue to risk, and expect always to win."

"Yes, I enjoy gaming—specifically, games in which I

can calculate the odds and pit my expertise against that of other players. I do not play those that depend solely on chance. But you mustn't fear that enjoyment will land us on the parish. Though I tremble to confess something so unfashionable, I'm afraid most of our income comes from deplorably bourgeois business activities.''

''Business?'' she echoed.

She must have seemed incredulous, for he chuckled. ''Ah, yes, you're thinking of Englemere's Luck. Though I've never made any secret of my activities in the city, the ton seems to prefer perpetuating the image of me as a wildly successful gamester. 'Tis partly true—I did have a phenomenal run of luck when I first came to town. Fortunately, a friend of my father's advised me to put most of my winnings into investments. My dear, we currently own shares in shipping, coal, canal projects—we've even thrown a bit into Mr. Trevick's horseless carriage experiments.''

Her immediate surge of relief quickly faded. ''Shipping and canals and horseless carriages? But are not such investments even more risky than the tables?''

''True, there are losses. A cargo of East India spices here, a coal shipment there may founder. The trick is not to sink all your capital in any one venture. Those that do succeed usually bring a handsome profit.''

His face lit with enthusiasm. ''Assessing the potential value, weighing the probability of success, choosing which projects to fund and which to refuse—ah, that is even more fascinating than gaming.''

Sunken cargo here, lost shipments there? Sarah blanched. 'Twas only the thrill of risk-taking translated to a different environment. She could see the gambler's fever she so feared glowing in his eyes as he spoke.

His excitement faded as he gazed at her. ''You don't trust me, do you?'' he said at last.

He looked more hurt than affronted. She opened her

mouth, closed it, searching desperately for words that were softer than the truth and yet not a lie.

He sighed. "I suppose 'tis not remarkable, after what you and your family endured. Sarah, I would never gamble with our security."

"I know you will do what you feel is right." That, at least, she could say honestly.

He smiled, the warm light she so loved back in his eyes. "And what would you sink our capital into, little Puritan? Land, I suppose?"

"'Tis ever there, Nicholas," she said fervently. "No flip of the dice or shipwreck can make it disappear."

"But land lying fallow earns nothing. You must harvest salable crops. How many years has the corn or wheat failed? All life is a risk, Sarah, none more so than farming."

She yearned to dispute that, but memories of the lean times came back all too vividly. "True, land may not always be profitable. But still it remains, with its potential for next year and the year after. Land remains to pass on to your children and grandchildren."

He laughed shortly. "My father passed all the Stanhope lands to me. And almost nothing in cash, having ever put his money back into his properties. After his death, when the price of grain plummeted, I could barely keep the household in coal and tallows." He shook his head. "That's a position *I* never wish to be in again."

She couldn't dispute that either. The image of wealthy, successful Nicholas in want of anything was so novel she could hardly credit it.

He grinned at her. "We shall make a bargain. I will teach you about investments, and you can instruct me in farm management. Deal?"

She winced. Even now, he used gambler's terms. "I shall try, Nicholas. It's just—oh, you cannot imagine what 'tis like to suddenly have your familiar world, your very future, collapse in the space of an instant into unsalvageable ruin!''

''Can I not?'' he said, an odd note in his voice. A strange, bleak expression crossed his face before he took her hand. ''Sarah, I will never risk our children's inheritance. Can you trust that?''

'Twas an honorable bargain. ''As you have trusted me. I shall do better, Nicholas! I shall apply myself to all my duties, be a model wife and never embarrass you again.''

''And so shall I do better, Sarah, I swear it. Now, about those 'duties,''' he murmured, his fingers going to the sash of her dressing gown. ''You can begin right now.''

Three weeks later, Nicholas sat with Hal at White's, sharing a convivial bottle of brandy after dinner.

''Excellent meal, Hal. Thank you.''

Hal nodded. ''Pleased to host you. Don't see you here much. Married, an' all.''

''Married indeed,'' Nicholas said with a sigh and drained his glass. ''I'm off to fetch Sarah for a party. Not that I can complain—I should have dined with her at the Dowager Duchess of Arundel's first.''

Hal shuddered. ''Good you shied off. Dreadful woman.''

''Sarah got me out of it, actually.'' He smiled wryly. ''Another of her courtesies.''

At Hal's baffled look, he continued, ''First it was the rumor about our star-crossed love, and then that silliness over the 'Farmer Bride.' Was Sarah upset over that!''

''You miffed about it, Nicky?''

''Devil a bit.'' Nicholas laughed. ''Sarah's much more concerned about my consequence than I am.'' His humor faded. ''So much so, she's throwing all her energies into being the perfect marchioness, the perfect chatelaine of my household and the perfect wife. To make it up to me for the rumors, she said.'' He groaned. ''I'm being 'perfected' to death.''

"Fretting you to flinders, eh?"

Unable to resist the temptation of unburdening himself, Nicholas poured another glass and eased back in his chair.

"You don't know the half of it. Take this function tonight. I doubt I'll manage half a dozen words with Sarah. She'll be too busy chatting up every dowager and dragon in the place—doing her 'duty' as a marchioness, you see."

Hal blinked. "It is?"

Nicholas sighed again. "I suppose. Mama does it, but then damn it, she's a dowager herself. I suspect she detests it—Sarah, I mean—but she still keeps on, function after function. I can scarcely drag her away for a waltz."

Hal gave an understanding nod. "Makes her testy."

"No, it isn't that. She does it cheerfully enough, and when I ask if she's enjoying herself, she assures me she is, now that the Farmer Bride business has blown over. Thanks to Sally Jersey, which—" he paused for a sip "—about evens the score with Sal for inviting Chloe to her ball."

Hal chuckled. "Manages doxies, too."

"Sally? She can't resist the urge to manage everyone."

"No, Sarah. At the Jerseys' ball. Heard her."

"She talked with Chloe at the ball?" Nicholas gasped.

"Not with the doxy. Weston." Hal chuckled again.

Exasperated, Nicholas nearly snapped at him. Willing himself patience, he tried to decode that cryptic utterance.

And gave up. "You mean Lord John Weston? What has he to do with this?"

Hal recovered from his mirth. "Bounder. Saw Mrs. Ingram enter. Went over to Sarah. Asked her how she liked being married to a chap with so beautiful a mistress."

"He *what!*" Nicholas exploded. "I'll wring his neck, the bloody bastard!" Suddenly he remembered Sandiford's warning—that Weston was Sir James's tool. Hadn't Sally also told him the man was responsible for that "Farmer Bride" epithet as well?

"Cool as you please, though. Sarah. Married handsomest and most accomplished man in London, she says. 'Course he has the most beautiful mistress.''

Nicholas's jaw dropped. Not a word had Sarah mentioned to him of the incident, or uttered a hint of reproach.

'Twas the response of a true lady of breeding, and more. 'Twas a clever deflection of someone's intent to wound. Anger stirred—and regret. He'd not considered others of malicious mind could use his liaison with Chloe to hurt Sarah. He really should end the relationship.

"She's the best of good wives, 'tis certain. I just wish she wouldn't overdo it."

"Overdo?" Hal looked puzzled.

"For instance, I said 'twould be nice to have macaroons with tea. Next day, the biscuit box was full of 'em. And every day since. If I see another macaroon, I'll puke."

"Invite me to tea. Like macaroons."

"Try this. I babbled something about Baines bringing me the wrong boots. She made the man take my wardrobe apart and reorganize everything in it. He sulked for a week."

Hal frowned. "Shouldn't truck with one's man."

"Quite right," Nicholas agreed with feeling. "I tell you, Hal, I'm in a quake every time I return home, worrying that she's seized on some chance remark and turned the house upside down. I swear, were I to express an interest in squid for breakfast, there'd be a damned rasher of 'em next to the bacon come morning."

"Couldn't. Come from—" Hal knit his brow "—some foreign place. Impossible."

"You underestimate Sarah. Did I breathe the word, I bet you a monkey I'd find them on the sideboard within a week."

"You're on."

"Well—" Nicholas sputtered "—I didn't actually—"

"What's this, a wager?"

At the vaguely familiar voice, Nicholas looked over his

shoulder. Lord John Weston lounged behind him, smiling. "Waiter, bring the book."

"Just a minute!" His grievances against the man sparked him from exasperation to anger in a heartbeat.

"Yes, bring the book." Hal motioned to the servant. "Sarah's a game 'un, but nobody'd do that. Saw 'em once—nasty things." He shuddered. "Got eyes on little sticks."

"Hal, I didn't really mean—"

Weston's loud halloo drowned out Nicholas's protest. "I say, gentlemen. A wager!"

Nicholas watched in consternation as, in a babble of voices, half a dozen club members ambled over.

"What's the bet?"

"I'll back Englemere, whatever the odds."

Nicholas cast Lord John a fulminating glance. Had the bastard been eavesdropping? 'Twas the worst of bad ton to make his own wife the subject of a vulgar bet—a recorded bet at White's, no less. But trying to explain to Hal, never nimble-witted, in the midst of this attentive crowd that he never intended to make a wager, would probably cause more gossip than letting it stand.

Damn Weston for trapping him like this—and his master, Findlay. Reluctantly Nicholas watched Hal scrawl a note.

"Squid by Friday, eh? Monkey says you're wrong."

"A monkey, then," he mumbled. It might be interesting to see if Sarah would really go that far. At least he'd have reason for once to anticipate with amusement rather than dread the results of a casual remark. And yet…

Hadn't he done Sarah enough disservice already? Hating himself, but driven to do so, after her midnight confession he'd made some casual inquiries at the club and verified Captain Sandiford's departure from the Sheffingdon rout immediately after his dance with Sarah. Having confirmed that, in a euphoria of relief—tinged with shame—he'd vowed to banish for good his ignoble, unworthy suspicions.

Sarah had been all that was honest and honorable. He owed her no less in return. After this, he swore with a dagger glance at Weston, he'd be on his guard.

The image of squid in a cooking pot, though, set him grinning. "Faith," he said with a chuckle. "Cook'll have palpitations."

A week later bedecked in a dressing gown, Sarah sat at her dressing table in the pale dawn light, the large cask containing the Stanhope jewels before her. Nicholas's mama had brought them, insisting rightly enough they were now Sarah's. She should choose something to match her gown for the presentation ball tonight.

Fumbling in her own small cask for the key to the larger one, she came upon Sinjin's signet ring.

Her chest constricting, she stared at it. She'd not worn it since the day she accepted Nicholas's offer. She should have returned it the morning Sinjin called, but in her agitation had forgotten.

As she lifted the heavy gold ring, its shiny surface caught and reflected an arc of morning sunlight. Suddenly she saw in the flash an ardent young man, his blue eyes blazing as he pressed the ring into her hand. Should she ever need him, he vowed, she need only send this, and he would move heaven and earth to come to her.

Tears stung her eyes and a great lump filled her throat. He came to see her often now—too often. Calling during regular hours, dancing with her at various functions, he'd adopted a teasing, elder-brother manner.

She still could not encounter him without pain, but the ache was dulling. Perhaps, given time, she could learn to consider him just a dear and valued friend. In another fifty or sixty years.

After each meeting with Sinjin, she seemed impelled to seek out Nicholas. Somehow, her husband's touch soothed the ache and made her feel—safe. Safe from Sinjin, or herself, was a question she didn't wish to examine.

If only she dared throw her heart, as well as her energies, into being Nicholas's wife, she might bury forever her lingering grief over Sinjin.

'Twas too risky a solution. She sighed heavily. Nicholas would support her, come what may, that she knew. But he would never, as Sinjin had sworn to do, ride *ventre à terre* to her rescue, words of love on his lips.

A breeze stirred the curtains, bringing with it a whiff of fresh green grass. The crops would be up at Wellingford. She felt a wave of homesickness.

Perhaps, after his mother's ball, she'd ask Nicholas's leave to go home. With a tremor of joy, she put her hand on her abdomen. She was certain now that Nicholas's nightly visits were no longer strictly necessary.

A pang marred her happiness. Once she broke the news, Nicholas would probably be more than willing to send her into the country. She closed her eyes to the image of a gloating Chloe Ingram.

Enough moping, she told herself, and rang for Becky. She'd make up a packet and mail the ring back this very day. Nicholas should be down for breakfast soon, and she had a little surprise for him this morning.

Nicholas smiled at Sarah as he entered the breakfast room. Attired in a gown of pale yellow, she looked like sunshine itself.

"You're up early, sweeting," he said as he dropped a kiss on her forehead. "I thought you'd be still abed, so fatigued were you last night. Have you recovered?"

"Quite. I've been up an age, and as you can see, was too famished to wait. Do help yourself, Nicholas."

She stopped eating and seemed to be watching with unusual intensity as he served himself eggs, bacon and toast. "Mama says you've been a great—what the devil?"

From under the lid he'd just raised wafted a hot breath with the distinct odor of tidal swamp.

"'Tis the squid you asked for. I hope Cook prepared them the way you like."

To tell the truth, he'd forgotten all about the wager. He eased the covered dish open cautiously, releasing another cloud of foul-smelling air. In the warmed dish, a congealed eye stared up at him. He felt last night's brandy rising.

"Good Lord!" he uttered with revulsion. Quickly he slammed the lid shut, vaguely noting a footman snicker. The stuff was every bit as repulsive as Hal had predicted. "James, take that—creature away!"

"But Nicholas, I thought—" Her anxious eyes on his face, Sarah bit back her reply.

Despite the closed lid, another pungent draft reached his nose, and he nearly gagged. "*Now,* James!"

"Yes, my lord," the footman said with trembling lips. As he hefted the chafing dish, he looked into Nicholas's revolted face, and a laugh escaped him.

Sarah stiffened. A rosy flush bloomed on her cheeks.

Glendenning cleared his throat and frowned at the footman, who converted his mirth to an unconvincing cough.

"The kitchen, James," Glendenning intoned with a curt nod toward the door. "Tea, my lord?"

Nicholas angled a glance at Sarah, but she was staring toward the open doorway through which the footman was now hastily removing himself. He followed her gaze.

To his consternation, milling about in the hallway were half a dozen footmen, maids and even a stable boy. Hell and damnation, he cursed under his breath.

Glendenning strode over and slammed the door. Sarah focused her gaze on her plate.

From behind the closed door, Nicholas could hear a babble of raised voices and the rumble of laughter. Sarah's flush deepened to brick.

Glendenning brought the teapot. As he poured, some of

the liquid spurted over the china rim onto Nicholas's wrist. With an oath, Nicholas jerked his hand away.

"Forgive me, my lord," Glendenning said in frigid accents. He gave Nicholas a totally unrepentant look before the usual mask descended on his features.

Staring straight ahead, Sarah took a sip from her cup. Nicholas might have been able to convince himself she was unaffected by the incident, were it not for the vivid color that still painted her cheeks, her ears—even her neck.

Guilt washed over him. He opened his lips to apologize, but the thought of confessing, before the obviously disapproving Glendenning, a wager that appeared more ill-judged and sophomoric by the minute was too daunting. He gulped tea instead, and scalded his tongue.

"That will be all, thank you, Glendenning," Sarah said. She took another precise sip.

The moment the butler closed the hall door, Sarah threw down her napkin. She was halfway to the French doors leading to the garden when Nicholas reached her.

"Sarah, I'm sorry!" he cried, catching her hand. "'Twas naught but a foolish wager. I'd told Hal you catered to my every whim, would even feed me squid for breakfast, did I but ask for it, and he couldn't believe—"

"Nor can I believe it. 'Tis true ours was not a love match, my lord, but never did I think to have you make a—a *May game* of me in front of the servants!"

Ripping her hand free, she sped to the door, wrenched it open and fled into the garden.

His mouth still open, Nicholas watched her go. After a moment, he slowly walked back and reseated himself. He sipped his tea. It was tepid now.

Feeling like the lowest beast in nature, he pushed his equally cold eggs around on his plate. He could, he supposed, ring for Glendenning to bring warm ones. Although, he thought with a gallows grin, he'd not be at all surprised should the dour butler report back, with suitable effusions of regret, that there were no more eggs to be had. He might even bring back the squid.

With a sigh, Nicholas went out to the garden. If he didn't find Sarah now, he'd probably not have another private moment with her until late evening. He didn't want to give her that long to brood over his boorish behavior.

Though ill-judged, at the time Hal proposed it the wager had seemed harmless enough. He hadn't considered the effort Sarah would have had to put forth to produce the blasted creatures, or envisioned so large and interested an audience gathered for their delivery. *In truth,* he told himself acidly, *you didn't think at all.*

As exasperated as he'd sometimes become with her these past few weeks, never would he wish to hurt or embarrass her. Without question he had just done both.

Calling himself names under his breath, he spotted Sarah on a bench facing away from him, and stopped short. From the set of her bent head and her shaking shoulders, he realized she was weeping.

''Hell and damnation,'' he muttered, feeling worse yet. Uncertain whether to apologize at once, or wait till she was calmer, he hesitated. Then he noticed a flicker of light.

She held something in one hand, something small and shiny that she was rubbing over and over like a talisman. He stepped closer—and saw the object she clutched so tightly was a man's gold signet ring.

Nicholas froze. The ring might be her father's, though he doubted it. 'Twas not his, certainly. He could imagine but one other owner.

Sarah hadn't heard his approach, for her posture didn't alter. As Nicholas silently backed toward the house, she sat weeping softly, her thumb rubbing Sandiford's ring.

Chapter Thirteen

Vacillating between outrage and chagrin, Nicholas repaired to the library. After a short glass of brandy and a lengthy bit of self-examination, he mastered the former.

Sarah must have had the signet a long time. Upon reflection, he dismissed his first angry suspicion that the captain had given it to her during their recent interview, as a pledge of future intent. As he had reason to know, she'd not had the ring on her person immediately after.

She should have returned it long since, but so intimate an item must be given back privately. She could hardly hand it over at a ball or in a crowded morning room.

Why had she been clutching Sandiford's ring? His lips twisted in self-mockery. After that humiliation in the breakfast room, even a boorish, insensitive fool like himself could understand she might wish for comfort.

And what could be more comforting than an object that reminded her of the gallant young man who—he gritted his teeth—*loved* her, who had no doubt pressed his token upon her with vows of undying affection? Unlike the husband who groused to Hal of her solicitude, made her the object of a vulgar bet and exposed her to the ridicule of the staff.

"Will your lordship require luncheon?" Glendenning interrupted.

"Will her ladyship be taking some?"

"Her ladyship has gone out."

Disappointed, but hardly surprised, he cast an eye at the butler. Disapproval positively radiated from him.

"Something simple might be prepared, though Cook did take to her bed when the s-squid," he choked out the word, "was sent back untouched. For the second time today, I must inform you, the first being after she vowed such a nasty foreign creature would never see the inside of her cooking pot. However, the mistress soothed her with a posset. And the boy who washed the pot, the maid who bought the—"

"Enough, Glendenning." Nicholas got the clear if tortuously delivered message that the inconvenience caused below stairs had been laid by the staff squarely at his door.

With the persistence of one who'd served his master since he was in short coats, Glendenning seemed determined that Nicholas not miss the point. "The mistress is held in the utmost respect and esteem by the entire staff."

Nicholas essayed a deprecating smile. "Which is to say, I should expect cold tea and burnt mutton?"

"Certainly not, my lord. One has standards. However—" he unbent at last "—'twas not well done, Master Nicky."

"No," Nicholas agreed with a sigh. "I fear I'm in the basket now."

"'Tis not my place to say so," Glendenning intoned and bowed himself out.

Formulating elaborate and heartfelt speeches of regret, Nicholas whiled away the hours until teatime. Every afternoon Sarah prepared his tea—and presented a blasted macaroon along with it. However, although his tea arrived hot as promised, Sarah did not return to share it.

For her to neglect performing that ritual, she must be even angrier than he feared. Munching his tasteless plain biscuits, Nicholas racked his brain for a gift lavish enough to convey his deep contrition. He was about to call for his curricle to go buy the largest diamond Rundell and Bridges possessed when a better idea occurred.

Sarah wore little jewelry—he suppressed a pang at that reminder of a certain signet ring—and showed no interest in useless gewgaws. Indeed, she'd stripped her allowance to send supplies to Wellingford. What better gift than to set up a fund she might use to restore her beloved estate? With luck, he could have the monies transferred and be back in time to catch Sarah alone before dinner.

Several hours later, Nicholas waited in the hallway for Sarah. She was "resting," Becky had informed him frostily when he returned from the bankers, and could not be disturbed. Since his only opportunity to apologize before the ball would be to waylay her before she came downstairs for dinner, he'd dressed hurriedly and now lurked about like a guilty schoolboy anxious to make amends for a stupid prank. Which, he sighed, was not far wrong.

At last Sarah emerged, a thin shawl of spangled gauze across her shoulders. Her simple gown of gold-frosted emerald silk clung to her curves and glittered as she moved, reflecting the light much more provocatively than the fine Stanhope emeralds at her neck and ears.

Tonight his family would present her to the ton as his bride. She looked magnificent, he thought with pride.

"Good evening, sweet Sarah."

"Nicholas!" she gasped. "You—startled me."

He let his appreciative gaze travel over her figure. "No one will have eyes for any other lady tonight."

To his surprise, she frowned. "The bodice is too low, just as I feared. I shall change immediately."

"No, the gown is lovely! Truly, Sarah." He caught her arm. "You've no need to change."

She stiffened at his touch and glanced up warily, as if she expected he might bite. "Are you sure?"

The open, trusting look he'd grown accustomed to had

vanished totally. He felt an almost physical ache. "You look stunning. I'll be the proudest man in London tonight."

Raising a skeptical eyebrow, she put her hand lightly, almost reluctantly on his arm. "Shall we go down, then?"

She took a step. Nicholas stood motionless, perforce halting her. "I came earlier to apologize, but Becky absolutely refused to let me in. I am sorry, Sarah, terribly sorry. I should never have played such a stupid, ill-judged trick. I expect you'd gone to a deal of trouble, and you have every right to be angry."

"I'm not angry," she replied, "not anymore. I suspect I've been…smothering you with my attentions. I don't have enough to keep me busy." She offered a small, polite smile. "I must confess, I did wish you'd chosen to bring the matter to my attention in a less, ah, dramatic manner."

Nicholas wished she'd rip up at him, call him a cad—she could scarce come up with a name he'd not already applied to himself. Anything but this distant wariness.

Had he only yesterday thought how nice 'twould be to distance himself from his oversolicitous wife? Well, Sarah had withdrawn from him, quite definitely. And he hated it.

As he fumbled for an apology abject enough to thaw the chilly caution in her eyes, his mother arrived. "How lovely you look, Sarah! Is she not beautiful, Nicky?"

"So I've just been telling her, Mama," he replied, trying to keep the frustration from his voice.

Setting the cap on his disgruntlement, Sarah turned to her mother-in-law with a smile of genuine warmth. "Not half so fine as you, Lady Englemere."

"Stuff and nonsense," his mother said, linking her arm with Sarah's. "Shall we go dazzle our guests?"

'Twas nothing for it but to offer an arm to each lady. Near fuming with frustration, Nicholas escorted them down.

Would the dratted ball never end? Nicholas thought as the night dragged on. As usual, he'd exchanged a bare handful of words with Sarah. After they'd been released from the receiving line, so assiduous had his mother been in taking Sarah round to chat with their many honored guests, he'd managed to nab her for only one dance. Since that had been the opening cotillion conducted under the attentive gaze of several hundred people, it had hardly offered him a chance for any private remark.

Perhaps he could steal her away now. He walked toward the head of the stairs where he'd glimpsed his mama greeting some late arrivals. The full figure and sinuous carriage of the lady now ascending those stairs caught his eye, and his heart nearly stopped.

Appropriately dressed in scarlet, the rubies he'd once given her flashing on her bosom, came Chloe Ingram. His horrified gaze expanded to include an all-too-familiar hussar on whose arm Chloe hung. What the devil did she mean coming here? Had Sandiford brought her?

Speechless with outrage, Nicholas stood frozen. He thawed quickly as his mother threw him a look of furious reproach. Mystified and seething, he hurried to her.

"So kind of you to include me, Lady Englemere," Chloe was saying. She turned to Nicholas, her eyes glowing. "My lord, I can't tell you how happy I was to be invited."

His mother looked at him accusingly. Wishing the floor would swallow him up, Nicholas prayed Sarah was in the refreshment room. While his mother murmured something polite to Chloe, Nicholas leaned to the captain.

"Did you bring her?" he said in a furious undertone.

"Me?" Sandiford lifted an eyebrow. "Certainly not. I came in while she was handing her invitation to the butler and she latched on my arm like a barnacle."

Chloe had an invitation, then. How in heaven had she gotten it? Never in this life would his mother have sent one. While he racked his brain, Chloe sent him a smoky, intimate glance, ending it with a pantomimed kiss.

Nicholas felt ill. There was no question what interpretation Chloe had applied to his bidding her, so she thought, to his wife's presentation ball. Save Sandiford, who'd just disclaimed with unfeigned disgust he'd had no hand in it, who could detest him—or Sarah—that much?

Even as he asked it, he knew the answer. How Findlay had gotten Weston to manage it, Nicholas had no idea, but this had to be his handiwork.

Never would Nicholas have believed himself capable of uttering the next words out of his mouth, but gritting his teeth, he managed it. "Would you watch Sarah for me while I get rid of—her?" he asked the captain under his breath.

His face contemptuous, the captain's chill blue eyes held Nicholas's impassioned green ones.

"I tell you, I had nothing to do with this!"

"Nothing?" The captain's glance traveled to the magnificent ruby necklace nestled between Chloe's breasts. "Oh, I daresay you had something to do with it. But for Sarah's sake, I'll do as you ask."

Nicholas didn't waste time arguing. "She may be in the refreshment room. Give me fifteen minutes."

Nodding, the captain took himself off. Nicholas groaned, thinking of Sally Jersey and her Almack patroness friends waltzing just beyond the open doorway. *Pray God I get her out of here before anyone else sees her.*

Dropping a fulsome compliment, he took his mistress's gloved hand off his mother's affronted sleeve and began walking her downstairs.

"Where are you taking me, Nicky?" she asked, her face still lit with triumph and pleasure. "Oh, you naughty thing. Not at your own ball, surely!"

"How did you come to be here, Chloe?"

"Why, I received an invitation, and knew immediately what you intended. How sweet of you to make so public a gesture, if a bit—indiscreet?" She gave him an arch look.

They reached the bottom of the staircase. "Summon Mrs. Ingram's carriage," Nicholas told Glendenning curtly.

Chloe's warmth cooled as she looked up at Nicholas's unsmiling face. "Nicholas?"

"Chloe, I regret treating you with such brusqueness, but we're both the victims of a particularly vicious practical joke. You must realize the last thing my mother—or I— would do would be invite you to my wife's ball."

Understanding dawned in the luminous dark eyes. "I take it that my presence is, shall we say, *de trop?*"

Nicholas nodded grimly. "I appreciate your understanding about this, Chloe."

"Oh, certainly. You'll find I can be wonderfully *understanding*. My friends were so surprised when I got the card. Whatever shall I tell them?"

Nicholas shot a glance down. Some strong emotion stormed across her face, but the smile that followed it was sweet—altogether too sweet. "I'll not forget this, Nicky."

A rigidly disapproving Glendenning handed Nicholas her cloak. Before he could drape it about her, Chloe stayed his hand. "Am I permitted to use the retiring room? Or must you have me ejected immediately?"

Nearly gnashing his teeth with impatience to spirit her away, Nicholas could hardly deny that request. He made himself smile. "Down the hallway, to your left."

An angry glitter in her eyes, she walked off. Chloe might be furious, but Nicholas had few thoughts to spare for that. 'Twould be nothing to the uproar in the ton should someone see her here. Nicholas paced as he waited, the loud ticking of the tall case clock in the entry sounding like a warning of approaching doom.

After what seemed an age, during which Nicholas kept throwing anxious glances from the front door to the stairway to the landing, Chloe finally reappeared. Strangely, her spirits seemed much revived.

"Thank you, Chloe," he said, relieved she'd not treated him to a full-scale scene in front of Glendenning and the attendant footmen. "I'll not forget your consideration."

She laughed. "Oh, I daresay you shall not."

Her humor fading, she wrenched her shoulder from under his hand. Glendenning already held the door open. Without further goodbye, she raised her chin and walked out.

Nicholas hastened up the stairs. He encountered the captain, minus Sarah, coming out of the refreshment room.

"I kept her as long as I could. Insisted then she must check the kitchens." He frowned. "She's worn to the nub, and ought to retire."

Despite his gratitude, Nicholas stiffened at the implied criticism. "Thank you, Captain, for your *concern*."

Just then Sarah appeared. She did indeed look so pale Nicholas felt a wave of anxiety—followed immediately by panic. Had someone seen Chloe after all, and told her?

Forgetting the captain, he went to her. "Sweeting, you look tired. I daresay some guests will stay till dawn, but there's no need for you to do so. Shall I take you up?"

To his immense relief, he could detect nothing more alarming in the smile with which she greeted him than fatigue. "Should I not remain?"

"Mama will say whatever is necessary."

Sarah made no further protest. "I have been rather fatigued this hour and more," she admitted. "If 'twould be no discourtesy, I should like to go up."

"I'll escort you, then, and inform Mama when I return."

She nodded. "Good night, Sinjin," she called over his shoulder. "Thank you for coming to the ball."

"Good night, Sarah. Rest well." Sandiford bowed to her and, after a brief accusing look, to Nicholas. With a fervent prayer of thanks for letting him escape so disastrous a situation unscathed, Nicholas led her upstairs.

* * *

Becky had readied her for bed, tucked her up and snuffed the candle, but despite her very real fatigue Sarah lay sleepless against the pillows.

She would make preparations to leave for Wellingford tomorrow. She simply must get away.

Sarah stared into the fire's glowing embers. She was still humiliated and furious over the squid incident, deeply hurt that Nicholas would repay her honest efforts so shabbily. And the manner of it! After she had bared her soul to him, gathered up her courage to reveal how deeply gaming distressed her, he had gone right off and made her, his own wife, the object of a wager.

The very thought of it still made her so angry she could scarcely breathe. He had not understood—he would never understand the lack of responsibility, the reckless toying with disaster that gambling represented to her.

And yet he could also be so kind. So thoughtfully attentive and considerate, she'd been completely unprepared for casual cruelty. She'd deluded herself into believing she was being wary, when in truth she'd been much too trusting—in too many ways.

As she discovered this evening after visiting the kitchens. Having ensured all was in train for the midnight supper, she stopped at the ladies' retiring room—and literally bumped into Chloe Ingram.

Chapter Fourteen

For a moment she was too astonished to say a word. Oh, Mrs. Ingram had been all that was polite. She complimented Sarah's gown and expressed her appreciation at being invited. As if Sarah had included her.

Only Nicholas could have done so. The full import of that invitation was just now dawning on her weary mind. That Nicholas had bade his mistress be present could only mean he was continuing their liaison. More than that—he was virtually trumpeting that fact to the ton.

Perhaps someone was competing with him for the favors of the beauteous Mrs. Ingram. Whatever his purpose, the lady herself made her own intentions perfectly clear.

"Of course, I expected your ball to be lavish and your gown lovely," she said after her pretty compliments. "Nicky is ever generous." And she smiled sweetly, lowered her glance and patted the magnificent rubies at her breast.

Though the woman insinuated nothing she did not already know, Sarah had been cut to the quick by that deliberate reminder of her husband's regard for another. And furious.

With the regrettable impetuosity she had thought long since mastered, she shot back, "Generous indeed, Mrs.

Ingram. Only remember, when all you have of Nicholas are those rubies to recall him by, I shall have his son.''

She swept out of the room, regretting as soon as they were uttered words as uncharitable as Mrs. Ingram's gesture. And as true. She must quit London.

Wellingford's rolling meadows and tranquil woods beckoned to her. Yes, she'd go to Wellingford tomorrow.

Too restless to sleep, she jumped up and paced to her desk. She would start her packing lists immediately.

She was drawing out pen and paper when the door opened. Nicholas stepped in and halted abruptly.

''Sarah, what are you doing up? I thought you asleep long since. I was just about to retire myself.''

How could I go peacefully to sleep after all you've done today? she wanted to shout. Aghast she'd nearly cried the words aloud, she bit her tongue and thanked the dim light that hid her flushing cheeks.

''Now that my presentation's complete, your mama will be returning to Stanhope Hall. I thought to visit Wellingford. The prospect was so exciting, I couldn't sleep.''

''You'll want to check on the improvements you ordered, I expect. And see about that—what was it, rapeseed?''

''Yes, I will.'' His immediate acquiescence shouldn't have hurt, but it did. Fool, she told herself crossly. Had she expected him to urge her to linger? Once his officially presented *wife* left town, he could take back up with his officially presented *mistress*.

''I'm pleased you were thinking of Wellingford, for I have a surprise for you that concerns it.''

She must have looked alarmed, for Nicholas winced. ''Don't distress yourself, Sarah. I'm reasonably certain this surprise you shall like.''

He cleared his throat. ''After my inexcusable behavior today, I wanted to express my heartfelt regret for upsetting you. I considered jewelry, but then I decided a fund for Wellingford would please you more. So I've set up an initial account of five thousand pounds, in your name only. You may draw on it when you wish, as you wish.''

Sarah sat stunned. Then she recalled Mrs. Ingram's sly words, and a pain twisted in her heart.

''I hardly know what to say. 'Tis wondrous generous.'' She managed a slight smile. ''The affront was hardly that great, my lord.''

''The affront cannot be measured, sweeting. You were only trying to please me, and I callously threw your efforts in your teeth. If that weren't bad enough, 'twas in the form of a wager, something you could not help but despise.''

The hard edge of her anger softened. Perhaps Nicholas did have some inkling of what his actions had meant to her.

''I know I can't buy your goodwill, Sarah, but I should earnestly like to have it.'' He took her hand and kissed it. ''Can you forgive me? I promise you, I shall do my utmost never to treat you so shabbily again.''

Whether he understood fully or not, he did realize he'd hurt her—and how. He was offering a handsome and unquestionably sincere apology. She should accept it in like spirit.

What of Mrs. Ingram? her heart whispered. She stifled the thought. When she accepted Nicholas, she had accepted Mrs. Ingram as well. 'Twould be dishonorable to go back on her bargain now, no matter how difficult she found the keeping of it. ''Of course I forgive you.''

He searched her face so intently she had to look away, then sighed. ''Your lips speak of forgiveness, but your eyes tell me no. I shall have to be at my most charming during our country sojourn if I hope to win back your regard.''

''Our? But you cannot mean to come with me!''

''Of course I shall come. As it happens, I have a minor holding not too distant from Wellingford. It's been under a cousin's management, and I've not checked on it in a great while. You can start on my lessons in estate management.''

Sarah was flabbergasted. Why would Nicholas wish to leave London, when he might take advantage of her absence to dally with Mrs. Ingram?

"You needn't escort me, Nicholas. I'll have Becky."

"Besides, you've told me so much of Wellingford, I'm quite anxious to see it."

Ah, he wished to discover if his money had been wisely spent. "The improvements I've ordered are necessary and well worth the expense. There's no need for you to inspect Wellingford personally."

"I'm sure you've done as you ought. I should enjoy seeing Wellingford, though, and visiting your family again."

He was being remarkably persistent, Sarah thought with exasperation. "I'm afraid the way I've described Wellingford—the way it lives in my imagining—and its current state have little in common. I'd rather show it to you after it has been restored. Besides, my stay might be rather extended, and you cannot wish to be gone long."

"But if you go, sweeting—" he lifted her hand to kiss her palm "—then of course I must be with you."

Ah, that. A bittersweet pain spiraled through her. Well, she could allay that concern. "You needn't trouble yourself," she said softly. "'Tis quite fitting that you stay in London whilst I repair to the country. Is that not where breeding wives are supposed to go?"

"Only wives who enjoy—" His teasing smile faded. "What did you say?"

"I said, breeding wives are supposed to—"

He seized her in a hug. "Sarah! Are you sure?"

She nodded, feeling suddenly shy. "Yes, I'm quite certain now. I hope you're pleased."

"Pleased? 'Tis wonderful news! Mama will be thrilled." His excitement ended abruptly. "But should you travel at such a time? Should you not remain and rest?"

Sarah laughed. "Nicholas, I'm breeding, not dying. 'Tis no reason I cannot travel or pursue any of my usual activities. Surely I will rest better in the country. So," she added soberly, "'tis no reason for you to accompany me."

Surely he understood her innuendo. Sarah held her breath, waiting for him to realize the truth of it, to cheerfully acquiesce and send her away.

"Sarah," he said quietly at last, "have I so offended you that you no longer wish my company?"

"No, Nicholas, 'tis not that at all! You prefer London. I'd not have you drag yourself away out of kindness and a sense of duty."

"'Tis not kindness or duty. Unless you truly find my escort repugnant, I wish to accompany you. So as not to burden the staff at Wellingford, we can stay at Stoneacres. Do say you'll let me come, Sarah."

"L-let you—!" She sputtered. "As if you needed my permission to visit your own estate. You truly wish to accompany me?" she asked, completely baffled.

Nicholas kissed her. "I truly do. But I've had to so coerce and cajole you into accepting my escort I'm certain you've not really forgiven me."

He was right—but she must make herself. "You're wrong, Nicholas," she said firmly. "I have forgiven you."

"Prove it, then," he murmured, and bent to trace his lips down the column of her neck.

"This isn't—necessary—any longer." She gasped, trying to stay coherent despite the flood of tingling warmth his kiss evoked. "You've already—done—your duty."

"Have I?" he whispered, his fingers at the laces of her nightrail. "Then let us take our pleasure."

A few days later they arrived at Stoneacres, the small estate Nicholas had inherited from his grandmother. True to his word, Nicholas accompanied her—not only accompanied her, but was at every stage so thoughtful and attentive that her remaining anger dissolved.

'Twas most difficult, she thought as Nicholas handed her carefully out of the carriage, to maintain a prudent distance from her handsome husband when he persisted in being so undeniably charming—and so irresistibly near.

Nicholas's cousin and manager, Hugh Baxter, along with the complete staff, came out to welcome them.

The neatness and comfort of the snug manor house impressed Sarah. Indeed, she was somewhat surprised to find the furnishings in the first style of elegance and the master's suite, which Mr. Baxter insisted on giving over to them, equipped with every modern convenience.

But upon closer inspection of that gentleman when they met again for tea, she was less surprised. Mr. Baxter was quite the dandy, she realized. His waistcoat of heavily embroidered gold silk, and the elaborate arrangement of his neckcloth and carefully pomaded locks, would have pleased the most meticulous Bond Street beau.

"Stoneacres looks to be most prosperous, sir."

Mr. Baxter shrugged. "I suppose. I'm not much interested in farming, myself, but my man Grimsby is a good agent. Most of my friends reside in London, and I bolt off to the metropolis as oft as I can."

Nicholas raised an eyebrow. "Do you, cousin? A wonder I've not chanced to meet you."

"Well, Nicky, I can hardly claim to move in such exalted circles as yours," Mr. Baxter replied with a boyish grin. "And I tend to favor—" he winked at Sarah "—more, ah, bachelor entertainments."

Sarah's smile thinned. Why did she feel his every word and gesture were calculated?

"Ah, here's the butler. Feeling you would both be fatigued, I took the liberty of ordering a simple meal. Briggs, take Lady Englemere's cup, man, and don't be so slow about it. My lord and lady?" He gestured toward the door.

If he meant to impress them with the alacrity with which he was obeyed, on Sarah his curtness had the opposite effect. He was beginning to strike her as an idle, self-centered man with little thought beyond his own comfort.

The hostile look she chanced to glimpse crossing Briggs's face underlined that opinion. To her surprise, though, his aggrieved glance encompassed Nicholas as well.

Not that the butler reinforced her suspicion by any word or action. Briggs's manner was deferential, as it should be toward his actual, if absentee, overlord, and his service impeccable. But after ten years of settling household disputes, Sarah's instincts were well honed, and the impression of discord lingered.

She shrugged. If there were problems at Stoneacres, doubtless Nicholas would discover and correct them during their stay. In the meantime, tomorrow morning they would go on to Wellingford. No disquiet could dampen her excitement at seeing again, very soon, her beloved home and family.

Nicholas continued to embellish his role of doting husband. Overruling her desire to ride, he ordered a light carriage for the journey, reminding her they'd need to carry more than saddlebags, and that she tired more quickly now.

Despite her resolve, she found her caution melting in the warmth of his solicitude. But as they approached Wellingford land, the joy of seeing familiar terrain displaced all other thoughts. Finally the carriage turned at the weathered gateposts and bowled down the long drive.

Sarah held her breath as the facade came into view. The sun shining upon the expanse of mullioned windows in the central stone block seemed to flash a welcome. The carriage halted at the entry, and before the footman could even lower the stairs, her sisters, along with most of the staff, poured out to meet them.

Meredyth herded everyone into the parlor, commanded Mrs. Cummings to bring tea, banished the dogs and directed her milling sisters to their places. After refreshments, Meredyth dismissed the children to the schoolroom, warning she'd inspect their lessons later.

"Shall you mind sharing Papa's chamber?" Meredyth darted a glance at Nicholas, her face flushed. "Mrs. Cummings says the linens in the mistress's chamber are past mending. Unless you'd like your old room with me, Sarah."

"Your papa's chamber will do nicely," Nicholas answered for them. "No disrespect, Miss Meredyth, but I much prefer Sarah share my room." He winked at Meredyth.

Blushing, she smiled back. "As you wish. I'll inform Mrs. Cummings. Make yourselves at home, of course, and if there is anything you need, please let me know."

Sarah's initial euphoria had dimmed. As logical as it was that Meredyth had assumed her duties with the staff and children, it still caused her a pang to be displaced. Her disquiet deepened as they proceeded to her mother's chamber.

Suddenly she saw Wellingford as Nicholas must: the paucity of servants, the closed-up rooms and threadbare hangings, the blank walls where once paintings hung.

Lady Emily lay propped against her pillows, eyes feverbright and startlingly blue in the pale oval of her face. It seemed to cost her great effort to raise the fine-boned hand for Nicholas's kiss, and her shoulders, when Sarah hugged her, were impossibly thin.

They stayed but a few moments, and even that taxed her. Leaving the sickroom, Sarah hastened down the hallway to a small landing. Through eyes blinded by tears she gazed out over the rose garden below.

"She has failed since the wedding," Nicholas observed.

"She is dying," Sarah said flatly. "The medicine she takes, though it costs dear, only d-dulls the pain." Her voice trembling, she said fiercely, "I would have married the devil himself to make her last days easy ones."

"I hope I'm not a devil," Nicholas said, drawing her into his arms. "But do promise me one thing, Sarah."

Trying to master the tears, she looked up.

"Anything that is needed at Wellingford—the governess your sister evidently hasn't yet recalled, medicine for your mama, gowns for your sisters, anything—you'll let me see to it? 'Tis not favors you ask, sweeting. Your family is mine now. I cannot profess to love them as you do, but I wish just as fervently that they be well cared for."

Over the lump in her throat, Sarah nodded. Then impulsively, she hugged him hard. London and Chloe Ingram be damned. Whatever the reason he came, Nicholas was with her now, and she was going to treasure every moment.

Several hours later, Nicholas accompanied Sarah on a drive. She seemed to glow with purpose, Nicholas thought, as she made knowledgeable comments about sprouting crops he could not even identify, and cast an expert eye on the condition of barns, fences and hedgerows. Each time they encountered a laborer about his task, she paused to compliment work and exchange greetings, never failing to ask by name after family and kin.

As the sun was setting, Sarah stopped the carriage atop a rise. Below them lay Wellingford Hall, its sparkling windows and burnished brick set like a jewel in verdant terraced gardens. A fine wood stretched to the horizon, and in the fields crops grew near well-kept cottages.

"How grand it will be, when Wellingford is restored." She turned shining eyes to him. "Which will occur all the sooner, thanks to you, Nicholas."

"You love this place, don't you?"

"Yes. Growing up, I always thought of it as mine. Papa treated me rather like a boy, taking me fishing and hunting, letting me tag along after the steward." Her smile faded. "Until Colton was born, anyway."

"His manner changed then?"

"It wasn't just Colton's birth." She frowned. "As I got

older, I...noticed things I'd not seen before. Fewer crops being planted, needed repairs delayed. And each time Papa made a London visit, some precious object—a Restoration wardrobe, a family portrait—would vanish.''

She shook her head, her face pensive. ''I wasn't very wise at thirteen. After learning one of our best fields was to lie fallow, I took Papa to task for not being a good steward of the land and for gambling away our wealth.

'''Twas no more than I deserved when he snapped back at me.'' She sighed. ''Managing Wellingford was not, and never would be, my concern, he said. Colton would have it all. Papa was willing the land I loved with every fiber of my being to a babe still squalling in the nursery.''

She turned her gaze to the far distance. ''Wellingford isn't entailed, and I had thought surely I would be given some part of it. I was—shocked.'' Her voice faded. '''Twas the second worst day of my life.''

''What was the worst?'' he asked, curious.

Sarah started, as if just realizing she'd made that admission aloud. She remained silent so long he thought she wouldn't answer. Then she whispered, ''The day Sinjin told me we could never wed.''

Before he could gather his rattled thoughts, she gave him a cryptic smile. ''So you see, I seem to have a long history of loving what can never be mine.''

The words left his lips before he could imagine whence they came. ''I'm yours. Love me.''

She looked at him searchingly. Then she took his hand and rested it on the slight swell of her abdomen. ''I suppose, in a way, you are.''

He stepped behind her and drew her close. With a sigh, she relaxed into him. Together they stood silently watching as the sun, trailing its gold and crimson cloak behind it, set before Wellingford.

Back at Stoneacres two days later, Sarah lingered over morning tea. Nicholas had ridden to consult with the local magistrate and would be gone several hours. Perhaps she'd take that time to review the Stoneacres books. On the drive back from Wellingford, Nicholas had teasingly reminded her he was ready to begin those lessons in estate management she'd promised him.

Seeking out Mr. Briggs, Sarah ascertained that Mr. Baxter was in the study. However, the butler added in a colorless voice, 'twas his master's unfailing custom to retire there after breakfast and nap under his London paper until luncheon.

A cautious peek inside the door confirmed Briggs's information. Her husband's cousin reclined against the gold-striped settee, his stockinged feet on a cushion, his snoring breath fluttering the edges of the newspaper perched on his lavishly embroidered waistcoat.

She hesitated, then continued on to the estate office. Everything at Stoneacres, including its ledgers, belonged to Nicholas anyway. She could in good conscience inspect them without Mr. Baxter's permission.

An hour's perusal left her troubled. According to the entries, the furnishings of the manor house had been refurbished three times in as many years, including the purchase of an expensive new cookstove. In addition, a hefty sum had been entered each season under unspecified "Estate Improvements."

Acting on instinct, she called for a gig and set off for a quick inspection of the closest farms.

She returned an hour later, her vague disquiet transformed to towering rage, and went directly to the kitchen. In a puzzled voice, Mrs. Briggs confirmed the serviceable but by no means modern cookstove was the same one she'd been using for "donnamany years."

Swiftly she proceeded to the estate office. After demanding Briggs turn over all the keys, she locked it. No one, she instructed the butler, particularly not the estate agent or its manager, was to enter that office until after Nicholas had inspected it.

"My husband is a fair and kind man," Sarah told Briggs as they awaited the footmen summoned to guard the office's door and window. "He will not tolerate the abuses Mr. Baxter permitted. He will put things right, I promise."

Briggs bowed, his stern face relaxing. "Indeed, I hope so, your ladyship. And may I say how powerful glad we are to have you at Stoneacres."

Once the footmen arrived, Sarah straightened her shoulders and headed for the study. She had a few words for the dandified Mr. Baxter.

Sarah entered and cleared her throat loudly. Mr. Baxter snorted awake, fumbled the journal from his face and sat up. "Ah, Lady Englemere. Luncheon, is it?"

Sarah looked at the costly waistcoat straining over his rounded stomach, the expensive lace trimming the lavish cravat that framed his plump cheeks, and felt a wave of revulsion. "Not quite, Mr. Baxter. But I have some food for thought for you."

He looked blank, then gave her a genial smile. "Ah, yes. Have you seen this morning's London journal? The most amusing criminal conduct case—"

"Mr. Baxter, the criminal behavior I wish to discuss has occurred much closer to Stoneacres. I understand the tenants have had their rents raised *three times* these last seven years."

Mr. Baxter nodded condescendingly. "Ah, I collect you've been conversing with the laborers. A rather worthless lot, I fear. Indeed, I'd hoped to raise taxes once more, but the wretches protested they couldn't pay another groat."

"Mr. Baxter, the people are starving."

"Lady Englemere, you must know how such low persons exaggerate. Surely you've seen much worse in London."

"This is not London, Mr. Baxter. This is one of my husband's estates, and you have the care of it. In my opinion, you have grossly abused my husband's trust, and so I shall tell him.''

Baxter was speechless for a moment, and then his eyes narrowed. ''What was it my friend Lord John Weston told me? That you consider yourself something of an agriculturist?'' His false-jovial smile turned nasty. ''Ah, yes—the 'Farmer Bride.' Let me inform you, your *ladyship*—'' he spat out the title with disdain ''—Nicky has, very properly, always considered farm management beneath him. As I am a gentleman, I must caution you—though your behavior toward me hardly deserves the courtesy—not to embarrass yourself bringing to Nicky's attention matters in which he has no interest. All he cares for, I assure you, is the money Stoneacres adds to his coffers.''

''And to yours? Tell me, Mr. Baxter, although the rental receipts trebled over the years, how is it that the amount forwarded to my husband's account has remained constant? Yes, I've inspected the ledgers, so pray do not insult my intelligence by telling me 'twas invested back in cookstoves or farms.''

For an instant, fury—and then fear—transformed his face. Quickly he mastered himself and uttered a strained laugh. ''I've always heard ladies who are increasing suffer absurd fancies. 'Tis true, I see.''

''The ledger entries are not fancy, Mr. Baxter.''

He opened his mouth, then closed it. One hand went to the lace at his throat, as if he were finding his neckcloth suddenly too tight. He straightened and curved his lips in a sneer. ''Lord John was right—you are sharp-tongued. Nicky must have wanted an heir badly to have married you, for he generally prefers his ladies beautiful and sweet—like his current love, Chloe Ingram. He invited her to your presentation ball, did he not?''

Despite herself, she winced. His nasty smile deepened. ''Oh, yes, Lord John sends me all the London news. Can you imagine how they laughed after you went up to bed and Nicky came back to dance with Chloe?''

She ignored the pain lancing through her. "We were speaking of Stoneacres and your management, Mr. Baxter."

His eyes gleamed and he leaned closer. "Take my advice, little lady. Nicky never tarries long in the country. Annoy him with matters like this, and when he returns to London he's like to leave you here—permanently."

Sarah forced herself to gaze at him calmly. "You waste your time making idle threats. You would do better to prepare an explanation—if you can—for Lord Englemere. Something that might prevent his laying criminal charges."

Baxter's eyes shifted uneasily, but he remained uncowed. "I am his cousin! Nicky would never serve me so." He took a rapid step toward the door.

And stopped short as Sarah held up a key. "The office is locked, Mr. Baxter, and the windows guarded. No one will touch those ledgers until after Nicholas sees them. I believe they will speak for themselves."

Rage mottled Mr. Baxter's already florid cheeks. Hissing a violent oath, he stepped closer and raised his hand. Then he caught himself, and instead of striking her, he raked her figure from head to toe with an insulting glance. "'Tis a good thing you're so ill-favored no other man would look at you. Else, with Nicky so bewitched by Mrs. Ingram, the ton might suspect you carry a bastard."

After the wretched poverty she'd seen and the taunts about Chloe, that slur against her honor was too much. Lost in rage, Sarah slapped Baxter's face.

Both of them stood shocked in the aftermath of the blow. Slowly Baxter raised a hand to his reddened cheek. "You'll regret that," he growled, and stalked from the room.

Chapter Fifteen

When Nicholas returned two hours later, Briggs delivered him a message to meet Sarah in the study without delay. Wondering what could have prompted such an unusual summons, Nicholas hastened to the room.

He entered to find Sarah pacing, looking pale but unhurt, and released the breath he hadn't realized he'd been holding. "What's the matter, sweeting? From the note Briggs gave me, I feared you'd suffered some harm."

Sarah faced him gravely. "I'm sorry to attack you thus before you've even had your tea, but something terrible has happened. Rather, has been happening, here at Stoneacres for the past seven years or more. Something that, I hope you'll agree, Nicholas, must stop today."

He took in her grim face and agitated manner. "Sit down, Sarah. Have some wine, and tell me what has distressed you."

"Oh, Nicholas, I hardly know how to begin! I went driving this morning, and the conditions I found on every farm I saw were appalling! Cottages falling apart, men, women, children in rags, and all of them thin to emaciation. It seems Mr. Baxter has, over the past few years, trebled the tenants' rents, leaving them in virtual penury."

"That cannot be correct," Nicholas objected. "I

checked before we left London, and the income from Stoneacres has remained constant.''

''The increase wasn't transferred to the Stanhope account. As I discovered when I checked them, the ledgers show all the additional sums entered under 'Estate Improvements.' Oh, 'twas cleverly done! Should you visit Stoneacres, you would see only the bathing facilities and the fashionable furnishings. The rest of the money—a considerable sum—was supposedly expended for repairs and consumables—seed, fodder and such. I imagine Mr. Baxter doubted you'd ever inspect the farms, and even should you do so, you couldn't expect to find 'consumables' still about.''

While Sarah stopped to sip her wine, Nicholas struggled to assimilate the implications of his cousin's bookkeeping.

''Aside from improvements at the manor, there have been no repairs at all that I can tell. Not even in Wellingford at its most destitute have I seen such squalor.'' She leaned over to seize his hands. ''Oh, Nicholas, people are starving, your people! Tenants who look to you for their livelihood and protection. Your own cousin has allowed them to be overworked, beaten—in your name! That he misused Stanhope funds is bad enough, but that I cannot forgive.''

Nicholas could only gape at her. The charges appeared incredible, yet Sarah was a sensible lady who knew much of farm management. If she said these things were true, she was undoubtedly correct.

''I must tell you what I've done,'' she continued, jumping up and beginning to pace. ''After inspecting several nearby farms, I had Briggs lock the estate office. Here is the key. Then I confronted your cousin, warning him you would shortly demand an accounting.''

She turned a pleading face to him. ''Cousin or no, you must discharge him, Nicholas! The way he has treated these people is shameful! And when I think how he's muddied your name with his callous deeds—oh, were I a man, I should run him through!''

Deeply troubled, Nicholas nevertheless had to smile at her fervor. He took her hand and kissed it. ''Thank you for you defending my honor, sweet champion.'' His smile faded. ''If what you describe is true, Hugh has disgraced me and betrayed my trust. I'd best see him at once.''

''Thank you for believing me, Nicholas.'' Her fierceness fading, she looked drained and weary. ''Before you go, there is something else I must disclose, for Mr. Baxter will seek to discredit me, and is bound to tell you.''

''Tell me what, sweeting?''

Avoiding his gaze, she commenced pacing again. ''I know 'twas wrong of me, and I regretted it in an instant, but he made some—rather distressing comments, and I…I lost my temper. I'm afraid I, ah, slapped his face.''

''I beg your pardon?''

She swallowed unhappily. ''I slapped him.''

Nicholas blew out a gusty breath. ''Are you telling me my dignified, gentle wife, whom I've never heard so much as raise her voice to a lazy housemaid, slapped my cousin?''

She nodded, shamefaced. ''I'm sorry, Nicholas.''

He studied her. ''Just what 'distressing comments' did Hugh make that caused you to so forget yourself?''

''Well—I told him I'd been through the books, and he realized at once what that meant. He tried to cozen me into thinking you wouldn't care how Stoneacres was managed, as long as the money came in, and that you'd be irritated with me if I tried to interfere.'' She gazed at her foot as she tapped it on the turkey carpet. ''When I refused to be cowed, he became quite enraged. At the last, he made an—insulting remark, and I—slapped him.''

A growing outrage at his cousin's perfidy put an edge to his voice. ''What remark, Sarah? I'm sorry to be so persistent, but if my cousin insulted you, I insist on knowing what he said. 'Tis a matter of honor.''

"A matter of honor," she repeated. "In truth, it was. Could we leave it at that?" She cast him a look of appeal.

She seemed so distressed, Nicholas nearly relented, but he felt strongly that his cousin could not be allowed to insult his wife with impunity. "No, Sarah. I'm sorry, but to deal with him properly, I must know."

She inspected the toe of her half boot. When at last she spoke, her voice was so soft he could scarcely hear her. "He said that, as all the world knows how—occupied— you are with your mistress, if I weren't so plain no other man would want me, the ton might believe I carry a bastard." Hearing his explosive intake of breath, she finished gruffly, "As if I would serve you such a trick."

White-hot anger burned all thought from his brain but the primitive desire to drag his cousin to the south lawn and demand immediate satisfaction.

After a moment, sanity returned. Much as the cur deserved so dire a reckoning, he wanted no public scandal. However, he vowed, his hands balling into fists, Hugh Baxter was about to suffer far more than a simple dismissal.

Nicholas gently raised her chin. "My dear, it grieves me exceedingly that a kinsman of mine could have so vilely insulted you. He will be dealt with."

"Deal with him about Stoneacres. The other doesn't matter."

"It matters to me." He touched her forehead lightly with his lips and went out.

On leaden feet, Sarah entered the sitting room adjoining their chamber. She sank into an overstuffed chair, faintly disgusted at having to use the same objects Nicholas's despicable cousin had touched.

She had done all she could. Though Nicholas might be more at home in a London drawing room than on a Hampshire farm, he was both intelligent and fair. The ledgers told the tale only too eloquently, and once he inspected them and the land, he would be as outraged as she.

Though she told herself they were uttered in pique, and came from Lord John, a most unreliable source, Baxter's words still lashed her. So all the ton had tittered at Nicholas tucking his wife away to dally with his mistress? She staggered at the rage and anguish that image brought.

Dismiss it, she told herself sternly. *What matter if the shallow sophisticates of the ton laugh?*

But that wasn't the real reason behind her pain, she forced herself to admit. 'Twas Chloe.

How complacent she'd become here in the country, secure in Nicholas's constant escort, lulled by his assiduous attentions. How easy it had been to put the lady out of mind. Baxter's ugly insult made her confront the fact that his woman—no, Nicholas's *mistress,* was still a reality.

Honor your bargain, she urged herself. *You told him he might go his own way. You told yourself it wouldn't matter. Live up to your agreement.*

But I don't want to! her heart cried. *'Twas a bad bargain, made in ignorance. I don't want to accept it now.*

Nicholas seemed truly content here with her. Though her experience in such matters was admittedly limited, she knew beyond doubt he enjoyed her as a woman. If she could find the courage to ask, perhaps he might be willing to give up Chloe—even once they returned to London.

Her spirits leapt at the thought. And immediately plunged. Why should Nicholas give up Chloe just because he also enjoyed his wife? Unfathomable as it was to her, the men of her class seemed quite able to keep both wife and mistress. Why should she expect Nicholas to be different?

'Twas only one reason compelling enough to induce him to dismiss his longtime paramour: he would have to be in love with his wife. She would have to fill his life so completely that he found taking another woman unthinkable.

An ache of sadness and regret washed through Sarah. That circumstance was the most unlikely of all.

She took a deep breath and squared her shoulders. No matter. She could stand whatever she must, including tolerating Mrs. Ingram. Why should she wish for the unreliable love of a gambler anyway?

Ignoring the raw spot that continued to bleed inside, Sarah rang for tea. Nicholas would probably report back to her after he'd talked with his cousin. She must regain her composure. If Mr. Baxter's brutal lesson finally taught her the value of maintaining a greater distance from her far-too-attractive husband, perhaps 'twas worth the pain.

His temper as raw as his bruised fists, Nicholas stormed into the small salon. After downing the meal and a mug of foaming home brew Mrs. Briggs had waiting for him, he felt calm enough to ask after his wife. The mistress was reading in the study, the housekeeper informed him.

Sarah looked like a little girl, curled up on the sofa by the fire, he thought with a smile. His amusement faded when she glanced up and he saw the wariness in her eyes. Nor did she make room for him beside her. His ire at his cousin reviving, he took the wing chair opposite.

"Hugh will depart first thing in the morning. After I examined the ledgers, we agreed it would be to our mutual benefit were he to seek employment in some other region of England. In fact, I highly recommended emigration."

He shook his head. "I can still hardly credit it. Hugh and I grew up together. Never would I have suspected he could have— Well, trusted cousin or no, I should have kept better watch. I intend to make amends to the tenants, insofar as I can. Will you ride with me?"

The grateful look she sent warmed him to his toes. "I should be honored."

He crossed to her and lifted her fingers for a kiss.

She stiffened, and as soon as politely possible, pulled at her hand. He held on, wincing slightly, and she noticed for the first time his scraped, oozing knuckles. "Nicholas," she said with a gasp. "You—"

Apparently surmising how he'd sustained the injury, she colored and looked away. "You shouldn't have."

"Shouldn't have punished a man who so vilely insulted my wife? Were he not my cousin I might well have shot him!"

"'Twas only pique, and fear over his future."

"Then I should have shot him for stupidity, to say such a thing to his employer's wife."

"I expect he realized that employment would shortly end. And I daresay he never imagined I would repeat it. Nor would I have, had you not forced me. I should like to forget it, and my own deplorable behavior, if you please."

She gently pulled her hand from his and rose. "You'll want some quiet after such a trying interview. Mrs. Briggs said you'd dined. I'll leave you to your port."

She was retreating again, just as she had after the squid incident. Well, he had no intention this time of letting her go. "Wait, Sarah."

She halted, her back to him.

"Sarah, come here."

She looked over at him, then at the door, every taut line of her body eloquent of a desire for flight. Her eyes implored release. Implacable, he held her gaze.

With slow, reluctant steps, she walked to him.

He took her limp hand and kissed it. "I only broke his nose, but I swear to you, Sarah, had I known his vicious comments would make you shy, I would have broken his neck."

She mumbled and tried to wiggle her fingers loose.

"I'm sorry he upset you. Surely you didn't heed his ridiculous words." She said nothing, and suddenly he realized she had indeed taken them to heart.

He remembered how, before their marriage, she'd promised not to *interfere* in his life. Remembered Hal telling him Lord John had accosted her about Chloe at Lady Jersey's ball—that she'd seen Chloe giving his arm an intimate squeeze.

Anger at his cousin warred with chagrin. "You did heed them, didn't you?" he asked incredulously.

She shrugged and shook her head.

Despite his discomfort in addressing the issue, he must put this to rest for good and all. Taking her chin, he gently forced her to look up. "You should *not* heed them, do you understand, Sarah? That—other matter—is settled. You're my wife, sweeting. No one can threaten your place."

"I know, Nicholas," she said softly.

But when he drew her into his arms, she remained wooden, neither inviting nor repulsing him.

Alarm shocked through him. Never before had she failed to respond. She'd been bludgeoned with Chloe's existence several times without offering a word of reproach. Had Baxter's nasty, wounding words been the final straw?

Surely he could still reach her, too intent upon doing so to ask why immediate reconciliation was so important.

He massaged her shoulders, willing her to relax and open to him. She sighed, leaned ever so slightly into his ministering fingers. But when he pulled her closer for an embrace, she held back.

An urgent need seized him to make her yield, to reaffirm the bond between them. Hands gripping her shoulders, he kissed her forehead, her eyelids, her cheeks. "Love me, Sarah," he breathed against her lips. "Love me."

At last she softened, opening her mouth and molding her body to his. Relief swamped in a tide of panic-sharpened hunger, he swept her up and carried her to the couch.

Sarah sat down to breakfast in the dining salon in solitary splendor. Though Nicholas had been gone only a few hours, she missed him already.

After Hugh's departure last week, he had asked her to start instructing him in estate management while they awaited a replacement. One day when the post brought him a parcel of papers from London, he teased her into the library and began explaining the complicated business of investing.

Much against her inclination, she was forced to admit that, risky as some ventures undoubtedly were, the business of choosing and balancing them fascinated. Their consultations, on both agriculture and finance, became a daily routine.

She sighed. Once again Nicholas was disarming her caution. But, she told herself hopefully, the longer he remained with her in the country, the better. She didn't know much about such arrangements, but perhaps after a time Mrs. Ingram would grow weary of waiting, and look for a more attentive protector?

It was thus with the greatest reluctance she'd reminded Nicholas of Mrs. Waterman's rout party. At this annual event, Hal's mama paraded before him her preferred candidates from the current Season's crop of marriageable misses for the position of daughter-in-law. Reminding Nicholas they had pledged Hal their support through this ordeal, Sarah convinced her husband to return alone while she stayed to tend Stoneacres.

He'd seemed genuinely reluctant to leave her, and agreed to go only after much persuasion.

She grinned at the memory of some of that persuasion. Would Nicholas linger in London? Her spirits sagged at that possibility. Firmly she put Chloe Ingram out of mind.

Then she felt it again—little fluttering pains, like tiny needles pricking her. Sarah grimaced and shifted her position on the chair. The odd, darting pains recurred as she ate, though, and a low ache started in her back. Perhaps, were she to lie down awhile, it would subside.

Reaching her chamber, she encountered Becky, but fobbed off the maid's concern by claiming she needed a nap. To her surprise, Sarah did manage to sleep. She woke to a sharper pain in her belly and a heavier ache at her back. And when she used the necessary, she saw blood.

On legs gone suddenly shaky, Sarah stumbled to the bellpull and back to bed. As she waited for Becky, a stronger pain gripped her. She breathed hard, fighting it and trying to stem a concern that was rapidly approaching panic.

Becky came so promptly Sarah suspected she must have been loitering in the sitting room. "'Twas a good nap, mistress. Are you feeling better?"

Sarah made herself smile. "Somewhat. I've a curious ache at my back, though, and…and I'm bleeding a little. I'm sure 'tis nothing, but I'd like to bring Dr. MacPherson from Wellingford. Just a precaution."

Becky strode to the bed and gripped Sarah's hands. "Don't fret yourself, Miss Sarah. You stay here with your feet up and we'll fetch that doctor." She paused. "I sent word to his lordship."

"Oh, Becky, you didn't!" Sarah protested. "'Tis but a trifle, and he particularly needs to be in London tonight!"

"That's as may be, but if there's even the smallest problem, the master would wish to be here, and well you know it. Anyway, 'tis done now."

"I suppose it cannot be undone, but I'm displeased nonetheless," Sarah grumbled. "If Lord Englemere speaks sharply to you, 'twill be only what you deserve."

"Yes, my lady," Becky replied, obviously discounting Sarah's every word. "I'll wrap you up and fetch some tea."

No longer sleepy, Sarah found the hours dragged as she lay staring over a book. The ache in her back continued, and the pains were sharper and more frequent. Finally she abandoned any attempt to read and stared out at the rain-darkened sky, straining her ears for sounds of the doctor's arrival. *Please God*— she closed her eyes to pray over and over —*please God, let no harm come to my babe.*

Just as night fell, she heard the welcome sound of the

doctor's hearty Scots voice. "What's this trouble ye be havin'?" the doctor boomed as he strode into the room.

Briefly Sarah told him. He frowned and shook his head. "Yer lady mother na had a bit o' problem carryin' her babes. Bleedin', ye say? I'd best have a look."

He finished his examination, his face sober. "I'll tell ye straight, lass. There's some that bleed, and carry the babe, and some who lose it. Ye must stay abed—no getting up for anything, hear? Stay abed, and we'll see."

Fear such as she had never known clutched Sarah. "Lose it?" she whispered. She seized the doctor's hand. "Surely you can do something."

The doctor's bluff face softened. "Dinna fash thyself, lass. I've known ye since ye were a wee bairn, and knew ye'd want the truth of it. 'Tis strong ye are, and likely all will be well. But there's naught to do but stay abed and keep yer mind easy. The rest is in God's hands."

Becky's summons reached Nicholas as he sat in his study fortifying Hal with brandy for the upcoming rout. Despite Hal's initial protests, he left at once. Becky was an older, experienced woman, not given to flights of fancy. If she thought the matter grave enough to recall him, 'twas likely to be serious indeed.

Within an hour he had strapped on a saddlebag and was guiding Valkyrie through the London traffic. Worry churned in his stomach. A barn-raising had been planned, and Sarah would doubtless have supervised. Had there been an accident? Becky's note provided no details. He pressed his horse harder.

When Nicholas calculated he'd reach Sarah before nightfall, he hadn't reckoned on the driving rain that began flailing him as soon as he left the environs of London, or on the pathetic condition of the hacks he was forced to hire after Valkyrie tired. It was past dark when at last, soaked through and jarred in every limb, he beheld the torches burning on the gatehouse at Stoneacres.

Never so glad in his life to surrender anything as he was to turn over the last sorry nag to a stable boy, he half fell from the saddle and stumbled up the front stairs. Briggs opened the door before he could knock.

"So glad you've come, Lord Englemere." The butler reached up to help him out of his sodden greatcoat. "The doctor's with her ladyship now."

"No!" Sarah's anguished cry ricocheted down the stairwell and lanced through him. For a moment after the echo faded, both men stood frozen, Briggs's hands clutching the collar of Nicholas's coat. Then Nicholas stripped off the dripping garment and took the stairs two at a time.

"No," Sarah repeated in a whisper. Even before the examination the doctor had just completed, she'd known the bleeding was heavier. The pains came often, and had intensified to wrenching spasms. Still, she refused to believe it. "There must be something you can do, Doctor— anything! I'll do anything to keep this babe!"

"Sarah, child, 'tis naught ye can do but accept. 'Tis young ye are, lass. There'll be other babes."

"You don't understand. My husband needs an heir. I owe it to him. I must carry this child!"

"Sure, and all men wish for sons, lass. But ye canna stop what's meant to be." He patted her hand, his eyes sorrowful. "Rest, now. 'Twill be over by morning, belike."

He turned to Becky, who stood by the bed. "Give her laudanum for the pain." He looked back at Sarah's rigid face and sighed. "Take some and rest, lass."

This isn't happening, Sarah told herself, locking her hands over her belly as if by so doing she could ward off the catastrophic process going on there. "No," she moaned.

Becky wiped her eyes with a corner of her apron. "I'll fetch you hot tea, Miss Sarah, and be back in a twink."

But when the door opened a few moments later, it

wasn't Becky with the tray. His wet hair plastered against his head, his sodden clothes steaming in the room's warmth, Nicholas paused on the threshold. "Oh, Sarah."

Sarah closed her eyes and turned her face to the wall.

Chapter Sixteen

She heard Nicholas shut the door, felt the mattress shift as he sat on the bed beside her. "The doctor just told me. I'm so sorry, Sarah."

She couldn't bear to face him. Struggling for control, she lay with her back to him, her eyes locked on the wallpaper. At last she managed to calm her breathing.

"I'm sorry, too, Nicholas," she told him, still facing the wall. "Dreadfully sorry. You didn't need a housekeeper, for your household runs like an oiled watch, or a friend, for you've many, or a lover, as—well, no matter. Only one thing did you need from me. And I have failed to provide even that."

"Don't, Sarah!" Nicholas cried. "Calm yourself, sweeting. Such things happen, the doctor said. You must dismiss such absurd fancies and rest."

She turned then. He looked distraught, she thought with numb detachment. As well he might. He'd bought a wife dear, and had no return yet for his investment. When he continued to gaze intently at her, she realized with a small shock he was genuinely worried.

With a supreme effort, she damped down the agony scouring her. "I shall be fine, Nicholas. I'm sorry you were dragged out of London to no purpose." She managed a weak smile. "You're dripping on the bedclothes."

Nicholas studied her. Seeming reassured, he smiled back. "Let me get food and dry clothes, and I'll return."

He stepped toward the door, then halted. "I wanted to come, Sarah—'twas no inconvenience. You should know, if anything happens, my place is with you." He wet his lips as if to say something further, then closed them. After a moment he said, "I'll be back shortly."

Sarah fixed her smile in place until the door shut. Then she fell against the pillows, and with a sigh that was half groan, half sob, turned her face back to the wall.

Finally dry in borrowed clothes, for the ones he'd packed in his saddlebag were scarcely better then those he'd arrived in, Nicholas warmed himself by the kitchen fire and hurriedly downed a plateful of food. As he drained the last sip of ale, Becky came in, her tearstained face anxious.

"Will you be going up to my mistress?"

"Directly, Becky." He put down the mug. "How is she?"

Becky's lips trembled and her hands twisted the ends of her apron. "The pains be stronger now. I tried to coax her to take the laudanum, but she'll have none of it. Powerful sorry I am about the child, your lordship."

"Thank you for caring for her. And for sending word. Did she read you a scold over that?"

"Aye, a bit. But I feared 'twas this from the first, and thought you'd want to be here." Her voice broke on a sob. "Oh, my poor lamb! She wanted this babe so much."

"I'll go up and see what I can do about the medicine."

When Nicholas entered, Sarah still lay facing the wall. Though she was motionless, he knew she wasn't sleeping.

She looked so small on that big bed. Seeing her still, her air of quiet competence vanished, Nicholas realized again how fragile she was. His heart cried out at her pain, and he wanted nothing so much as to comfort her.

He eased himself beside her on the bed, took one limp hand and chafed it. "Sarah, sweeting, how can I help?"

She turned to him slowly, infinite sadness in her shadowed eyes. "Nicholas," she murmured. "You must be exhausted. A miserable ride through the rain, only to learn of the l-loss of your child."

"'Tis you who concern me. What can I do?"

"Nothing." She took a ragged breath. "There's nothing anyone can do. Go to bed, Nicholas."

Her flat, emotionless voice moved him more than tears. He fumbled with the laudanum bottle. "Sarah, at least take some medicine. 'Twill ease—"

"Go, Nicholas," she repeated in a whisper. "I'll be better by morning." She pulled her hand from his and once more turned toward the wall.

"Sarah?" He cupped her shoulder, yearning to gather her into his arms. She held herself stiffly, resisting.

"Go get some rest, Nicholas." Her muffled voice was barely audible. "Please—for me?"

He sat immobile, stricken that she refused the comfort he wanted so badly to give. Finally, though the urge to embrace her almost consumed him, he forced himself to honor her all-too-plainly stated wishes.

"All right, Sarah, I'll go. Rest, sweeting." He kissed her averted head.

Settling for maintaining a sort of vigil in the adjoining room, he had Briggs place a cot by her door and, unutterably weary, dropped onto it. He was too distraught to be surprised at the ferocity of his need to hold and console her. Only by stern effort of will did he restrain himself from sleeping by her bed.

When next he thought at all, wan dawn light filled the sitting room. He jumped up and eased her door open.

Sarah lay quietly, and he could tell by the relaxed line of her body that she slept.

She looked peaceful. Would that serenity last when she woke? Stubborn, strong-willed, courageous—under her serene demeanor she was all that, and more. But from the first, she'd been openly passionate about one thing only—giving him a son. Without doubt, she'd take this loss hard.

Stretching his cramped muscles, he went to the bellpull. He'd get a shave, put on his own hopefully-dried-by-now clothing and be ready to attend her when she woke.

"Get out! Get out and leave me alone!"

At his wife's shriek, Nicholas started so badly he cut himself. Swiping at the shaving soap with a towel, he threw down the razor and ran. "Mistress, you mustn't!" He heard Becky's voice.

"I will ride this morning, I tell you! 'Tis a morning like any other!" The sound of a chair overturning followed.

Nicholas charged through the open door and stopped short. "What the devil?"

Becky stood by the bed, weeping. Propping herself on her forearms, Sarah lay on the floor by the toppled chair.

As Nicholas entered, she looked over at him. "I will r-ride," she repeated, but her voice faded and broke. Pressing clenched fists to her head, she began to weep.

"Leave us," he barked. Sobbing, Becky hurried out.

Gently Nicholas gathered Sarah in his arms and carried her to the bed. Holding her tightly, he rested his cheek on her tangled hair while she wept with deep, wrenching sobs that cut to his heart. He held her till his arms and shoulders ached, though that paltry ache couldn't begin to approach his anguish at her misery. Finally, the sobs subsided, and he eased her back a little.

Pulling up a corner of his half-tied cravat, he wiped her tear-blotched face. "'Twill be all right, sweeting."

"W-will you h-hold me, j-just a little l-longer?"

He kissed her red, swollen eyes. "Of course."

She'd been limp in his arms before, but she clung to him now, as if he were her sole support in a crumbling world. Ignoring the protests of his already cramped limbs, he hugged her close, murmuring incoherencies until at last the tension left her and she slept. When her breathing was deep and regular, he gently laid her against the pillows.

Sarah sat over a tray several hours later with a dull sense of calm. *It's over,* she thought. *My precious babe.*

She had no more tears, for she'd cried them already— all over Nicholas, soaking his coat and ruining his cravat. *Ah, Nicholas,* she thought, sighing, *what a sorry wife I've been.*

She'd reached another equally bleak conclusion. In the solitude of her room after that bitter night, Sarah finally accepted the fact she'd been evading this month and more. Despite their unemotional bargain, despite her apprehensions about his gaming, she'd fallen in love with Nicholas.

That was why she could no longer view with detachment his liaison with Chloe Ingram. Why she missed him after a mere hour's absence, why her heart warmed and her whole being quickened when he so much as walked into the room.

Fool, fool, a thousand times fool, she told herself savagely. *How could you stupidly succumb to an emotion Nicholas doesn't want, an emotion that will make it impossible to remain the cool, detached wife he does want?*

The very idea of Nicholas in Mrs. Ingram's embrace was enough to curl her fingers into claws and tighten her chest with outrage. How could she encounter his mistress at a rout, at the opera, with even a modicum of distant courtesy, when all she wanted was to tear the woman's hair out? How could she politely send Nicholas off to his club, wondering every time he left if he were going to visit *her?* And if he should not return of an evening, how could she face him calmly over breakfast the next morning, Chloe's cloying scent on him, and not rant like a fishwife?

Sarah covered her face with her hands. Countless highborn wives managed to carry on in perfect charity with, or at least feigned indifference to, their husbands' other lives.

She had promised Nicholas she would do the same. But she couldn't—not now that she loved him.

If she'd carried the child, she might have managed. She could have channeled all the love she felt for the father into his son, absorbing herself so completely that she had little time to consider her husband's pursuits.

But now there was no babe. The idea that the arms that held her so gently while she sobbed out her grief might, in just a few hours' time, be holding Chloe Ingram, sent a lancing spear of rage and pain through her. How could she share her husband with that woman—any woman?

Would she really have to? her ever-hopeful heart asked. Had Nicholas not been passionately attentive, even after he learned she was breeding? Perhaps he was ready to dismiss Chloe. She could summon her courage, and ask.

Almost, she could believe he might pledge fidelity, if not love. But what if she were wrong? If she broke their agreement, demanded a change in the terms of their arrangement, Nicholas might be annoyed, even outraged.

She remembered his anger the night of the Sheffingdons' rout, and shuddered. She didn't want to live with coldness and distance the rest of her life. If she hadn't won his love, she dared not risk destroying their friendship.

He had bidden Chloe Ingram to her ball. All London saw the woman there, Mr. Baxter said. Kind gestures and passionate interludes could not argue away the only logical explanation for that very public display of favor.

I've settled it, Nicholas had told her. Yes, he'd settled it all right, clearly demonstrating he'd not relinquished his claim on the woman. *You're my wife, and no one can threaten your place.* He meant, of course, that he would protect and provide for his wife and children, regardless of where his attentions might wander.

What else had he said, standing there dripping on the carpet? *My place is with you.*

No ardent vow of affection, that. The statement he'd made mere hours ago would not support the faint hope that, during their country sojourn, she'd managed to capture his heart so completely he'd happily discard his mistress.

Which led to the bitterest truth of all. For if her husband had a duty to her, she owed him one as well: a son and heir. As soon as the doctor said 'twas permissible, she must try again. No matter how much her heart ached, she'd have to bid him come, listen to his love words and lie with him, knowing he might go straight from her bed to Chloe's.

Her whole bruised, heartsick being revolted. *I can't do it,* she thought, tears beginning to slide down her cheeks. *Maybe later. Next month. But not now.*

Send him back to London alone, the thought flashed into her head. *Get Dr. MacPherson to tell him I must recuperate here, and let Nicholas return without me.*

It shouldn't be too difficult—he'd never intended to remain in the country. The ploy could buy her at least a little time. Sarah set aside her tray to summon the doctor.

"Better now, are ye?" the doctor asked as he entered. "I'll be on my way, then. 'Tis nothing amiss with ye time canna heal, and I've sick ones to tend."

"I must speak with you about—healing, Doctor."

He gave her an inquiring look. Sarah took a deep breath. "Please, Doctor, will you h-help me," she said in a faltering tone, "convince my husband to return to London alone? Tell him I need peace and quiet to, ah, recover, and that it would be best for me to stay in the country. He'll be wanting to leave here immediately, and I cannot face London just yet."

"Aye, 'twould be good to avoid the fevers and congestion of the city, lass." The doctor nodded his head approvingly. "Ye should recover fully within a fortnight. Surely yer man would be willing to wait that long."

"I was thinking of a more extended stay, actually. A month or more. I'd not wish to tie him here that long."

The doctor gave her a shrewdly appraising glance. "'Tis

not uncommon to lose a first babe. In most cases, such women have no trouble after. Dinna fear to try again.''

''I know my duty, and I shall do it. But I'd like to…wait. Longer than a fortnight, at any rate.''

''Surely yer husband will understand that, too. Doubtless 'twill be difficult at first, but I think it best if ye return and get on with yer life.'' He patted her hand. '''Tis a comfort in such times to have yer man about.''

''But it isn't!'' The words burst out. Dr. MacPherson raised an eyebrow at her and waited.

She bit her lip, for the first time regretting the doctor knew her so well. He'd not press for an explanation, but if she wanted his help, she'd have to confess the whole.

Pride warred with desperation and lost. ''Ours was a marriage of convenience,'' she began, ''but over the course of it my—emotions have become rather strongly engaged.''

''And yer man's have not?''

''There's another woman,'' Sarah whispered.

''Ah.'' The doctor gave a sympathetic nod.

''Do not misunderstand—my husband is everything considerate.'' She swallowed and willed the tears away. ''But I cannot go back to London now, knowing who—what I will find there. Not yet. Please, will you help me?''

''What is it ye wish me to do, lass?''

''Just tell him my health requires an extended convalescence in the country.''

''And if he wishes to remain?''

Nicholas might well think that his duty, so she'd already prepared her argument. ''Could you not tell him I feel I've failed him—'tis true enough—and that his presence would be a constant reminder of that failure? Tell him I need some time alone to…recover my spirits.''

The doctor stayed silent so long she feared he would refuse. Finally he said, ''To my thinking, if it's his affections ye wish to engage, ye'd do best to get with child again at the earliest opportunity.''

Sarah blanched. "Oh, but Doctor—"

"There, there, dinna fash thyself. I'm but a man, and lacking in sensibility, or so my wife is always telling me. I suppose, after what ye've suffered, if 'tis solitude ye wish, ye should have it. Mind, I'm not agreeing 'tis best."

Sarah gave him a tremulous smile. "No doubt you're right, and in a week or two I'll come to my senses and pack my trunks. Thank you for giving me the choice."

He nodded brusquely. "I'll talk with yer man, and be on my way. Keep thyself safe, lass."

Weary but relieved, Sarah leaned back against her pillows. She'd have a month, perhaps more. Surely in that time, she could reconcile herself to her duty.

Nicholas was finishing his repast when Dr. MacPherson entered the breakfast room.

"I've just checked yer lady wife. 'Tis my opinion she'll make a good recovery, given time. As she has no further need of me, I'll be going."

Nicholas rose to shake the doctor's hand. "Thank you for tending her."

"No need for thanks. I've a great regard for Miss Sarah. Everyone about Wellingford does." The doctor hesitated, frowning, and motioned Nicholas back in his chair. Seating himself, he said, "I must tell ye, she's taking this hard, just as I feared. I strongly recommend ye let her stay here, or at Wellingford. Keep her out of the noise and filth of London."

"Of course. Is there anything else?"

The doctor paused a long moment. "Yers was what they call a marriage of convenience, was it not?"

Nicholas cocked his head at the unexpected question. When he thought he understood the doctor's intent, he stiffened. "It was not a love match, if that's what you are asking. I assure you, however, I hold my wife in the greatest respect and esteem."

"Never inferred ye did not. However, in such cases, the

wife is bound to feel she has failed in her duty.'' Nicholas flinched and the doctor nodded. ''Aye, I can see she's talked of it to ye. Some husbands, in such cases, can be quite brutal—'' he held up a hand when Nicholas would interrupt ''—not that I'm suggesting ye would. What I mean is, even when the husband is understanding, the wife often feels her failure strongly, as strongly as she feels grief for the child. The two feed on each other.''

''What are you trying to say, Doctor?''

''That each time she sees ye, Lord Englemere, she's remembering her failure, and thinking again of the child she lost. Having ye here is, ye might say, a constant reproach. 'Twould be better, I think, were ye to leave without her.''

''Leave her? But surely my place is here with her.''

''Not if your presence will prolong her pain.''

''Would it not be better to stay and divert her from that pain?''

''Divert Miss Sarah when her mind's set?'' The doctor sighed. ''Change the course of the Thames as easy, I'm thinking. Understand now, 'tis miracles she's used to making. Half a dozen times she's saved her family from the workhouse. Why, she was scarce sixteen the first time. Her poor papa, God rest his soul, tried to auction off some land the girls' grandmama had left them for dowries. A rare foiter it was, and whispered about the county what a shame for the lasses to be left penniless. But not for yer wife to stand by and do naught.''

The doctor shook his head and laughed. ''No, what must that halich do, but ride to the auction and tell the crowd did they buy the land, she went with it, for without dowry she was as good as ruined anyway!''

''Wait!'' Nicholas had been listening impatiently, but a vivid memory shocked him alert. ''This auction—did it take place seven years ago, near the village of Picton?''

''Aye, that would be the place.''

''But I was there,'' Nicholas burst out. ''The land

marches with a corner of Stoneacres, and my father had sent me with a sealed bid. I saw a girl ride up on a lathered horse…and talk the buyers out of bidding! That was Sarah?''

"Aye. Ye did not recognize her?''

"I never saw her up close.'' Nicholas gazed out the window, watching in his mind's eye as a tall girl in a faded cotton dress, hair hidden under a chip straw bonnet, climbed the stile. Bracing herself, she confronted the curious, gawking buyers like a warrior defending the ramparts.

"What a Trojan she was. I was too far away to hear every word, but she convinced them. When the auctioneer insisted on proceeding, not a single man bid. The caller was furious, and stormed over for my father's offer.'' Nicholas smiled. "I tore it to pieces in front of him. What a risk she took!''

"Aye. Right fearless she was—'twas the talk of the neighborhood, some holding as 'tweren't fitting for a well-bred lass to put herself forward so. Most, though, thought her resourceful, and uncommon brave.''

"Yes. She's surely that.''

"So ye see, my lord, having done the near-impossible, 'tis powerful hard for her to accept she's failed in this. 'Twill take time for her to forgive herself and go on.''

"You truly think it better if I just abandon her here? I tell you, Doctor, that flies in the face of both duty and inclination.''

"Let's just say 'twould make the lady easier in her mind. 'Tis not the body that worries me, 'tis her spirits.''

Nicholas sighed heavily. Every instinct told him to stay, and he wanted desperately to help soothe the grief he'd seen in her eyes and felt in her anguished body. But if the doctor, who had known Sarah much longer than he, felt he should not remain…

Defeated, he said, "I suppose I must leave, then.''

The doctor nodded. "Don't be fretting yerself, my lord.

Yer lady wife is resilient, in body and spirit. Give her but some time, and she'll come back, and I daresay present ye with a brace of sons ere long.''

''Sons I would have, but 'tis Sarah that concerns me now. Thank you for your advice, Doctor.''

As he was mounting the stairs, another memory recurred, and his hand clenched on the balustrade. He saw a second rider galloping up *ventre à terre* on a lathered horse…reining in at the fence rail…leaping from the saddle and pulling the girl down. From his gestures, and the murmurs of the dispersing crowd, Nicholas had surmised the newcomer was a brother giving the girl a thundering scold. Until she threw herself in the lad's arms and kissed him passionately. He'd chuckled, thinking the young lovers would soon be making use of that dowry.

He didn't chuckle now. After leading the girl apart, the young man came to thank him for destroying his bid. The handsome youth's skin was fairer, his hair a lighter ash. Still, Nicholas had no doubt the grateful suitor had been St. John Sandiford.

Surely the captain would visit his mother before returning to the army—and Sarah would be here, just a few hours' ride away. When he heard of her tragedy, would he ride *ventre à terre* to her, as he'd ridden to her rescue that day long ago? Would Sarah welcome his comfort?

Another image flashed in his head: Sarah sitting in his garden, weeping over a gold signet ring.

Chapter Seventeen

Nicholas sat at the desk in his London library, his eyes on a book but his thoughts back at Stoneacres. Three weeks after his return, he still felt uneasy and displaced.

Sarah had been so cool and distant when he went to see her after the doctor left, her face a blank mask, her manner that of the ice maiden they'd once joked about. He might have thought her angry with him for some unknown misdeed, had it not been for the stark agony in her eyes.

An agony that called to him to discard the doctor's advice and take her in his arms. To nurse her back to health, then to ride and joke and laugh with her, warm her in his bed, until the misery faded and she began to forget.

But when he took her hand, she drew back, as if anticipating a blow. Shocked, he merely stood there while she slowly pulled her fingers free.

She wouldn't look at him. Her voice as distant and impersonal as her manner, she stared at some point beyond him and said, politely as if to a stranger, that she was sorry to have been such a burden and she would try to make it up by tending Stoneacres until a new manager arrived. Of course, she had no desire to tie him to an invalid in the dull fastness of the country—he must return to London as planned. She wished him a safe journey. Pleading fatigue, she leaned back upon her bed.

He sat with her after dinner, but his one-sided conversation lagged and finally died out altogether. She lay silently, her eyes fixed straight ahead, and never once looked at him.

There was no need for words. Her rigid body and averted eyes said only too eloquently, "I don't want you here."

So the next morning he left. She was sitting, motionless and silent, a book on her lap, in the window seat that overlooked the drive when he came to say goodbye. She turned her face to take his kiss on her cheek instead of her lips. As he rode away, he saw her there still, silhouetted against the light of the opened window. She didn't wave.

Almost, he could have been angry with her, except the look of numb misery had intensified, rather than diminished with the passing hours. To his dismay, she was retreating ever further into some private world of grief.

Why could she not have accepted the comfort he wanted so badly to give? It was his loss, too. Surely she could not believe he would reproach her. And if, in the raw grip of grief, she couldn't yet bear the thought of conceiving another child who might expose her to similar pain, did she not imagine he could understand that, too? Did she think him so unfeeling he could not restrain himself until she was ready? Why must she reject him?

As Lydia had.

But then, 'twas not the same. Lydia left him for spending too little time with her. In her frantic search for frivolity, she had ever needed to be the center of attention. Sarah, so much stronger and more independent, chose to bear her burden of grief and pain alone. Or at least, without *his* help.

Would she let Sandiford mourn with her? As well he might, since until Sarah delivered sons the captain had forsworn any claim on her.

The captain's lands marched with Wellingford, not so very far from Stoneacres. Was he there even now, holding her weeping against that broad, blue-coated shoulder, as Nicholas had held her the morning after she lost the babe?

He slammed the book shut. *Stop it,* he told himself furiously. *You'll drive yourself mad.*

With a sigh, he jumped up and paced to the window. The dull gray fog swirling outside matched the restlessness within. When he'd first returned, still smarting from Sarah's cold dismissal, he'd contemplated seeking out Chloe. The briefest of reflections revealed he now found the idea of bedding Chloe—or indeed any other woman—distasteful.

He sat down straightaway to pen a cordial farewell note. Charging his secretary to deliver it personally, along with a handsome sum of cash, he dismissed Chloe from his life with no regrets.

Nicholas traced a raindrop's pattern along the window glass. He could look up Hal, or perhaps go work off his fit of the dismals at Jackson's. Invitations to an assortment of dinners, routs and musicales sat heaped on his correspondence tray, but he could muster no enthusiasm for any of them. Perhaps he would dine at his club.

Nicholas smiled grimly. In the inscrutable way servants have, the household had learned of his loss, and upon his return, Glendenning had expressed the sympathy of the entire staff.

Though the starchy butler would probably have choked before allowing any sign of emotion to cross his face in the presence of outsiders, when he saw his master had returned without the mistress, he unbent enough to express surprise, and then shock when he discovered Nicholas meant to leave Sarah in the country for some weeks. The butler's clear disapproval had speedily been conveyed throughout the household. He could dine at home without fearing the horrors of burnt roast and cold potatoes, but did Glendenning not pride himself on his standards, Nicholas half suspected such might be his fare.

'Twas bad enough, he thought sourly, to have one's wife

send one away, without then having to suffer one's household treating one like an insensitive boor.

No, his club didn't appeal. What he needed was Sarah. He'd given her almost a month of doctor-recommended solitude. Perhaps he should go to Stoneacres and fetch her.

The idea brought a rush of excitement, as quickly dashed. What would he do, should he arrive and find that look of cool reproach still on her face? A stabbing pain lanced through him at the thought. No, having been so definitely dismissed, he'd not return unbidden.

Then a happy idea broke through his despondency. Sarah seemed to find solace in the country—why should not he? Not at Stoneacres, if she didn't want him, but at the Hall. He could, he hoped, count on a warm welcome from his mother. More than that, Mama had lost two babes herself. Mayhap she would know what he could do to reach Sarah.

The idea touched some chill, aching spot in his heart and warmed it. Feeling better than he'd felt in three weeks, he decided to depart on the morrow.

"Nicky, darling, how wonderful to see you!" Emerging from his embrace, the dowager held him at arm's length, her lovely eyes scanning his face. "Where is Sarah? Is something wrong? I thought you said she was recovering."

"She is, as far as I know." He released her hands and paced past the tapestry frame to the morning room window.

His mother seated herself on the brocade sofa and patted the place beside her. "Come, Nicky, and tell me what is troubling you."

He laughed shortly and ran a hand through his hair, disordering the carefully brushed locks. "Is it so obvious? I expect it is to everyone. I'm afraid my care-for-nothing society image is in the process of being ruined."

She raised an eyebrow at the bitter edge in his tone and paused, as if uncertain how to continue. "Is it the loss of the child? As I wrote in my note, I was so sorry to hear of it.''

He acknowledged her sympathy with a nod. "Partly, though it's difficult to grieve over what was scarce more than an idea. Sarah had been breeding for but a few months. No, it's Sarah herself who concerns me.''

She handed him a sherry and he took a sip, struggling for the right words. "She's always handled everything with consummate composure. Even Findlay, and he's as nasty a business as I'd ever care to meet. I expected the baby's loss would disappoint her. I was disappointed myself. But she was much more than that—she was devastated.''

"Oh, Nicky," the dowager said, a catch in her voice. "My son, no pain in life approaches the loss of a child!'' She patted his hand, remembered sorrow in her eyes. "Sarah will grieve—'tis only natural. A mother must, whether she loses her child at two, or twenty, or before birth.''

"'Tis more than that.'' Nicholas paced to the fireplace and held out his hands to the flames. He dreaded broaching the rest of his dilemma, truly didn't know how to begin. His mother waited patiently. Sighing, he turned to her.

"Sarah's taken this ridiculous idea in her head that she failed me. That our marriage brought her every advantage, and she had but one boon to offer me—an heir. And she has failed to provide it.''

"Ah—'' his mother nodded "—well, in simple terms, 'tis true. You married for an heir, and she to rescue her family. Not an uncommon bargain, but a bargain nonetheless. My marriage to your father was a love match, so I can't pretend to know how Sarah feels, but I think I can imagine.''

"When I reached Stoneacres that first night, she was lying alone in her chamber, her face to the wall. She wouldn't even look at me.'' Staring into the fire, he felt a pang of remembered anguish. "She said I'd needed only

one thing from her, a son. She apologized for being such—
and these are her words—a 'sorry bargain' of a wife.

"Lord, Mama!" The words burst from him. "She was
in such pain, and I didn't know what to say! 'Quite, my
dear, but I hold you in respect and esteem'?" He kicked
savagely at a log on the grate, sending sparks flying. "Paltry, don't you think, in the face of her grief?"

"So you came back to London," his mother said softly.

"No! Did you think I just abandoned her for the diver-
sions of the city? Mayhap you do, since even my own
butler seems to believe that. Well, it's not true—rather the
opposite. She sent me away, Mama."

When his mother made no comment, he continued,
"She even got the doctor, an old stick of a Scotsman
who's known her practically all her life, to add his bit.
Insinuated I might chide her for failing in her duty, the
impertinent sawbones! Well, I set him straight. He seemed
to believe me, but said Sarah couldn't accept or forgive
herself, yet." He drew a ragged breath. "He said just looking at me shamed her. That I should give her time to
grieve, and heal."

"Poor child," the dowager murmured. "His advice
sounds sensible, Nicholas. She probably just needs time."

"But it's been nearly a month! How much longer can
she need?" He leaned his hands on the hearth, focusing
on his own signet ring winking in the firelight. "She's my
wife, Mama. If she's distressed, I should be with her."

"From what I know of Sarah, she'd not want you to
stay out of duty."

Nicholas smiled wryly. "You'll not let me off so easily,
will you? All right, I admit it. I miss her, Mama. True, the
household runs smoothly enough, but 'tis somehow…
different without her. And I don't mean only Glendenning's disapproval."

He looked back at the fire, his lips curving of their own
accord into a smile. "It's not just that she makes me comfortable, though she caters to my wishes far too much.

There's a kind of—serenity—about her, and yet, at the most unexpected moments, such fire as well. She's so easy to be with, almost like a man who knows when to speak and when to be silent. We are friends, as I'd hoped we would be.''

He drained the last of the sherry. ''The staff misses her, too. Not a day goes by that someone, from the butler to the lowliest tweeny, doesn't ask if I've had word of her return.'' He laughed shortly. ''Glendenning positively quivers with disapproval every time he greets me.''

''Why don't you go fetch her?''

Uncertainty, distress and resentment swirled in him as it had so often this past month. ''I don't know if she'd receive me,'' he admitted, and felt a pang at that avowal.

''I see.''

He looked back at her and was shocked to find a little smile on his mother's face, so inappropriate to the gravity of the moment that anger stirred. Then the smile vanished, and she said, ''Would you like me to visit her for you?''

''Would you?'' Irritation forgotten, Nicholas strode over and seized her hands. ''Would you go to Stoneacres? Her notes say she is recovering, but I cannot be easy about her. Would you check her for me and find out—well, you'll know how to go about it discreetly—if she's ready to come home?'' He kissed her fingertips and released them. ''Tell her I miss her,'' he added gruffly.

''Excellent,'' his mother said, rising in a swirl of skirts. She returned his sharp look with a guileless one. ''Excellent notion, I meant. I'll be happy to carry a note for you, that you might tell her yourself. And now, you must excuse me. It seems I have a journey to prepare for.''

Nicholas caught her up in a fierce hug. ''Thank you, Mama. I know you won't fail me.''

She touched his cheek with a finger and gave him a faintly amused smile. ''Certainly not, dear son. After all, what are mothers for?''

* * *

Three days later, when Sarah returned from riding to the village, Briggs informed her the Dowager Marchioness of Englemere had come to visit.

Surprised and curious, Sarah smoothed her windblown braids. She felt a stir of foreboding. What brought Nicholas's mother all the way to Stoneacres? Had something happened to Nicholas? A shock of fear pierced her. She whirled and ran down the hall.

"Lady Englemere," she said as she burst into the morning room. "What a delightful surprise! I'm sorry I was out when you arrived. Everything is well, I trust, with you, and—and Nicholas?"

"Sarah, dear. Yes, we're both fine." Her mother-in-law came over to envelop her in a hug. Enormously relieved, Sarah returned it warmly.

The dowager looked at her appraisingly. "Have you fully recovered? I was so sorry to hear about the babe."

Sarah swallowed the lump in her throat. Even now, it was impossible for her to talk about it. She nodded.

The dowager had been watching her face. Her lips trembled and her eyes brimmed over. "Oh, my dear," she murmured, and drew Sarah back into her arms.

I will not weep, Sarah told herself fiercely. *Weeping cannot change things, and I will not weep.*

Despite her best efforts, a few disobedient drops leaked out the corners of her eyes. "Sorry," she said gruffly, swiping at them with a trembling hand.

The dowager led Sarah to the sofa. "You needn't apologize, Sarah. I've lost three children, you know. A babe, a man, and one before b-birth." Her voice wobbled. "'Tis the most crushing blow life can deliver."

Sarah thought of the pain she felt, multiplied by three. Suddenly her grief seemed less overwhelming. "I'm sorry, I didn't know."

"Nicky didn't tell you? I suppose it didn't occur to him. Much as he may love his children, a man cannot know how it feels to carry a child under his heart. But men do grieve, you know. Nicky surely is.''

Sarah looked away. "I'm so sorry I—"

"You didn't fail him, Sarah, though I understand how you might think so. When I lost my first, I considered it the most monstrous injustice in the world. Any ignorant housemaid could carry a child—indeed, unmarried ones had a habit of doing so with alarming frequency. Yet for all my health and wealth and desire, I could not do that for the husband I adored.''

Sarah could sympathize only too well, but dared not say so. "It is difficult,'' she said finally.

"I know just how difficult. Time will dull the pain. But Sarah,'' she said gently, compassion in her eyes, "nothing will take it away. Not blaming yourself, or hiding away in the country. I don't wish to interfere, but I tell you from bitter experience, you must accept your loss and go on. God willing, you'll have other babes.''

Sarah could hardly tell Nicholas's mother that 'twas the idea of sharing her son in such intimate creation that prevented her doing just that. "I...I don't feel ready.''

"Nicky is worried. And he misses you, Sarah.''

A dull ache squeezed Sarah's heart. "Did he send you?''

"Yes. Not that I haven't been concerned, but I wouldn't have intruded, had he not asked. He's suffering, perhaps more than you can guess. You see, he's taken this absurd notion you can't tolerate the sight of him.''

"I can't—'' Sarah gasped. She felt a pang of guilt. "But 'tis ridiculous! 'Twas my fault, mine alone!''

"'Twas no one's fault, Sarah. But if you're not angry, will you not go back to him?''

You don't understand, she wanted to shout. *I can't go back and be the meek, disinterested wife he wants. The jealous, possessive shrew I've become he wouldn't want.*

She put a trembling hand to her cheek. "I can't,'' she whispered, rebel tears escaping again. "Not yet. He is dearer to me than you can imagine, and I would hate to cause him a moment's anxiety. You must tell him that!''

The dowager stared at her for a long moment. ''Has Nicky ever talked about Lydia?''

''Lydia?'' Sarah asked, startled. ''His late wife?''

The dowager nodded.

''No, ma'am. Clarissa told me that after she died in an accident he mourned her for years. Nicholas has never mentioned her and I—I didn't wish to pry. He must have loved her very much.''

Again the dowager sat silent. Finally, with a sigh, she began, ''Nicky never speaks of her. Only his two closest friends know, and 'tis not my story to tell, but I think it important that you hear it.''

Mystified, Sarah watched the dowager rise and pace to the window, distress clear in her face. She turned back to Sarah. ''Yes, Nicky mourned, but not just for the reasons you think. You see, when Lydia's carriage overturned, she was leaving Nicholas.''

''Leaving him?''

''Yes. She was unhappy in their marriage, apparently, and left a note saying she went to one who loved her more. He set out after her, and came upon the wrecked carriage.''

Incredulous, Sarah shook her head. ''I cannot imagine any sane woman leaving Nicholas.''

That earned her a smile. ''Nor can I, darling Sarah. But Lydia,'' she spat out the name with distaste, ''apparently found some nameless soldier—Nicholas never learned who—more to her fancy.''

She strode from the window to grasp Sarah's hands. ''Can you not see? The situation is scarcely the same, except that once again, someone he cares deeply about has turned him away. He's my son, Sarah, and I feel his pain.''

Agonized, Sarah gasped. ''But I never meant...! How could he think...?''

''You couldn't have known. And Nicholas does understand, at least in his head, your need to grieve alone. It's been a month now. Perhaps 'tis unfair of me to ask, but if you truly care for him, could you not try to put aside some of that grief and go back to my son?''

Nicholas, rejected by the wife he loved. Nicholas, betrayed and abandoned. The enormity of it exceeded the bounds of comprehension. But anguish she could understand, and his pierced her to the core. ''Oh, N-Nicholas,'' she whispered, her voice breaking on a sob.

The dowager hugged her close, and when she released Sarah her own eyes were wet. ''Forgive me, I didn't mean to distress you further. I won't press. Consider returning with me, 'tis all I ask.''

She dabbed at her face with a lace handkerchief, started to put it in her reticule and stopped. ''I nearly forgot! I have a letter from him for you. And the latest London papers.''

She pulled the articles out of a large embroidered bag beside the reticule. ''I'll leave you in private to read them. Now I should like to rest before tea.''

Sarah remained in the study, still struggling to accept the dowager's incredible information. Then a shocking thought sent her flying to her feet.

Lydia had left Nicholas—for a soldier. Whatever must he have felt about her reunion with Sinjin?

Even a husband with no particular apprehensions would have been less than happy with the situation. She could not begin to imagine the dismay it must have caused a man whose wife had run off to a soldier.

He'd seemed stiff around Sinjin, but not more than she would expect of a husband dealing with his wife's former suitor. Other than that, never by word or deed had he displayed the anxiety or resentment he doubtless felt.

Gamester that he was, Nicholas must have accepted the risk inherent in remarriage as the cost of fulfilling his duty. But nothing she had endured in the past or feared for the future could compare to the gamble he had taken in trusting her to behave honorably about Sinjin.

He had shown rare courage and consideration. She owed him no less. Whether or not he would ever love her, despite the situation awaiting her in London, she must return.

Three days later Sarah saw her mother-in-law off to London. During the remainder of her short visit, the dowager did not once refer to the matter of Sarah accompanying her, nor did she show a single sign of reproach when Sarah confirmed she would stay on alone.

Just until the new estate manager, due the end of the week, settled into the job, Sarah had assured her. 'Twould give her at least ten more days to prepare herself.

Sarah wandered into the library and picked up the London paper, but her eyes wouldn't stay on the page. She'd kept her sorrow close in a sort of righteous anguish. Yet rare was the woman who saw more than half her babes grow to adulthood. Who was she to shut herself away, as if she alone had ever suffered such a loss?

Nor, selfishly wrapped up in her own misery, had she ever thoughtfully considered how Nicholas must feel. No, she'd discounted his grief as mere disappointment. Then, unable to stomach keeping the bargain she herself had made, she'd banished him, compounding one failure with another.

It shouldn't have taken the dowager's heartrending history to make her realize how her dismissal could wound her husband. Worse yet, in her selfish preoccupation, she'd ripped open the scars of betrayal. "Oh, Nicholas," she whispered, a tear sliding down her cheek, "never would I wish to deepen your pain."

Unquestionably she owed it to Nicholas, as well as to duty, to return to London. Somehow she would just have to tolerate Chloe Ingram.

Chloe, with her hand possessively on Nicholas's arm, smiling with satisfaction as she patted the magnificent rubies adorning her equally magnificent bosom. Sarah slammed her mind shut against the image.

Her restless fingers rustled the paper in her lap. With a sigh, she scanned it. One name seized her attention.

Sir James Findlay, the entry said, had the pleasure to announce his engagement to Miss Angela Buxley, daughter of Baron Buxley of Windfeld Manor, Kent.

Sarah sat up straight, running through her mind a catalog of the Season's debutantes. Then a face came to view, and consternation gripped her. She saw a pale, slender girl with long golden curls and a gentle, almost frightened expression that made her look younger than her years. A girl with a gamester father deep in debt.

Sarah closed the paper and looked down to the scar at her wrist. She smelled again the stench of hot candle wax and scorched flesh, felt the agonizing rasp of Findlay's tongue against the raw wound, heard him warning her to submit. She remembered with a sickening shock the vile practices he'd described to her on her wedding day.

At the time, she'd had only a hazy idea what he meant, but as a bride of several months her images of what Findlay's wife could expect were revoltingly clear.

'Tis none of your affair, part of her argued. *The girl has parents to protect her.* But Sir James could be charming when he wished—only see how he'd turned Lady Beaumont up sweet. And if the father were drowning in debt, and the girl had been pressed to do her duty, she might be too frightened to tell them what her suitor was like.

That Findlay had revealed something of his nature to Miss Buxley, Sarah had no doubt at all. He'd feed on the terror he could inspire in her.

A cold calm descended on Sarah. Ready or not, she must go to London the minute her bags were packed.

If her sense of obligation to Nicholas had nearly been enough to push her into returning immediately, this announcement made it imperative. She could not live with her conscience if she let Sir James marry such a vulnerable innocent without doing everything possible to prevent it.

Chapter Eighteen

In the late afternoon two days later, Sarah's traveling coach pulled up at Nicholas's London residence. The footman handed her out, and with a deep breath, she walked up the steps.

At her rap, Glendenning opened the massive door. His eyes lit and his austere face creased with the hint of a smile. "Lady Englemere! Come in out of the chill!"

He bustled her in and helped her out of the traveling pelisse. "Your message must have gone astray, for we didn't expect you. May I say, 'tis a pleasure to have you home."

"Thank you, Glendenning. I didn't send a message. My decision to travel was rather—sudden." She ignored a sniff from Becky, who passed by with her jewel case. The maid, until finally silenced by Sarah, had nattered on at length that, much as she approved Sarah's decision to return, the mistress should have sent for her husband's escort.

In truth, Sarah was so uncertain about Nicholas's reception she'd not dared send a note. What if he had grown so…comfortable with his London arrangements he preferred she remain in the country?

"What's all the commotion, Glend—Sarah!"

Nicholas stopped short and stared at her. Cursing herself

for a fool but unable to help it, Sarah stood there like a looby, drinking in every dearly remembered detail of her husband's handsome face.

The crisp dark hair she loved to curl her fingers in. The deep green of his eyes that sometimes glowed like molten emeralds. The sensuous lips that could make her thoughts dissolve into longing.

She forced herself to look away. Shocked he certainly was, but when that faded would he be pleased—or angry?

"Are you weary, my dear? Should you like to refresh yourself, or can you take tea with me?"

His voice sounded welcoming. Though her hair could stand brushing and she felt the dust of the road, she'd not had her fill of gazing at him. "I'm not tired, Nicholas."

"Tea in the morning room, then, Glendenning." Taking her arm, he led her in.

"When Mama left yesterday, she warned not to expect you for several weeks. You should have let me know you'd changed your mind, Sarah. I would have come to fetch you."

"You're not angry I returned?"

"Angry? No! I'm delighted!" He raised her hand and kissed it. "I've missed you, Sarah."

"Have you?"

"Very much indeed." At the quiet intensity of his voice, she could not help but look up. And met an equally intense gaze whose warmth was unmistakable. With a little cry, she went into his arms.

He murmured her name and held her fiercely, his cheek against her hair. So sweet was it to be in his embrace, she wasn't sure how long they stood thus, but after a time he moved her back an arm's length.

"Does this mean I'm forgiven?"

"Forgiven? For what?"

"Whatever sin I committed that made you banish me." Guilt flushed through her. "Don't be nonsensical. I didn't wish to tie you to an invalid's bed. I'm a terrible patient, I must confess. And you prefer London.''

''I'm not so sure. You were beginning to teach me a great appreciation for country matters, and studies, and—''

The pain cut so deep, she could scarcely breathe. ''Don't, sweeting,'' he cried, consternation on his face.

She forced a wobbly smile. ''I'm all right, truly. It's just that I d-did—'' she made herself say the words ''—so want to give you a s-son.''

With infinite tenderness he kissed away the one tear that escaped the corner of her eye. ''You will, Sarah. I'll take great pains to ensure it.'' And then he was kissing her forehead, her cheeks and finally her mouth.

Any thought of maintaining distance vanished. With all the hunger of love long denied, she kissed him back.

Sometime later she vaguely heard the sound of a throat being cleared. Nicholas pulled away, and blinking in bemusement, she saw Glendenning with a tea service, James bearing another tray beside him. Judging by the grin on the footman's face, they must have been there some time.

With a grimace that might have been annoyance, Nicholas guided Sarah to the sofa.

Glendenning followed with the tea. ''Not knowing how long ago you'd had sustenance, your ladyship, Cook took the liberty of sending along more substantial refreshment.'' The butler gestured to the overladen tray James was depositing.

Sarah looked at the assortment in awe. Cold ham and roast beef, three kinds of cheese, fresh biscuits, jam, honey, scones, cherry tarts and an assortment of fruit met her astonished eyes. No macaroons, however.

''Cook must not believe I took nourishment the whole of my stay at Stoneacres!'' She smiled at Glendenning. ''Tell her it looks delicious, and I thank her for her concern.''

''All the staff have been concerned, if I may be permitted to say so, your ladyship. Very happy we all are to have you safely back with us.''

Sarah felt a lump in her throat. ''Thank you, Glendenning. I'm very happy to be here.''

The butler and footman withdrew, leaving them to their feast. As they ate, Nicholas regaled her with what had been going on in society during her absence. He did not, she noted, mention Sir James Findlay's engagement.

When they'd finished their tea, he came to sit beside her on the sofa. ''Are you happy to be back, Sarah? I hope so. For I'm devilish happy to have you here.'' He took her hand and kissed it. ''I trust you've gotten over the absurd idea you failed me. Such things happen, as Mama surely told you. I still consider myself the most fortunate man in England to have married you.''

Joy, pain and a wild hope she tried hard to restrain surged through her. ''Thank you, Nicholas,'' she whispered.

''Sarah, I may be only a man, but I have some idea how difficult this has been for you.'' He cleared his throat. ''I want to assure you, I won't…ask anything of you until you're ready.''

Feeling unaccountably shy, she looked away. Though she'd not expected he would force himself on her, she was nonetheless touched. Over her days of packing and travel, however, she'd decided that it was foolish to deny herself any longer the pleasure and comfort of intimacy with him.

Fiercely she pushed aside the thought of Chloe Ingram. While Nicholas loved her, he was hers alone, and she'd been stupid to forgo that ecstasy simply because she could not have him exclusively. Besides, perhaps the doctor was right, and if there were another child…

But first, she must deal with Sir James Findlay.

Reluctantly breaking their warm intimacy, she asked, ''What entertainments are planned this evening? Would your hostess be offended to accommodate an extra guest?''

''Hardly, when that guest is my wife. But are you sure

you wish to go out? You've had a long journey, and so recently after—well, I don't want you tiring yourself.''

"I'm fully recovered, Nicholas. And after living in London, the country can get a bit dull.''

She told that plumper with barely a quiver. 'Twas true for some people, even if it was not her own opinion, she silently justified herself.

"Certainly we'll go out if you wish it, sweeting. Hal's coming to dine. We've cards for several functions, Lady Richardson's ball being the most important.''

Clare had once informed her nothing less than a deathbed illness would keep a member of society from this exclusive fete, whose invitation list was sometimes laughingly described as the membership roll of the haut ton.

Surely Findlay, who prided himself on his lineage, would be there—with his betrothed and her parents.

"I think I should like that, if you care to go. Clare's told me so much about it.''

"If we're to attend, you must rest before tonight.'' Nicholas kissed her hand one more time and retained it, as if reluctant to let go. "Hal arrives at eight. Shall I walk you up?''

Reveling in his touch, Sarah could not force herself to refuse. "Thank you, I should like that.''

Nicholas tucked her hand in his arm and went slowly up the stairs, as if he feared a more vigorous pace might overcome her. After escorting her to her sitting room, he rang for Becky. He glanced toward the door of the adjoining bedchamber, and his eyes took on a well remembered glow.

Sarah felt her pulses quicken, but Nicholas straightened. He took a deep breath, then made her a bow. "I'll leave you to Becky's care. Rest well, sweeting.''

Sarah watched him go with regret. Tempted as she was to give him some signal she was ready for the interlude his heated glance promised, she did need to rest. More important, she needed to plan.

Given his opinion of the man, Nicholas would doubtless want her to avoid the baronet. Sarah had thus decided to attempt resolving the matter of Findlay's marriage unassisted. As wedding plans were already in train, she must begin tonight.

Sarah found it easier than anticipated to get a private chat with Miss Buxley. Spying the young lady headed for the withdrawing room, she sped after her.

As they reached the corner, Sarah bumped into the girl. "Oh, how clumsy of me. I do beg your pardon!"

Miss Buxley turned to her a pale, blue-eyed face even younger than Sarah remembered. "'Twas nothing."

"Miss Buxley, is it not? I'm Lady Englemere," Sarah offered a hand and a friendly smile. "I've just returned to town. Let me congratulate you on your engagement."

Was it a trick of the light, or did the girl pale? "Thank you, Lady Englemere."

"You might know that before my marriage, Sir James was much in my company. I came to know him rather well."

The girl shot her a glance from under a heavy fringe of lashes. Sarah saw caution—and fear. "You did?"

"Yes. Forgive my bluntness, and any offense this might cause you, but do you wish to marry him?"

The girl's lips trembled and she looked away. "'Tis a good match, Mama says. He will make a handsome settlement."

"'Tis shockingly intrusive of me, but I was very nearly compelled to marry Sir James. I *know* him. And so I ask again—do *you* wish to marry him? Trust me, please!"

"No, I don't wish it!" the girl burst out, and clapped a hand over her mouth. She looked around wildly, as if afraid someone might overhear. "No," she repeated, "but what can I do?" Her face crumpled. "He—he frightens me!"

Silent sobs shook her slender shoulders. Sarah looked

at the childish face with its flaxen curls, the delicate frame, and knew whatever it required, she could not allow Findlay to get control of this innocent.

"I told Mama." Miss Buxley raised tear-spangled eyes. "She just said all brides suffer from nerves, and if I pleased Sir James, he would treat me well." The girl paused, mingled fear and loathing in her face. "But I don't want to do—what he said."

A bolt of pure rage tempered Sarah's concern. The despicable sadist. Could he not choose a more worthy adversary? This poor child wouldn't last a fortnight.

"They can't force you to marry him, you know. 'Twill be difficult, but simply tell your father you will not have him. Lovely as you are, you must have other suitors."

"But none so rich." The girl sighed unhappily. "And Sir James gave Papa a large sum of money when the betrothal was announced, he told me. So that I should not think to cry off." She twisted her handkerchief between her fingers.

"Tell your papa what Sir James said you must do."

"I could never!" Miss Buxley gasped, scarlet flushing her pale face. "I did *try* to tell him I could not like Sir James, Lady Englemere, but he only said I should be a good girl, and not bother him, and sent me off to Mama. I want to be a credit to Papa, but—but I can't please Sir James." She gave a helpless sob. "And they will not listen."

Frowning over the golden head, Sarah patted the girl soothingly. Clearly, she was too weak-willed to flatly refuse Findlay. Sarah would have to approach her parents.

"Don't despair, Miss Buxley." She handed over a fresh handkerchief. "I shall contrive something."

"Oh, Lady Englemere, if only you could!" Miss Buxley clasped her hand fervently. "Sir James mentioned you to me, you know." A puzzled look crossed her guileless face. "He said you owed him a debt, but I would repay it. I cannot imagine what he meant."

A chill ran through Sarah. The ton had followed Findlay's assiduous courtship of her, had doubtless snickered over her last-minute preference for Nicholas. A man of his pride could not forgive that.

That he might take out his rage on this child sickened her. Without doubt, she must prevent their marriage.

Being a marchioness had its advantages, Sarah thought ruefully. Miss Buxley's mama was only too happy to stroll with her on the terrace.

Lady Buxley's pleased look at being singled out faded rapidly, however, when after listening to a lengthy discourse about wedding plans, Sarah pressed her about her daughter's feelings toward her intended.

"Having spoken with Miss Buxley, I received the distinct impression she held Sir James in aversion."

"Surely you misunderstood, my lady," the mama protested. "Sir James has been everything courteous."

"She has never mentioned feeling ill at ease?"

Lady Buxley shifted uncomfortably. "Well, if she is a bit nervous, 'tis only normal. She's been well brought up, and is rather—uninformed about the duties of matrimony."

"Lady Buxley, I believe your daughter fears Sir James. And I must tell you, she does so with good reason. Do you not know his two previous wives died, under what can only charitably be called *mysterious* circumstances?"

Lady Buxley twitched her shawl. "I'm sure I don't listen to gossip, Lady Englemere. Nor, with all respect, can I see that this is any business of yours."

"Please, Lady Buxley, it may be improper of me to interfere, but I was once nearly engaged to Sir James. Having every expectation of marrying me, he revealed aspects of his character that, I implore you to believe, render him unfit to be the husband of a delicate young girl! I cannot claim to know your daughter well, but this I do know—if you care for her, do not force her to wed Sir James."

"But the trousseau is ordered and the preparations in train!" Lady Buxley twisted her hands. "And Sir James is so charming. Surely you are mistaken."

Sarah fixed a grim gaze on the lady. "I wish I were, Lady Buxley, but I promise you I am not. Sir James is a widower twice over. 'Tis her very life at stake."

Strong emotion flitted across the woman's face. Then she flung off Sarah's hand, as if by breaking that contact she could erase the disturbing picture Sarah had sketched.

"I appreciate your concern, Lady Englemere. But Angela's papa has conversed extensively with Sir James. He has his daughter's welfare at heart, I assure you, and if there were anything untoward in Sir James's character, he would have discovered it. Now, if you will excuse me."

With a nervous glance, as if she feared Sarah might compel her to remain, she hurried back across the terrace. Sarah ground her teeth.

The woman was uneasy over the match. But she obviously preferred to pass responsibility for it onto her husband. Sarah would have to seek out Baron Buxley.

Fortunately, as it had been nearly half an hour since she left the ballroom and her solicitous husband would soon be searching for her, she'd already concocted a plan for accosting that gentleman. And the card room was probably the last place Nicholas would think to look for her.

Sarah found Lord Buxley just as a hand of piquet broke up. Quickly drawing him into conversation, she praised his skill and begged he might engage her for a game.

Lord Buxley preened a little. "Be happy to take you on, your ladyship. I'll endeavor not to fleece you too badly." He laughed heartily at his own joke.

Sarah chatted of idle matters until the cards were played out, herself losing heavily, before broaching her subject. "I wished to speak with you about a different lamb, Lord Buxley. Your daughter Angela. She's to marry Sir James Findlay, I understand."

"Yes, a fine man. Excellent family."

"Lord Buxley, do you know of Sir James's past?"

The baron's genial glow dimmed. "I've heard some nonsense. Nothing to it. Have only to speak with the man to know that. True gentleman."

"My lord, much as I regret it, I must disagree. I was once nearly promised to Sir James, and I assure you those—rumors you heard are not exaggerated."

Lord Buxley looked annoyed. "See here, your ladyship, I've talked with the man, and I'm satisfied. I expect your husband is waiting for you." Nodding a dismissal, he rose.

Sarah grabbed his sleeve. "Sir James may be charming, but he is dangerous as well." At her last hope, she unbuttoned her glove to the wrist and held her arm out. "I displeased Sir James once, and he did this."

He glanced at her wrist and quickly away. "Sir James is a gentleman. Yes, and a generous one. I've no doubts about my daughter's safety and happiness, none whatsoever." He scowled at Sarah. "*She* will not displease him." He tugged at his sleeve.

Sarah did not release it. "And if he cannot be pleased? Do you care for her so little you will risk that?"

"This is ridiculous," the baron said in a furious undertone. "Of course I care for my daughter. I begin to think you deranged, my good woman."

Then his face lit. "Ah—just remembered. Lost a child a month ago, didn't you? Poor lady. You're still distressed, naturally. Such a thing's bound to upset a female." He patted her shoulder.

"Have your husband take you home to rest, that's the ticket. And don't worry, my gel's future is well in hand."

With a fatuous smile, such as the nervous bestow on lunatics, he pulled loose his sleeve and walked off.

Slowly Sarah refastened her glove, despair settling over her. So much for dissuading the Buxleys. They either could not, or would not listen.

She looked up to find Chloe Ingram's dark eyes on her.

The woman gave her a mock-sympathetic glance and smiled.

I have Nicholas, the smile said. *What do you have?*

It needed only that to cap off the evening. Her eyes brimming tears, she brushed past the woman, sped blindly down the hall and ran headlong into a tall, blue-coated figure.

Sinjin steadied her. "Sarah, whatever is wrong?"

"N-nothing."

"Was it Mrs. Ingram?" he persisted, his eyes searching her face. "I saw her at the doorway to the card room. Did that doxy say something to upset you?"

"Not at all. She merely smiled at me."

Sarah had never been a good liar. Sinjin took another look at her face, steered her into an adjacent room and handed her a handkerchief.

With admirable compassion, he looked away while she mopped her eyes. "Thank you, Sinjin. I'm better now."

"Are you better, Sarah? I was so sorry to hear about the child. I didn't dare write, but I grieved for you."

Sarah had recourse to his handkerchief again. After a moment, she got her emotions under a modicum of control.

"You should count yourself fortunate." She attempted a smile. "I've turned out to be a rather wretched wife."

"I could never think so."

"'Tis true, nonetheless. Thank you for assisting me, but I must get back."

"No, it wouldn't do for *Lady Englemere* to be found with Captain Sandiford," he said with bitter emphasis.

"Nicholas would not like it."

Sinjin looked at her searchingly. "'Tis more than that, isn't it, Sarah? I've felt the change for some time. You love Englemere, don't you?"

She didn't attempt to deny it. This was Sinjin, and he knew her too well. "Yes," she whispered.

He swore softly.

"Oh, Sinjin, you mustn't feel that diminishes the love I

had for you! Do you believe our hearts so poor and mean they can admit affection for one person only? You will always be dear to me, so dear that, regardless of my husband's views, I dare not trust myself alone with you.''

She gave him a tremulous smile. ''Can you truly say you would settle for the illicit affair that is the only relationship possible for us? I could not so dishonor the love we shared, and neither could you!''

''Could I not, Sarah darling?'' For a fraught moment, she feared that, after her rash admission, he might pull her into his arms. But he merely stared at her, a gentle sadness slowly replacing the bitterness on his face.

''I leave London the end of the week,'' he said at last.

''To rejoin your regiment?''

''Yes. Who knows, after we've beaten Boney, I might stay on soldiering. There's little enough for me here.''

''Your mama wouldn't like that.''

He curled his lip. ''No, Mama would doubtless give me an earful, were I to see her.''

''You've not visited her yet? Oh, Sinjin!''

''I'll post down to Sandiford before I leave. I've that much sense of duty.''

''Have compassion on her, Sinjin. In her own way, she loves you very much.''

He gave her a twisted smile. ''What a fortunate lad. Blessed with two ladies who love me 'in their own way.'''

He put a finger to her lips before she could protest. With a hungry gaze so powerful she could feel its heat, he whispered, ''One last time I will say it—I'll love you till I die, Sarah Wellingford. If ever I can serve you, send for me.''

She could not have spoken had she wished to. Once again, her eyes brimmed with tears.

''Easy, sweetheart. I'll not distress you further.'' He offered her the handkerchief. ''Tell that handsome husband of yours he'd best make you happy, or he'll answer to me.''

''Sarah, there you are—Sandiford!'' Stopping short on

the threshold, Nicholas's anxious expression turned to surprise, then anger.

"Lady Englemere was distressed." The captain indicated the soggy handkerchief that Sarah had used to wipe her tears. "I escorted her here to compose herself."

Nicholas glared at Sandiford. How dare that blue-and-silver-braided popinjay secrete himself with Sarah! Nicholas had half a mind to call him out for his effrontery. And what had Sarah been thinking, to let him? What if Sally Jersey had walked in on them? "If my wife is *distressed,* I am fully capable of assisting her."

"Then why were you not nearby to *assist?*"

"Nicholas, Sinjin, please!" Sarah burst in. "You are both distressing me now."

"I'll take you home, Sarah. You look tired."

"I am, Nicholas. Perhaps I should not have come. Sinjin, thank you for the handkerchief."

"Keep it, Sarah. Should I not see you before week's end, goodbye. My lord." He bowed curtly and walked out.

Seething, Nicholas propelled Sarah from the room.

"Sinjin did assist me, Nicholas," Sarah said as he hurried her down the hall. "Someone reminded me of—of the child. He found me a private place to recover, and offered his own condolences, which he wanted to do, he said, before leaving London. He rejoins his regiment next week."

"Next week?" Nicholas couldn't stem an upsurge of gladness. He struggled to come up with some sincere expression of regret, and failed. "I'm sure his unit needs him," he offered finally. "He's a fine officer."

"Yes, he is. He's a fine man as well, Nicholas. I had hoped you two might be friends."

When pigs fly, thought Nicholas. "Here's the carriage. I feared going out tonight would be too much for you."

Sarah was quiet on the ride home, from fatigue—or distress—Nicholas could not tell. Was it the thought of her lover's departure that made her shoulders sag and brought that numb misery to her eyes? His anger revived.

He handed her out of the carriage and marched her upstairs. "I'm sure you'll wish to retire immediately."

Sarah looked at him wearily. "I'm sorry, Nicholas. I should have better control. People will comment about—about it. I can't be dissolving into tears every time someone offers me condolences, no matter how sweetly false."

Becky bustled in, clucking and fussing over Sarah, and Nicholas withdrew. She had not, he noted, apologized for the indiscretion of slipping off with Sandiford. His brow puckered, he walked moodily back to his own chamber.

He poured himself a brandy and flung into his chair. Then a phrase echoed: "and offered his own condolences."

The implications of the remark hit him like a blow. Sandiford hadn't visited her at Stoneacres. Relief and a savage joy flooded him.

Shame stemmed the flood of gladness as he recalled Sarah's wan, strained face. After swearing to himself upon her return that he would not—*he would not*—ever again let his jealous imagination fly away with him, at the very first test he once again succumbed. How could he be idiotic enough to doubt Sarah's distress when someone mentioned her lost child? Had he not himself witnessed over and over the depth of her grief?

Instead of jumping to inane conclusions regarding the captain, he should have offered her comfort, a warm shoulder and a sympathetic ear.

Regret stabbed at him. He would apologize at once, before she fell asleep.

Sarah reclined against the pillows, her braided hair under a frilly nightcap. The depth of the curtsy Becky gave him as she exited indicated the maid held him responsible for his wife's pale weariness.

Nicholas handed her a glass of wine. "'Twill help you sleep. I hoped an apology might help as well. I'm sorry for my brusqueness tonight."

"You've no need to apologize. Even though upset, I should have realized I must not allow Sinjin to assist me alone." She gave him a small smile. "He's been a friend so long, 'tis sometimes hard to remember the meaning—others might attach to his attentions. I shall do better, I promise. Now, is that not a familiar theme?"

"We shall both do better. But you look exhausted, sweeting. Perhaps we should remain at home a few days. I don't think you're recovered enough for the late nights one keeps in London."

"I'm not tired, really. 'Twas the incident that upset me, and the sooner I learn to deal with it, the better. I cannot spend the rest of my life hiding in Stanhope House."

Nicholas drained his glass and went over to the bed. "You mustn't push yourself. You do that, you know. Give yourself time, Sarah." He picked up the end of the long plait and stroked his fingers along its satiny length.

The slippery softness recalled the feel of her bare skin. During their marriage he'd become delightfully accustomed to sharing her bed nightly. He'd not done so in nearly five weeks, and at the thought of her silken body under the thin veiling of nightrail his heartbeat quickened and a tremor spiraled in his gut. Reach out his arm, and the little buttons could be undone, the fabric pushed back—

He realized he'd been reaching out in truth. Clenching the hand into a fist, he jammed it at his side. Sweat broke out on his forehead. If he meant to leave her untouched, he'd best remove himself with all speed.

Instead of her lips, he leaned to kiss the tip of her braid. "Sleep well, sweet Sarah," he said through a tight throat. He forced his reluctant legs toward the door.

"Nicholas."

He halted to look back at her.

"Are you still angry with me?"

"No, sweeting. I thought I'd told you that."

"Then, can you not—stay?"

Heat, like the blast from an opened oven, suffused him. He stilled, his pulse frantic, his ears roaring, and tried to keep his eyes from lingering on her lips, her breasts.

"I don't want to injure you, sweeting."

"I'm fully recovered, Nicholas. Stay, please?"

So much for good intentions. Before the plea left her lips, he reached the bed.

Smiling, Sarah put the last pin in her coil of braids. What a fool she'd been, hiding away at Stoneacres. Nicholas had been particularly tender, especially passionate last night, and she had no doubt as he loved her that his mind had room for no one else. If she could lure him to her nightly, when would he have time for Chloe?

And as he had at Stoneacres, he'd not left her after their joining, but gathered her close and slept in her bed. Surely there could be no more wonderful feeling under heaven than waking in the arms of the man you love.

Her euphoria dimmed as she headed for the breakfast room. Her attempt to dissuade the Buxleys had failed totally. Though she hated to risk breaking their lingering contentment, she must talk to Nicholas about Findlay.

His eyes lit when she entered and he rose to kiss her. "Fill your plate, sweeting. If you're like me, you must be famished." He gave her a naughty grin.

She couldn't help grinning back. She allowed herself to delay the discussion until they finished their meal and were pouring a last dish of tea. In what she hoped was a casual voice, she asked, "Did you see the notice of Sir James Findlay's engagement?"

Nicholas grimaced. "I did. And wondered about the taste—or intelligence—of his affianced bride."

"I doubt she had much choice about it. Do you not recall her, Nicholas—Miss Angela Buxley? Shy, slender, blue-eyed with golden curls? She's scarcely more than a child. And her father is a debt-ridden gamester."

Nicholas raised his eyes to hers, suddenly grave. "Appears to be a pattern, does there not?"

"Except the intended victim this time is much younger and more vulnerable than I. Oh, Nicholas, she's a delicate little thing, and she's terrified of him! I tried to talk with her, and then her parents last evening, tried to make them see what he is, but they wouldn't listen."

"You spoke frankly to the Buxleys?"

"Yes, and you may spare me the lecture that 'twas not my place to do so. I know Sir James as perhaps no other woman—still living, that is," she inserted grimly. "How can I let some poor innocent be delivered into his hands?"

"Sarah, I admire your courage and concern, but this truly isn't your problem. The girl *does* have a father. 'Tis his task to protect her."

"Not when the glitter of gambling money beckons," Sarah said bitterly. "I tried to reason with him, warn him—I even showed him my scar. But Findlay has him charmed—and well paid. Baron Buxley would hear nothing against him."

"Then you've done all you could. And proceeded much further than most would have been willing to go."

"But it isn't enough, Nicholas. I suddenly realized last night that, even had I succeeded in dissuading the Buxleys, Findlay would only seek another victim, until he found one gullible or unprotected enough."

She looked away from Nicholas's disapproving face. "Should I manage to blacken his reputation among the ton so thoroughly that none would countenance a union with him, it would still not be enough. He would merely target one poorer and more vulnerable still. Does not a maidservant or a shopkeeper's girl have just as much right to protection from such as he as the daughter of a baron?"

"I concede the point." Nicholas frowned. "But I fail to see what you can do about it."

Sarah took a deep breath. "Is not assault a crime punishable by law? And is this—'' she pointed to the scar at her wrist ''—not evidence of assault?''

Nicholas stared at her in horror. ''You cannot mean to bring him to the dock upon assault charges!''

Nicholas took her hand and kissed the scar fervently. ''My darling Sarah, I applaud your spirit and good intentions, but I could not permit you to expose yourself in a public courtroom in such a manner.''

''Tis only my wrist, Nicholas.'' She smiled.

He wasn't amused. ''Tis a great deal more, and you know it,'' he snapped back. ''The mere thought of the vulgar display a trial would occasion—cartoons in the press shop windows, crowds in the courtroom—makes me shudder. The family would clamor for me to divorce you. No, you must not consider it.''

The urgency of the task and her desire to please him battled within her. Could she not convince him to help?

''When I spoke with Miss Buxley, she told me Sir James said I owed him a debt that she would repay. She had no idea what Findlay meant, but I do. Do you not see? As inconvenient, as scandalous as it may be, I am responsible. I cannot just turn away and forget.''

Nicholas looked grimmer than she'd ever seen him. ''How could you think to prove assault? The scar is old now, and there were no witnesses to the attack. Sarah, as your husband I absolutely forbid you to proceed in this matter.''

So searing had the experience been, she hadn't considered her scar might be worthless as evidence. Before she could ponder the implications, Nicholas pinned her with a gimlet glare. ''Don't even think of approaching Findlay himself, Miss Save-the-World! I swear, if you so much as look in his direction, I'll—I'll lock you in your room.''

Sarah stared. ''On bread and water?'' she asked dryly.

His severity softened into a grin. ''Bread and tea, perhaps. And—'' he winked at her ''—I would *visit* often.''

Then his face sobered. ''This worries me, sweeting. If

Sir James does harbor a grievance, we must be careful. I'll not underestimate his menace, for I should never forgive myself were something to happen to you. The other maidens of this world will have to find another champion. I will not bend on this, Sarah.''

He grasped her scarred wrist and rubbed it gently, frowning. ''We should take precautions. I'll escort you to any functions we attend, and if you wish to go out shopping, you must take the carriage and two extra footmen.''

She agreed without argument. Then, pleading the need to prepare for just such an expedition with Clarissa, she put down her cup and slipped from the room.

In the refuge of her chamber, Sarah mulled over Nicholas's words. She yearned to believe him, to abandon her dangerous enterprise. The warmth with which he'd treated her since her return, the ecstasy of their loving last night, made every fiber of her being protest proceeding in a mission that might forever destroy any hope of happiness together.

She could pursue this only over Nicholas's most adamant disapproval. Should she press a court action, 'twould likely mean all the vulgar scandal he'd predicted, and more. *I should have to divorce you,* he'd said.

Would he go that far? Dare she find out?

What other choice did she have? In her heart she knew her treatment of Sir James had, however unwittingly, added fuel to the fire of the demon that drove him. Because of her, did she not succeed in stopping him, innocent girls would suffer, and perhaps die.

If she had a duty to Nicholas, she owed her conscience an even greater one. She could not live with herself knowing she had allowed the maiming or death of blameless fellow creatures. She must go forward.

Then she recalled Nicholas's other objection. She carefully inspected her wrist.

The scar, thin, white and puckered, ran for scarcely an inch. As Nicholas had said, 'twould be difficult to judge its age. Findlay might well claim her charge was spite, that she carried the scar from some earlier mishap.

The implications of that realization frightened her to her bones. If she intended to stop Sir James, she would have to present fresh evidence.

She thought a long time before the plan came to her. Her turmoil settled into a cold, firm resolve. *Forgive me, Nicholas,* she said silently. *I love you, and I'm sorry. But I must do this.*

Chapter Nineteen

That night they attended Lady Cunningham's rout. As the Cunningham daughter was a friend of Miss Buxley and the party honored both girls, Sarah was certain Sir James would be present. How she would manage to slip away from Nicholas long enough to have a private word with Findlay concerned her, but it proved easier than she expected.

Nicholas's Aunt Amelia and the Odious Archibald chanced to be attending. When Archibald, ostensibly a suitor to the hand of Miss Cunningham, left his mama, Lady Stanhope latched on to Nicholas's arm and declared he must escort her to the refreshment room.

Sarah realized this was her best chance. As soon as Lady Stanhope steered Nicholas out of the ballroom, Sarah scanned the crowd.

She saw Sir James at the far side. It seemed he was watching her, for his eyes met hers and he nodded.

Findlay pulled Miss Buxley forward. From the pained look on the girl's face, he was holding her hand in a merciless grip. As he bent and kissed her fingertips, the girl's eyes widened. She tugged at her hand. When Sir James released her, she cradled her hand to her bosom and fled from the room.

Sir James watched her go. Then he raised his fingertips, touched them to his lips and waved to Sarah.

A rage greater than her loathing filled her. He'd staged that incident just for her, she was certain of it.

He was still gazing at her—doubtless awaiting her reaction. Clenching her teeth, she inclined her head toward the terrace. He smiled and shook his head.

Would he refuse to meet her? Somehow she must goad him to it. She looked toward the refreshment room where, had he truly been watching her, he would know Nicholas had gone. She turned back to stare at Findlay, and when he did nothing, raised an eyebrow scornfully. Then she made her way deliberately to the terrace.

Would he take the challenge? He had only to ignore her, and she could truly do nothing. Her heart pounded in double time as she waited on the darkened terrace, and despite the warmth of the evening, she shivered. Almost, she hoped he would not come, and she could return with a light heart to Nicholas—

"So, little dove, you seek a meeting. Tired already of your new husband? Or is it that he neglects you too often for one of—how shall I put it—superior charms?"

Sarah gathered her courage. "'Tis not of Nicholas I wished to speak, but of your betrothed. She's a child, Sir James. Hardly worthy of you."

"True. She has none of your spirit, and taming her will be a paltry business." He stepped closer. She forced herself to stand firm. "That slender little body is lovely, though, so frail and—delicate. And I do have a man's... appetites."

A door slammed, and Sir James looked back sharply. "Charming as this interlude is, I mustn't linger. So unreasonable of Englemere to restrict your movements, little dove, whilst feeling himself free to entertain Chloe. But alas, I have learned to respect his displeasure."

He bent his head until the light from the ballroom windows illumined his face. The Grecian perfection of his nose, she saw with a shock, was marred by a crooked bump.

"Yes, your lord husband is rather close with his possessions. He counts even a dance an effrontery."

He ran a finger along the fracture, and suppressed rage roughened his voice. "I shall collect for this, never doubt." Falling back into his languid pose, he smiled at her. "From someone." He turned to walk away.

"I've not yet said what I wished," she called after him. "Perhaps if I call on you tomorrow?"

The baronet halted. With slow deliberation he turned back to her. "You would visit my home?"

She took a deep breath. "The proposition I wish to deliver is rather—private."

He stared at her, and she could almost see him weighing the risk of retribution from Nicholas against the prospect of having her once again in his power.

"But—if you fear Nicholas..." She shrugged. "'Tis nothing for it, then. Good evening, Sir—"

"I fear no man," he barked. He smoothed his cravat, frowning. She held her breath and waited. Just when she thought she must scream from suspense and frustration, his lips curved and that hot glow she had always found so disturbing began shimmering in his eyes.

"I don't suppose I could be held responsible for your visit," he said, half to himself. "Come if you wish, my lady. I shall be at home." He raked her body with a hot glance. "Perhaps you're deciding you made a mistake."

She watched him walk away. "Someone has," she whispered.

Too late now to question the wisdom or necessity of her plan. He'd taken the bait. Tomorrow she must spring an airtight trap.

Before that, though, she had one last night with Nicholas. Casting aside every restraint but love and need, she intended to make the most of it.

* * *

Sarah heard Nicholas approach her chamber door, and a shiver of anticipation tingled along her spine. He had come to her eagerly last night, and their loving had been joyous and passionate. Even so, ever mindful of her pledge, she had held back, responding rather than seeking a response.

This time there would be no holding back. If, after this night, she were fated to leave Nicholas, she would bear what she must. At least this once, though, she intended to touch and taste and love him with full abandon.

He closed the door and stepped into the candle-bright room. She would have preferred daylight, to see him more clearly, but the massed candelabra on the mantel and the bedside table would have to do.

Nicholas looked around in bemusement at the extravagant array of wax tapers. Then his glance reached her. His eyes widened, his breath caught and he stopped short.

Sarah reclined against the pillows, the coverlet at her ankles, clothed only in the shimmering fall of her hair. She'd fanned it loose, and like a pale ocean it flowed up over her breasts, down into the trough of her belly, breaking here and there over an elbow, a boulder of hipbone, before subsiding in a satin pool above her knees.

"I'm glad you've arrived," she said, her low voice loud in the charged silence. "I was getting chilled."

"L-let me warm you," he rasped. In two swift strides, shedding his dressing gown as he went, he reached the bed.

She let him kiss her, reveling in the taste of him, but when he reached to pull back her hair, she caught his wrists. "I want to look at *you*," she whispered. "Let me."

With an inarticulate sound, he dropped his hands. His eyes focused on her, he let her guide him back against the pillows, adjust them behind him. Still half concealed, half revealed in her robe of tresses, she knelt beside him and simply looked.

His gaze followed hers as she studied his naked body

with a thoroughness she'd never before been able to indulge. That hollow at his throat looked made for kisses, she noted, and the little dimpled places beneath his collarbones. She wondered how the flat, rigid nipples would taste, whether the fine dark hair of his chest would tickle against her cheek, and felt a wicked delight that soon, she would find out. She drank in the sinewy curve of arm, the bony bend of wrist, the concave plane of abdomen.

Then she feasted her eyes lower, on the crinkly ruffle of curls, the tensed thighs from which his erection projected, a marvelous construction of taut length and smooth skin. Though she moved nothing but her eyes, his shaft leapt under her gaze.

"S-Sarah," he groaned. Perspiration had broken out on his forehead, his chest. He pushed to sit up.

She stopped him with her palm, gently insistent. "Stay, my lord. I'm not finished."

With a murmur, he subsided, but propped himself on his elbows to watch as her glance traveled lower still, to the plump sacks at the junction of his saddle-muscled thighs, the sharp angles of his kneecaps, the round of calf and bump of ankle, the toes splayed with tension.

"Do I turn over?" he asked.

Her secret places throbbed with heat and damp at the knowledge of what she would do. "No," she replied unsteadily. "I want to see you watching me."

She moved a fraction, and he tensed. Hands clenched on the bedclothes, he stared at her, the pulse beating visibly at his throat. In the candlelight, his moist skin glowed.

But she didn't touch him, not yet. She merely bent her face to his foot and exhaled over it, watching as her warm breath ruffled the tiny hairs of his toes. Securing her trailing hair behind her, she traveled slowly back up his body, blowing over his ankle, calf, knee, thigh.

Her whole body was pulsing, her nipples burning and tender, her passage drenched and ready, by the time she reached his rigid member. She had to stop, draw in a deep breath, before she could direct a long continuous flow of air over it.

Nicholas cried out, and her heart exulted with sensuous joy and lascivious power. Though his face contorted, his eyes squeezing tight and his shoulders writhing, she knew it was sweet torment and delicious agony that held him prisoned, prone before her.

"S-Sarah!" he begged, his voice strangled.

"Soon," she promised.

He opened glittering eyes to watch her, sucking in his belly at the soft erotic wind of her passage, hissing through clenched teeth as it crossed his nipples. He arched his neck back at its touch on his throat, thrust his head forward again to take the breath of her on his jaw, opened his mouth to feel it on his tongue.

And then she kissed him.

With a growl he grabbed her, slick against his chest, his mouth devouring. She kissed him back just as hungrily, but when he tried to roll her over, move her under him, she pushed him away. After a moment, his grip loosened.

He glanced at her, his eyes wild, unfocused. "Sarah, please! Now!" But when she sat back, he let her go.

She wanted more. She wanted him beyond control, transported out of mind and senses, lost totally in her and her loving of him.

"I want to touch you," she said. "Let me."

"Touch," he said hoarsely.

She bent and kissed him, not his mouth but the skin just beyond it. Holding his chin, she traced her lips along his brow, his jaw, nibbled at his earlobe, feeling him exhale hot against her face. She touched her tongue to the pulse at his throat, tasted the hard ridge of collarbone, the tickly curl of chest hair.

When her lips reached his nipples, he clenched her buttocks, kneaded them as she nipped her way across the taut skin of his belly.

She paused before his rigid shaft. "Sarah," he gasped, a plea.

Gently, sheathing her teeth, she took him in her mouth. His skin was velvet under her tongue, his taste heat and salt. Then he was moving, thrusting against her, his breathing frantic gulping pants, like a runner nearly spent. She adjusted to his rhythm, pulling him deep, sliding him free. A moment later he convulsed, crying out her name.

Her own heart doing a rapid tattoo, she released him. Murmuring, he pulled her to his chest, wrapped his arms about her and held her close. She felt his stampeding heartbeat steady, then slow.

A ferocious exaltation flooded her. Hers. This time, he was fully, completely hers.

Finally, with a low moan, he sat up. He gazed at her a moment, as if he couldn't quite believe what had just transpired, and drew one finger gently down her cheek. "Oh, Sarah, that was…" He shook his head. Then he slid his hand to her breast and grinned wolfishly. "My turn."

She pulled his fingers away. "Not just yet."

"More?" He gave her a theatrically exaggerated look of horror, but reclined readily back upon the pillows. "Lady, I am yours to command." He laughed, sounding bemused. "I begin to believe I'm enchanted, and you're a handmaiden sent straight from Aphrodite to drive me to madness."

"Believe it," she whispered.

She shook out her tangled hair and dried him with it, from his damp shoulders downward. By the time she reached his toes, his flaccid manhood had begun to stir. Wrapping a fistful of hair around her hand so the massed ends became a brush, she slowly dusted him with it, all along the length of his body, each plane and crevice, made him turn over so she could sweep his back and thighs and bottom.

She reveled in the muffled sounds she brought forth, in the way his buttocks puckered when she played the whisk of hair over them and down between his legs. When she turned him back over, he was fully ready.

But she again commanded him to stillness. Beginning at his toes, she slowly kissed her way up his lower body. She licked the balls of his feet, took his toes into her mouth and nibbled them. She tongued the soft soft skin below his ankle, the hollows beside his kneecaps, drawing from him deep, strangled groans.

When she reached his upper thighs, he was slick with sweat, his breathing once again a hoarse panting. He'd gone up on his elbows to watch her, expectant. But when her mouth moved from smooth muscled leg to suckle the pebbled sacks at the junction of his splayed thighs, he bent his head back and emitted a toneless, primitive wail that made her body surge with wetness and her heart exult.

Hers, hers, his body stretched and ready, and hers the power to bring him to such a pinnacle of anguished joy.

Grasping him, she took his sleek heated flesh deep in her mouth and carried him over the edge into ecstasy.

Afterward he lay limp. "Sarah," he sighed, a mere whisper of sound, and half raised a hand to her. Then his wrist fell back, his eyes flickered closed and he dozed.

The candles had burned down to thumb-sized wedges, dimming the light to a misty glow. Her heart filled with a piercing, bittersweet sadness, she lay beside him, rested her head on her crossed arms and watched him sleep.

She had given him every pleasure her love and imagination could devise. Forever and always, come what might, she would treasure those moments.

A short time later he awoke. He smiled at her and drew her atop him, molding her hips against him. "Now," he whispered, "you cannot say me nay."

Gladly she let him claim her. Following her lead, he stimulated, stroked and tasted every inch of her, bringing her over and over to the summit, drawing her back, and finally joining her in luxuriant fulfillment.

Near dawn, satiated, they at last pulled the damp sheet

up around them. Nicholas propped her against the pillows and gazed down at her, awe, tenderness and something else she dared not name in his face.

She waited, but after a moment he merely shook his head, as if at some great mystery. "Sarah," he said on a breath of wonder. "Sarah."

Nonetheless, after he gathered her against him, she fell asleep certain that whatever happened tomorrow, however far he might send her on a journey through courts and divorce and shame, he, too, would never forget this night.

Smiling in bemusement, Nicholas sat at his desk the next morning reviewing with relish every delightful, astonishing detail of his night with Sarah.

Such a blend of well-bred restraint and unbridled passion, he marveled. Over breakfast, as he poured tea, she sat cool as an untouched virgin. When he made an oblique reference to their near-sleepless night, she blushed.

In memory he traced his fingers the length of her satiny skin from collarbone to ankle. He could hardly wait till this evening. He was aroused already.

A knock sounded and Sarah entered. He beamed at her. Tremulously she smiled back and crossed to the desk.

"I've some commissions to complete, dull household matters, else I'd ask your escort. I'm meeting the factor to inspect the quarter's dry-goods supplies."

"I'm to be abandoned for meal, flour and coffee?" He sighed in mock outrage. "Will you be back for tea?"

"I'm not certain. Probably not."

Taking her hand, he drew her to him for a lingering kiss. "Can I not tempt you away from your duty?"

She gave him an odd smile. "So easily, I must depart forthwith." She stepped back as if to leave, then halted.

Placing her fingers on his temples, she gently traced his face from cheekbone to chin, as if he were an object infinitely dear. Her face glowed with such tenderness, such soul-searing warmth, that his breathing suspended.

"Goodbye, Nicholas," she whispered.

Nicholas sat motionless. He'd never seen such a look on her face before. A dancing spark of excitement licked up his veins. Could Sarah love him?

Hal seemed to think so. As they sat over port after dinner two nights ago, Hal had announced in his usual enigmatic fashion, "Dotes on you."

"Dotes?" he said, at sea.

"Sarah," Hal replied patiently. "All April-and-May with 'er. Eyes follow you around the room, watches you when you don't know she's lookin'." He made a sweeping hand gesture, as if closing an argument. "Macaroons."

"You mean," Nicholas said, as he pieced it together, "you think Sarah *loves* me?"

"See it in her eyes. Dotes on you."

Dare he believe it? He replayed every detail of that glowing look and came up with no words short of "love" to describe it. And last night—surely she must entertain the warmest of feelings to behave as she had.

Exhilaration flooded him. He'd never thought to want that emotion from her, but he found himself delighted.

Glancing down, he discovered Sarah's glove on the desk, where she'd evidently forgotten it. He lifted the soft leather and inhaled.

The scent was chamois and lavender, its touch silky soft. Like Sarah.

He couldn't remember what task had brought him to the library. Whatever it was, he was no longer interested in it. Or anything else. He should have gone with Sarah.

He was acting like a besotted bridegroom, he thought with a chuckle. Then much-belated illumination finally cracked him over the head like a cricket bat.

Could it be he loved Sarah as well?

The shocking idea froze him to his chair. After Lydia, he hadn't thought it possible he could love another woman—the hurt and distrust went too deep. His feelings for Sarah had built imperceptibly, layer upon layer, from a base of admiration and friendship. But upon assessing the depth of his concern for her, the strength of his desire to be with and protect her, and his unslakable passion, no other word seemed adequate.

Still marveling, he grasped the idea cautiously, like a precious goblet too fragile for handling. Could Nicholas Stanhope, wary, world-weary Marquess of Englemere, truly have fallen in love with his own wife?

My, how the ton would laugh. He didn't give a damn.

Already impatient for Sarah's return, he wandered into the hall, paused at the cheval glass to check his cravat. His face sported an idiotic grin. How many hours until tea?

Sarah checked the watch in her reticule. Delivering the package to Sinjin's batman had taken little time, but she'd had to purchase gloves before meeting the factor. That merchant would have thought it strikingly singular for the marchioness to arrive gloveless, and she hadn't dared risk returning to Stanhope House—and encountering Nicholas.

She couldn't have endured another goodbye. Would she ever see him again? Her heart seared with longing, she ordered the carriage to proceed to Portman Square.

Almost, her courage failed her. She made herself envision Angela Buxley's face and the nameless faces of all the innocents who would suffer if she did not act.

The carriage slowed to a stop. Her heartbeat already speeding, her fingers clammy in her new gloves, she climbed down and dismissed the carriage. When Martin, the footman Nicholas had detailed to protect her, protested the master instructed she wasn't to go anywhere without him, she replied at her most imperious that she was calling on a friend, and another friend would see her home.

Before mounting the stairs, she handed him a folded note. He should deliver it to Nicholas, but not until after tea, she instructed.

She must do this—and she would. She climbed the stairs and rapped firmly.

A thin man with a scarred face bowed her in without comment. Over the sudden thundering of her heart, Sarah heard the neigh of horses and the clatter of wheels as the Stanhope carriage drove away. Then the door closed behind her.

Leading her up a graceful cantilevered stairway to a reception room, the gaunt butler intoned in a colorless voice that he would inform his master of her arrival.

Knowing she was now enclosed with Sir James sent a shiver up her spine. This room, like its master, was on the surface perfectly appointed and polished. Were she to press it, she wondered a little hysterically, would she find rot under the satinwood inlay, mold beneath the brocade sofa?

Would Sinjin come? *Portman Square No. 13, Four of the clock. Do not fail me. Sarah,* she'd written. And inserted the note in his signet ring.

Now she must provoke Sir James. Could she control his violence once she unleashed it? Having no wish to become a martyr for the sake of conscience, she could only hope so. And pray that Sinjin would be on time.

"Well, well. So you did come."

Sir James stood in the doorway, impeccable in a black coat over buff breeches and a cream figured waistcoat. "Some wine, Manners," he called over his shoulder as he entered. "Surely, on such an auspicious occasion, you will take a glass with me, my dear."

Sarah had chosen a wing chair near the fireplace. Sir James approached it, smiling faintly. "Shall we observe the amenities, or do you wish to proceed immediately to this proposal you hinted at?"

"Let us begin. It is simply, as I said last night, that I cannot permit you to marry Miss Buxley."

"Having robbed me of a more fitting bride, you can hardly object if I seek matrimony with another. Have a few months of dull propriety with Englemere made you recognize your error? How sad 'tis too late."

He sighed. "Regret cannot alter my need to marry. So

pleasingly permanent an arrangement. Despite any—disagreements—a wife cannot go running off.''

''Or lay testimony against you?''

''Precisely. Such a discerning wit you have, little dove. 'Tis one of the things I've always admired.'' He smiled that slow, mocking smile she detested and walked toward her. The hair on the back of her neck bristled.

He reached for her, then checked his hand as the door opened to admit the butler with wine and glasses on a tray.

''On the side table, if you please. That will be all, Manners. Please note, we don't wish to be disturbed.''

Sir James poured wine and handed her a glass. She accepted it, willing her fingers not to tremble.

''A toast to you, my dear. Quite brave of you to come with nary a maid to lend you countenance. Why did you, I wonder? Has your toplofty husband washed his hands of you, now that you've lost the brat?''

Sarah gritted her teeth, fighting the pain any mention of her loss still caused her. She took a sip of wine.

Sir James sighed in mock sympathy. ''I warned he wanted you only for breeding, did I not? Of course, I've taken some pains to accelerate his disgust—my 'Farmer Bride.'''

She stared in shock. Findlay had schemed with Weston to discredit her? ''You—''

''Ah, yes.'' He waved a negligent hand. ''A trifle, perhaps, but one misstep does build upon another. Though you quite cleverly avoided several of the traps Weston set. Did you not realize I would never passively accept Englemere's theft of you?''

He touched a finger to her chin. She made herself pull back slowly, without flinching. Findlay laughed softly.

''We are well matched. Have I not always said so? Your dull but exacting husband cannot appreciate, as I do, your many qualities. Your wit and courage. That irrepressible urge to do good. 'Twas why you came today, was it not, little dove? To flutter your pretty wings and lead me away from Miss Buxley?

"And so," he said triumphantly, his blue eyes chilling, "does my ultimate plan succeed. I had hoped choosing the very young, very innocent Miss Buxley would bring you back to me. Not, had that purpose failed, that she hasn't merits of her own. Such a lovely bud about to unfurl."

He paused, a distinctly lascivious look coming into his eyes. Sarah felt sickened.

"Not of your caliber, of course. However, marriage doesn't preclude additional, quite satisfactory arrangements, does it, my dear? One need only ask your assiduous captain. How fortunate he returns to Spain."

Before Sarah could think or move, Sir James closed the distance between them. "We are fated to be together, don't you feel it, little dove? You bear my mark." He seized her arm and stripped down her glove. "Ah, yes, there it is."

His smile faded. "And I bear yours." He touched his fingers to the crooked bridge of his nose. "What retribution should I exact, I wonder, for this?"

Sarah ignored the impulse to appease him. "I had nothing to do with that."

"Did you not? True, that lummox Waterman perpetrated the outrage, but you cannot deny you were the cause."

He stepped back, making an elaborate show of studying her. Sarah forced herself to meet his gaze squarely. He wanted her to be afraid—he thrived on it. She would not allow him the pleasure.

"I doubt you do anything," she said evenly, pleased at how coolly disdainful her voice sounded.

He laughed, a nasty sound. "My dear, are you that careless of your reputation? I have but to detain you while I call a few friends. How long do you think it would take before the news galloped round the ton that Lady Englemere paid an unescorted call to my bachelor dwelling? Your very proper husband might well divorce you."

"He'd be more apt to shoot you."

"On what grounds? Manners, and your own coachman, would attest you came here willingly. Besides, do you really think Englemere would exert himself over a wife who not only failed to provide an heir, but has already embroiled herself in several tawdry little scandals?"

He tightened his grip. "Of course, you may be right. I take a risk. But 'tis what makes it interesting."

Although she strained away, he raised her wrist and kissed the scar. "A divorce might be convenient. I could install you here. And Miss Buxley, of course. What has Englemere taught you, I wonder?" He jerked her nearer and looked in her eyes. "Would you enjoy a *ménage à trois?* I shall likely have to tie her down. Such a little thing, 'twill be bloody. Shall you want to watch?"

"You are disgusting."

He smiled as if she'd paid him a pretty compliment. "Shall I call in those friends—or let you go? Even do I release you, I must extract payment. What would be fitting, do you think?"

He forced her arm up and ran her bare hand down his damaged nose. "Not your own sweet nose. No, we need something that would be our little secret. One slender finger, perhaps?" Holding her rigid, he waited for her reaction. For her fear.

She laughed, albeit shakily. "You wouldn't dare."

"Wouldn't I? My servants are both well paid and… deaf, when it suits me."

"I am Nicholas's wife. Injure me, and he'll kill you."

He nodded, as if she'd just scored a point at whist. "Perhaps. Something more subtle, then."

Suddenly light glowed in his eyes. "Why not enjoy what was stolen from me? And what better mark, than to plant a tow-haired bastard to be Englemere's heir?"

Hauling her against him, he trapped her in his arms. "Now, this," he groaned, rubbing the hardness in his breeches against her, "I can truly enjoy."

For an instant, Sarah panicked. She forced herself not

to struggle. To be raped had been no part in her plan, but if she resisted, he would quickly overpower her. *Think*, she told herself furiously.

Making herself move slowly, she strained away from him. Immediately he tightened his hold. Still pressing him away, she uttered a low, passionate moan.

Findlay stilled and gave a triumphant laugh. ''Yes, moan for me, little dove.'' Noticing the opening she'd made, he slid a hand down to fondle her breast. His breathing erratic, with his other hand he fumbled at the buttons of her gown, shifting his body back a few precious inches.

It was enough. Bracing herself, Sarah slammed her knee up against the bulge in his breeches.

He broke away with a howl and doubled over. Sarah retreated toward the fireplace, heart hammering, every instinct screaming at her to flee.

She glanced at the clock. Three-fifty. Whatever Findlay did next, she prayed she'd survive it. And that Sinjin would not be late.

Slowly Sir James straightened. In his expression, nothing of humor or lust remained. ''You little bitch,'' he whispered, his eyes blazing. Then he smiled, and from his waistcoat pocket extracted a small knife. Flicking the blade open, he advanced on her.

Chapter Twenty

Still grinning, Nicholas loped up the stairs of Stanhope House. Too restless to work until Sarah's return, he'd borne Hal off to Jackson's. He'd astonished master and disciples alike by allowing an untried fledgling to land a glove on him, and then laughing over his lapse.

Jackson reproved him for lack of concentration. Hal looked at him strangely. He smiled genially back.

Now it was teatime, and although Sarah had said she would probably not return, he'd come back just in case.

Glendenning brought tea and ushered in a footman.

"Mistress says I was supposed ter give ya this, but ya weren't to read of it till after tea."

Nicholas took the note. From its paper wafted the faint scent of lavender he always associated with Sarah. He inhaled deeply. "You left Lady Englemere somewhere?"

"Aye, master. Said as how she was avisitin' a friend in Portman Square, and would be brung home by anudder."

"Portman Square?" he repeated, trying to recall who of their acquaintance lived there. Probably some old dowager in precarious health Sarah was paying a duty call on.

"Thank you, Martin," he said, and propped the note on the tea tray.

What was Sarah proposing? Another little tryst, dare he

hope? He tapped the scented envelope. She said to wait until tea. Surely he had that much patience.

As he stroked and gentled her tonight, would she murmur out her love? In the aftermath of passion, should he confess first? Despite the newly discovered fervor of his emotions, he was still hesitant about voicing them. Awkward as a green boy in the first throes of infatuation, he thought with a chuckle.

"Sweet Sarah, I love you," he whispered experimentally. But then, 'twas nothing urgent about saying it—they had years and years, the rest of their lives. The idea of being in love, of Sarah loving him in return, was still so novel he felt a sense of awe and joy at the thought of it.

Probably he was letting his imagination run riot, and the note was merely a reminder of which function they were to attend tonight, or a message from the factor.

But with Sarah, he couldn't be sure. Only think of his reception last night. Biting into a macaroon, he leaned back against the chair, reliving once more his entrance into his wife's bedchamber.

Some niggling sense of unease clouded that arousing vision. Then the memory surfaced.

Did the job right. Broke his nose for sure. Bled all over m'carriage when I carted him back to Portman Square.

For a moment, he froze. Then Nicholas grabbed the note and ripped it open.

My dearest Nicholas, You have forbidden me to interfere in the matter of Sir James Findlay's marriage. After much reflection I must conclude I have a duty to my conscience that transcends even that which I owe you.

I beg you will understand, dearest husband, that I cannot turn away and allow the death or molestation of young innocents, knowing it is within my power to halt it. Thus, I must gather the evidence that will prevent Sir James—

His heart stopped and a bolt of sheer terror shocked his body. Turning so abruptly he knocked over his chair, he yanked on the bellpull and dashed from the room.

He nearly ran down Glendenning in the hallway. "Send Martin to the mews, and have Valkyrie saddled immediately!" he shouted as took the stairs two at a time. Careening into his chamber, he kicked off his tasseled Hessians, pulled on his riding boots and raced for the stairs.

Please, God, he prayed to the pounding cadence of his footsteps. *Please, God, don't let him hurt her.*

He sped past the astonished Glendenning and out to the stables. Spying Martin leading Valkyrie, he shouted, "Which house on Portman Square?"

The footman broke into a trot, bringing the horse to meet him. "Number thirteen, master."

"Have John Coachman send the carriage. Hurry."

Grabbing the reins of the snorting, sidling horse, he jumped into the saddle, applied both spurs and whip and galloped off.

Carts pulled aside and pedestrians scattered as the stallion thundered down the street. Images jumped out at him from the blur of faces. Lydia, lying broken beside her broken carriage. Edmund, his eyes staring sightlessly from a face white as river foam.

He clutched the reins, scoured by anguish. *Please, God, this time don't let me be too late.*

Then he remembered the colt in the stall at Tattersall's. Bitter gall rose in his throat. Applying the whip again, he bent low over Valkyrie's back.

Portman Square appeared quiet as he brought his lathered horse to a plunging halt. He leapt from the saddle, ran up the steps and put his shoulder to the door. To his surprise, it opened easily. He shoved it to the wall and raced into the marble entryway.

From the top of the staircase, he could hear grunts, the crash of crockery and the clash of steel on steel.

"Sarah! Sarah, where are you?"

He'd leapt up two steps when Findlay, sword in hand, backed onto the landing, hard-pressed by Sandiford.

The captain lunged, Findlay countered. As the force of the check rang out against the stone floors and wall, Findlay shoved the captain back and ran for the stairs.

Perhaps seeing Nicholas startled him, or mayhap his boot caught on the carpet. Whatever the reason, he seemed to check at the top of the stairs, then fell headlong.

Nicholas stepped aside. Findlay reached out as he tumbled past, frantically clawing at Nicholas's boot. He continued to bounce and slide until he reached the bottom.

With a sharp crack, Findlay's head hit the marble floor. He emitted a long, low groan and lay still.

Swiftly the captain sheathed his sword. "I'll finish this." He jerked his thumb toward Findlay. "Look to your wife. First chamber on the left."

Nicholas scrambled up the stairs. "I've a carriage coming," he called back. "Will you watch for it?"

At the captain's nod, he turned and ran down the hallway. "Sarah! Sar—oh, my God."

Facedown and motionless, one hand outstretched, his wife lay on the floor before the fireplace.

In two bounds he reached her. "Sarah," he whispered, his heart racing as he picked up the hand to check her pulse.

He recoiled, for her arm lay in a crimson pool. With each faint pulse, a spurt of warm blood gushed from her wrist to stain his gloves and drip onto the floor.

Gasping in his panic, he clawed at the knots in his cravat, finally tearing it free. He doubled the cloth and bound it tightly around her wrist.

Holding her hand to the floor, he pushed his whole weight against the pulse point. Not until the tips of her fingers turned bluish did he dare decrease his force.

It appeared the bleeding had slowed. Clamping a hand over her wrist to maintain the pressure, he rolled her over, intending to lift her into his arms.

Her head lolled back, and as he reached down to support it, he saw the bodice of her gown had been sliced to ribbons. A crisscross maze of small cuts covered her chest.

With a trembling finger he pushed aside the ruined material. The cuts all appeared shallow, and though the skin still oozed, none bled actively. She lay limp and lifeless, but a faint pulse throbbed at her throat.

His chest tight in an agony of rage and pain, Nicholas carried her to the sofa. He sat, one hand still clamped about her slashed wrist, and cradled her against him.

She had not submitted tamely, he noted as he tried to wrap himself around her chilled body. The room was a chaos of broken knickknacks and overturned chairs. With each puff of breeze from the open doorway, downy feathers wafted from a jagged gash in the sofa cover.

His fingers numbing, he shifted her bandaged wrist. 'Twas cut at the same place as the burn scar, he realized.

How could you think to prove assault? His impatient words burned in his ears.

He should have known she would not abandon so important an enterprise. He should have known, and helped her, instead of goading her to this deadly confrontation.

"Forgive me, Sarah," he whispered. "Forgive me, forgive me." Laying his face against her braids, he wept.

Through a silent eternity punctuated only by the steady ticking of the mantel clock, Nicholas waited.

Finally he heard boot steps echoing down the hall. Sandiford strode in. His swift glance took in Sarah's unconscious figure, and his jaw clenched. "Can you carry her?"

Nicholas nodded.

From behind an overturned chair, Sandiford produced a military cape. "I have no idea where her pelisse might be. Seems the servants bolted. Best wrap her in this."

Nicholas covered Sarah and lifted her gently. Sandiford frowned. "You're a pretty ghastly sight yourself."

Nicholas looked down. A ragged tatter of neckcloth hung from his collar, dark stains spread from his lapels down his stiffened shirtfront, and the cuffs of his jacket were soaked a blackish red.

Sandiford tucked the long ends of the cloak up over Nicholas's shoulders, masking the damage. "Let's go."

Within moments they had her in the carriage. The captain had primed the coachman, for he stood with his whip at the ready and gave them no more than a glance.

Once the carriage rolled forward, Nicholas looked over to Sandiford. "I owe you a debt I can never repay."

The captain waved away his gratitude. "I would do anything for Sarah," he said simply.

"What happened back at—" A black rage fired in him, and he couldn't choke out the name.

"I'm afraid I don't know much. My batman found me about teatime with a package from Sarah. It contained my signet, wrapped in a note demanding I meet her in Portman Square at four of the clock."

He held out the ring. "I'd given this to Sarah three years ago, telling her if she ever needed me, she had only to send it. Naturally, I came at once. But Findlay had already—" Sandiford's voice broke, and he swallowed hard "—already cut her when I arrived. Why she went there, or why Findlay attacked her, I have no idea."

Guilt and bitter regret scalded Nicholas. "She knew him well. When she learned he meant to wed a very young girl, she felt she must at all cost prevent it. He had—hurt Sarah before."

"He what?" Sandiford exploded.

"Just before their engagement was to be announced, Sarah displeased him in some way, and he burned her wrist. She carries the scar still. 'Twas one of the reasons I married her." Nicholas laughed without humor. "To protect her. What a bloody botch I've made of that."

"'Tis not the first time she's flung herself into peril, doing what she felt she must," Sandiford soothed. "You've known Sarah only a few months. You couldn't have dreamed she would be so foolhardy."

"But I should have guessed," Nicholas cried. "She told me of her anxiety. I knew what Findlay was capable of and wanted Sarah nowhere near him. So when she suggested she bring charges against him, I, arrogant fool that I am, flatly forbade it. I even said, God help me, that her scar was too old to serve as e-evidence."

He gritted his teeth, too anguished to speak. After a moment he whispered, "I didn't think...I never suspected—" He closed his eyes and bent his cheek to her head.

Sandiford said nothing, but the sting of his own reproach was goad enough. A few moments later they reached Stanhope House. Sandiford assisted him out, then distracted Glendenning while Nicholas carried Sarah up. He was helping Nicholas lay her on the bed when Becky rushed in.

She halted, her face paling. "Oh, my lady!"

Sandiford caught her arm. "Steady, Becky. Remember when she was ten, and fell out of that apple tree I dared her to climb? Looked a sight then, too, I remember."

"Master S-Sinjin?" Becky clutched the captain's arm. She took a deep breath and straightened. "I'm all right now. Let me get her out of that h-horrible gown. You'd best step outside, young master."

"May I call tomorrow?" he asked Nicholas humbly.

"Of course."

Sandiford nodded. He stepped toward the door, but then, as if drawn by an irresistible force, walked instead to the bed. The expression on his face as he gazed down at Sarah left no doubt of the depth of his emotion. With a half apologetic, half defiant glance at Nicholas, he bent to brush a wisp of pale gold hair from her forehead. "Wake soon, dear Sarah," he said huskily, and strode out.

Nicholas helped Becky ease Sarah out of the ruined gown. By the time she had bathed away the crusted patches of blood and bundled Sarah into a soft flannel nightrail, Becky was weeping silently. "My poor, sweet lady."

Nicholas collapsed in a chair. Already the day felt years long, and night had not yet fallen.

In the predawn stillness, Nicholas sat on a chair by Sarah's bed. During the long, interminable evening he had had his physician check Sarah.

Keep her warm and get fluid into her if you can, the doctor had advised, adding she would likely not regain consciousness for some time. Then, if she hadn't lost too much blood and if wound fever didn't set in... Tonight would probably tell, he concluded soberly. Leaving a powder to administer in case of fever, the physician promised to return in the morning.

Some time ago, Becky had brought him supper. Knowing he needed food to maintain his strength, he'd eaten mechanically, the meal like dust and ashes in his mouth. While Becky dozed in the sitting room, he sipped brandy-fortified coffee, able only to wait—and think.

Sandiford's reassuring words could not ease his guilt. Sarah had spoken to him of this, concern eloquent in her voice. Instead of bending every effort to assist her, he'd played the dictatorial husband.

So naturally, when in peril she sent to Sandiford. A wise choice, was it not? Unlike him, the captain had neither argued nor questioned, but come at once.

An equally dismal thought struck him. She must have returned from Stoneacres to confront Findlay—not because she missed her fool of a husband.

With a heavy sigh, he looked down at her note and read it once more to the end.

I hope it is within your power to forgive. If not, I will understand, thank you for the happiness you have brought me and pray fervently that a merciful Provi-

dence may in future bless you with a wife more worthy than I.

She had believed his threat to divorce her, apparently. Would she welcome it, and fly back to Sandiford, the man who trusted and supported her? Nicholas had no doubt the captain would be delighted to receive her, and would care naught for the ruin divorce would bring her reputation, and his.

For perhaps a second, Nicholas entertained the idea of standing nobly aside—and then angrily rejected it. She had pledged herself to him, and he would hold her to it. Damn it, he loved her!

After Lydia, he had built such a wall of suspicion and distrust around his heart he'd not believed any woman could broach it. Yet, somehow Sarah had.

Given his past, he might never be able to trust her completely. But he also knew beyond any doubt that, even were the obnoxious captain to reside next door, a permanent thorn in his side, keeping Sarah's warmth and passion in his arms and his bed and his life would be worth every risk.

Surely she cared for him a little. The tenderness in her face when she bade him goodbye—was it just this morning?—the way she touched him, loved him that rapturous night, must mean she cherished some warm emotion.

He would woo her passionately until he won back her respect and earned her affection. Until she no longer regretted the loss of her former love. He'd begin, he vowed, the moment she woke.

Feeling more hopeful than he had since tearing open the note twelve hours ago, he leaned over to stroke her cheek. Hot, dry skin scalded his hand.

Panic drying his tongue, Nicholas stumbled to the door and called for Becky.

While the maid ran for water and cloths, Nicholas mixed the powder the doctor left and carried it to Sarah. Raising her by the shoulders, he shook her gently, then with more vigor, to no avail. He could not rouse her.

For several hours, he and Becky dipped, wrung out and applied the cold cloths to her face, chest and arms. Becky had the fortuitous thought of tearing a strip from one of them, soaking it in medicine water, and trickling it in her mouth. From time to time she swallowed and they managed to get at least a fraction of the drug in her.

As his hands worked feverishly, his mind confronted the reality Sarah might die. Wretched as he'd felt before, the agony of that idea made his previous anxiety pale.

Disconnected images of her flitted through his fear-fogged mind: how she tilted her head and looked at him inquiringly…her charming gurgle of a laugh, and the golden lights that danced in her eyes…her head nestled on his shoulder as, after loving, she drifted asleep.

He thought of her independence, her stubborn pride, her insistence on driving herself to fulfill what she saw as her duty. He thought what a desert his life would be without her.

Most of all, he had never in his life regretted anything more than not having told her he loved her.

Finally, pale dawn light peeped through the curtains. Sarah's fever seemed lower, though she lay unconscious still. Nicholas's body ached in every limb and his hands were numb from wringing out cloths.

Becky glanced at him and must have read the weariness in his face. "Master, will you not lie down? I've slept some, but you've not had a wink all night. You must rest. The mistress will be needing you when she wakes."

In truth, Nicholas wasn't sure he could force himself to continue much longer. Funny little lights were dancing before his eyes, his head felt as if it might float to the ceiling, and his ears buzzed. But the thought of leaving her terrified him.

"All right, Becky, I'll sleep. Here, by her bed." He

dragged a wing chair over. ''Wake me at once if—if anything happens.''

Wrapping up in a blanket, Nicholas leaned his head on the chair's padded arm. Despite his anxiety and grief, he was asleep in a moment.

Slowly Sarah rose to consciousness to discover her chest afire, her wrist throbbing and her parched mouth filled with a bitter taste. Wanting nothing so much as a drink of water, she reached toward a glass.

Her hand fell back, startling her. She realized she was in her bed at Stanhope House, and terribly weak.

Oddly, Nicholas slept in a chair beside her. His shirt wrinkled and cravatless, his hair untidy, he rested his unshaven face on one hand. Dark circles, black against the pallor of his skin, shadowed his eyes.

Concern jolted her awake. And then she remembered.

Findlay had come after her with a knife, his lips curled back in a snarl as he called her names she didn't even recognize. Though she dodged his first furious lunge, inevitably, he caught her.

Trapping her against the fireplace, he pinned her arms behind her. Still mouthing obscenities, he methodically slashed her bodice, making the cuts shallow so that some rent only cloth, some pierced skin. Finally, growling this time he'd make his mark indelible, he forced her wrist up and sliced open the scar.

Faint with pain and terror, she heard Sinjin roar her name, saw him burst in, sword drawn. Findlay shoved her aside and grabbed his own sword from above the mantel.

She seemed to remember a clash of steel before a cold faintness stripped her fingers from their hold on the fire screen and she fell into darkness.

Had Sinjin brought her home? She felt a rush of gratitude. Dear Sinjin, who had come without question, and without question saved her life. Thank Providence he would be out of the country so the horrific scandal sure to follow this escapade would not touch him.

It would tarnish Nicholas. No wonder he looked ill! Probably he was waiting for her to wake so he could tell her where he meant to send her during the court case. Where she might stay while a divorce bill went forward.

Was this the last time she would see him? Despite the fire in her body and the ache in her heart, she cherished this one, lingering chance to gaze at him.

Through her despair a tinge of humor emerged. Never had she seen her impeccable husband look so unkempt.

He stirred, groaned and opened his eyes. Sarah noted how bloodshot they were, how pale and drawn was his face. Her alarm revived.

"N-Nicholas," she croaked. "Are you all right?"

He jolted upright. "Sarah? Oh my God, Sarah!"

He stumbled to the bed and touched her forehead with trembling fingers. "The fever's nearly gone, praise heaven!"

"Are you ill? You look dreadful."

Nicholas seized her uninjured hand and kissed it fervently. "If I do, 'tis all your fault. What a scare you've given me! But you must be thirsty."

He caught up the bedside glass and held it to her lips. She drank it down without stopping.

"Thank you, Nicholas. I tried to reach it, but I seem to be amazingly weak."

"'Tis not surprising after what you've been through."

Cold reality snuffed the joy of seeing him. "I'm so sorry, Nicholas, I—"

"No, Sarah, 'tis I who am sorry! When I read you intended to confront that madman, I was never so frightened in my life. You sweet, courageous fool."

"I had to, Nicholas. I tried to think of another way, but nothing less would stop him." She sighed unhappily. "The scandal will be dreadful, I'm afraid."

"No one knows you went to Findlay's. I gave out to

the servants that the activities of London proved too much, and you collapsed at a friend's. 'Twill be no scandal.''

Sarah took a deep breath and regretted it as hot prickles blazed across her chest. "I must go forward with this, Nicholas." Bittersweet longing and regret filled her. "I expect you will divorce me, and I don't blame you. I've been a shockingly poor bargain of a wife."

"Don't say that," Nicholas cried. "I know when you needed me most, I failed you. But I promise to do better. I don't want a divorce, and I won't let you marry him."

"Findlay?" Sarah shuddered. "I wouldn't consider it."

"Sarah, Findlay is dead. That's why there will be no scandal. You don't need to testify."

"Dead?" Shocked, she sagged back against the pillows. "Did Sinjin—?"

"No. They were dueling on the landing. Findlay tried to break for the stairs, and fell." Nicholas made a noise that sounded like a growl. "More's the pity! I should have taken great pleasure in driving a blade through his heart."

"Bless Sinjin," Sarah murmured.

"Sarah, I know how you feel about him, how you've always felt, and I know he cares for you. But we took vows. I want to honor them. This time, won't you let me stay and nurse you? Can we not begin again?"

A wild, impossible hope soared through her. "Do you mean, after all the trouble I've caused, you still want me?" Her heart commenced to beat at double time, and she dared not look at him as she awaited his response.

"More than ever."

Her glance shot up. Nicholas was smiling, his sincerity unquestionable. Exultation robbed her of breath.

Then her conscience prodded. "Before you decide, Nicholas, I must confess I can no longer keep our bargain. You see—" she twisted the coverlet between nervous fingers "—I'm sorry, but I'm afraid I've fallen in love with you."

To her surprise, Nicholas grinned and eased himself on

the bed. "Have you, now? The prospect sounds delightful."

"But you don't understand," she wailed. "You've seen how—impassioned I become about those I care for—my family, the tenants at Stoneacres. I shall be demanding and possessive." Her courage nearly failed her, but she forced herself to make it plain. "What I mean is, I—I can no longer tolerate your mistress."

"What mistress?"

She gave him an aggrieved glance. "Nicholas, do not trouble to deny your understanding. I saw her there, at my presentation ball."

His grin vanished. "You saw—! No, 'tis impossible!"

"Then her twin sister accosted me in the ladies' withdrawing room—wearing a necklace of robin's-egg rubies. Besides, from what Mr. Baxter said, several hundred other guests saw her dancing with you as well."

"He told you that? No wonder you were so angry! Believe me, my darling, 'tis a lie. First, I never bade her to your ball. I've not been able to prove it, but I suspect Findlay had Weston forge an invitation, just to foment trouble. Second, I hustled her away before she ever reached the ballroom."

Before her disbelieving brain could comprehend the full impact of that, he seized her hand. "I swear to you, I've not seen Mrs. Ingram except at social functions since I asked for your hand. I love you, sweet Sarah. I want no woman but you."

She stared, her mouth falling open. Could she have heard him aright? He loved her? Her heart swelled.

He grinned again. "You could kiss me," he suggested.

She leaned eagerly toward him—and remembered the last, worst part of her confession. *Must* she tell him? Yes, her conscience insisted.

"There's one other matter." She felt her face flush. "I must warn you I may sometimes f-forget myself." He looked at her blankly. "As I did our last night."

Nicholas sighed. "Our last night was wonderful."

"Now, Nicholas, you told me most plainly you didn't want a spirited, passionate wife!"

"Not want—?" Nicholas shook his head violently. "I never said anything so cloth-headed!"

"You most certainly did!"

"I must have been foxed." An arrested look crossed his face. "You mean every night of our marriage might have been like the last, had I not made that bacon-brained remark?"

"Perhaps not *every* night. You did teach me—things."

Nicholas cupped her face in his hands. "So did you teach me. That I wanted no other—I dismissed Chloe weeks ago! That in spite of the past I could love beyond doubt. Yes, let us forge a new bargain."

He slipped off the bed and went down on one knee. "Will you take a chance on loving me, my one and only darling? I promise a return you will never regret."

Gambler's words still. Sarah gazed at the earnest entreaty of his eyes. Could she really commit herself, heart and soul, to this unrepentant gamester?

Had she not already made that decision? "My dear husband," Sarah said as she urged him back on the bed, "that's the one gamble I'm prepared to take."

* * * * *

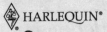

COMING NEXT MONTH FROM

HARLEQUIN HISTORICALS

- **BRIDE OF TROUVILLE**
  by **Lyn Stone**, author of THE KNIGHT'S BRIDE
  A Scottish widow agrees to marry a French count, believing he'll
  live in France. Yet when he stays, she must contrive to hide her
  secret—as well as her love.
  HH #467 ISBN# 29067-5 $4.99 U.S./$5.99 CAN.

- **CONOR**
  by **Ruth Langan,** author of RORY
  In the second book of *The O'Neil Saga,* a diplomatic Irish rebel
  falls in love with an Irish noblewoman as they both entertain
  Queen Elizabeth I.
  HH #468 ISBN# 29068-3 $4.99 U.S./$5.99 CAN.

- **THE MERRY WIDOWS—SARAH**
  by **Theresa Michaels**, author of THE MERRY WIDOWS—
  CATHERINE
  Half-Apache, half-Irish avenger Rio Santee's heart is captured by
  a landowner who takes his family into her home, in the final
  book of *The Merry Widows* trilogy.
  HH #469 ISBN# 29069-1 $4.99 U.S./$5.99 CAN.

- **THE RANCHER'S WIFE**
  by **Lynda Trent**
  A young wife abandoned by her husband moves in with her
  widower neighbor to help care for his daughter, but they soon
  find they want a union together based on love.
  HH #470 ISBN# 29070-5 $4.99 U.S./$5.99 CAN.

DON'T MISS THESE FOUR GREAT TITLES AVAILABLE NOW:

HH #463 TAMING THE LION
Suzanne Barclay

HH #464 THE WEDDING GAMBLE
Julia Justiss

HH #465 THE MARRIAGE KNOT
Mary McBride

HH #466 A COWBOY'S HEART
Liz Ireland